INSIDIOUS

THE MARKED MAGE CHRONICLES

VICTORIA EVERS

Cover Art By: CivilAnarchy
Photo Credit: http://lisajen-stock.deviantart.com/

ISBN: 1540491005
ISBN-13: 978-1540491008

INSIDIOUS

CONTENTS

PROLOGUE

The headlights barely penetrated through the blanketing fog as the school bus continued down the winding bends of the forested streets. Visibility was not more than ten feet at best ahead, and the continual groaning from the anxious passengers only grew louder as the minutes ticked by.

"I can't take it anymore," declared Brittany, reaching up and unlatching the top of her window.

"What are you doing? It's not even forty degrees outside," whined the point guard seated behind her.

The rest of the bus crankily shared in the sentiment.

Brittany simply settled back in her seat, unrelenting in her decision despite the upheaval.

"I know it doesn't take you girls much athletic ability to wave a bunch of pompoms around, but the guys here can't afford to stiffen up before the game," remarked another basketball player.

"Screw you, Travis!" snapped one of Brittany's fellow cheerleaders. "You could walk on the court after coming right out of a sauna, and it wouldn't make any difference.

You're still gonna shoot bricks."

"Guys, knock it off back there!" Coach Masters finally barked just as the insults and name-calling reached its crescendo.

"Then tell Britt to close her window!" moaned half the bus to its driver.

"How about someone tell you guys how to wash your pits," the brunette shot back. Everyone knew it smelled rank in there. The same bus was used for every sports outing, and it always smelled like stale sweat. Mix that with the hideous combination of perfume from the girls, and the bus was downright sickening. "I'm sorry, but some of us need fresh air here. It's like a stink bomb went off."

Travis threw the hood to his sweatshirt over his head and begrudgingly settled back into the crepe brown leather seat. "How much longer is this gonna take, Coach?"

"Hard to say. At least another fifteen minutes," replied Masters from behind the wheel.

Groans echoed through the bus all over again.

"Hey, if you guys want to wind up trapped in a ditch, then by all means, I'll speed up." The coach kept his eyes fixed on the road, or at least, what could be seen of it. The sun had set an hour ago and streetlights were far and few on this stretch of back roads, leaving nothing but the headlights to guide their way.

"We should've stayed on the highway," remarked another passenger.

"You saw the traffic. With all the construction going on, we would've been stuck out there forever," Travis admitted. The young man put his ear buds in, trying to let Saliva's "Ladies and Gentlemen" get him back into the zone. He rested the side of his head on the window, heaving out an aggravated sigh.

Just as he shut his eyes, a thunderous eruption blasted over the power of the music and his head thumped against the window as the bus suddenly shimmied. Everyone yelped, gripping onto whatever they could find. Yanking out the headphones, Travis snapped up to his feet, seeing the vehicle slow to a stop.

"What the hell was that?" he demanded.

"Everybody, just stay calm," ordered Coach. "I think we just blew a tire." Once the bus was placed in Park, he pulled the lever to open the door and climbed out with a service flashlight in hand.

Curses resonated across the bus as everyone took out their phones.

"Is there someone we can call to tell them what happened?" asked a power forward. "They can't call a forfeit on us if we're stuck, can they?"

"We're about to find out," said Travis, scrolling through his contact list.

"I don't have service. Do you?" queried Brittany, holding up her cell and moving it around in vain.

"I've got nothin'," said a player.

"Me neither," confirmed another.

The whole bus groaned as everyone else shook their heads.

"Say goodbye to our record," grunted the point guard.

"Now what?" asked Brittany. "We haven't come across another car on this road for the last ten minutes."

"'Cause no one else is stupid enough to drive in this," confirmed Travis, pointing out the window.

Brittany took notice to the dense fog that now gently billowed into the cabin from her cracked window. "Are we even safe in here? I mean, what if another car does come along? Even with the hazards on, it'd be almost impossible for them to see us."

Paleness washed over everyone's faces at the acknowledgement.

"Coach?" called out Travis, sticking his mouth up to Brittany's opened window. "Coach?"

"Everybody, shut up!" demanded Brittany, straining her ears to hear Masters' reply. Nothing.

"Coach?" she yelled. Her voice echoed off into the mass of trees surrounding the street, but no one returned her plea.

"Where the hell is he?" Travis climbed over his friend seated beside him and made his way to the back of the bus, scanning the scenery outside. "Anyone see Coach?"

When no one confirmed, he hastened to the front end, heading down the stairs to the base of the door. "Masters!"

Unease tightened around his nerves as his feet dropped to the gravelly shoulder of the road. His sneakers grinded against the worn, pebble-coated blacktop, and the sound seemed all the more amplified now that everyone had gone wholly silent onboard. He made his way to the back tire, seeing the whole wheel stripped of rubber. Travis knelt down and peered beneath the undercarriage, finding nothing but a black rod tucked behind the blown tire.

He strained to reach the object, but finally managed to grip his fingers on the very end. A small shard of glass clanked to the ground as he pulled it out, and he turned over the object to see the broken screen of the service flashlight. The sweat layering his palms almost made him drop it as he rose to his feet. He quickly wiped his hands on his sweatpants, but the flashlight still felt slick in his grasp.

"T-Travis," stammered Brittany.

He looked up to see the brunette's eyes trained below

his waist and instinctively dropped his own gaze. "Shit!"

His grip immediately loosened and the flashlight fell to the ground as a low growl fixed behind him. Fear whirled the shooting guard around, but nothing could be made out through the dense fog. He shot off to the front of the bus and practically fell inside the cabin, barely managing to pry the door shut with his grimy hands.

The boy collapsed on the slated flooring of the aisle, and everybody froze as they observed the red smears painted across the side of his white pant leg.

"That's not what I think it is..." muttered one of his teammates.

Travis raised his hand, seeing more of the mucky liquid staining his skin. "There's something out there."

"What are you talking about?"

"There's something out there," he reiterated shakily, pulling himself up.

Brittany laid a hand on his shoulder, and he startled at the touch. "Travis, what did you see?"

He wordlessly plowed past her and the other members on the bus, heading toward the backend.

"What did you see, man?" begged his friend.

"Nothing."

"Will you just tell us?" bellowed Brittany.

"Nothing!" snapped Travis, peering out the large rear window. "I didn't see anything. It's what I heard."

"What?"

"It's some kind of animal," he muttered, more to himself.

"Like what? A coyote?"

Travis shot the cheerleader a dirty look. "You honestly think a forty pound coyote attacked Coach and managed to drag his body away?"

The bus fell silent again.

"Did you actually see his body?" asked Brittany. "I mean, we don't know what happened to him. Right?"

"What? You think he got mauled by a rabid dog and then decided to ditch us to go play Animal Echo in the woods?" remarked a player.

"Can we still drive with a flat?" queried a small forward. "There could be a gas station or something just down the road for all we know. We get there, we can call for help."

The team's point guard went to the front and plopped into the driver's seat and sighed in relief that Coach had left the keys in the ignition. He turned the engine over and put the vehicle into gear, letting the bus slowly coast down the stretch.

One of the girls suddenly screamed, and not a second later did the vehicle suddenly jolt at the annihilating impact that registered on the left side. A sharp shudder followed and the point guard could hear the other rear tire blowout. The backend buckled down, scraping along the asphalt before the bus came to an eventual halt. It didn't matter how hard the point guard pushed down on the accelerator. The bus wouldn't move.

"Anyone hurt?" called out the point guard, turning to look back at the rest of the passengers.

"What the hell is this thing?" demanded Travis, looking at the concaved siding of the bus that received the impact. The collision even managed to break several of the windows.

An aching howl erupted outside, and the whole bus was met with another blow. The backend slid off the pavement, and the cabin tilted down toward the deep trench. Everyone tried scrambling over, hoping to rebalance the vehicle, but another ram hit, sending the bus toppling off the road. The helpless passengers crashed onto the roof as their world turned upside-down.

Buried beneath a mound of her classmates' limbs, Brittany achingly tried prying herself up, but fear paralyzed her as heavy breathing stirred her untidy brunette locks. She only managed to shift her eyes over to the broken window beside her head, seeing an enormous, long muzzle and snarling white teeth just inches from her face. A scream lodged in the poor girl's throat as the monstrous creature lunged into the cabin.

CHAPTER 1
Animals

"I'm on the verge of eating notebook paper," Carly declared, eyeing the composition journal in my hands.

I laughed. "I believe that's a sign of iron deficiency."

"Or just extreme hunger."

We both stood on our tiptoes, trying to gauge an estimate of how many more people were still ahead of us in line.

"Okay, keep my mind off my ravenous appetite by spilling some goods. Is it true you're seeing Blaine Ryder?" Carly urged.

Feeling my cheeks blush at the mention, I turned from her, and she gasped.

"Ooooh, I take that as a big, fat YES!"

"No, no. I wouldn't say 'seeing,' per se. We're taking things slow," I clarified.

"You and the Golden Boy, huh? Me likey." Carly couldn't wipe the Cheshire smile now glued to her face. "So, where's Prince Charming? Shouldn't he be here?"

"He had a family thing to take care of. He'll be meeting us at the bonfire though," I confirmed.

"That's so adorable!" She was downright giddy. Sadly, I couldn't share in the sentiment. Not as long as Becky Sorensen kept throwing visual daggers at me.

Carly turned, taking note of my annoyance. "Just ignore her."

"That'd be easy if it was just her. I'm public enemy number one. Hunted like Dillinger and loathed like a Kardashian." I should have known better. I was fresh meat to Belleview High. An outsider. Sure, I'd been here a year, but you still can't just roll into town and snatch up the golden boy. "And just when I thought public schools would be more laid back than boarding ones."

"That's the thing about the public school system. They bring out the worst in everyone. Sweet girls become nice girls. Nice girls become bitches. Bitches become Queen Bees. And Queen Bees become See-You-Next-Tuesdays."

"People are acting like I clubbed a baby seal using a freaking panda. I broke up with Adam weeks ago, yet Becky's still fuming from the ears. If she wants him that bad, he's free!"

"She wanted him to break up with you. Not the other way around. If she went out with him now, she'd just be getting your sloppy seconds," clarified Carly. "And a whole new batch of trouble is brewing now that Blaine's putting the moves on you. Ava Ashford has been trying to sink her claws into him since freshman year, and she's not gonna go away quietly." My friend's stomach growled so angrily that I could hear it even over all the chatter. "I knew I shouldn't have listened to you."

I'd convinced Carly to hold off getting in line before the basketball game, because the crowds around the concessions usually plummeted after tip-off. Thanks to the visiting team being a no-show though, boredom sent everyone to the refreshment stand, leaving us at the end of a very long line.

"I said I was sorry," I lamented, "but I still don't get why you didn't just eat before we came here."

"Because, my mom ordered all this gourmet food earlier for her dinner party, and there's no way in hell I'm trying any of that crap again. Remember last time? Her caviar tasted like ass."

"What's this I hear about tasting some ass?" A burly set of arms rested on each of our shoulders from behind.

"Oh, God help us," groaned Carly as Mark stepped between the two of us.

"Is this an offer by any chance?" He winked at my friend, igniting an immediate eye roll from her end.

"You forget I'm dating your best friend?" she retorted, pointing to Daniel, the handsome point guard sitting on the bleachers inside the gym.

Mark pouted exaggeratedly before turning to me. "What about you, Kitty Kat? Interested in letting me toss your salad?"

Carly outright gagged and slugged him in the shoulder. "Well, there goes my appetite."

"I'm not hearing any objections." He beamed a charming smile at me that seemed to work on all the clueless girls of my class. Thank the Lord I knew better.

"Carly would have a better chance getting with me than you," I countered.

My blonde bestie grinned wickedly, gently vibrating her tongue to make a sarcastically sexy purr directed at me.

"You start playing for the other team all of the sudden?" Mark retorted.

"No, but at the off chance you were the last guy on the planet, I'd strongly consider it. Or celibacy," I clarified.

"Ouch, Montgomery. You little spitfire."

Carly squirmed under his hold, fanning her nose. "Jeez, Mark, you start boycotting showers?"

"It's a part of my scoring strategy," he laughed. "No one wants to guard someone who smells rank."

"Well, you achieved your goal admirably. Onions make me tear up less," I remarked.

"Please, just do us all a favor and shower after the game. I'm not spending the whole night around Pepé Le Pew."

A high-pitch whistle blared, bringing the gym to a standstill, and the pudgy referee waddled to the middle of the basketball court. "Due to Hersey High's absence, we have no other choice but to rule this as a forfeit on their behalf."

Mark quietly rejoiced, and no one could blame him. Sure, we wanted to win the old-fashioned way, but Hersey's team was our biggest competition and the easy triumph only helped our record.

Daniel came up and shared his trademark handshake with Mark. "Look at that. Triumph, and we didn't even have to break a sweat."

"Yeah, but now what do we do? The bonfire doesn't start 'til nine," said Carly.

Mischief painted her boyfriend's face. "Oh, I have an idea. But we're gonna need to call in the whole troop for this one."

***

"Everybody ready?" called out Eric as he rolled the van to a stop behind a thick set of bushes.

"This is so stupid," muttered Kelsey, looking at the house just down the way.

"What? You lose your nerve?" challenged Eric.

She sighed, knowing it was too late to change her mind. "No, let's just get this over with."

"Guys, lighten up. This is gonna be fun," said Mark, handing each of us a black garbage bag from the trunk. "Okay?"

"This is also Principal Harris's place," corrected Kelsey. "If he catches us, we're gonna end up more screwed than a cork."

"Get out," laughed Mark, pushing her out of the backseat as everybody started unloading from the vehicle.

Eric motioned to the house with tactical hand signals like we were all on a military field operation. The six of us couldn't help but giggle under our breaths as we skulked up to Harris's front lawn. Between the amusement and the fact that Mark had lit up in the van, he lost his footing and rolled across the grass in a laughing fit.

"Idiot." Eric pulled him back up to his feet with a snicker as we approached the massive maple tree in the middle of Harris's front yard. "Go," he mouthed.

We all opened our garbage bags and pulled out a roll of toilet paper. Mark was the first to throw his. It flew through a mess of branches overhead, but it tumbled back down to the ground still intact.

"Seriously?" snorted Daniel. "You're supposed to unwrap it first, you goof."

Vanessa and I doubled over with stitches as we tried not to burst out laughing.

Eric and Daniel unwound each of their rolls a few feet and heaved the toilet paper over the top of the tree. Tangling in the branches, the rolls winded back down with two perfect white lines dangling above us. "That's how it's done."

Everyone else followed in suit and unraveled the rolls. In no time at all, the entire tree was dripping in streams of toilet paper. The guys continued in their vandalism as they chucked the last of their stash over the front of Harris's house.

Euphoria set in as the fear and excitement of it all burned through our veins. We danced across the yard, waving our hands through the flood of Charmin and Angel Soft. I pulled out my phone and took a shot of the scenery for our proof as the other girls ran around Mark. He held the ends of their rolls so that they could wrap him up mummy-style. He did his best Hulk impression as they finished up and burst through the paper with an animated roar.

A light turned on from one of the upstairs windows, and we crashed to a halt. Just as the curtains pulled back, Eric shouted, "Abort! Abort!"

We all grabbed our bags and dashed in hysterics off the property. Everyone piled back into the van, and Eric tore off down the street. As Eric took a turn off onto another road, everybody let out a massive sigh. Suddenly, the whole van broke out into a laughing fit.

"Good work, team!" declared Eric, drumming his hands on the steering wheel.

Mark rolled down the window and stuck his head out, howling into the night air.

"I can't believe we just did that," I sighed as Vanessa and Carly wrapped their arms around me, ensnaring me in a sandwich hug between them.

"You get a decent snapshot, Montgomery?" asked Daniel from the front passenger's seat.

I pulled up the photo in question and handed over

my phone to him.

"Perfect, baby girl!"

Eric cursed under his breath, and everyone in the van looked up front to see steam emanating from the hood.

"Relax," Eric assured as Vanessa and Carly began panicking. "It's just overheating."

Thankfully, there was a gas station at the end of the block and we pulled right in. Eric cut the engine, and the guys climbed out to assess the situation.

"Unless you want second degree burns, don't touch the cap yet," warned Daniel, slapping Mark's hand away from the radiator. "It's gotta cool off first."

"Doesn't look like there's a leak in the cooling system. It's probably just low on coolant," said Eric. "Not a surprise. The guy I rented it from didn't exactly look like he was rolling in the Benjamins. Lucky he even had gas in the tank."

"Why didn't we just take your Escalade?" moaned Kelsey.

"I'm sorry, did you just miss what we did back there?" laughed Mark. "With the way the neighborhood watch is around here, someone was bound to see the van. If we pulled up to Harris's place in the Cady, we may as well have just left some Polaroids of ourselves on his doorstep."

We waited awhile until the car cooled off, and the guys confirmed it. The van was low on coolant.

Eric ran inside the gas station to pick up some, and the rest of us continued moseying around the van in boredom.

"Come on," Kelsey whined impatiently.

"Pop a Valium," said Mark, watching her pace about. "We'll get to the bonfire soon enough."

"Yeah, but Zack's already there, not to mention Tiffany," she moaned.

"I don't get why you date Zack," said Carly. "The guy's an experiment in Artificial Stupidity, and his eyes wander more than someone with strabismus."

"Strabismus?" laughed Mark. "You become a doctor all of the sudden?"

"Well, she did give me a pretty thorough body exam last night," cracked Daniel, immediately receiving a backhand to the chest from his girlfriend.

The theme from *Dracula* blasted in the air, causing everyone to jump.

"Cheese and rice!" bellowed Carly. "You really need to change your ringtone. That is so creepy."

"Sorry," I laughed, pulling out my phone to read the new text.

Carly eyed me curiously. Snatching my phone clean from my grasp, she stole a look at the screen and gasped. "Oooooh, look at what we have here."

"Car, don't be nosy," said Vanessa.

"What? I can't help it. I think it's cute she has an admirer."

"That's hardly a newsflash," laughed Mark.

She rolled her eyes. "I'm not talking about Adam."

Everyone paused in curiosity.

"Oh?" Vanessa, who never minded in gossip, even seemed intrigued by the development.

"It's-"

"Don't," I warned.

Carly sucked in a breath. "Blaine," she mouthed wickedly, receiving an immediate backhand to the forearm from me.

"Holy crap!" spat Eric. "Blaine Ryder? You gonna be hooking up with him tonight?"

I groaned. "It's nothing serious. Honest."

"This is still gonna break Adam's heart," Vanessa pouted. "You two were so cute together. Childhood best friends, separated from each other for years, only to be reunited and become lovers. It was so romantic."

"Yeah, well, it's all the more proof that Nicholas Sparks didn't write the story of my life," I grumbled, unable to hide my hurt. "If he had, I still wouldn't want to put a fist-sized hole through Adam's face."

Vanessa merely sighed. "I still think you're moving on rather quickly. And with the resident Golden Boy no less. You little heartbreaker, you."

Carly shot her a glare. "V, will you knock it off? She had to move on eventually."

"I'm still surprised Kat stayed with him as long as she did," commented Daniel. "Let's face it. The guy was flakier than a Pillsbury biscuit. He deserved what he got when she dumped his ass."

"And that's precisely why she needs to move on," said Carly, wrapping an arm around my shoulders. "Kat deserves only the best."

"Thanks," I finally laughed.

Tires squealed as a souped-up Dodge Challenger roared into the lot. The car did a quick 180 and pulled up right in front of the first available pump.

The guys couldn't help but admire the quality driving, not to mention the beautiful wheels.

"Hot damn," muttered Mark.

"You got that right," confirmed Carly, outright gawking at the striking driver as he exited the vehicle. "On a scale of one to ten, that boy's an eleven."

"I'm right here, you know," scoffed Daniel.

"Oh, lighten up, babe. You know you're my sirloin steak. I'm not ordering anything else off the menu." She batted her eyes innocently before a wicked grin broke through. "But...that doesn't mean I can't peruse the dessert selection every now and again."

Standing at a cut and athletic six feet, the stranger's physique could barely be contained in his wife beater shirt and workout shorts.

"The guy's gotta be freezing," said Vanessa, watching her breath vaporize in the cold. "How could you be out in this weather without a jacket?"

"I'm not complaining." Carly outright swooned as a lock of hair escaped from behind the stranger's ear, falling onto his chiseled cheekbone. Daniel eyed her with obvious annoyance.

"Car, didn't you say you were hungry?" I asked, clearing my throat loud enough to catch her attention.

"Uh-huh," she sighed, not bothering to take her eyes off the guy. Her obliviousness to Daniel's irritation was downright epic.

"Why don't you go inside and grab something? A bag of chips. Maybe a candy bar. Or something...*anything*," I remarked, now nudging her.

She blindly dug around in her purse, pulling out a wad of crumpled bills, and handed it over. "Surprise me."

I stole a glance back at Daniel who just shook his head. "Sorry, man, did my best."

He forced a small smile. "Valiant effort."

I took the wrinkled cash and flattened it out the best I could before heading inside the gas station. Scanning over the assortment of snacks, I grabbed a couple bags of potato chips and decided on getting a Snickers bar for myself. I figured it wouldn't hurt to have something edible on hand, given that bonfires were more notorious for having liquid refreshments than actual food. The bell above the entryway rang as I made my way up to the register, and the pleasant mixture of honey and musk engulfed me, masking the noxious smell of ammonia from the recently applied floor cleaner.

Curiosity got the better of me as I looked over my shoulder, only to find the last human being I ever wanted to see heading towards the back of the store. That familiar, damned knot formed in my stomach, as it always did anytime Reese Blackburn was near. I rocked back and forth on my heels, trying my best to keep my patience in check as the old guy in front of me continued buying virtually every lottery ticket available.

Come on, come on, come on. I needed to get out of here. PRONTO.

Footsteps started making their way to the counter from the back of the store, and I immediately deflated, knowing a confrontation was now inevitable.

"Montgomery," spoke a silvery voice directly behind me.

I regrettably turned to face the ass-hat in question, giving him my best artificial, Pan Am smile. "Blackburn."

The guy always looked like he'd just waltzed off the set of a Tim Burton movie, and tonight was no different. He was dressed in his typically peculiar attire, sporting a gothic knee-length horseman's jacket laced in chains, a pair of black slacks, a silk tapestry vest, and dark brogue boots adorned with skulls on the metallic buckles.

"Never thought I'd see you south of Providence Street," he remarked in the sarcastic fashion he always saved for me. "Get lost on your way to the country club?"

"No, I was actually out looking for your heart. Should've known better that it's long gone," I retorted. "And what about you? Never thought I'd see you out in public on a full moon. Get lost on your way to your cult meeting in the woods?"

"That's later in the evening," he chuckled, flashing me that dimpled smile and perfect set of pearly whites. Such infectious, boyish charm seemed misplaced, considering he was stab-worthy. It really was a shame, because Reese wasn't half bad looking.

And by 'half', I mean *not entirely.*

Sure, he had cheekbones that could cut glass, not to mention bedroom eyes so amber they looked to be stowing flames inside them, but still...

Okay, okay. Even I had to admit, Blackburn was hardly an eyesore.

Even with my heeled boots, I still stood a good half foot shorter than him, but his lean frame thankfully made him less imposing.

The old guy in front of me started ordering cigarettes as well, causing my fisted fingernails to start biting into my palms. Knowing how quickly our conversations always descended into verbal smack downs, I grasped at anything I could think of to divert us back to small talk until I could move to the register.

"Did you go to the game earlier?"

Reese shrugged. "I considered it, but then I started thinking of other excruciating things I'd rather do, like have a root canal, and I decided to pass."

"You heading to the bonfire?" I tried again. He merely cocked a brow, and I realized how ridiculous I sounded. "Oh, that's right. You don't do anything fun. How could I forget?"

"If you call watching a bunch of drunken idiots gyrate around and trash a field while you suffocate from smoke inhalation 'fun,' then yes—I don't like fun."

"It wouldn't kill you to be normal, ya' know."

"Maybe, maybe not. Haven't tried it."

"So, Mr. High and Mighty, what superior plans do you have this evening?"

"Test my alcohol limits, take off my clothes, and harass innocent bystanders." He thumped the side of his head. "Oh, wait a minute. No, that's *your* friends."

"At least I have some."

He stole a look outside and leered. "With *friends* like that, I consider myself grateful that I don't."

"Bite me."

"I probably shouldn't. Wouldn't want to get rabies."

"I beg to differ. Foaming at the mouth would probably be an improvement for you. Anything to get you to stop talking."

He smirked. "Touché, Princess."

My jaw impulsively clenched. How silly of me to think I could get through a conversation without him calling me that. I obviously did a horrible job at hiding my distain for the moniker, because he halfheartedly tried to bury his laugh, causing the front strands of his long, razor-cut coffee-brown locks to fall into his eyes as he looked down. And to think, I thought he was cute…once upon a time.

I still couldn't figure out what the hell his problem was. The two of us met not long after I moved to town last June. I thought things had gone well, but I was obviously wrong, seeing as how anytime I saw him after that, he treated me more and more like a festering fungus. He actively went out of his way to avoid me—as in literally fleeing in the other direction—anytime I was with Carly and the others. So I took the hint and made an effort to keep my distance.

That cruel bitch otherwise known as Fate seemed to

have other plans, as Reese and I were forced into becoming science partners for Physics come senior year. Then to add insult to injury, I joined the school paper, unbeknownst to me at the time that Reese was Belleview High's chief photographer, not to mention a fellow journalist. He didn't go out of his way to talk to anyone at school, and he seemed to prefer it that way. Except when it came to me, apparently. Nowadays, Reese never got tired of throwing shade at me for some inexplicable reason. The guy seemed incapable of having a civil exchange.

Oh, lucky me...

The bell above the doorway rang again. "So we're good for tonight?" said Daniel.

I looked over to see his cell pressed against his ear just as the customer in front of me finished paying.

"Yeah, we'll see you at the bonfire," Daniel finished, lowering the phone as the call ended. He waved over at me. "Gotta get rollin', Kat. The van's cooled off, and Kelsey's about to blow a gasket of her own if we don't get a move on."

"I'll be there in a sec." I handed over Carly's crinkled money to the cashier, and the guy behind the counter laxly gathered my change. "Never the pleasure seeing you," I remarked, turning to face Reese. All the color had suddenly drained from his face, and he even took a half step back as he returned my stare.

"You okay?" I asked.

"Kat, can you hurry it up?" called out Kelsey impatiently from outside the opened doorway. The girl seriously looked like she was about to burst a blood vessel, even from this distance.

"You heard the girl," laughed Daniel, beckoning me to follow him.

Reese still stood there, looking back at me like I had spontaneously turned into a flesh eating zombie. When he didn't respond, I self-consciously skulked away, muttering a quiet 'bye' under my breath before gathering my purchased items.

"What's his deal?" whispered Daniel as I met him at the door.

"Hell if I know."

We headed back out to the van, and I caught sight of Reese's old beater truck parked a few spaces down from us. The thing had more rust on it than it did paint.

Carly waved her hands enthusiastically at the sight of the chips in my hands. "I'm open!"

I jokingly imitated a fake out before throwing one of the bags to her like it was a football.

She caught it, whaling out an animated, "Touchdown!"

"Goofball," I laughed, suddenly feeling fingers wrap around my upper arm. The contact caused me to whirl around, and I was met with amber eyes again. Reese's grip wasn't hard by any means, and he immediately let go as I faced him.

"Hey." The natural bravado in his voice had been undoubtedly replaced with quiet discomfort.

"...Hey."

"I don't want this to sound weird, but...you want a ride?"

Of all things, I actually laughed. "What?"

"Sorry, it's just...that doesn't exactly look too safe," he remarked, nodding over to the van that gurgled unnaturally as Eric turned over the engine.

"I thought you of all people would be thrilled to see me locked in a high-speed deathtrap."

He didn't laugh.

"Thanks for the offer," I politely amended. "But my mom taught me to not accept rides from strangers. And I don't really know you all that well, so..."

Unrest stirred behind his eyes as he closed the distance between us in one swift, unnatural motion. "Please, don't get in the van," he whispered.

"Excuse me?" I tried backing up, but his hands gripped my arms again, this time with a much firmer hold.

"Please, just listen to me. I know this sounds crazy, but you can't get in the van."

In any other circumstance, I would have already screamed bloody murder, but there was something about the earnestness in his voice that seemed to paralyze me.

"There a problem here?" Daniel and Eric started heading over to our sides. I tried pulling away, but Reese again wouldn't release his grip, and the guys immediately charged over at the sight.

"Let her go!" barked Eric.

"Don't do it," Reese pleaded again, refusing to take his eyes off me.

A force ripped between the two of us, and Daniel slammed Reese against the side of the truck as Eric safely pried me away.

"What the hell's going on?" begged Carly, seeing Mark quickly meet up to aid Daniel.

"Please, don't get in the van!" Reese repeated.

"Why?" scoffed Carly.

"'Cause he's a freak," spat Eric.

"Kat, don't—"

"Give me one good reason not to bust your teeth in," barked Daniel, shoving Reese back against the vehicle as he tried to step forward.

"She's going to die!" Reese suddenly blurted.

The entire parking lot came to a standstill.

What did he just say?

"Okay, the guy's clearly bat-shit. Let's just get out of here," howled Mark.

No one else hesitated, but Daniel was forced to practically lift me up into the vehicle as I remained paralyzed in place. Mark grabbed hold of Reese's coat, feeling around the pockets. Sure enough, he pulled out his car keys and hurled them into the oblivion of the woods bordering the parking lot. Mark used the distraction to race back over to us, and he hopped into the front passenger seat. The van took off before he even had a chance to close the door.

"Shit," Reese muttered. He charged at the van, and we all unreservedly screamed as his fists hammered the back window right where I was sitting.

Daniel managed to shift the van into third gear, and we finally gained momentum.

I stole a look at the speedometer, seeing us already pushing over twenty miles an hour.

"This dude's gotta be on PCP or some shit," said Mark, watching Reese unrelentingly race beside the van, not losing ground.

He kept hollering, pleading for me to get out.

It wasn't until we clocked thirty that we finally started pulling away from him. Only once he became nothing more than a speck in the distance did anyone else breathe.

"You okay?" asked Vanessa, giving me a hug as I sat frozen in my seat.

Eric looked over his shoulder and sighed. "Hey, don't let that freak get to you, okay? He was just trying to scare you."

"Mission accomplished," said Carly shakily.

"Don't let him ruin the night. The guy's nuttier than a peanut butter factory," assured Mark.

CHAPTER 2
Bad Moon Rising

"You need to loosen up!" Everyone continued to tease me as we all sat on bales of hay, watching the massive bonfire blazing nearby.

Music coursed through the air, and a bunch of our classmates drunkenly gyrated away to the beat in the middle of the open field. Screams sounded off in the distance by the waterfront, which drew my concern, until I realized it was from a bunch of moronic guys throwing their girlfriends into the pond. I shivered at the thought, not just because it was a little chilly outside, but because that pond was murky beyond belief. I was pretty sure the creature from the black lagoon lived in there.

"If it isn't my favorite people," chuckled a pleasant voice as hands draped over my eyes from behind. "Can you guess who it is?"

"Given that you sound happy to see us, I think it's safe to say it's not Principal Harris," I finally laughed.

Everyone else shared in the amusement as my admirer removed his hands from my eyelids, poking his head over my shoulder to cast me a charismatic smile.

"Well, if it isn't Mr. Blaine Ryder."

"The one and only." He beamed a bright smile, sharing the seat beside me. Blaine always looked suave, and tonight was no exception. Not a single strand of his midnight black locks lay out of place. The sides and back were cut short while the top layers were longer and slicked back to perfection. Between his hair, formal fashion sense, and unmistakable charisma, he was like a modern-day Jay Gatsby. And that was precisely why every female classmate was shooting me visual daggers, seeing him cozy up closer to me.

"So, Blaine, weren't you saying something earlier about how you wanted to ask a certain someone to dance?" grinned Carly, nodding obviously in my direction.

"Car," I growled in embarrassment.

Blaine chuckled, obviously sighting the redness in my cheeks. "Well, as a matter of fact, I did mention something along those lines." He rose up, taking my hand into his, and even added in a small, playful curtsy for good measure.

"Awww," Carly mused as he kissed the top of my hand.

Blaine grinned down at me, trying best not to laugh. "What do you say?"

"If you don't say yes, we're all gonna take turns kicking your ass," remarked Daniel.

I buried my hands into my face, sharing in Blaine's amusement as we both laughed. "Sure."

"Amen!" everyone howled.

In no time at all, the dread from earlier eased away and I finally relaxed. After a number of rounds of dancing and partying though, the merriment seemed to catch up to me.

VICTORIA EVERS

I excused myself, pushing my way through the throng of people.

"Kat? You okay?" called out Blaine, following after me.

My equilibrium gave way and I stumbled, falling right into his arms.

"Whoa." He chuckled slightly as he adjusted his hold on me. "You know, I've been hoping you'd show me some interest for awhile now, but I never imagined you'd literally throw yourself at me."

I attempted to steady myself again, but my legs felt like they didn't even have bones to offer me support. My body started to sink down to the ground, and Blaine thankfully eased me back up.

"Kat? How much have you had to drink?" he asked, concern raking through his muffled voice.

I opened my mouth, trying to force the words out, but for the life of me, nothing would come. What was wrong with me? I hadn't drunken anything, except soda from a closed can.

"Oooh," howled Vanessa and Carly giddily in the distance, clearly getting the wrong impression. "Seems you two are getting cozy!"

The bass of the music suddenly pounded in my eardrums, and a guitar shriek sent my hands clawing over my ears. Everything sounded so distortedly loud.

"Hey, how about I take you home?" offered Blaine, safely snuggling me into his embrace. "You don't look so hot."

I barely managed to nod my head.

"Good." He turned us around, keeping a taut arm held around me to ensure I wouldn't stumble.

I continued to stagger, practically dragging my feet

28

across the trampled grass. My vision blurred as a bunch of parked cars came into sight.

"Here we go."

I heard a set of locks pop up, and a door opened to my left.

"Watch your head," cautioned Blaine as he helped me into the passenger seat of what I assumed was his car. He gingerly propped me upright to put my seatbelt on properly, and I suddenly heard what I thought was someone calling out my name.

The passenger door closed and I looked up through the windows, but my eyes refused to focus. Blaine joined me a moment later, hopping behind the wheel.

"We'll be home in no time. Okay?" His voice sounded so serene that it helped soothe the disarray running through my head.

The engine roared as he turned the car over, and the blurred scenery started rolling past the side window. I woozily tipped to the side, my body resting against the door of the car. As the vehicle drove down the hillside, I started sliding forward, but Blaine eased me back into my seat.

"Hang in there. You're doing good," he continued to assure.

I had never felt so drunk in my entire life. My lungs even seemed to struggle taking in air. Panic began rising up inside me, and I only managed to moan out something that sounded more like a whine than actual words. What if I suffocated to death?! A cry escaped my lips, and it caught Blaine's attention.

"You're gonna be fine."

"No," I croaked. I needed help!

The car banked down another hill, and Blaine swiveled the steering wheel to accommodate the deep, winding bends in the road.

"Shit!" He suddenly jerked the wheel and the vehicle skid so severely that my head slammed into the passenger window with an excruciating wallop.

A distorted, large black mass on the road swept past my vision as the car spun out of control. One full rotation later and a boulder came into sight, illuminated by the headlights. My neck snapped forward as the front end smashed into the rock head-on. Talcum powder engulfed me as the air bag deployed, but the impact didn't relent. In an instant, the metal of the hood was pulverized in one swift crunch and the glass from the windshield blasted into my face. The power of the compression forced the front of the car to impede the inside of the passenger cabin, and my entire body was met with an annihilating blow as I felt my insides shatter apart.

Darkness.

That's all there was. Searing pain raking through every inch of me, and I couldn't move.

"Come on," I overheard a distant voice grunt. "Just hang on."

Cold hands pressed to my neck and someone's fingers cradled my head.

"You're gonna be alright." The words were nothing more than a whisper, and then everything fell silent.

I couldn't feel anything.

Subtle sounds slithered their way back into my world. After a moment, it became clearer.

"Miss? Miss?"

Lights blazed into my eyes as my right cheek lay against the dampened pavement. A bloodied hand rested in my line of vision, and I willed myself to move, seeing the fingers twitch. It was mine. There was also a line of rubber from a busted tire, mangled pieces of steel, and broken glass fragments splayed in front of me. A pair of thermal conductive gloves came into sight, and my head was readjusted to look straight upward.

"Can you hear me?" asked the middle-aged man crouched over me.

I could see the Star of Life emblem on the front of his hat, and I realized he was a paramedic. After failing to verbalize a response, I achingly nodded my head. Everything seemed to move in slow-motion with a disorientated haze clouding my eyes. People raced all around me, and I was eventually lifted up onto a stretcher.

"Blaine?" I tried angling my head back in the direction of the wreckage, but an EMT turned me forward again and placed an oxygen mask over my face.

***

Every inhale felt like I was trying to lift an elephant off my chest. The bleariness slowly eased from my vision, and the collection of screens and wires looming overhead finally came into focus. A green line continuously spiked up on one display before falling back to its baseline, and I realized it was a heart rate monitor. I didn't remember the ambulance ride or my admission, but I was apparently now at the hospital. Only a small light in the corner illuminated the space, and blackness blanketed the sky outside the window. It was still night. Or maybe a whole other day had come and gone.

"Shhh," cooed a male voice beside me. "You're okay now."

A familiar scent wafted in the air, overpowering the concentrated odor of disinfectant. I tried looking over at the individual, but the pain that shot through my neck kept me from fully turning. The only thing I could see in the limited light was a tall figure donned in hospital scrubs with a matching blue cap and surgical mask.

"Get some rest," whispered the male nurse, heading out the door.

Not an inch of me seemed to be spared from the agony tearing through my body, and I prepared myself for the worst as I looked down at myself. A full body cast, an amputated limb, mangled features, deformity. I knew the impact, felt its devastation. I didn't delude myself into believing it could be better than expected.

My breathing faltered as my eyes traveled down my body, my pained arm tearing away the blanket covering my legs. It couldn't be. Deep purple stains painted the exposed skin in large splotches, greenish hues spreading across the edges before bleeding into healthier, untarnished flesh.

How?

Despite the horrid bruising and the pain that came with it, I could still bend my joints without opposition. My body remained intact. Not even a trace of a bandage. I tried calling out for help, but my parched throat merely made me cough at the attempt. Scouring the space around me, I failed to find anything with a reflective surface I could use to look at my face. My right cheek throbbed and my temple felt like someone had taken a baseball bat to the side of my head. I stifled a cry as I forced myself to sit up.

The aching pull inside my left arm made me acknowledge the needle shoved in my vein. I was attached to an IV. Grappling for the pole with the clear liquid bag hooked at the top of it, I planted my bare feet on the cold linoleum floor. Vanity outweighed the agonizing pain scorching my body as I struggled to stand. Where were my clothes? My jacket, pants, shirt, boots, and even socks were gone, replaced by a hideous hospital-issued gown.

One step, and I woozily collapsed to my knees. The room tilted as a new sickness washed over me. I must have just been administered a sedative. If this was how it felt with heavy painkillers raging through my veins, I shuddered to imagine what fresh Hell I was in for when it wore off. Struggling back upright, I grasped the IV pole, using its ball bearing wheels to slowly guide me toward the bathroom.

Batting away the matted locks of hair obscuring my face, I gazed into the large mirror, sighing in relief. Further bruising extended from the right side of my temple across my cheekbone down to the corner of my lips, but there didn't appear to be any swelling. Dark smudges encrusted the skin along the side of my hairline, and I grabbed some paper towels from the dispenser beside the sink to clean it off. Dampening the cloths, I dabbed them over the area, gently scrubbing the surface. The stains slowly washed from the skin, bleeding into a muddied soup across the paper fabric. I dropped the moist heap at the realization.

It was blood.

Achingly lifting my arms, I pulled up the hospital gown, seeing more bruising...and more dried blood. But not a single scratch maimed my skin. Where did all the blood come from?

CHAPTER 3
Mad Hatter

A light knock registered at the bedroom door, and it only caused me to roll over and bury my head into my pillows. Another knock followed, along with my mother's voice.

"Kat?" She opened the door and stepped inside after my failure to acknowledge her. "Hey, you have some company."

I cringed at the painful tug in my ribs as I turned and looked up at the entryway. Vanessa and Carly both gave me a small wave. "How's she been?" asked Vanessa softly to my mom.

"Hasn't left her bed with the exception of eating and using the bathroom. That's about it," Mom affirmed intentionally louder.

"At least she's eating," sighed Carly.

"That's what's so strange. Normally when she's down about something, it's like having to extract teeth to get her to eat," said Mom. "Now, Kat's like a human garbage disposal. I've seen her eat more in the last week than she usually eats in three months. She polished off two pints of ice cream, downed a bag of Lays potato chips, had an entire bucket of fried chicken, and then ate a large pizza. This was just yesterday, mind you."

"Damn, girl." Carly came up to me and ripped my comforter right off the bed, exposing me in my Batman boy shorts and tank top.

"Hey!" I curled up into the fetal position as the brisk air bit at my bare legs and arms.

"Seriously? You've been pigging out like Garfield the cat, and you look thinner! If I so much as dream of French fries, I wake up five pounds heavier!"

"Just leave me alone," I groaned, jamming a pillow over my head.

"You need to get out of this room," sighed Vanessa.

"I like this room."

"You haven't returned any of our texts or phone calls, and no one else has heard from you. Being a hermit isn't healthy, babe. We all think you could use a little fresh air."

Carly and Mom nodded.

"And you just so happened to pick today to do this?" I scowled at all three of them. "I'm not an idiot. I know what today is. And even if I didn't, Johnny Cash's entourage here is pretty much like a neon sign in my face," I remarked, pointing at Vanessa and Carly's all black ensemble. Neither wore the color frequently, and never did they wear it head-to-toe.

"The funeral starts in about an hour," Vanessa confirmed.

Mom nodded to my friends, as if silently passing the baton to them. "I'll leave you girls be."

She exited, and Vanessa slowly made her way over to my bedside, smoothing out the ends of her dress.

"How's your mom been?" whispered Carly. "When we saw her at the hospital, she was wound up tighter than a ten day clock."

"You guys were at the hospital?" I asked, my voice muffled as I buried my face into my pillow.

"Yeah, so was Adam," replied Vanessa.

My head shot up from the fluffiness with surprise. "He was?"

I looked over at Carly who unreservedly shot V an ugly glare.

"The nurses wouldn't let any of us come see you though," added Vanessa, obviously ignoring Car's anger.

"Anyway," Carly growled.

"Mom's been...well, Mom," I clarified. "Thankfully, I'd been sedated in the hospital, so by the time I'd woken up, the doctors had already assured her that I was fine. Though, I could've used a little more mother and a little less public relations liaison."

Carly gave me a sympathetic smile. "That bad?"

"Imagine the worst case scenario and multiply it by twenty," I moaned. "She was in full-blown damage control mode. My mom convinced the police to release an official statement saying that I hadn't been drinking that night, but by the sounds of the conversations she's been having with my dad, it doesn't sound like everyone in town is buying the story."

"Where is your dad?" queried Vanessa. "The garage door was open when we pulled up, but I didn't see his car.

"He's still in Arizona," I said.

Both Carly and Vanessa's eyes widened at the clarification.

"Wait, you mean he flew back there, right? He did come home to see you," Carly urged.

I shook my head. "It's not that big of a deal though. My mom couldn't get a hold of him until after she already found out I was okay, so by the time they talked, I guess he figured it wasn't worth flying all the way home. It's fine."

Carly gritted her teeth. "Yeah, right."

"It is, really. He's in the middle of finalizing a huge merger, so...you know." The room fell silent, forcing me to address the elephant in the room. "I can't go."

"Not feeling well?" asked Vanessa, gently brushing the hair from my eyes.

"It's my fault." I hadn't actually uttered those words out loud since the accident, and the moment I heard them, I buried my face back into my pillows with a sob.

"That's not true," Carly assured as V ran a hand up and down my arm. "You weren't the one behind the wheel."

"Yeah, and he wouldn't have been either if it wasn't for me," I cried. "Blaine's dead!"

Vanessa tried soothing me as Carly returned my comforter to the bed.

"It's all my fault," I sniveled.

"No one thinks that, and neither should you. The police even said so. There was an animal in the road. It could have happened to anyone," Carly confirmed. "You can't blame yourself for that. Accidents are just that; Accidents. We can't control them no more than we can control the weather. It's out of our hands. You're obviously going through survivor's remorse, but that's exactly what you should be grateful for. You're a survivor. Considering how bad the crash was, it's a miracle you walked away at all, let alone with next to no injuries." She plopped down next to Vanessa on the bedside. "You don't have to stay if you don't want. If at any time during the service you feel like it's too much, we'll go."

"It might be good to, you know, be around others who are grieving as well," added V. "You're not alone."

"I'm a total mess," I murmured.

"We'd figured you would be," Carly chuckled, flashing me a large department shopping bag.

***

I took a quick shower, and Vanessa helped do my hair as I applied some makeup at my vanity mirror.

"How long were you in the hospital?" she asked hesitantly, continuing to wrap sections of my blonde locks around the barrel of my curling iron.

"About a day and a half."

"That's it?"

"Yeah, the doctors said I only suffered superficial injuries, so they just kept me for observation."

"You're lucky," Vanessa sighed as Carly kept sorting through the lot of clothing options she brought with.

"How about this one?" Carly pulled out a low-cut, black mini dress from the bag.

"Car, it's a funeral; not a nightclub," remarked Vanessa. "She cannot go in that."

"Why not? I'm wearing this." Carly disrobed from her pea coat, revealing a black haltered dress with a dangerously plunging neckline.

"Are you kidding?" barked V.

"What? It's still black," she argued. "And what's wrong with wanting to look your best?"

"Your best doesn't require your boobs to be propped up and put on display for everyone to see."

"Please just give me something," I finally mumbled. "I'll take a freaking poncho at this point."

Vanessa took control from there, handing me a black brocade dress that fell respectfully to the knees. I headed over to the bathroom to change when a loud thud struck the window closest to me. We all shrieked, jumping back from the pane.

"What the hell was that?" yelped Carly.

I hesitantly made my way over to the window, looking down at the ground. A small black clump lay beside the flowerbed below. "You've gotta be kidding me."

"What is it?"

"It looks like a bird flew into the house."

"Oooh." Carly had a total soft spot for animals, so she promptly jumped to action.

"V, can you-"

"Sorry, Car," Vanessa interrupted. "I love your go-to attitude and everything, but I'm not good with blood and all that. Besides, isn't that, like, a bad omen or something? A bird hitting your house?"

"That's just an old wives tale," huffed Carly. "Kat, would you mind helping me?"

"No problem," I said, following her out of the room.

"V, can you at least get a blanket or a large towel along with a box? If the bird's still alive, I'll need to handle it properly."

I gave Carly a pair of handy gloves to use as we headed outside. We walked down the front porch over to the small garden, seeing the little broken body resting beneath the window.

"Oh, you poor thing." Carly crouched down in front of the fallen bird, observing its body. The animal lay motionless, and it didn't appear to be breathing either. Car still picked it up for good measure, just in case there was something she could still do.

"How does it look, Doc?"

"Her neck's broken. She's already gone." Carly set the body back down. "I'm gonna go grab a plastic bag so we can dispose of it."

She took off the gloves and headed back inside.

R...R...Ruff-ruff!

"Oh, no."

Paws clacked up the driveway, and no sooner when I turned did a big, wet snout come barreling into my face.

"Stanley!"

The black and white spaniel bounced about like Tigger the Tiger on crack cocaine. He started sniffing my shoes, and the dog's eyes then pinpointed to the raven's body.

"Stanley, don't!" I lunged for the bird, narrowly managing to sweep up its tiny frame and raise it above my head to ensure Stanley and his drooling chops couldn't reach it.

"Stanley," whined Mrs. Corvets two houses down. "Stanley, get over here, and stop harassing the poor girl!"

The dog's ears drooped at the command.

A cracking noise erupted from my hands, and I immediately lowered the bird back down to eye level. The raven's once crooked collar was now snapped into place, and its contorted wing suddenly twisted and set itself back into the socket.

"What the...?"

The bird's chest puffed up quickly and deflated a beat later.

Puffed up and deflated.

Again.

And again.

Mrs. Corvets howled something, and Stanly seemed

to finally relent to the order, trotting slowly across the lawn back to his owner.

A soft tweet resonated from within my hands, and the bird's eyes flung open.

"Holy crap!"

The bird shot out of my hands, its wings fluttering crazily. I instinctively began swatting, trying to get the frightened creature out of my face. Last thing I needed was a plucked eyeball!

"Oh my God!" exclaimed Mrs. Corvets as the raven finally flew away. "Are you okay, sweetheart?"

I nodded dazedly, still unsure as to what the hell just happened.

"Hey."

I jumped, turning to see Carly standing behind me again.

"Where's the bird?" she asked, looking over my shoulder to observe the flowerbed.

I still couldn't find an answer.

Car's eyes settled on Stanley as he galloped back over to his owner's yard. "Eww. He didn't...you know, take it, did he?"

It was an easier explanation, I suppose, so I just nodded again.

"That's so gross."

***

"I can't do this." I started backpedaling through the mass of people in the main aisle when Vanessa and Carly both caught hold of my arm, coaxing me forward.

"Yes, you can. You're doing fine," V assured.

"Why the hell did I agree to this? Everyone's staring

at me," I muttered.

"No, they're not."

It wasn't my imagination. Everyone was. The entire congregation seemed to pause in the midst of their actions the moment my presence was made aware. The Ryders weren't particularly religious, so Blaine's mother had chosen to hold the service at their family's sprawling estate. And no expense seemed to be wasted by the looks of it. The entire banquet hall had been refurnished with everything from pews to even an altar. Whispers filled the hall's warm, stagnant air as V and Car ushered me to a vacant section of a nearby pew.

I heard an indistinct murmur come from behind me as I headed over to the space, and a sharp whack echoed immediately after. I turned around to see Tiffany Albright rubbing the top of her head before my eyes caught sight of the rolled up brochure in Carly's hand. I cut Vanessa a look, and she grimaced as the three of us sat.

"Should I ask what that was about?" I whispered.

"Nothing."

"You're a terrible liar, V." I leaned over to see Carly giving Tiffany a slew of crude hand gestures.

"Yeah, like I'm the only one here thinking it," Albright remarked back.

"Hey," Carly finally snapped, her voice sneering above a whisper. "Unless you want us all to be hearing *your* eulogy next, I'd shut it!"

Everyone within ear distance turned their attention to us.

"Will both of you knock it off?" said Vanessa, nodding up at the altar.

Up until that moment, I had made it a point to not look up there, but alas I finally did. Clawing my fingernails into my thighs, I felt my stomach drop and chest tighten. Beside the closed casket, there was a massive placard with Blaine's yearbook photo on display, his striking blue eyes and infectious smile beaming back at me. I immediately shielded my eyes with my hand, trying to control the inevitable sob that erupted from my throat.

Vanessa insisted she switch seats with Carly to put some distance between her and Tiffany, and I couldn't be more grateful as tears spilled off my lashes.

Car didn't miss a beat, immediately coddling her arms around me. I buried my face into her sleeve.

"It's okay," she hushed softly.

As if someone had gripped my shoulders, I suddenly wrenched upright. The involuntary movement almost caused me to scream. A soothing warmth began spreading across my chest, leaving me in a deeper state of bewilderment.

"Do not let your heart be troubled." The words came in a gentle whisper, breathing right into my ear. I whirled around, finding nobody on my opposing side. In the far back of the banquet hall, however, stood a most curious guest. They lingered in the entrance of the corner passageway, an oversized black hoodie hiding their features. The person merely nodded, disappearing into the shadows of the corridor. The warmth was swiftly ripped from my chest, leaving an aching, hollow chill in its place.

***

Mystic Harbor divided into three sections. I, along with the Ryders, lived in the East End where a majority of the upscale residents resided. Some were newer homes, but most were century-old estates, and they all looked like

43

something eerily out of *The Stepford Wives*. The cemetery was on the whole other side of town, resulting in an exhaustingly long funeral procession. We drove north to the rightly named Old Port, a 19th-century district made up of historic buildings and cobblestone streets. Quaint shops lined the boulevard, moss clinging to the thick roofing slates. With all the antique mold trimmings, handmade bricks, and carved molding doors, it looked just like the design of one of those old novelty village puzzles. It was a particularly gloomy morning, and a heavy blanket of fog had traveled down to the district to cast a subtle glow across the dewy streets. Complimented by the warm gaslights lining the stretch, Old Port remained a place paused in time, like an idyllic English town untouched by modern hands.

The same couldn't be said about the south and west ends of town. On the other side of Old Port were all the shopping centers, restaurants, and bars tourists reveled in visiting from just off the harbor. The businesses brought in revenue, but it also brought what my mom's country club society called "the unfavorable." Mystic Harbor was built on old money, and the tight knit community didn't leave much welcomed room for outsiders. So when new businesses boomed, the flock of neighboring locals from less respecting areas gravitated to Mystic Harbor, becoming thorns in the country club's side.

One of those said thorns happened to be the Reynolds. Adam's dad opened up a popular waterfront bar a few years ago off the river, and it had become the local watering hole for those who didn't drive Porsches and live in seaside castles. I loved it, not only because it gave me a reprieve from Mom since she and the rest of her country club goers refused to travel west of Bowen Street, but because it had become my home away from home...up until recently. It was dubbed The Office, after a running gag. Their novelty shirts read, "Sorry, honey, I'm still at The Office."

At last, we arrived at the cemetery.

"Hey, sweetheart."

I froze at the sound of the deep, burly voice. Sure enough, it was Mr. Reynolds. Standing there in beaten up boots, worn jeans, and his iconic racing jacket, he stood out like a sore thumb amongst the other black-clad mourners. I hadn't seen him at the service, so it came as a surprise to see him here. And I couldn't be more relieved.

He opened his arms, and I practically tackled him with his invitation for a hug.

"Hey, Papa Bear." I nuzzled my face into his chest, welcoming the comforting aroma of cinnamon and cigarettes that always lingered on his clothes. He easily dwarfed me, which wasn't that hard given I was only five-three, but he took it to a whole other level. Mr. Reynolds used to be an ultimate fighter, and the years hadn't robbed him of his muscular physique. The only indication of his age was the sparse gray strands riddled in his copper brown locks and cultivated facial hair. Top the fact that he was six-foot-five and looked like he could take down Wolverine with his bare hands, and I honestly felt like a little kid hugging him.

It had been hard not being able to have the same relationship with him that we had before Adam and I broke up. He'd become something of a second father to me since moving to town.

"I didn't see you at the estate," I said, peering up at him.

"I didn't go. I'd just spotted you in the procession on the way back from the hardware store, and I wanted to see how you were doing." He planted a kiss on top of my head as I finally pulled away.

"Been better," I admitted, noting the handful of mourners eyeing me as they passed by.

"Hey." He perched a finger on my chin, redirecting my head in his direction. "Don't pay any mind to them, okay? Things will get easier. I promise."

I gave a meager smile.

"How about you swing by the bar sometime, give us a chance to talk."

"I'd like that," I affirmed.

We both noted the last of the cars pulling into the lot, and Mr. Reynolds sighed.

"I'll let you go," he said, giving me one last hug.

We said our goodbyes, and I fell back into step with Carly and Vanessa. As we walked along with the others to the burial plot, a few girls ahead of us shared in a less than discrete conversation.

"Why didn't they have an open casket? My brother knew this one guy who was in a car crash, and his folks still had an open casket," said one of the girls.

"Yeah? Was this guy decapitated, too?" remarked her friend sourly.

"Are you serious?" Her two friends gawked.

"From what I heard, that wasn't the only body part that got taken off," she confirmed.

They gagged at the thought, and I immediately slowed my pace.

"They're gonna need closed caskets when I'm done with them," growled Carly as she and V noticed me lingering back.

"I need some space," I affirmed. "I'll see you guys after."

"You sure?" asked Vanessa.

I nodded, heading across the cemetery. A massive black oak tree sat nearby, so I made my way over to it, resting my back against the ridged bark. The funeral was still close enough that I could observe it, but I thankfully couldn't overhear anything being said by the pastor...or anyone else.

"Nauseating, isn't it?"

I whirled around and stumbled back as a figure appeared from behind the tree. "I'm sorry?"

Reese Blackburn pushed off the tree bark and strolled out towards me, sporting an expression I couldn't quite decipher. Resentment? Frustration, maybe. He ruffled a hand through his bed-head brown hair. His clothes weren't in much better shape. Reese appeared to have pulled his black slacks and matching blazer out of the hamper, as the articles were pressed with wrinkles. It was by far the most disheveled I'd ever seen him look. "The bloviating," he affirmed.

There was a large camera dangling from his neck, and when he lifted it up to take a distant snapshot of the service, I caught a better look at his AC/DC 'Highway to Hell' t-shirt. Not exactly what you'd call funeral-friendly attire.

"Obviously no one wants to cast dispersions on some dead guy, so you always hear the same things. 'He was the nicest, gentlest, sweetest person,'" he drawled flatly. "All a funeral really is is just a social facelift. Put 'em six feet under and any asshole becomes a saint. Just once, I'd like to see a little honesty."

"Excuse me?" I finally uttered.

"What? You disagree?"

"To your blatant psychosis? Yeah," I blurted, my tone swiftly shifting from stunned to downright anger.

He smirked as he lifted his camera again, but I

swatted the lens away, ruining the shot.

"Why the hell are you even here?" I demanded.

"Trust me; I had better things planned for my morning, but our editor insisted I come here to cover the service. You know, write a touching article about my firsthand account of the tear-wrenching memorial of our beloved quarterback. Yada, yada, yada."

"Are you really that stupid, or just that insensitive?"

"I prefer the term honest. Prince Charming on that placard over there wasn't the Golden Boy everyone insists on advertising."

"Oh, I get it. Residual trauma from swirlies has got your panties in a bunch," I shot back. "I suppose it is easier to badmouth someone who can't defend themselves, right? How manly that must make you feel."

He grinned, but it didn't mask his obvious aggravation as he got a better look at me. Reese suddenly chuckled to himself.

I ignored the gesture and turned around.

"Look, I'm not judging you or anything," he remarked.

"Judging me?" I queried, spinning around.

"Yeah, you and Ryder...you know."

"No, I don't know," I growled.

"He put Percy in the playpen, am I right?" Reese scoffed.

I could feel my cheeks burning, but it wasn't from embarrassment.

"It's a pity that's not a video camera," I growled, pointing to the device in his left hand. "Because that would've been the only piece of evidence to record what I'm about to do to you."

"You offering to go twenty-toes with me, too?" He

still wasn't amused. What was this guy's problem?

"I was thinking something more along the lines of a Colombian necktie." I closed the gap of space between us, and he stepped back, but that stupid smirk of his wouldn't subside.

"You're a little hostile, you know that?"

"Maybe you didn't hear, but I was the one in the car with him—"

"I know." His jaw was set unnaturally tight as his eyes bore down at me.

It wouldn't do me any good starting up a full-fledged fight with him, so I stepped backward. "Just stay the hell away from me," I growled.

Reese's gaze redirected over my head. "Careful now."

I suddenly spun at the sound of leaves crushing beneath someone's boots directly behind me, and Carly and I collided into one another.

"Holy hell!" she yelped as we both stumbled to the ground.

Brushing the mess of hair from my eyes, I looked back behind me at the tree, only to find no one in sight. "What the hell?"

"You okay?" asked Carly.

I shot back up to my feet and rounded the oak, finding nothing on the other side but more tombstones. "Where did he go?"

Car just looked at me perplexedly.

"Did you see where he went?"

"Babe..."

"Did you see him?"

"Kat, nobody else was out here," she finally muttered.

CHAPTER 4
People Are Strange

When Monday morning rolled around, I was forced to face the inevitable. I had to return to school. After the accident, I stayed home during the whole next week to recuperate from my injuries, which unbeknownst to anybody but my immediate doctor, were purely superficial. The trauma I suffered was mainly localized across my chest and abdomen from where I'd been wearing my seatbelt. The bruising was so bad that all the doctors working in the ER were certain that I had internal damage of some kind. There was also swelling over the center of my chest which prompted everyone to keep mentioning the distinct possibility that I had a "sternal fracture."

By some sheer miracle though, I was given a clean bill of health. My absence from Belleview High was admittedly for emotional recovery. Sadly though, isolating yourself from the world while wearing your comforter around the house and pigging out on Ben & Jerry's doesn't remedy heartache. If anything, it put me into a deeper funk. I needed to reintroduce myself to society.

Anxiety hit me though as I observed my fellow classmates pulling into the school parking lot come 7:23 a.m. Everybody congregated around their cars, and all eyes were on me as we drove into our designated space. Indistinct whispers circulated, and I couldn't tell by their grim expressions if everyone pitied or blamed me for what happened. Desperate for a distraction, I finally tuned into Carly and Vanessa's conversation. Since they picked me up this morning, they'd been giving me the lowdown on all the steamy gossip I'd missed out on over the past week, but I admittedly checked out of the conversation a whole thirty seconds into it. Thankfully, by the sounds of it, Carly's rant about unfair school dress code violations was done as she was now talking about her boyfriend. Given her proclivity for over sharing however, it may not have been a much better subject matter, as the conversation risked taking a sharp turn into an NC-17 rating.

"My mom's going postal about me being out at night now, even if I'm with Daniel," moaned Car.

"Your mom should be worried if you're out with Daniel, especially alone," Vanessa cracked.

She laughed. "True. But after everything that's happened, she's trying to turn the house into Fort Knox. Got a new alarm system, put up cameras around the property, and she's calling in these guys to reinforce all the doors and windows. Seriously, we could survive *The Purge* if it came down to it."

"After everything that's happened?"

"Yeah, you know. With Hersey."

"What about Hersey?"

Vanessa and Carly both exchanged awkward glances.

"Okay, what am I missing here?" I demanded.

"You seriously don't know?" asked V.

"How could you not know?" begged Carly. "I mean, I know you've been locked up in your room and all, but you never watched the news?"

The blank look on my face must have said it all, because she sighed. I'd made it a point to avoid the news at all cost after my stay at the hospital. Channel 5 was bleeding coverage about the accident, plastering Blaine's face along with mine across the screen every chance they got.

"The night of the bonfire, one of the buses heading to the basketball tournament…it vanished. It had Hersey High's entire basketball team and cheerleading squad onboard. Everyone across the county went crazy. We even set up search parties around here. You should've joined us. Would've been a good distraction. The guys came with V and me to go through Tyler Park and the surrounding woods."

"Did they find the bus?"

"The bus, the driver, the students. Gone."

"Our own team and cheerleaders were reported missing as well," whispered Vanessa.

"What?"

"Yeah, but it turned out to be nothing," she quickly added. "Apparently, after the tournament was over, everyone decided to skip the bonfire and go to Jacob Marshall's lake house to party. They all crashed there for the night, so when news about Hersey broke the next morning, everyone's parents went nuts thinking their kids went missing too. It was a whole fiasco."

My stomach somersaulted. Blaine had mentioned something about the lake house and how he'd blown it off going so he could come to the bonfire instead…to see me.

"You okay?" asked Carly.

"I just want to get this day over with," I murmured as

we walked past another group of gossiping classmates.

Calculus and Bio both went by in a blur. My attention on the assignments was nonexistent and by third period, I felt sick. I'd tried convincing myself that it was all in my head, that anxiety was simply getting the better of me. Even sitting in my desk, I felt lightheaded, and my stomach lurched achingly. It felt like I hadn't eaten anything in days, despite having had a full breakfast of eggs, bacon, and a whole stack of pancakes just a few hours ago. Maybe my blood sugar was on the fritz.

The moment class let out, I staggered down the hallway and practically tackled the vending machine as I dug around in my pocket for change. Reassurance escaped me though as the coil pushing my purchased protein bar stopped just short of letting the snack fall. My dignity was nonexistent as I batted the glass before crumpling on the ground beside the machine, trying to find more coins in my book satchel.

"Hey, you okay?" Gentle blue eyes greeted me as I looked up.

"Adam…hi. No. I mean, yes. I'm fine. I-I'm just trying to find some money. The machine didn't give me my bar." I hadn't seen or spoken to him since before the night of the accident, and things hadn't ended particularly well.

"May I?" He gestured at the vending machine.

"No, it's okay. You don't have to waste your money. I've got some quarters in here somewhere," I insisted, rummaging through my bag more determinedly.

He smiled. "Lean forward."

I looked at him questioningly, but did as he requested. Securing both arms around the sides of the machine, Adam gently rocked it back and forth. A soft thump registered, and he coaxed it back on all fours like it weighed nothing. He plucked out my protein bar from the bottom slot and handed it over.

"You really shouldn't do that," I said. "Statistically, you're more likely to die from a vending machine crushing you than being killed by a shark."

He grinned. "Yeah, you told me that the last time I did that."

"Oh..."

"And I looked it up. It's still only a one in a hundred million chance."

I hated it when he said things like that, because it was oddly sweet. He failed spectacularly at delivering on the important things when we were together, but in all earnestness, he always recalled the little things...like he cherished them enough that he'd take the effort to do a fact check.

And I highly doubted he'd get flattened by the vending machine, though I admittedly use to fantasize about it when he'd do things like ditch me out of nowhere. Adam was really strong. Not in a beefy sort of way, but he was solidly built. He really enjoyed working out, especially kickboxing and strength training; though you couldn't tell how muscular he was just by looking at him. He dressed rather demurely, hiding his frame beneath flannel shirts and loose jeans.

I could tell he'd just worked out too, observing the dampness of his thick, slicked back ashy brown hair. He always showered after gym class and practice, and the fresh scent of mint lingered on his skin as he extended his hand to me.

I'd always loved the way he smelled.

Snap out of it, I ordered myself, climbing back up to my feet.

His gaze softened all the more as I met his height, or at least as close as I could get to it. He was just shy of six feet, so he still had almost nine inches on me.

"I never had a chance to ask you, how're you doing?" He quickly diverted his eyes at my failure to reply. "Sorry, I didn't mean to put you on the spot like that."

My mouth managed to open, but I couldn't force the words out. I'd been telling everyone all day long that I was "okay," but Adam was different. He knew better than anyone when I was lying, and it seemed pointless to try.

"I tried calling you after..." He cleared his throat. "But you didn't get back to me, so..."

He'd done more than that, and I knew neither he nor my mom would admit it (though for very different reasons). Mom was never particularly fond of him, even before she knew about his flakiness. The woman tried living her high school glory days again vicariously through me, and a ruffian such as Adam didn't fit the profile. She wanted me to find someone like my dad. The Golden Boy. That guy who reeked of sophistication and charm. A yuppie-in-training if you will. Not a grease monkey who looked like he'd just rolled out from under a car. She wanted me to be with someone like...Blaine.

"Hey, you ready to hit the gym?" announced Carly, suddenly appearing at my side. She eyed Adam like he was Satan's Spawn, hooking her arm around mine and pulling me away.

"Thank you," I managed to say, holding up the protein bar in appreciation to Adam before she gave me a good yank. "Oww."

"What're you doing?" she groaned.

"Besides having my best friend rip my arm out of its socket?" I jabbed, knowing full-well of her condemnation. "Lighten up, okay? He was just being polite."

"And you were totally falling for it."

"Was not."

"Oh please, every time he gives you his *Puss in Boots* eyes, you're on your ass."

"Well, then be thankful I'm not you. Otherwise, I'd be on his mattress," I laughed.

***

"There's this thing you may have heard of called chewing," remarked Carly, seeing me practically inhale my protein bar as we exited the locker room.

The gnawing pains in my stomach grew fiercer, and I prayed it wouldn't take too long for the small serving to curb my aching appetite. I headed over to the bleachers and lay flat across the unoccupied first bench.

"Don't take this the wrong way, but you kinda look like crap," said Carly, brushing my unruly strands of hair out of my face as she took a seat beside me. Her hand rested on my forehead, and she hummed.

"What's your diagnosis, doc? Do I have the plague?"

"You're not hot."

I half laughed. "Well, that's not very nice."

"You're really pale though."

"Tell me something I don't already know." I'd noticed it the first time I'd faced a mirror after the accident. The rich tan I'd inherited from all those long summer days was now nonexistent, replaced by an alabaster so light that it rivaled Snow White's complexion. Hating my new Casper the Friendly Ghost look, I tried concealing it under some bronzer and blush, but the makeup didn't seem to be holding up.

"You have any chills? Sore throat? Aches?"

I shook my head. "I just feel like my blood sugar has crashed, like I haven't eaten."

"Were you prescribed pain meds or something? Last year, after I broke my arm, my doctor put me on some stuff that completely messed up my stomach."

"No." I'd been given a couple different prescriptions at the hospital, but I hadn't taken any of it. The masochist in me wanted to feel the pain. What right did I have to numb myself after what happened? Someone had died, and all I had were some bruises and a few minor scratches.

"Look alive," announced Coach Gleeson, and we all straightened at the command. The man was ex-military and about the last person you wanted to piss off. While other schools treated gym class like freaking recess, Coach ran P.E. like it was Army Basic Training. "The radar is showing us that the rain will be taking a short break before the new system rolls in. And on a day as oddly warm as today, it would be a shame to let such fine temperatures go to waste. If you all hurry, we may just get back inside in time before we get drenched."

"What are we gonna do outside? The grass is sopping wet," challenged Carly. "You want us to play in the puddles?"

Gleeson grinned. "Nope, you'll be running the track. The mile, actually."

Everyone groaned.

"Isn't that a safety hazard? Someone could slip out there."

"Yes, and by sitting here, all your stationary limbs could start tingling from poor blood circulation, and who knows what kind of horrible residual aftereffects you may suffer from?" Coach cracked. "Up, people!"

We all moaned again as we followed his instructions.

"Perfect," I muttered. "Nothing better than lots of cardio to help make me feel better."

"You know, I've come to find that rigorous bouts of exercise can be a great way to work off stress," laughed Carly devilishly, helping me to my feet.

"Oh, yes, I can only imagine how deeply therapeutic 'exercising' with you must be," I chuckled, shoving her.

"Yow! Get your mind outta the gutter there, tomcat," she teased.

"Oh, I'm sorry," I laughed. "You weren't implying an overtone of sorts there?"

"Race me."

"What?"

"On the track," Carly clarified. "I want to see some of that gumption of yours, and it just might be what the doctor ordered. Nothing helps me feel better than a good endorphin rush."

She had a point, and she knew my inner overachiever couldn't stand the thought of losing.

Everyone started filing out of the side exit, and an unexpected burst of adrenalin hit.

"Prepare to lose," I challenged, shaking her hand.

"You honestly think you can beat me?" She was one of the top runners on the track team, but I was nevertheless pretty fast myself, though I'd never run competitively.

"I'm saying I'm gonna mop the track with you when I'm done," I said heartily.

"What's this now?" asked Daniel, catching up with us.

"Your girlfriend here is gonna give some therapeutic

relief via me crushing her ego on the track," I declared.

"Take it easy there, Prefontaine," laughed Carly.

Taking the gravel road out to the track, Car and I pushed our way through the pack of classmates to the front of the line.

"You wanna place a wager on this?" asked Daniel.

"I'd say it's best not to."

"Oh? Someone's confidence wavering?" he remarked.

"No, I just doubt Carly's ability to play by the rules," I said, stretching out. "Wouldn't want to put any real stakes on the table, only for her to pull a Rosie Ruiz on me."

"Hey, running is one thing I'd never have to resort to cheating on," she corrected.

"Yes, because I imagine fleeing from your nightly conquests must require considerable speed and strong endurance," I whispered jokingly to her.

"Your mouth certainly doesn't seem to tire easily, but the question is, can your feet keep up?" Carly laughed as the two of us prepared for Coach to commence the race.

"Remember, four full laps. And I will be keeping track, so don't even bother trying to pull anything, okay?" warned Gleeson. "On your mark… Get set…" He hesitated, seeing the two of us overly eager for him to call it. "Go!"

Carly and I both rocketed off down the stretch and neither of us lost pace over the course of our trek. My muscles were on fire, the strangely humid air posing no help in letting the sweat perforating my skin to evaporate. The two of us kept in stride with one another, but on the final lap, an adrenalin rush exploded within my veins. I managed to sneak my way into the inner lane, rounding the first turn sharply. My legs propelled me faster and faster, and I heard Carly's footsteps fading behind me. I plowed through the packs of people in front of me who were still on their third lap, and my pace didn't relent. If anything, it felt like I was gaining momentum.

I finally raced past the finish line where Coach was standing on the grass field inside the track's perimeter. Decelerating gradually, I finally came to a halt and trotted back over to Gleeson to clock in my completion. Something foreign inside me clawed desperately for me to keep running, soaking up the high from my endorphin rush.

"I've got a question for you," said Coach as I approached. "Why in good health aren't you on the track team?"

"What was my time?"

"5:24."

"What?" Carly exclaimed, just now passing the finish line.

"Cue some 'Eye of the Tiger,'" I declared, jogging in place and throwing up my burning arms Rocky-style. "'Cause I'd call that the sweet taste of victory."

"Yeah, by a long shot," she huffed exhausted. "How the hell did you do that? You made me look like a grandma out there."

"Haven't a clue," I admitted, not feeling the least bit winded.

Something didn't feel right, in the fact that I now felt fine. Better than fine. I felt phenomenal. We'd run the track not even three weeks ago, and I struggled to beat the 6:30 mark in perfect health.

Lightning suddenly crackled overhead, followed by a thunderous roar, startling us all. The thought of being trapped out on the track in the rain made even the laziest runners pick up the pace, and we thankfully got back to the gym before the downpour commenced.

"Alright, we'll dial things down a notch." Coach

opened the equipment storage room and dragged out a bin full of hockey sticks. He split the class up into four teams, letting the last two take a breather on the benches as the first hit the court.

"You've got this, baby!" cheered Carly to Daniel, who took to center court for the face-off.

Metal clacked overhead from the newly installed overlook that housed our new weightlifting space. Half the girls were sitting at the top of the stands so they could steal peeks between the railings at the shirtless guys working out overhead. My mind seemed elsewhere however, as that invisible pull inside me hadn't lessened. My body wanted to keep moving, but I was now stuck on the sidelines. Gazing unfocusedly across the gym, my vision suddenly centered on Brenda Hardy.

I nudged Carly. "Do you see that?"

"Hmm?" She somehow managed to stop making googly eyes at Daniel long enough to glance over at where I indicated. "What am I looking for?"

"Brenda Hardy."

Of all things, she laughed. "Yeah, you'd think she'd stop trying to fit into her little sister's clothes by now, but what the hey."

Okay, yes, Brenda was notorious for wearing shirts that looked about three sizes too small for her, but that was beside the point. I highly doubted a fashion faux pa took precedence over the freakish red cloud floating around her.

"You don't see anything else weird?"

Carly shrugged. "No. Why?"

Like a dog eagerly yanking on a leash, I felt an inexplicable inner urge pulling me toward Brenda. The longer I sat there, the stronger the sensation became. I was forced to claw my nails into the underside of the bench to keep my ass planted down.

"Hey, you okay?" asked Carly. "You look like you've got ants in your pants, or something."

A pang suddenly punched me in the gut as Daniel relinquished a slapshot, sending the rubberized hockey ball across the court. Right at Brenda. She attempted to hit the ball away when another girl came barreling down on her. Their sticks collided, and the two girls ran into each other. A gasp escaped my lips just as a rogue hockey stick drove right into Brenda's left ankle. She tried to catch herself, but the force sent her sideways, leaving her accompanying knee to give out at an unnatural angle.

Brenda yelped, crashing to the floor in an agonizing heap. Everybody on the court raced over to her, blocking Coach's path. He blew his whistle, leaving us all half-deaf by the painfully high pitch. The crowd parted, and everyone on the bleachers caught sight of Brenda as she rolled over with a scream.

Carly outright gagged, and I covered my mouth at the grisly image of Brenda's kneecap protruding from the side of her leg!

As a player ran out of the gym at Coach's command to fetch a nurse, I saw the red cloud slowly dissipate from around the girl.

"That is so messed up," croaked a classmate behind us.

Heat spread throughout my body, and my heart started throbbing against my rib cage. What the hell was happening to me?

The invisible force within me grew into an all-out rage, pounding against my flesh in a desperate attempt to literally break free from my skin locking it inside.

"You don't look so good, babe." Carly hesitantly put

her hand on my shoulder, and I involuntarily shuddered at the contact, recoiling away from her like a frightened animal. "Kat, what's wrong?"

"I...I have to go."

As if a spring was planted beneath me, I launched up from the bleachers and flew out the side door to the outside. Despite the humidity, a breeze still coursed through the air, batting my clammy skin. I remained under the brick canopy that shielded me from the downpour, but that same feeling continued tugging against my chest.

I needed to run.

The singular craving brought a wave of clarity over me, and everything around me fell mute. I took off, loving the thrill of the water splashing around me as my feet pounded against the flooded cement walkway lining the building. The parking attendant hollered something at me as I eventually made it to the school lot. She hustled out with her umbrella, trying to catch up with me. The bestial frenzy roaring through my veins laughed at the pathetic attempt as I blew past her in nothing but a blur.

CHAPTER 5
The Nobodies

I ran for nearly an hour straight without any objective before I eventually found myself nearing my house. The high I had gotten must have worn off, because grim death blanketed me as I staggered up my front steps. I barely managed to unlock the door as my body collapsed against the frame. Surely I had the flu. Even with the unseasonably warm temperature, I was freezing. My hands felt weak, and it took a considerable amount of effort to just move my legs. Could I get upstairs? I made it as far as the foyer rug before everything went black.

The ground gave out from beneath my feet, sending me into a freefall. I had the wind knocked out of me as my body slammed into the surface below. Desperately struggling to refill my lungs, I gasped as my fingers curled, clawing up what felt like brittle dirt. The blurriness slowly eased from my vision, but all I could see was a billowing cloud of ash looming overhead, illuminated by the light atop of the hole.

Wait...

The hole?

The ends of my hair battered my face as I sat upright, seeing shadows cast amongst the rough stone wall beside me. Three grottos lined the space ahead, each entryway pitch-black. Was I in...a cave? The light at the surface burned coolly from an angle, and the sky above was dark. If it was already sunset, I'd be losing that last ounce of light in a matter of minutes, leaving me trapped in the dark. I screamed, hollering at the top of my lungs for help until my voice gave out. I scrambled back across the ground, kicking up the filth around me. Something about the dirt felt odd. Having spent time in Mom's garden bed, I knew the feeling of mud and dirt all too well. This wasn't the same. I lifted a handful, letting the material sift out between my fingers. Even with the minimal light, I could see the charcoal coloring. It wasn't dirt. It was soot.

A low grumble echoed overhead, and a flash of lightning followed, highlighting the space. All the shadows vanished in that split second, leaving every inch of the hole exposed. My body slammed against the grated façade behind me as I fell into a frenzy, desperate to keep cowering back despite having no place left to go. Off-white fragments lay spewed across the cavern ground, and the intact structure in the corner solidified my fear. Long shafts rested beside the base of a vertebra, the ribcage and skull framing the outline of the skeleton.

"Somebody! Please!" My raw vocal chords barely choked out the words as my fingers clawed desperately into the cavern wall. I tried scaling the rutted mass, but my fingers kept slipping on the moist rock face, sending me on my ass as I repeatedly fell back down to the ground.

"Don't be afraid."

I wrenched around, my vision straining to see

through the darkness. The draft coursing through the hollowed space swelled, pushing a pall of dust out from the faint corridor in front of me as footsteps echoed from within the tunnel. The remaining light overhead dimmed in an instant, and I sprang forward, ready to blindly race into one of the other passageways when the large shadow stealthily materialized. I shrieked, stumbling back into the wall.

The sweeping draft took hold of the flowing black robes, ushering the ends out like expansive bat wings as the hooded figure emerged from the tunnel. I tried to move, but something was holding me in place. It didn't matter how hard I internally wrenched at my limbs; I was trapped. A severe chill prickled down my spine as the stranger drew closer. Struggling to see beyond the shadows of their hood, I couldn't make out any distinguishable features. A gloved hand reached out towards me, and I choked on my own scream. I couldn't even open my mouth.

"Noli timere," whispered a low, silky voice. Each word hissed with an unnatural, serpentine quality, making every syllable all the more bone chilling. "Sponsa mea."

Amid the bleak space, a startling surge of warmth radiated from the figure as his sweeping cloak engulfed me from all sides. Leather-bound fingers grazed the bottom of my chin, tilting up my head. The angle had me looking square in the face with the stranger, but I still couldn't see anything. Not until he inclined his own head back did a pale, angular chin peek out from under the guarded veil. Pearly white canines gleamed in the limited light, the teeth elongating the further his jaw opened.

"Noli timere."

***

I shuddered awake with a violent jerk, finding thin silk fabric looming not more than half a foot above my face. My mind reeled as it slowly regained its full consciousness. Where was I? All I could see was the desert gold linen, so I rolled over to get a better view of the living space. I shrieked, finding nothing but air beneath me. At the realization, my body suddenly dropped, and I hammered down onto the mattress. The cushiony springs bounced me off as I hit the comforter, sending me hurtling off onto the carpet beside the bed.

Achingly sitting upright, I looked up to see the familiar surroundings. I was in my bedroom. My first thought would have naturally been, **how did I get up here?** if not for the bigger question: **how did I get up *there*?** The canopy of my bed hung just below the ceiling, and I'd awoken mere inches from it. I'd been…floating.

"Kat?"

I jumped at the voice, and my nerves didn't relax much as I realized it was my mom.

Heels clacked up the hall before she knocked on my door. "Kat?"

"Y-yeah?"

She didn't wait for an invite as she twisted the knob and waltzed into the room. "You've got a lot of explaining to do-" Mom paused, looking down at me confusedly as I still rested on the floor. "What is going on?"

Holy crap! How long had I been floating like that? Had she seen me?

"Where have you been?" she yowled.

"W-what?" I turned to look at the alarm clock on my nightstand, seeing it was six o'clock.

"You were supposed to meet me at the country club after school let out. Why didn't you answer your phone? You know how many times I called?" Her voice ticked up to a whole other level with each new sentence. "I called all of your friends, and none of them knew where you were either! You know how scared I was?"

"I'm sorry..."

"And after all the trouble I went through to get you that appointment with Mrs. Marin." Mom rubbed her temples aggravatingly. "We needed this. With everything that happened with Blaine-"

She stopped herself, taking a moment to catch her breath.

"I know none of this is your fault, but the accident has left a lot of scorched earth for us around here. Mrs. Ryder has a lot of sway in Mystic Harbor, and we need to do everything we can to get back on her good side. Right now, we're all the town's pariahs, and especially with your father's business, we can't have that kind of rep."

Against all better judgment, I rolled my eyes. I couldn't help it. I was in the midst of a nervous breakdown, and all she could think about was her reputation. The gesture didn't go ignored. Mom heaved a sigh and muttered something about going to Mrs. Banisters's.

"And don't forget that your father's coming home tomorrow. He'll be taking your car into the shop to get an oil change in the morning." As quickly as she came, she was out the door.

Crap.

I'd completely spaced out on that tiny detail, and that put a wrinkle in my plans. Having made a mad dash out of school, I didn't have any of my things. No books, no homework, no purse, no phone. And the last proved the most problematic.

I knew I couldn't wait another thirteen hours until getting back to school. My cell only had a third of its charge left when I'd checked it this morning, so the damn thing would be long dead by the time I got to it tomorrow. And I couldn't go without that lifeline, especially if I wasn't going to have the car. For how increasingly shitty I felt, a call to the hospital seemed inevitable.

Asides from the anxiety attack still stirring in my chest, I thankfully didn't feel too bad. If I hauled ass, I could get to the school before it closed for the night. Climbing off the floor, I ambled my way to my closet to get changed. Last thing I needed was more strange looks from fellow classmates when I waltzed back into Belleview still wearing my gym uniform. And I shuddered at the thought of lying in bed with the sweaty clothes, but it was a hygienic issue I'd have to wrestle with later. I started peeling off my shirt, expecting to feel the cotton athletic wear. Instead, my fingers grappled at loose polyester. I looked down at the hamper in the corner, and sure enough, the black and purple gym clothes rested at the top of the container.

Spinning around on my heels, I retreated from the closet to the mirror beside my dresser. I was now donned in one of my off the shoulder sweaters and a comfortable pair of black leggings. Given that I'd passed out in the foyer, I doubted my ability to make it upstairs, much less change my outfit. But this was coming from the girl who'd swear she was just levitating above her bed a minute ago...

Surely, I was going mad.

The lights suddenly dimmed. Lightning crackled outside, flashing white into my room from the open window shades. My mind immediately snapped back to the dream, and my stomach coiled. Not a moment later, rain began pelting the windows, urging me to throw on a pair of knee-high flat boots. They were always perfect for a rainy day, managing to keep my legs and feet dry while also giving me good traction on slick grounds. I then instinctively searched for my purse, realizing a few seconds past having a blonde moment that it, too, was still in my locker.

To add insult to injury, the storm outside only seemed to be getting worse. Sure enough, tiny specks of hale pelted the windshield as I rolled my tiny red Civic out of the garage. Maine's magnificently abysmal weather appeared to have come out in full force. Our house sat on the hillside corner of DuPont Lane and Rochester Drive, where the fog continuously rolled down each street, flooding our lot in the crossfire as the two bends converged. Tonight was no different, making visibility pretty much nonexistent as I drove down the main drag.

Between the poor driving conditions and the fact that I got stuck behind a sluggish, phantom-breaking minivan, the typical ten-minute drive to the school wound up taking me an exhaustible twenty. Boxing had become kind of a big deal at Belleview over the last couple years, and by the looks of the occupied parking lot, the guys were still inside training. At least one thing had panned out in my favor.

I took the closest parking space I could find near the gym doors and cut the engine. It wasn't more than a thirty foot trip, but I still ended up completely soak from head to toe by the time I made into the building. Sneakers squeaked across the gymnasium floors as hollering overpowered the thunderous echo of the rain pounding against the vast rooftop. I rounded the end of the drawn-in bleachers to see the basketball team practicing on the court, and I immediately recoiled.

Crap. They'd changed their schedule.

If Carly had resorted to calling my mom, she sure as hell had told Daniel, and Mark, and Eric all about my vanishing act. The last thing I wanted was to have to talk to anybody, let alone explain myself. And all three were right there. I didn't have a choice though. There wasn't another way to get to the hallway. All the other doors would have been locked and chained up hours ago.

I remained hidden behind the bleachers, waiting for the game to head to the other end of the court. When my opening came, I darted across the gym. Heaving a sigh of relief, I entered the hallway, thankful that no one seemed to have noticed me. The janitorial staff must have already done their rounds, because the lights were all off. Only the faint glow of the street lights outside illuminated the shadowed corridors. The creepy atmosphere did nothing to calm my nerves as I pulled open the doors to the stairwell. Thankfully, one of the dim light fixtures remained on at the half-landing, allowing me to safely travel up the steps. I made it to my locker on the second floor, but failed the first five attempts to get the stupid thing open. There weren't any windows or doors nearby, so I had next to no visibility to see the numbers on the combination dial.

When I finally did get inside, I blindly reached up into the top shelf, feeling around for my cell. As soon as I pulled it down, the theme from *Dracula* erupted from within my hands, startling me back.

Damn, I really did need to change that.

It came as no surprise that I had 52 text messages and 21 missed calls. I scrolled through the texts, seeing messages from pretty much everyone begging to know where I was. What was surprising was the fact that Vice Principal Wallace hadn't raided my locker, given how often my phone must have been going off throughout the day. I could've sworn I'd set it to vibrate…

The phone played its sinister ringtone once again, and I noted another incoming text message.

That was odd. The name of the user was listed as *Unknown*. I tapped on the message.

"Good to see you bounced back so quickly."

Another message immediately popped up, and I nearly dropped the phone as a picture came up on the screen.

Broken glass lay spewed all over, the bits seeming to stick to the masses of blood splattered across me as my lifeless eyes bore into the void above. I was on the pavement, the damp asphalt gleaming under the flash of the camera. It was…from the accident. My trembling fingers zoomed in on the photo. It wasn't the blood that was keeping the glass in place. It was burrowed in my skin, a particularly large shard protruding from the front of my temple. How could that be? I didn't have any cuts on me when I woke up in the hospital, mere hours after the accident.

Who the hell would send something like this? Or the better question, how did they even get a hold of it?

The floor rumbled as a vicious bout of thunder resounded outside. I frantically tossed a mass of textbooks and notes into my satchel before slamming the locker shut. Lightning crackled again, and I froze, catching sight of the figure lurking at the end of the hallway out of my peripheral. Slowly turning, I faced the individual, unable to see anything down the long, shadowed corridor. My feet backpedaled toward the stairwell as lightning struck again. Between the distance and brief illumination, all I could make out was a tall frame hidden behind a massive black sweatshirt with the hood drawn over the person's head and dark pants. No features were distinguishable, but the frame was relatively tall. Around six feet, give or take.

Each step I backtracked, the figure advanced.

"Hello?" I called out shakily, just like all the dumbasses chased down and brutally murdered in every horror movie...ever.

It came as no surprise that I didn't get a response. I whirled around and darted toward the stairs, practically falling down the dual flights as panic reduced my legs to shaky twigs. Footsteps echoed from the top of the stairwell just as I hit the bottom landing. The vast distance this person covered in such a short burst was ridiculous, and I outright screamed as I raced out into the ground floor hallway.

The light from the open gymnasium doors came into sight. Only a little further.

A large shadow suddenly loomed in the entrance just as I rounded the bend, and I smacked full force into a strong, bare chest. The individual didn't budge, holding me in their grasp.

"Kat, what's wrong?"

I instinctively shrieked back, still trying to wrestle away until I noticed the gel glove wraps protecting this person's hands. My eyes snapped up as recognition landed with the voice.

Adam.

"What are you doing out here?" He looked over my shoulder, gazing up and down the hall.

"There's someone in here," I spat.

"Not surprising. The place is swarming with jocks," my ex remarked.

"No, I think they were following me."

"What are you talking about?" The look on my face must have said it all, because any hint of amusement fell from Adam's face. He backed up and ushered me into the safety of the gym. "Where are they?"

"In the stairwell," I muttered.

Before I had a chance to protest, he disappeared into the shadows of the hall.

"Thought that was you," panted Mark, startling me from behind as he trotted over from off the court. "Sorry about tattling on you to Adam, but the way you zoomed through here, I wasn't sure what was up and Coach wouldn't let me leave."

Adam reemerged from the hall not a moment later, shaking his head. "Nobody's out there." He slung the fresh towel hanging off his shoulder and unfolded it, ruffling it through his sweaty locks as he parked a seat on the bottom row of the bleachers still drawn out.

Mark exchanged a puzzled look between the two of us. "Oookay, what did I miss?"

"Nothing," I quickly countered. "It's nothing."

Even amid my mental bedlam, my eyes couldn't resist traveling over Adam's taut frame. His bare, broad chest glistened with sweat, and the lighting overhead lay emphasis on the dips and contours of his chiseled body. The only clothes he donned were knee-length mesh shorts and shoes, and the sight made a field's worth of butterflies flutter in my stomach.

The guy seriously looked like an MMA fighter, which wasn't entirely off. Adam "dabbled," as he put it, in mixed martial arts. I silently laughed at the thought. Not because he was bad at it. He was freakishly good, in fact. It was how he so offhandedly referred to "hobbies." While others may dabble in, say, something like cooking or playing guitar, Adam oh so casually practiced the art of double-leg takedown body slams.

Mark smirked as he caught me stealing the long

glance at my ex. Thankfully, Adam didn't seem to notice as he removed the gel wraps from his bound hands, flexing his fingers stiffly. My guilty thoughts were interrupted by Coach blowing his whistle.

"Hey, McDowell! Get your ass back on the court. I didn't recruit you so you could stand around lookin' pretty."

"That's my cue," laughed Mark, giving me a soft elbow to the arm. "Don't do anything I wouldn't do."

In Mark's book, that didn't exactly narrow things down. At all.

I shot my friend a testy glare as he trotted off humming, "Bow chicka wow wow," with a rhythmic beat straight out of some generic 80's porno.

That didn't escape Adam's attention as he finally looked up at me with slightly reddening cheeks. "I'll walk you to your car."

As much as I appreciated the offer, I hastily said, "No. It's okay. I'll be fine." I wanted to kick myself for not taking him up on the kind gesture, but stubbornness ruled against the logical half of my brain. Even now, amid my frantic thoughts, I still didn't want to have to depend on him.

My words came out a bit snippier than they should have, causing Adam's soft smile to turn upside down. "I mean, you're in the middle of practice. I don't want to be a bother," I clarified a bit more politely.

"It's really no problem. Practice ended about a half hour ago. I was just in the weightlifting room getting a little extra time." He looked up at me with those deep, soulful blue eyes of his, and it was all I could do to nod.

An appreciative smile tugged at his lips, and it still confused me. I had been the one to officially end the relationship, but Adam was the one who made it clear that he wasn't invested for the long haul. Yet he seemed to have taken the breakup like a wounded puppy dog. Carly was right. He did regret what happened, and the thought hurt all the more. If he still cared, why did he do any of it in the first place? And why did he continually hurt me when we were together? The whole scenario made no sense.

I was left to digest those questions as he said, "I'll be right back," before disappearing into the damp concrete stairwell leading up to the weightlifting room.

"I'll be right back," I reiterated to myself, still finding no humor in the horror movie clichés that seemed to be playing out all too frequently. Thankfully, my life wasn't entirely like Scream, because Adam did in fact return a moment later with no stab wounds in sight. He pulled a large hoodie on over his head, subsequently covering up the ab-tastic awesomeness that was his stomach.

I followed him across the gym to the side exit, and thanked him as he held the heavy metal door open for me against the batting winds. We raced over to my car, and Adam cupped his hands over his eyes, stealing a look into the backseat through the rain splattered windows.

"You're all good," he confirmed as I hit the UNLOCK button on my key ring.

"Thanks." Still shaken, I returned his smile as best as I could, climbing into the driver's seat.

"If you have any problems, just give me a call."

"Will do." Unlikely.

He closed the door and saluted me before trudging his way back up to the building. I started the car and turned out onto the main drag. The windshield wipers swiped at the highest setting, but it didn't do much good as the rain hammered down harder than ever. Maine's swiftly changing weather constantly kept its inhabitants on their toes behind the wheel, and it was giving me a run for my money. A knot had formed in my stomach earlier when I'd woken up from...whatever that could be called, and it hadn't gone away. The further I drove, the knot only grew.

I was being paranoid. Simple as that. The weirdo in the hall was probably just some brain-dead jock who'd seen me in the gym. Hell, if I hadn't known Mark was still on the court, I'd bet my life that it was him. He did stupid things like that all the time, no matter how insensitive they were. So it stood to reason that another one of his basketball buddies got the same idea.

But what about the picture?

And how I'd been feeling?

Or me...levitating?

I could chalk up everything to PTSD and some cruel, obnoxious prankster. But that last bit...it didn't have a rational explanation. Either hysteria was causing my imagination to wreak havoc on my sanity, or something else was really, really wrong.

Refusing to let my thoughts run away to a very dangerous place, to which there was no return, I pressed my foot down harder on the accelerator. The sooner I got home, the better. I'd take a shower, get something in my stomach, and lose my thoughts in homework until I fell asleep. Sounded like a solid plan.

Warmth spread across my chest, yet I could feel the hairs on my arm stand on end beneath my sweater. If there was such a thing as spidey-senses, I was pretty sure this was it. That, or I was having a panic attack unlike any I'd ever heard of. An inexplicable dread washed over me, and I looked in my rearview mirror to see no headlights behind me. There weren't any cars in front of me now either. Knowing that I wasn't going to get creamed by some reckless SUV barreling down the street should have been comforting. Yet, my hands instinctively gripped the steering wheel till the whites of my knuckles looked like they were about to tear through my skin.

The wipers continued racing across the windshield, but it was getting harder to see. I turned on the defrosters, hoping to clear away the steam on the windows. It was then I realized that the mist wasn't on the inside. The fog seemed to cling to the glass as I raced down the stretch. I could barely make out the red light hanging above the upcoming intersection, relieved to see it switch to green just as I started to slow down. I let my foot off the brake, rolling right through the juncture to the town square.

Lightning waged overhead, and sparks suddenly spewed from everywhere. All the bulbs from the shop windows to the streetlights exploded, sending the village center into total darkness. It wasn't until I was right on top of them that I saw the silhouette standing right in the front of the car.

"Holy shit!" I yanked the wheel to the right, sending the car into a tailspin as it hydroplaned on the flooded street. The backend bucked up from what I guessed was the Civic jumping the curb, but I didn't hear any other impact as I jolted to a stop. Just as I blew out a sigh of relief, the front end buckled with a heavy wallop. I shrieked, seeing a pair of booted feet standing on top of the hood.

What the hell?

The figure knelt down, seeming to peer inside the car. I still couldn't see their face, but by the all-black ensemble adorned by the large hood, it didn't take a rocket scientist to put two and two together. It was the creep from the hallway!

I was pretty sure that I'd locked the car doors when I got in, but I wasn't taking any chances. My shaking fingers fumbled with the side panel, reinforcing the locks. I still couldn't peel my eyes away. Had I hit this person? They didn't appear to be the least bit injured. A leather clad hand suddenly pounded down on the frontend, igniting a strange crackling sound from beneath the hood.

All of the gauges above the steering wheel suddenly died, leaving the entire dash pitch-black. I frantically tried restarting the engine, but I was only met with a rattling click. What did they just do? Looking back up at the stranger, I choked on a scream, seeing two blazing red lights flash beneath the shrouded hood where the eyes should have been. My eyes crazily blinked, trying to rid themselves of the obvious mind trick, but it wouldn't go away. This person's eyes were...glowing.

Through the rapid hustle of the windshield wipers, I could also see the other hand move behind the stranger's back.

No.

No.

No.

An L-shaped rod came into view, and I quickly realized it was a tire iron.

Crying out every curse word imaginable, I kept twisting the key in the ignition without any luck. The hood hoisted back up as the individual leapt off it to the ground in one fluid motion.

"Come on, come on!" I slammed my palm against the steering wheel as my other hand tried one last time to turn over the engine. As if answering my prayers, the vehicle roared back to life. My foot slammed down on the accelerator, not particularly concerned with whether or not I plowed this psycho down. The car lurched forward, but jolted back to a stop just as quickly.

"Shit!"

The figure loomed toward the driver's side of the car, and I throttled the gears into reverse. Punching down on the accelerator, the Civic floored back. An ugly crumpling sound scratched the undercarriage, but the car didn't stop as I drove up onto the sidewalk. The shattered remains of one of the large potting plants lining the town square spat out of the frontend. Apparently, that was what I'd hit. Angling the car parallel to shop windows, I threw the gearshift into drive and sped off down the sidewalk. As the next intersection came, I jumped the curb and swerved back onto the street, stealing a look behind me in the rearview mirror. The rain made it impossible to see much of anything, but I could still make out the singular shadow looming across the road as lightning struck again.

CHAPTER 6
Emperor's New Clothes

Apparently, word about the police cruiser out front spread like wildfire among the Real Housewives of Mystic Harbor, because not five minutes after Officers Blake and Stevens arrived did Mom storm in the house. I told the police all about the attack—with the exception of the whole glowing red eyes bit—and even showed them the photo I received when I retrieved my cell phone. They exchanged nervous glances.

"Could we have a word with you in private?" asked Stevens, motioning to my mother.

"Whatever it is, you can say in front of her," snapped Mom.

Both officers grimaced.

"Officer Stevens here also checked with local hospitals to see if anyone came in from a hit-and-run. Nobody matches the case," said Blake. "And on our way up here, we passed over the bridge where your daughter claims this all happened. The only thing there was a dead coyote on the side of the road."

"Is it possible you may have been mistaken about what you saw?" Stevens directed to me.

"Unless this coyote happened to be six feet tall and wearing a black sweater, I wouldn't say it's likely, no." I tried answering as politely as possible, but from the moment they walked in the door, their stance was made pretty clear. Either they were a part of the massive conspiracy, or they just thought I was bat-shit. Safe to assume the latter.

"Look, I went to Belleview High, too," said Blake, who looked to be no older than twenty. "So I know how immature the guys there can be. The whole thing with the text and chasing you was probably just some moronic prank gone too far. When I was in school, my friend was forced to shave his head after another member on the basketball team put glue in his hair gel."

"It's not uncommon for people to see things after going through the kind of trauma you did. PTSD isn't something to be ashamed of," added Stevens.

The conversation didn't get any better from there. If anything, everyone became more and more convinced that I was fit for a straitjacket. Blake urged me to come back with him and Stevens to the precinct, where a therapist would be more than happy to speak with me. Mom insisted that it wouldn't be necessary, practically shoving them out the door.

At first, I mistook her anger, thinking she was mad at the officers for not taking me seriously. She made herself pretty clear however the moment we found ourselves alone. The whole of Mystic Harbor would hear about 5-O paying us a visit by morning, and the town was fixed with eyes and ears. It was only a matter of time before everyone learned that I was *Shutter Island*-grade certifiable. Considering Dad had only been with Barker & MacLeane for less than two years, the last thing he needed was bad press to overshadow his work, especially with him in the midst of closing a merger. Then there was the matter concerning Mom's upcoming run for Regency Board President of the Woodstone Country Club. Apparently, I was making a P.R. nightmare for the family.

***

After spending a sleepless night flopping about my bed like a fish, I assumed I'd be in full-on zombie mode by second period. Instead, I was wired. Coupled with my hypersensitivity and growing paranoia, I was kookier than Mel Gibson in *Conspiracy Theory*. Or maybe just Mel Gibson in general. And this peculiarity didn't go unnoticed by my friends. I didn't help my case at lunch when I practically devoured everything I could get my hands on.

"Seems someone's been tokin' some reefer," laughed Mark disquietly. His usual amusement was absent as I torn into my second turkey sub.

"She's not using pot," defended Vanessa. Sadly, I couldn't dismiss the apprehension in her voice. I was scaring them, or at least making them uncomfortable. And I couldn't blame them. Between the bloodshot eyes from running on no sleep and my recent, ravenous case of the munchies, I'd think I was high too if I didn't know any better.

Daniel gave me a small, sympathetic smile and managed to change the subject. I started to let my eyes wander aimlessly amongst the sea of fellow classmates when a particular individual grabbed my attention.

"Earth to Kat." Mark waved a hand in front of my face, snapping me out of the trance I hadn't realized I'd fallen into. "What's up?"

Reese started moving across the cafeteria with an empty tray in his hand, and my eyes naturally tracked him. It didn't exactly take detective work to figure out what—or rather who—I was gawking over as Carly stole a look over her shoulder.

Her jaw dropped so far, I'd swear it should have disconnected from her skull. "Blackburn?"

Everyone at the table seemed to freeze before slowly turning their attention to me.

"What about Blackburn?" Vanessa said his name like he was freaking Voldemort. "You're not crushing on him, are you?"

"What? No..." I shook my head nervously, seeing an unnatural sense of relief shared across the table.

"Thank God," sighed V.

"Why? What's the big deal?" I asked reflexively.

Carly stiffened. "Your funeral," she muttered.

"What's that supposed to mean?"

"Dating someone like him is social suicide," laughed Mark.

Someone like him? Sure, Reese wasn't typical by Mystic Harbor's standards...or society's, but it didn't seem that taboo.

"Seriously, your popularity rating would take a nosedive," said Vanessa. "Not to mention, it would give your mom a heart attack."

"Why?"

"Well, he's a West Ender for starters," she further clarified, and it took everything I had not to roll my eyes.

'West Ender' was the label given to those who lived in the less-than-reputable part of town by the riverfront. In Mystic Harbor, you bought your way into the in-crowd. Unless they were a star-studded athlete, every West Ender was pretty much resigned to social leprosy.

"That still doesn't explain why you're all acting like he's Beetlejuice."

Mark snickered. "Have you gotten a look at the guy? That's really not that far off."

Reese was sporting a Victorian-era militia tailcoat, accompanied by a black silk dress shirt, matching pinstripe slacks, and even pointy toed Steampunk boots. Yeah, even I had to admit, he had a point.

"Blackburn could walk onto the set of *Sweeny Todd* and not miss a beat. You don't think that's...odd?" said Mark.

The guy did stick out like a sore thumb amid all the preppy, future Ivy Leaguers and Abercrombie model wannabes. He was strangely refreshing; an attractive quality...if not for the fact he was also a stab-worthy jackass.

"And he's always doing weird things during class," said Vanessa.

"Like what?"

"I don't know...like magic tricks and stuff. He's usually fiddling with a deck of cards or making coins disappear from his desktop. It's a bit out there. Plus, I've never seen him really talk to anybody around here."

"And it really is a shame," huffed Carly. "The man's not half-bad looking. With a makeover and some green in his pocket, the boy could have some serious potential."

"Yeah, because what girl can resist an anti-social David Copperfield?" mocked Daniel.

"We share French class with him," said V.

"We do?" That was news to me, and Vanessa knew it.

She chuckled. "Yeah, but you'd never guess it since the guy's always a no-show. I'm surprised he even bothers coming to school at all. His GPA's probably in the toilet."

"But how?" I posed. "That's an AP class, and Physics is an honors course. You don't just get into those by accident."

Everyone just shrugged.

"Did they ever figure out what happened to Blackburn's old man?" asked Mark.

Daniel shook his head, noting my confusion. "Blackburn's dad disappeared right after Reese was born. The police looked into it, but there wasn't a Christopher Blackburn even on record. There were rumors that he was maybe a part of WITSEC or something. Regardless, it was obvious that the name was just an alias to hide from his past. Everyone figured it must have caught up with him, 'cause the guy was like Keyser Söze. Gone without a trace."

"Gives me the willies just thinking about him," shuddered Vanessa.

"Which one? Reese or his old man?" Eric clucked.

"Like it makes a difference." She laughed. "After the whole gas station incident, we thought for sure that's why Kat ran out on P.E. yesterday."

My brows furrowed. "What'd you mean?"

"You didn't notice Blackburn in the gym?" asked Carly.

I shook my head.

"Yeah, he was standing in the doorway by the cafeteria, staring at you."

"When was this?" I muttered, drawing a total blank.

"Right before Brenda got hurt. And he disappeared right after you left," she said.

"I heard some of the girls in the locker room talking about it later. They were saying that he was somehow responsible for Brenda's injury," scoffed Carly. "People are so stupid. They were saying he used, like, black magic or something." She snorted at her own remark.

"I know it's just a bunch of garbage, but still...the guy's a freak," said Vanessa. "And weird, bad things always seem to happen when he's around."

"Better keep an eye out," cautioned Daniel. "I think he has a thing for you."

"Trust me, he doesn't," I immediately countered. "The guy can't say so much as a sentence without insulting me in the process."

"The fact that he even speaks to you at all is a marvel," said Mark. "We've gone to school with him since we were in kindergarten, and the number of words I've heard him say before the night of the bonfire can be counted on one hand."

I looked around the table, and everyone nodded in agreement.

Despite still being hungry, I got up and dumped my tray once the conversation somehow transitioned into plans for the upcoming weekend. Seeing no one at the table paying mind to me, I stole a glance around the cafeteria. Reese wasn't there, and that verity was comforting. I wanted answers, yes. But I didn't want to go seeking out trouble to get them. One thing I couldn't ignore: Reese's handy camera. Could he have possibly taken that picture of me after the accident? I spent the rest of lunch with my nose buried in my phone, seeing if there was a way to find out what camera model took the image that was sent to me. Unfortunately, there wasn't any EXIF data from the image, which would have acted like a digital fingerprint. My detective skills could've used a little more work too, because despite all the times I'd seen Reese with his camera, I never bothered to make a note of what brand he owned, let alone what model it was.

By the time Study Hall rolled around, I was about to jump out of my skin. Hoping to distract myself, I headed to the library to work on my physics report. Plopping myself down at a vacant cubicle in the computer lab, I logged on, finding my fingers hovering over the keys as I stared at the Google search page on screen.

Focus: Energy transfer and conversion. That's why you're here.

I started to type, and before I knew it, the search engine results page gave me loads of websites on levitation.

Stop.

Just don't go there.

I shoved that nosey little voice of reason aside and began scrolling.

I got hit with a bunch of useless results ranging from cheesy magician breakdowns all the way to some kind of music festival venue. The deeper I ventured into the findings, the weirder it got. By the time I reached studies on humanoid aliens and Wiccan spell casting, I knew I'd gone bonkers. This was stupider than trying to self-diagnose on WebMD. I doubted the art of Harry Kellar and his "Levitation of Princess Karnac" illusion held the answers to my rabbit-hole madness. I pushed the keyboard back, letting my forehead drop down on the desktop.

"Hey, stranger."

My entire body stiffened as a shadow suddenly cast over the cubicle. Sure enough, as I looked up, I was met with a pair of striking amber eyes and a smirk stretched from ear to ear.

"I'm really not in the mood, Blackburn," I said, straightening back up.

This ~~sexy~~ crazy individual rounded the side of the desk and plopped down in the vacant seat beside me. He poked his head around the cubicle wall to observe my computer screen and chuckled. "Doing a little light reading, I see."

"Please. Leave," I gritted, noting the absence of his camera.

"Thinking of developing a new hobby?" He still couldn't take his eyes off the ridiculous illustration from the website.

Embarrassment reddened my cheeks, forcing me to close the browser. "What do you want?"

"Well, to quote Freddy Mercury, 'I want it all,'" he laughed. "But for now, I'll settle for some answers."

"I don't know anything, especially the reason why you're stalking me!" I sneered.

"Stalking?"

"Yes, that's what you call it when you repeatedly harass someone and follow them around!"

"I beg your pardon?"

I looked him over, seeing he was dressed in his long militia coat. "What? You decide to leave your hoodie at home?"

His brows furrowed confusedly.

"Don't even deny it."

"Okay, I won't...as soon as you clarify what the hell you're talking about," he countered.

"Last night. You're really gonna stand there and tell me you weren't the hooded psycho who nearly ran me off the road?"

"Yes, I am—going to tell you that, because I *wasn't*."

"Can't say I'm particularly swayed."

"Trust me, if I was there, you'd know. It'd be a real shame to rob you of the sight to all this awesomeness," he laughed halfheartedly, making an invisible circle around his face with his pointer finger.

"Personally, I think the ski mask better suits you."

A couple students nearby turned in their seats, eying me weirdly.

Neither the stares nor remark seemed to faze the magician though as he leaned in closer, forcing me to scoot as far over in my desk chair as I could without falling off onto the floor. His head tilted down as his eyes bored into mine, causing shadows to forebodingly cascade beneath his sharp cheekbones. With his teasing grin, the look was somehow menacing...in a frighteningly sexy way. And that thought churned my stomach. Sure, he was what society would call 'odd,' but Reese wasn't scary by any means. There was still something about him. An enigmatic quality that made him mysterious. And in Mystic Harbor, where everyone knew everything about everyone, the odds of finding someone like Reese was about as good as stumbling upon a unicorn grazing on your front lawn.

"You know what I am," he said lowly.

"Yeah, psychotic."

His eyes narrowed, seeming to scrutinize every microexpression on my face, before traveling back over to the computer monitor. A mystified look fell over his own features. "Hold on. You...you really don't know, do you?"

"That you're crazier than a bag full of cats? It's not that hard to miss," I shot back.

That weird, studying expression of his didn't fade. "Feeling a bit different lately?"

My heart rate ticked up to a whole other level. How could he possibly know that?

I apparently didn't have much of a poker face, because his eyes expanded as he read my expression. "You've gotta be joking."

"Get away from me," I growled.

"Or what?"

"Or I'll scream," I countered.

Of all things, he laughed. "Well, good luck with that. I can assure you, you'll just look crazy."

"And why's that?"

"Because as far as they're concerned, Princess," he said, gesturing to the rest of the room, "you're just arguing with yourself."

"You're bat-shit."

"No, I'm invisible," he countered. "Well, that's not entirely accurate. I'm only invisible to normal humans, when I wish to be. And mute."

I snatched my book bag off the floor and started throwing my things inside. "I don't know what the hell's wrong with you, and quite frankly, I don't care. My advice, up your dosage and leave me alone. And investing in a straitjacket wouldn't hurt you, either."

"You don't believe me?" He grabbed a highlighter off the desk I hadn't gotten to yet and suddenly flung it behind him, smacking some hipster guy in the back of the head across the way.

"Owww!" The student yelped, whirling around in his seat.

Reese sauntered over to him, waving his hand in front of the innocent bystander without any reaction. The hipster just shot *me* a dirty look.

"You wish for me to further demonstrate?" the magician taunted, picking up the guy's chemistry textbook next.

"What? No!" I blurted.

Everyone now turned their attention to me.

"I'm sorry, I didn't quite catch that!" Reese declared,

his voice booming across the entire room.

Still, not one person paid this psycho any mind.

Holy crap…

I had gone bat-shit! I was hallucinating invisible people!

"Is there a problem?"

I jumped at the voice behind me, only to face one of the library aides as I turned around. Without another word, I grabbed my remaining materials off the desk and slung my bag over my shoulder before bolting out the side exit.

That bottomless pit feeling resurfaced in my stomach, and I was hit again with a sudden dizzy spell. Bracing myself against the row of lockers beside me, I pinched my eyes shut and blindly stumbled down the empty hallway until I knew I'd reached the stairwell. I yanked the heavy metal door open and staggered inside, letting my body slide down the wall once I moved to the side of the landing.

"'There are two ways to be fooled. One is to believe what isn't true; the other is to refuse to believe what is,'" remarked the voice that suddenly registered beside me.

I snapped back upright. "Jesus Christ!"

"No, that was Søren Kierkegaard, actually," confirmed the magician, laxly leaning against the wall with his arms crossed. "And in your case, truer words haven't been spoken."

I lurched forward in an attempt to reach the stairs when my equilibrium gave way, throwing me off balance.

A pair of strapping arms secured me from behind, helping me back upright. "Easy there, Princess."

"Get off of me," I demanded, batting my hands against his hold.

"That's an odd request to give the person stopping you from taking an involuntary swan dive down a flight of stairs." It didn't seem to take him much effort as he swept me off my feet and started heading down to the ground floor, setting me back down on the bottom step like I weighed next to nothing. "Be back in a sec."

And just like that, Reese ducked out, leaving me all alone again. A moment later, I felt a little steadier, so I rose to my feet. There was no way I was hanging around here waiting for my psychotic hallucination to return. I poked my head out into the main hall, still seeing no one else around.

I started making my way towards the front offices, praying that the nurse would be in. I still wasn't sure what she could do to help me, since all anyone ever seemed to get was a thermometer in the mouth and purple spots burned in their vision from her flashlight, but what else could I do?

"God, you're stubborn."

It took everything in me to not scream out at the top of my lungs as footsteps galloped up from behind me.

"Which do you prefer? Granola bar or M&M's?" the magician queried as he fell into step with me, holding up the two options.

I eyed the snacks, acknowledging the pit in my stomach only growing deeper, and I admittedly grabbed them both.

My mother would have been appalled at my poor etiquette as I tore the M&M pouch open with my teeth. I guzzled them down in a frenzy before treating the protein bar to the same fate. A moan escaped my lips as I closed my eyes, feeling the food already taking effect in only a matter of a minute.

"Better?" he queried.

I nodded.

Realization suddenly hit, and my eyes flew back open.

"Wait, how did you know…?"

The magician's brow piqued. "That you were hungry?"

I never said I was, and there were countless reasons for feeling dizzy. So how could he possibly have guessed? Better yet, why did he keep staring at me expectantly?

"The cravings will lessen with time. Your body's just adjusting to the changes," he followed up, so matter-of-factly.

Fear rippled through me at the remark, and without warning, I throttled my hands into his chest, shoving him back.

I wanted to scream at him, tell him just how psychotic he was, but everything felt *off*. I couldn't ignore that something was wrong with me. I couldn't ignore what he had said that night at the gas station.

Panic sent blood pumping into my ears to the point that I could hear my pulse thumping inside my head. All I could do was run. I took off down the hall, but I didn't get more than ten feet before he snatched my arm, whirling me back around to face him.

That strange feeling in my core returned, and instinct suddenly took over. I drove my opposing arm down on his hand, breaking the hold. I threw my elbow up at his face, and he barely managed to dodge it. Just when I thought I'd gained an edge on him, he swiftly snaked away from me. I spun around, losing sight of him, when hands ensnared me from behind, pinning my arms down in the process.

"You're a natural. I'll give you that much," he mused in my ear, his breath cascading down my neck. "But not the face, Princess. That's just cruel."

I drove my heel down on the top of his foot, but it didn't seem to do any good as he turned me around again.

My back suddenly met with the wall. The psycho pinned my hands above my head, holding me there with just one arm as his body pressed up against mine.

Before I could find the will to scream, he covered my mouth with his free hand. "I wouldn't recommend it," he warned. It wasn't a threat. More like a helpful suggestion, given that nobody else could apparently see him. I'd only look all the more stupid, especially after my display upstairs.

Still wrestling against him, I managed to bite down on one of his fingers.

He retracted his hand glaringly, but a grin quickly replaced the flicker of pain. "I'm a fan of biting, Princess, but it has its time and place. This isn't it."

"You call me 'Princess' again, and I'll do a lot worse than bite you."

"Well, I appreciate the vigor. You're going to need it, but not against me."

"Says the psychopath assaulting me," I sneered, wreathing uselessly about in his hold. For a guy with arms thinner than a rake, he sure had some muscles…somewhere.

He finally seemed to recognize how truly scared I was, because he loosened his grip. "I think we've gotten off on the wrong foot here."

More like he chopped off the entire freaking leg!

"You don't need to be afraid of me. If anything, I can help."

"I highly doubt that, on both counts. All you've proven is that I'm going crazy," I jeered.

The teasing nature that seemed to be a staple in his personality dissipated as his features darkened. "Deluding yourself into believing that none of this is happening to you won't change the fact that it is. And I, more than anyone, can assure you that willful ignorance here is only going to get you killed."

My body fell rigid against his frame.

"How do you think you survived the crash? You heard what happened to Blaine. Is there even a smidgen of you that believes you walked away unharmed by pure providence?"

He drew in closer, and heat rushed over me. But not in a bad way.

If that wasn't a clear indicator that something was *really* wrong with me... Sure, the guy was attractive, but he was also cra-cra beyond description.

Curiosity clawed at my insides, begging me to ask him the questions swirling in my head, but I couldn't bring myself to do it. Indulging in his lunacy didn't seem like the smartest move.

"Ms. Montgomery?"

My head snapped to the right, seeing Vice Principal Wallace coming towards us from the offices at the end of the hall. The magician peered down at me with that teasing grin of his plastered to his face as he slowly retracted from me, leaving me frozen up against the wall with my arms still raised over my head. I immediately dropped them, imagining just how idiotic I must have looked. By Mr. Wallace's expression, *pretty stupid* seemed like a safe assumption.

The rotund man stopped halfway down the hall and knocked on one of the doors. Dr. Fritz, the school psychologist, stepped out from what I now realized was her office as the two whispered to each other.

"Uh-oh, looks like somebody's in trouble." My stalker winced, but it was more sarcastic than concerned.

"Ms. Montgomery, if you'd please," beckoned Vice Principal Wallace.

Crap.

I pushed myself off the wall to head toward the office, but Reese cut in front of me, blocking my way. He reached into his back pocket and fetched out a worn leather wallet, removing a business card. Against my will, I couldn't take my eyes off his mouth as he placed the paper between his lips, using both his hands to tuck the wallet back into place and remove something else from inside his jacket.

A smug grin tugged at his delicious lips as he grabbed the card again, palming it as he scribbled something down on the blank backside with what I saw was an old-fashioned fountain pen. "I have the distinct feeling you'll be in touch," he whispered impishly.

In your dreams, I wanted to sneer. But Mr. Wallace and Dr. Fritz were still just down the hall, and they continued eying me strangely as I managed to steal a look over the magician's shoulder. The distraction caught me off guard, and I gasped at the hand that grabbed at the front of my jeans. I looked down, realizing Reese just tucked the business card in the front pocket.

He winked, and I forced myself forward, trying to head around him.

Bad idea.

He was the one in control here, and my little act of defiance seemed to spark deeper amusement in him, because he took a step back and positioned himself in front of me once more. His brows piqued in challenge.

I took a step to his other side, but he met me once again. Three more attempts, and I now looked like I was trying and failing miserably at doing some spontaneous line dance sidesteps.

"Will you stop?" I finally growled, trying to move my mouth as little as possible.

He smiled a ridiculously full, closemouthed smile and glissaded away. "Good luck with the shrink."

I hustled down the hall as fast as I could, afraid that he'd change his mind and harass me further. Vice Principal Wallace addressed me, but I darted right into Fritz's office before he could finish his thought.

CHAPTER 7
Don't Threaten Me With a Good Time

As you can imagine, talking to yourself draws unwanted attention. Yeah, I'd landed in the seventh circle of Hell. Dr. Fritz continued dropping a bunch of psychobabble about post traumatic stress, and Wallace just kept nodding and staring at me with widened eyes, trying to—I'm guessing—appear thoughtful. In actuality, he kind of just looked deranged. Though, given my present condition, it's not like I had room to talk. His toes kept tapping and I quickly realized he wanted out of there as much as I did, so I confessed to talking in the library, but somehow convinced them that I'd been on my phone. I even pulled out my ear buds from my book bag, showing them to Dr. Fritz. She noted the microphone built in, and I explained that the conversation had just gotten out of hand.

Doctor Fritz scrunched up her nose as she glanced between me and the file open on her desk. "Well, if that's the case, I suppose this is up to you on how to handle this," she said to Wallace.

He huffed, stealing another look at his watch. "You

know very well about our cell phone policy."

"Yes, I'm sorry," I lamented.

Before he even said it, I knew what was coming. His impatience was a dead giveaway. "But I suppose I'll let it slide. Just this once."

"Thank you, sir." I sprang up from my seat and bolted for the door.

By the time I got out of there, there was only a couple minutes left before the final bell rang. Keeping a watchful eye, I made my way back to my locker. No sight of Reese. It should have given me comfort, but I could still feel the business card burning a hole in my front pocket. Wrestling with the urge to pull it out, I seemed to space for a moment, because I didn't even realize classes let out until the hall was in hysterics with students barking and laughing about.

Just as my fingers started to slide into my pocket, Carly appeared at my side, throwing herself in the most theatrical fashion against the gray sheet metal of the locker beside mine. She whimpered, slowly sinking down to the floor.

I immediately retracted my hand. "What's with you?"

She shrugged, as if that constituted for an answer.

"Cough it up. Why do you look like someone just murdered a basket of puppies?" I asked.

"Abrams's making me stay after school."

"Why? Did you fail a test or something?"

"Who knows? Probably."

Carly wasn't dumb by any means, but she unfortunately had a proclivity to focusing her attention on the wrong things. The girl could quote the latest issue of *Cosmo* from cover to cover, yet didn't bother studying for most of her classes. Against all odds, she still somehow managed to squeak by with a C-average. Our physics teacher, Mr. Abrams, was a hard-ass though. If his radar picked up on untapped potential, he harped on the student in question until the person finally relented and put in the effort. In the end, it was less of a trouble to study than not. And by Carly's melodramatic agony, it seemed Abrams had singled her out as his next pet project.

She pulled out her keys and tossed them at me. "You're gonna have to take my Baby home. With all of the endless yammering, I could be stuck listening to one of Abrams's lectures till dawn."

"But how are you gonna get home?"

"Daniel can give me a lift," she confirmed, seeing her boyfriend heading down the hall towards us. A little bit of her natural pep returned as she hopped back up to her feet and ensnared him in a kiss. "Speak of the devil."

"Hope you've been saying nice things," he laughed. "What's up?"

"I need a ride home," she pouted.

Daniel cringed.

"What?"

"Shit, I thought I told you. I have a game up in Winnetka. We're heading out at four."

"It's okay," I said, handing the keys back to Carly. "I can catch a ride with someone else."

Her eyes narrowed at the mention. "Like who?"

We both knew everyone close to us was already busy. If there was a game, all the guys were out of the picture. And Vanessa and Kelsey had early dismissal, because they both worked at the country club bistro.

"Don't think Mark didn't tell me about your little run-in with Adam."

Busted.

"Danny Boy," hollered one of the other basketball players at the end of the hall. "Come on. Coach wants to have a meet with us before we leave."

"Gotta go. Love you," he said, giving Carly one last kiss.

"Kick some ass," she laughed, smacking him in the butt as he walked away.

I turned back to my locker, putting all my text and notebooks in their proper order. A weird rippling effect suddenly swept into my vision. I kept blinking, trying to rid of it when vertigo hit in full force. My body immediately wrenched backward. Expecting to hit the floor, I gasped, suddenly finding myself still standing upright.

"Daniel can give me a lift," Carly said beside me, once again on the floor.

"What are you talking about?" I muttered, noting my vision was once again intact. "He's got a game."

She looked up at me quizzically. "He does?"

"He just told-" My mouth clamped shut, seeing Daniel making his way back down the hall that he just came from.

"Speak of the devil," said Carly, climbing up to her feet. Once again, she met him with the same overly affectionate kiss.

They were having the exact same conversation from a minute ago. I numbly slammed my locker shut, finding Carly's keys magically clasped in my left palm. *What the hell?*

"...I have a game up in Winnetka. We're heading out at four."

Carly looked at me, and I dazedly handed the keys back to her for the second time. "It's okay. I could use a walk," I muttered, staggering away. She called out something, but it was lost on me as I disappeared down the hallway. I burst out of the front doors, letting the cold breeze bat me in the face. What just happened?

Reese's words ran feverishly through my mind, and I found myself yanking out the business card from my pocket. Dialing the number on the back, I raced down the cement steps to the sidewalk.

"Y'ello," answered a silvery voice on the third ring.

"Where can we meet up?" I blurted, trying to steady my own voice against the anxiety shooting through my veins.

"I'm sorry?"

"It's Kat. Kat Montgomery. Where can we meet?" I clarified.

A beat of silence.

"Hello?" I asked, checking my phone to see if maybe he'd hung up.

"You know where Slippery Pete's is?" he finally said.

"What?"

He sighed. "It's a restaurant, down by the pier. Think you can find it?"

"Yeah."

"Meet me there at 4:30."

Good. The pier was on the whole other end of town, but he'd given me enough time that I could make it there easily via public transport.

Mystic Harbor catered to the tourists that flocked to the city from May through November. The beaches and oceanic properties made the city a hot commodity during the summer, and the autumn colors and rustic scenery made it idyllic for cozy lodging. Because of this, a tourist trolley could be found on nearly every street corner of the downtown. I jogged my way down to Jefferson Boulevard and grabbed the green line that took me to the shopping center right by the pier.

The trip took a good forty-five minutes, due to the constant stops and scenic detours that the visitors reveled over, but I'd made it there no less. If Google was correct, Slippery Pete's should have been at the very end of the road past the store fronts. The afternoon crowds flooded the streets and sidewalks, forcing me to push my way through the throng of people. As I maneuvered around a group of seniors, someone knocked shoulders with me, their hand brushing my own.

"Sorry," I said, looking behind me. Everyone buzzed in different directions, making it impossible to determine who I'd run into. I walked about a dozen steps or so when a searing pain suddenly pierced the inside of my left arm. I buckled over, gripping the skin, only to see a soft pale light spreading across the back of my hand.

A couple onlookers took notice to me, their faces contorting in bewilderment. "You okay, hun?" asked an elder woman.

The light on my hand started growing brighter and brighter, going from the intensity of a glow stick to a tiny strobe light.

What was happening?

As more bystanders started paying mind to me, I suddenly darted out into the street, narrowly dodging traffic as I raced to the other side. Running down the alley between two nearby storefronts, I came out into the woods backing the shopping center. The ground sloped, and I galloped downhill till I was out of sight. I bit back a grievous scream, feeling the flesh on my arm sear like someone was holding a torch to it.

Elaborate swirls and symbols took shape in the light, akin to an expanding, glowing tattoo. And a string of small shimmering tethers curled around my ring finger, wrapping about and knotting into an intricate design. The strange, shining patterns continued to grow upward underneath my sleeve. I pried off my coat and yanked at the material of my long sleeve shirt, hiking up the fabric as far as it could go.

Was this going to consume my whole body?

My heart throbbed as I cowered over to a tree trunk, slumping against the rough bark. The pain was too much. Tears stained my cheeks as I toppled over, seeing the world fade out as I hit the dirt.

***

A loud, dull roar blasted through the nightly air, and I shuddered awake to realize it was a foghorn from the nearby lighthouse. I clumsily climbed back up to my feet, aches rifling through my entire body. The light...

I looked down, seeing the pattern on my hand had at last reached my elbow and thankfully stopped.

The light had faded, revealing metallic black ink resting in its place. My entire arm was now covered with a massive tattoo! The pain too had subsided, but a faint red glow remained over a small section of the skin. It was a symbol that looked like an upside-down Y. My vision swayed woozily as I knelt down to grab my jacket. Barely managing to make it down to the nearby clearing, I stumbled out onto a bridge to what looked like a reservoir. The only manmade lights I could see were streetlights resting on the other side of the lake. By the sickening wave of nausea rolling over me, I knew I wouldn't have been able to climb all the way back up the steep hill to the shopping center, so I headed across the bridge.

Halfway, I froze.

"I see you." The words echoed with a lingering hiss, carrying themselves to me in the chilling wind.

"I see you."

Whirling around in every direction, I didn't see another soul in sight. Whether this was a sick prank or something worse, I wasn't about to wait around to find out. My feet pounded across the wooden planks of the dock as I took off across the harbor. Making it safely to the other side of the waterfront, I raced toward the upcoming street.

Warehouses and ramshackle residents came into view, and I could faintly make out the distant city lights radiating from the downtown. My legs were propelling me so rapidly that I feared tripping, given the dampened conditions, but fear only urged me faster.

"I...see...you."

I trampled to a halt as a large dark mass walked onto the road at the end of the block in front of me. Snarling white teeth showed from the black mass of fur, and I staggered back at the sight of blazing yellow eyes. It was a wolf! The beast lowered its head, emitting a low snarl as the hair on its back stiffened along with its straightedge tail. A revolting odor hit me in the face, making me gag at what reeked of rotting eggs.

Just as I pivoted my foot back a step, the animal barked, springing forward. An ear aching scream erupted from my lungs as I darted down the garbage cluttered alley right beside me, coming to a large chain link fence. If I managed to climb it just enough, I'd be safe. My feet gained traction at the bottom of the barrier as I ran up the fence, gripping my fingers into the steel wire diamond patterned openings. The gate shuddered as the animal ran at it, yapping and snapping up at me. Frantically scaling to the top, I was just about to heave my weight over to the other side when something grabbed a hold of my calves, wrenching me downward. I expected to feel the stabbing of sharp teeth tearing into my skin, but the force felt more like...hands.

I tried maintaining my clutch on the top bar, but when I was met with another solid yank, my fingers lost grip and I fell backward. Landing in an accumulation of garbage bags, I tried rolling out of the mass, preparing to see the wolf. Instead, a brawny masculine figure looked down at me. The chilling winds rushing off the waterfront coursed through the air, causing the ends of his long, black trench coat to sweep around him. Bare-chested and donning leather riding gloves, the stranger removed the hood shading his face, revealing long blonde locks of bone straight hair.

"Well, well, well. Look what we have here," he cooed, standing over me. "A newbie."

I brought up my leg, preparing to hit him in the groin, when he ever so swiftly caught a hold of my foot before I could execute my attack. He thrust all his weight down on me, pinning every limb under his own.

"Don't struggle, sweetheart. I promise, you tell me what I want to know, and I'll do this fast. You'll barely feel a thing," he hummed almost tenderly, running his nose alongside my face with ease. "Where is your Maker?"

"My w-what?"

"Who turned you?"

"I...I don't know what you're talking about," I choked out as tears rushed down my cheeks. "I have credit cards and money on me. You can have them! Please, just don't hurt me."

"Ignorance isn't going to get you anywhere," he

suddenly snarled, an animalistic growl emanating from the back of his throat.

His grip around my wrists tightened, and I whimpered out another plea as he brought his gaze to meet mine. His once brown eyes suddenly smoldered into a radiating gold before casting an unnatural, iridescent shade of yellow across the entirety of his irises.

"Such a pity we didn't get to you first." The man pried off his gloves, revealing a strange pentagram tattoo on each of his palms. He rubbed them together, and the metallic ink suddenly burned bright red as the guy started chanting something foreign. Despite my constant fighting and flailing, he didn't seem the least bit affected by my desperate attempts. He even snorted out a laugh at one point.

"Producite eam ad inferos," he hissed at the end, raising his hands up. Smoke rose from out of the tattoo as the skin underneath the symbol rose like cauterized flesh.

"End of the line," he grinned.

"Yeeeeah, I don't think so," remarked a familiar voice behind us at the mouth of the alleyway. I painfully angled my head in the direction, seeing an upside-down view of a dark frock militia coat and riding boots.

"This doesn't concern you," remarked my attacker, homing his gaze on our surprise guest.

"Hate to bust your chops here, but your whole penance stare thing doesn't work on me," said Reese. "Now, before you hurt yourself, why don't you run along back to the Underworld?"

Something thin and long gleamed in the magician's hand, and my attacker clawed at my jacket. In one swift motion, he flung me off the ground and hurled me backward clear out of the fabric. My body pounded against the chain-link fence before succumbing to gravity. I dropped back to the cement, letting out a painful yelp from the impact. Something dug into my leg, and I reached down, prying out a sizeable shard of broken glass.

The attacker met Reese's proposal and suddenly removed some kind of sword from a sheath strapped around his waist. Light caught the blade in the magician's hand, and I realized he, too, was armed. As if things couldn't get any weirder…

"You seriously think you can beat me?" the blonde snickered.

Reese's eyes surveyed the sheer bulk of my attacker, and he grimaced. "Probably not. I'm really not a swordsman myself," he huffed, suddenly putting his blade back into its sheath. The attacker dropped his own sword with a low laugh, sliding off his trench coat. Snapping noises emanated from his back, and I shrunk against the fence, seeing the discs in his spine punching out against the skin as the white flesh darkened to a sickly gray.

A long dagger suddenly manifested in Reese's hand. "I'm more of a marksman." He hurtled it through the air, and I lost sight of the blade as my attacker gasped. The blonde staggered over to the wall, revealing the handle of the dagger sticking out of his chest.

"Others will come," the blonde spat, crumpling to the ground.

"And you can rest assured, I'll do the same to them," said Reese, making his way over to us.

I all-out screamed, seeing him plunge the steel so far in the blonde that the tip came out through his back.

My attacker howled in agony before…turning to ash?

In an instant, his entire body became brittle, crumbling apart and falling to the pavement in a mass of what looked like sand.

What the f*@#?
What the f*@#?
What the f*@#?

I pried myself off the ground and frantically climbed up the fence again. This time I managed to heave myself over the top, and I leapt off the other side, barking out a few curse words from the impact my ankles took.

"Not again," muttered the magician, racing after me.

I sprinted off out of the alleyway, hearing the chain-links rattling behind me as I assumed Reese was heading over the fence as well.

"Kat? Kat!"

I tried to ignore his words, but I couldn't ignore how close they sounded. With each declaration, it was obvious he was gaining speed on me. Cutting across another street to make it back to the main boulevard, I screamed out, begging for help. No one met my plea, except Reese.

"Kat, will you please just stop?" he huffed as his footsteps trampled closer and closer.

I continued to give it my all and tore off down the main drag. Was this guy an Olympian or something? I'd beaten one of the fastest runners on the track team just yesterday, and yet it seemed like Reese wasn't exhausting himself nearly as much as I was.

"My sincerest apologies for this, but you're not exactly leaving me with another choice here," he finally said.

Just as we raced past a park, his hands hooked around my hips and he drove me sideways to the ground. Crashing into the grass, I furiously wrestled against him. I tried climbing back up to my feet, but Reese managed to pry me back down and pin me to the lawn by the base of my wrists.

"I'm not going to hurt you," he said softly, peering down at me. "I'm just trying to help."

"You just killed someone!" I howled.

He merely sighed. "Would you have preferred that he kill you instead?"

I fought against his hold, and Reese scoffed.

"Well, that's one hell of a thank you. Not sure if you noticed back there, but I saved your ass."

"What the hell did you do to him? His body..." I muttered.

"It's what happens to the unholy when you kill them with an Angelorum blade."

"Who the hell are you?"

A grin pulled at his lips. "I'm pretty sure we exchanged introductions some time ago."

"*What* are you?" I better clarified.

Of all things, he actually smiled. "Ah-ha. At last, you ask the right question. Same as you, in a sense."

"...Which is?"

"Some might refer to you as a Changeling, though there are a variety of nicknames nowadays."

My continual struggle against him wasn't getting me anywhere. My chest continued to frantically heave, but I at last forced the rest of my body to settle down. Reese felt the tension fall away from my once combatant arms, and he finally loosened his grasp on me. I didn't hesitate prying my hand out of his hold, grabbing my tiny pepper spray key chain out of my pocket. Confusion flashed across his face as he caught sight of the small black tube, and the delayed reaction gave me just enough time to flick off the lid with my thumb and spray the mace into his eyes.

Thank you, Amazon!

It didn't matter how strong he was. Tear gas took down even the best, and Reese was no exception. He howled, letting go of me completely as his hands shot to his burning eyes. The change in his balance allowed me to kick him upward, tossing him off me. I clawed my way back up to my feet, racing off down the street back to the downtown.

CHAPTER 8
Carousel

"Excuse me." The phrase served as more of a warning than a polite pardon as I rushed past a group of people exiting the front of the police station.

I heaved one of the heavy glass paneled doors open and the stench of musty old carpet hit me in the face. I'd never been inside a police headquarters before, so I wasn't sure what to expect, but this certainly wasn't it.

Clearly, the crime rate around here wasn't too high, because it didn't seem concerned about accommodations. The station was small. Really small. Only a handful of worn maroon chairs sat in the lobby with a water cooler positioned in the corner. Yet, the place was a bustling madhouse. Phones rang off the hook, people hustled about the crammed space, and someone suddenly threw a stack of flyers into my hands.

"Give these to Karen," the guy remarked over his shoulder.

"What?" I looked down at the papers to see that they were missing person's adverts.

Brittany Lynch, a Hersey High cheerleader. Age:17, Missing since October 7th.

"What'd you need, hun?"

My eyes snapped back up to the front desk to see a uniformed woman staring at me. "Ah...yeah."

She took notice to the flyers in my hand and motioned me to the right. "Supplies are down the hall. Second door. Put duck tape on each corner of the back, and then use the laser printable labels to make sure they don't stick to each other."

"Oh...no-"

"Della, we need copies of that report!" shouted an officer from a backroom.

The woman huffed and hustled away before I had a chance to correct her. The adrenalin still coursing through my veins left me shaking and at a whole new level of frustration.

"Here." I tossed the stack of flyers into the hands of the first passerby as 'Della' returned to the front desk.

She gave me a pointed stare. "What's the problem?"

"I'm not here to volunteer. My name's Katrina Montgomery. I'm here to report a crime," I clarified.

Her eyebrow ticked up. "Montgomery, ay?"

I'd become all too familiar with the expression she returned. I was officially a persona-non-grata, and her cool shift in demeanor affirmed it.

"What kind of crime are we talking about here, Ms. Montgomery?" She annunciated my name with obvious distain. "Stolen vehicle? Missing persons? Harassment?"

"For starters? Assault."

Both her tone and expression remained flat. "Are you in immediate danger?"

"Not presently, no," I remarked, now with equal

crass.

"Well, I'm afraid I can't help you."

"Excuse me?" I took a derisive look around me. "Well, my apologies, but I was under the impression I was in a police station. Not a goddamn Chuck E. Cheese!"

She stared down at me from above her reading glasses and continued smacking her gum as she turned away from the counter. "I'm a civilian employee, which means I take reports for misdemeanors. To report a felony, you're gonna have to wait to speak with an officer. And as you can see, things are a bit hectic at the moment. In the meantime, you can fill this out." She handed me a clipboard with paperwork pinned under the clip at the top and motioned me to the chairs in the corner.

"Thanks for all the help." Snatching the clipboard, I caught a glimpse at the personal photo on the desk of her affectionately kissing a giggling little boy who I assumed was her son. The sight only made it more disheartening at the evident lack of empathy she was showing me at the existing moment.

Was this really going to be my life now in Mystic Harbor? The town's pariah? A local leper? My mind suddenly digested the facts of what just happened. Who the hell was going to believe me? What was I even going to say?

'Yes, Officer. A gigantic wolf chased me down, turned into a man, and tried to kill me, but he was then murdered by a crazy invisible guy. You won't find the wolfman's body though, because he was somehow incinerated into a pile of kitty litter. Any questions?'

Might as well just fit me for a straitjacket now and spare anyone the trouble.

"Miss?"

I snapped out of my trance to acknowledge the elder

woman sitting across from me. She looked back at me expectantly, and I realized she must have said something that I'd completely missed.

"I'm sorry?"

"You're bleeding."

I followed her line of vision to my left leg to see a dark, damp stain running down the length of my shin, and a small trail of blood leaked out onto the top of my white sneakers. My adrenaline high must have muted the pain, because I'd barely paid mind to the pain after I'd gotten away from the weirdo from the alley. I muttered a thank-you before setting down my clipboard and darting to the hallway. Even then as I walked on the injured leg, it barely hurt.

I scanned the labels on the doors, finally finding the one with the sign of the restroom stick people stamped on it. It was a unisex bathroom with only one toilet, so I was able to lock the door for privacy. Last thing I needed was to make some innocent bystander sick at the sight of me mopping up a bunch of blood from a gushing wound.

I gingerly rolled up my pant leg, seeing blood encrusted all over the side of my calf. Thankfully, the bathroom was stocked with paper towels and not just a hand blower, so I pumped the lever and collected a mitt full, soaking them under the running faucet. With a little soap lathered up in the towels, I gently started rubbing the fabric over my skin, awaiting the painful sting as I'd eventually run over wherever the wound was hiding beneath the caked mess.

Where was it?

Disbelief washed over me as I finished cleaning up the majority of the blood, finding not a single cut.

I hadn't imagined it. I'd pulled a huge shard from my

leg. And I held the evidence in my hands. I'd been bleeding. Profusely.

Grabbing another set of paper towels, I scrubbed the skin again, removing every last morsel of blood. This time I discovered a faint pink line running down the side of my leg. Was that...a scar?

The doorknob suddenly rattled, forcing me out of my trance. A knock followed, along with a plea to use the facilities.

"Just a second!" I collected all the bloody cloths and tried my best to clean up the mess I'd made around the sink, tossing the evidence into the trash bin. For safe measure, I grabbed some more unused towels and dumped them into the garbage as well, using them to hide the reddened fabric resting on top.

Darting out of the bathroom, I made a beeline straight for the exit. I instinctively dug around in my purse for my phone, coming to the realization once again that it wasn't there. My mind scrambled, trying to figure out my next move.

How could I file a police report about an assault if I didn't have any evidence? How did a three-inch gash miraculously heal in under an hour? What the hell was happening to me?

For the first time, I honestly wished my crazy stalker would show up. He seemed to be the only one who may have answers. And that acknowledgement hit me hard. If I told Carly and Vanessa about what was happening to me, they'd think I was having some PTSD episode, and I shuddered to even consider what my mom and dad would do. The only person I could turn to who probably wouldn't wish to wrap me up in a straitjacket over my hysterical rantings was a killer.

Wait...

Adam.

The thought came out of nowhere, and nothing honestly sounded better. Even if I couldn't tell him everything about what was happening, I still knew he'd be there. Adam always reserved judgment, and I could trust him enough to know he wouldn't go blabbing about this to anyone. He'd always been able to comfort me in the past, and even all things considered, I doubted he'd disappoint me now.

If memory served me right, there was a payphone inside the café just down the block. I jogged over to Nan's Diner, breathing a sigh of relief at the red vintage phone booth tucked in the corner as I walked in the restaurant. Slinking past the tables and booths, I made my way to the back, opening up the glass encased door and stepping inside the kiosk. Thankfully, it wasn't just a novelty piece, because I was met with a dial tone as I lifted up the phone receiver upon feeding it change.

Three rings passed, and my hopes began plummeting.

"Hello?"

I nearly jumped in elation at the sound of his voice. "Adam!"

"Kat?" He paused, and I guessed it was to check the number. *"Whose phone are you calling from?"*

"I'm at a payphone-"

"Is everything okay? You don't sound right."

I could hear the concern in his voice, and I silently thanked God that I'd gotten through to him. "Honestly, I don't know where to start. I seriously feel like I'm trapped in *The Twilight Zone* here," I blurted with a grievous laugh. Just as the sound escaped my lips, an involuntary cry immediately followed.

"Kat, what's going on? Where are you?" Music blared on his end of the call.

"Are you at work?"

"Yeah, my shift ends in about forty minutes, but I can take off now if you want."

I caught sight of the street outside. "No, I can meet you at the record store."

"You sure?"

"Yeah, I'll see you in forty," I confirmed, hanging up the receiver.

I bolted from the box and ran out of the diner to the other side of the street where a taxi was parked. The guy in back exited the cab, and the driver rolled down his passenger window as I approached the car.

"Need a lift, hun?" the old man inquired.

"Yeah, can you take me to the Deer Park Mall?"

He waved me inside, and I was met with the sickening combination of body odor, spilled coffee, cheap cologne, and an assortment of ineffective air fresheners. Rolling the window down, I tried best to breathe through my nose and touch as little as possible over the course of the ten minute trip. The devil on my shoulder cursed me for not inconveniencing Adam to come get me as I forked over a staggering thirty-two dollars to the cabby when we pulled up to the mall's front entrance.

With still about a half-hour to kill, I made my way up to the second floor where I took a seat in the food court. My table overlooked the plaza below, so I had a clear view of Sterling House Records. All the delicious scents from nearby venders overwhelmed my senses, urging me to indulge my appetite. I finally caved in and made a beeline to Auntie Anne's Pretzels. It wouldn't come as a surprise if I'd broken a world record for how fast I downed three large originals.

"Jeez, nobody at school can ever accuse you of being anorexic," laughed Daniel, startling me as he suddenly appeared beside me. "Chew much?"

I gave a feeble, close-mouthed smile as I finished swallowing the last of my meal. "I kind of forgot to eat dinner," I lied.

"Still trying to catch up on schoolwork?"

"Yeah."

"So what brings you here? Can't remember the last time you took a break from your studies to do some shopping, especially during the week. Trying to give your mom an ulcer?"

I forced out a small laugh.

"You're not gonna get a 4.0 shopping at Victoria's Secret."

"I'm just here to see someone."

"Oh?" He looked around, and his eyes homed in on the front entrance of the record store. "No..."

I grimaced.

"Kat, you can't be serious."

"It's not like that," I assured.

"Try telling that to Car."

"She's not here, is she?"

"Yeah, she's buying perfume or something at Bath & Body Works. I couldn't take the smell in there, so I bailed. She's gonna be here any minute."

"That's my cue to hightail it to safe ground." I really wasn't in the mood for a lecture right now. I collected the pretzel wrappers and headed over to the trash to discard them.

A force collided into my shoulder as I turned around, and I outright gasped, shrieking back at the sight.

"Sorry, you okay?" asked the Goth. The guy was a towering presence. His stilt-high black and blue spiked hair only exaggerated his 6'3" stature. And that wasn't the only spiky thing that could be found on him. His entire jacket and even sections of his shirt were garnished in small metal spiked studs. That wasn't what took me aback though. It was the fact that his eyes were black. Not just the irises, but the entire freaking eye! No whites, no color. Pure black!

"I'm fine," I managed to mutter.

The Goth smiled sweetly, and it only made the sight all the more horrific. He turned and continued on his way across the food court, leaving me to gape mindlessly in his wake.

"What was that?" asked Daniel.

"You saw that? You saw his eyes?"

He laughed. "Yeah, it's called guy-liner. I know you're a bit of a stickler for conventionalism, but some folks like to be a bit more eccentric."

"No, I mean the color of his eyes," I whispered.

A look best guessed as confusion distorted Daniel's features. He suddenly gaped, imitating my apparent dismay. "I know, right? When was the last time you saw brown eyes? That's only, like...half the population, including me." He laughed, but still looked at me in bafflement when it was clear I didn't share in his amusement. "Seriously, what's up with you? You look like you've just seen Pennywise the Clown."

"I have to go."

"Kat-"

I pushed past him, making my way toward the escalator. As I made my way down, I spotted Carly sauntering over to Daniel. Knowing he'd tell her about my mini freak-out, I maneuvered between the inactive people standing on the stairway and ducked into the first store I could get to when I reached the ground level. Hiding behind a clothing display near the shop window, I saw Carly and Daniel walk out of sight after a couple minutes toward the other end of the mall.

At last, I'd caught a break.

I exited the boutique and started heading over to the record store when a figure cut into my path.

"Hey, again." It was Black Eyes!

For the life of me, I couldn't say anything. I just stood paralyzed, looking up at him with eyes the size of saucers.

"I haven't seen you here before, and I never forget a pretty face," he mused, perching his elbow up against the wall beside us. His other hand suddenly teased through the ends of my hair.

I shied away, but a woman leaving another store suddenly plowed into my back, hurtling me right into Black Eyes's chest!

He grinned down at me, clearly pleased by the development. "How about we take this somewhere a bit more private?" he cooed, his hand cradling my chin.

Just as I was about to run for dear life, another arm suddenly slung across my shoulder. "What a little maverick this one is. I leave you alone for ten minutes, and you're already seducing your next victim."

Both Black Eyes and I turned to see my Psychotic Hallucination beaming down at me devilishly, and I'd never welcomed the sight as much as I did in that moment. The Goth reluctantly backed up as Reese planted a kiss on the side of my head.

"Seems we need to have a little talk," the magician jabbed lightly, pulling me away.

His arm dropped down to the middle of my back, and

he steered me across the plaza. Temptation urged me to look behind us, but he tightened his grip. "Don't. You'll only draw more attention."

"Is he the same thing as the guy from the alley?" I asked under my breath.

"No, he's a demon."

Well after we were in the clear, I tried moving out of his hold, but he wouldn't let up.

"What the hell is going on?" I insisted, slamming on the brakes. The effort did me little good as he continued on, practically dragging me across the marble floor. "Will you stop? Just talk to me!"

We passed the Cineplex, heading down toward a side exit. I further protested, but Reese pushed the door open and hauled me through. The exit took us out to a vacant section of the parking lot where only a few sparse cars were scattered across the spaces by the closed automotive department. I immediately spotted the old beater truck resting under a streetlight just down the way.

"What attacked me in the alley?"

"Hellhound."

I looked at him incredulously.

"Trust me, it's a long story. I'll fill you in once we get you somewhere a bit safer."

"I'm not going anywhere with you!" It still amazed me that I was even bothering to put up a fight at this point. I'd have better luck taking down a great white than this guy.

"Hey!" a voice barked from behind.

Reese's hold on me ripped away as I caught sight of a hand clasping around his throat. The power behind the individual sent the magician hurtling away, driving him into the brick wall beside us.

Adam?

"Don't!" I bellowed. Seeing firsthand just what Reese was capable of, I didn't doubt for a second that he'd skewer Adam like a shish kabob.

Adam ignored my plea as he charged at the man, grabbing a hold of the front of his shirt. Reese instantly nailed his foot into Adam's left shin, making him retract. The magician pushed up in front of him and whirled around to catch him off guard as he caught him in a chokehold. Adam's face started turning red as he tried and failed to break free. I sprang forward in an attempt to intervene when I saw Adam at last pry out something from his pocket. Was that a black marker? He swiftly thrust the ballpoint right into Reese's bicep. The magician barked out a string of curses as he released his grip on my ex.

Just as I'd seen Adam practice in the gym countless times, he delivered a spinning hook kick, striking Reese right in the jaw. The impact of his boot had apparently broken the skin on the magician's face, because a trail of blood ran from the reddened mark beside Reese's mouth.

Bile threatened to rise up in my throat as blood literally spurted from the wound like a popped ketchup packet as Reese ripped the pen from his flesh as well.

Adam wasted no time and grabbed him from behind, locking Reese's arm behind his own back. He began lifting him off the ground when Reese threw his weight back, catching Adam off guard. He forced a step forward before driving his left hand around, nailing Adam right in the temple with his elbow. As Adam crumpled over, Reese continued bringing his hand over, placing it on the other side of Adam's arm. He straightened, locking up the appendage and getting right in Adam's face. Reese all-out sucker punched him in the ribcage, knocking the air right out of him.

I cried out, but the magician wouldn't relent. He threw Adam against the wall, pinning him in place with his forearm digging into Adam's throat.

"STOP!" I wrestled my way between the two, but Reese still wouldn't budge. "Let him go!"

Reese shot me a bemused glare. "Why in perfect health would I do that?"

"That's my ex, you idiot!"

His stare only hardened all the more as he looked back at Adam. "Oh, I think he's much more than that."

"What are you talking about?"

"He can see me," Reese growled. "Only those who are supernatural have the sight to see past mental manipulations. The only question is, which breed is he?" Reese fetched out a long slender knife from inside his coat.

"What are you doing?" I snapped.

"If one of the unholy comes in contact with silver, it scorches their flesh. Let's see if he burns." He removed his arm from Adam's throat, only to put the knife in its place. The steel pressed into the skin, nicking it ever so slightly. Asides from the trickle of blood that escaped, there didn't appear to be any other reaction.

"That's enough! Get off of him," I demanded, seeing no resolve. I finally managed to push Reese away enough so I could step between the two.

"Seems you get to keep your head," huffed the magician, tenderly holding his injured arm. "At least for the moment, anyway." He examined the hole in the fabric where Adam had stabbed him and groaned. "Though I might change my mind, being that you ruined my jacket."

"You both have some serious explaining to do," I barked, looking back over at Reese. "And I'm pretty sure you need a doctor."

"He'll be fine," muttered Adam, fingering the knick on his own throat. "The wound will heal within the hour."

"And you know that from personal experience, I take it?" remarked Reese, still watching him guardedly.

"Something like that." Adam's eyes shifted behind him, and he grimaced. "Though, this might take a little longer."

I gasped, and Reese didn't even have a chance to turn as a tire iron suddenly throttled into the back of his head. The magician's body limply collapsed on the asphalt, and the figure standing behind him stepped into the light.

My jaw practically detached. *"Mr. Reynolds?"*

"Hey, sweetheart."

CHAPTER 9
The Wretched

Mr. Reynolds promised he'd give me the answers I needed, but first, he had business to tend to. By the looks of it, that business was Reese, who was now bound and handcuffed to an iron chair in the Reynolds's basement.

Every time I stole a glance at Adam, he quickly diverted his own gaze, and I knew this wasn't going to be good. Footsteps pounded down the stairs, and Mr. Reynolds headed over to the landing to greet the visitors. Everyone else's backs were turned towards me, but I could still make out the strapping figures and short haircuts to distinguish that they were all men. Mr. Reynolds whispered something indistinct, nodding over in my and Reese's direction. The group turned, and the whole room froze.

I instinctively cowered back over to the recliner in the corner, unable to read everyone's faces. Were they taken aback by Reese or *me*? I recognized the men from around town, but didn't know anyone by name with the exception of Russell, one of Mr. Reynolds's security detail buddies. He was a burly man with a military crew cut and arm muscles the size of cannonballs.

"What'd we know about him?" asked Russell, eying the magician.

Reese was still out cold. His long locks swept over his eyes as he sat slumped over in the chair, and my own neck hurt just looking at the crooked angle his was unconsciously positioned in.

"He goes to school with Adam and Kat," confirmed Mr. Reynolds. "It's Christine Blackburn's son."

The name drop didn't improve the mood.

"Do we know what he is?" asked one of the men.

"No, but he was carrying quite the arsenal when we took him out," remarked Adam, motioning to Reese's jacket that was now slung over the back of the loveseat by the landing.

The men eyed the garment curiously, opening up the inside compartments.

"Holy shit," muttered Russell, pulling out over half a dozen different blades and tactical tools. There was even a set of silver throwing stars. "He's definitely packing."

"What're we thinking? Purebreed? Hellhound?"

"I don't know," huffed Mr. Reynolds. "But I don't like it."

Adam finally approached me, but it wasn't without hesitation. "You might want to wait upstairs. This could get ugly."

"*Ugly?* What are you planning to do to him?"

"He's right, Kat. You won't want to see this," affirmed his father.

All eyes were on me, and the discomfiture was enough to get me to leave. But before I could move, I heard a low grumble. Everyone looked over at Reese as his head bobbed a couple times before he wearily peeled his eyes open.

"Motherf...." He wrenched his neck sorely, wincing at the pain I could only imagine was radiating from the back of his skull.

"Well, look who decided to grace us with his presence," remarked Russell, walking over to Reese with a folding chair in hand. He propped it open and set it down backwards, so when he sat on it, he could rest his enormous arms across the backrest.

Reese finally gave a good look around the room, and of all things, he chuckled.

"You know who we are?" queried Russell.

"Let me take a guess..." The magician seemed to take deep consideration in the question as he scrutinized each of the brawny men. "An underground steroid coalition?"

No one appeared pleased by the remark, but that didn't stop Reese from sharing in his own amusement.

"Shut him up," growled one man, pulling out a blade from an ankle holster.

"No," barked Mr. Reynolds. "There are other means of doing this." He pulled out a flask and unscrewed the lid, heading over to Reese.

"What? You wanna become drinking buddies?" Reese scoffed.

"Depends. How do you feel about holy water?" Mr. Reynolds suddenly hurled the contents of the container right in Reese's face. "

"Ah!" the young man howled, triggering everyone else to unsheathe a variety of different blades aimed at him.

Perturbed, Reese shook his head, causing the water dripping off the front strands of his hair to spray across the floor. "Right in the eyes."

The men lowered their guard at last, apparently not

getting the reaction they had anticipated.

"What? Were you expecting me to burst into flames?" Reese chortled. "Sorry to disappoint you all, but you're barkin' up the wrong tree."

Russell growled, getting up from his seat and walking behind Reese. The magician cringed, expecting some kind of blow to follow. Instead, Russell shoved his head forward, brushing away the hair covering the back of Reese's neck. Unsatisfied, he grabbed the collar of Reese's shirt, taking turns exposing each shoulder. "He's clean."

"Where did you get these?" asked Mr. Reynolds, stepping forward with one of Reese's filigree knives in hand.

"eBay," the magician retorted. "Or was it Craigslist? Door-to-door salesman, perhaps. Can't really be sure. That hit to the head is making my memory a bit fuzzy."

Still, no one else seemed amused.

"You a Purebred or Changeling?" asked one of the other men.

"What difference does that make?"

"Are you a part of a charter, or not?" growled Mr. Reynolds.

Reese sighed, fidgeting at the restraints around his wrists. "Is this really necessary? Or is this how you treat all your guests?"

"Just answer the question. Were you turned or not?"

The magician stole a sideways glance at me, a restrained grin tugging at his lips. "No good deed goes unpunished, aye?"

Russell grabbed a handful of his hair, wrenching Reese's head back.

"No," he confirmed.

"So your old man was a Reaper then, I take it? Is this his collection?" Mr. Reynolds didn't really need him to answer, observing the knife in his hand. "Impressive steel. You know what happened to him?"

"Your guess is as good as mine."

"Did he teach you how to use these?"

"Well, he walked out on me when I was two weeks old, so if he did, I can't say I remember much," said Reese, flatly. "The only reason I even figured any of this out was because I found his weapons and journal buried in our basement when I was thirteen."

"Can someone just explain to me what the hell's going on?" I finally demanded. "Who...and what are all of you people?"

"Care to clarify?" mused the magician. "Or do you wish for me to do the honors?"

Eric and Adam only exchanged uneasy looks.

"I'll take that as the latter," huffed Reese, turning to address me. "Back in the day when Lucifer and his legion fell from Heaven, these fallen angels fornicated with human women, bringing about a new breed called the Nephilim, otherwise known as Mages."

"Mages?" I uttered.

"Historically, a Mage is the equivalent of a sorcerer. They possessed the powers of an angel and wielded the darkest, demonic magic. Drank the blood of their victim to steal their life source. Vampires. Nearly indestructible. To counteract the reign of terror they brought upon mankind, God flooded the Earth, wiping them all out," Mr. Reynolds clarified. "Their spirits remained earthbound though, in the form of demons. Asides from your casual possession, they didn't pose any threat. That is, until some occultists a few hundred years back managed to resurrect a demon, by the name of Azazeal, back to our world in bodily form. He repopulated the world with Mages, forcing Heaven to combat the movement. A small band of benevolent angels willingly fell from Paradise to bless the strongest and pure-hearted of men with the abilities to fight these new Mages, therefore creating Reapers. Us."

"There's a delicate balance between the living and the afterlife. Reapers escort souls to the hereafter, but they also have the power to resurrect the dead under certain circumstances," added Adam. "If they do this, the person brought back is no longer human, but a Changeling. Half-Reaper, half-human—i.e., you."

"Wait, you're saying I *died*?"

"In a less than flattering sense, yes," confirmed Reese.

"*Who did this to me?*"

"That's the million dollar question," growled Russell, cutting a glare at Blackburn.

"Don't look at me," said Reese. "If I was her Maker, I'd put everybody's minds at ease and confess so I can get the hell out of here." He continued fidgeting at the binds with no luck before looking to me again. "But back to my original point, Changelings have pretty much all the same skills and abilities as full-blooded Reapers, yet they're still not heralded as equals to most Purebloods."

Mr. Reynolds's face contorted, and I couldn't tell if it was the comment or the truth behind it that upset him.

"Why's that?" I asked.

"It's not that Changelings are looked down upon; it's just that they pose a risk to Reapers such as ourselves," said Adam. "Hellhounds were created by the demon Ba῾al Berith, a chief prince in Hell. He tempts men and women alike to commit murder and destruction by way of a demonic virus. When an ordinary human is infected, it opens them up to possession. A malevolent earthbound spirit can take over the body of the host. Reapers are immune to the disease, as they were blessed by angelic blood. Changelings, however, still have human DNA, which makes them susceptible to the virus. If infected, the Changeling turns into a Hellhound."

The growing pit in my stomach deepened as I looked over at Reese. That's why I was attacked in the alley. "How do you get infected?"

"You have to be bitten," said Adam. "Hellhounds generally go for the neck. Their fangs pierce the jugular vein, so the venom gets into the system faster."

"Wouldn't you bleed out?" I asked.

"You'd think, but it's said that something in the venom causes the wound to immediately heal after the fangs are removed."

Well, that didn't sound too pleasant. "What happens if you get turned?"

"We can't be turned, because we're pureblood Reapers, from birth. If *you* get bitten," clarified Russell, "then you become a member of Hell's chief assassins. A shape-shifter with an uncontrollable blood lust."

"Hellhounds don't have any feelings. No remorse, no sense of pain. They kill at will, and the only thing they care about is carrying out their mission. We're the only ones strong enough to defeat them, so taking us out is a Hellhound's top priority," said Mr. Reynolds. "And since Changelings can be turned, they seek out the likes of you in the hope of increasing their numbers."

"What about all the Mages? If they're really as powerful as you claim, then wouldn't they have already taken over by now?" I asked, uneasy. "I mean, they've had hundreds of years."

"There hasn't been a Mage for over two centuries," said Mr. Reynolds. "You may have heard of what most would refer to as the '18th-Century Vampire Controversy.' A Mage is said to have had the ability of telekinesis, along with resurrection, among many other talents. And they could just as easily infect a Changeling. Hysteria broke out all across Europe as people reported reanimated corpses terrorizing towns and cities. It wasn't until a renowned physician by the name of Gerhard van Swieten investigated the claims that the epidemic finally ended. He concluded it was nothing more than fear and inane superstition that drove the hysteria. What the books leave out was the fact that he was a Reaper. Under the guise of night, he and his men led a crusade to eradicate all Mages stalking the whole of the continent. By the end of the 1700s, all existence of these so-called vampires had been wiped out."

"So, are any of you Changelings?" I asked.

Everyone went rigid.

Mr. Reynolds finally shook his head. "We don't fight alongside Changelings. Don't get me wrong, they're just as capable as Purebloods when it comes to killing Hellhounds, but..."

"You're a liability no less," finished another man. "The last thing we want is for a Changeling to be turned into a Hellhound with the knowledge of where to find all of us. They'll bring Hell with them and slaughter us all."

"So, you can bring people back from the dead, but you don't have any relationships with them? Not even a loved one?"

"We prefer not to sustain close friendships with Changelings, for security sake. And Reapers know better than to mate with someone outside of their order," said Russell. He stole a hardened glance over at Adam, and it stung. Had that been why Mr. Reynolds warned me about dating his son when I moved to town? Is that why Adam had pushed me away? Because I wasn't a Reaper?

"We've strayed off topic," said Mr. Reynolds. "The point here is, we need to be more vigilant than ever. Demonic activity in these parts has increased greatly over the past few weeks, and we need to know why. Kat, do you remember who resurrected you?"

I shook my head.

"Shame." Mr. Reynolds tucked Reese's blade back into his jacket.

"What difference would that make?"

"Well, for all we know, there's a rogue Reaper out there, making Changelings without our knowledge. Anyone who's brought back is now a target for demonic infection. We could be overrun by a new army of Hellhounds and not even know it until it comes to our doorstep." Mr. Reynolds ran his hands through his hair, ruffling up the thick mass. "We all have to be diligent from here on out. Any sign of a Hellhound, report it to me."

I opened my mouth, but Reese threw me a warning look. *"What?"* I mouthed.

He shook his head ever so slightly.

"How do you spot one of these things if it hasn't gone full-on Wolfman on you?" I asked instead.

"Unfortunately, they're not easy to spot. Unlike demons inhabiting a human vessel, Hellhounds don't have obvious telltale signs, like black eyes. If it's someone you know, you'll probably notice a change in their personality. They're generally charming, to lure in their victims, but they're incapable of displaying any real emotions other than rage. Crying is impossible."

"Charming, void of feeling, and murderous," I pondered. "So basically Patrick Bateman meets Hannibal Lecter. Lovely."

"Folklore concerning both the Werewolf and Vampire are reasonably accurate depictions to that of a Hellhound. A member of the infected will bear bite marks from when he or she was attacked, most likely on the side of their neck, but it can be anywhere. They'll also be branded with a pentagram on the back of their neck as a mark of their master," confirmed Adam. "Crucifixes make Hellhounds agitated, but only holy water and silver hurts them. And you can only kill a Hellhound by either decapitating them or piercing their heart with a silver blade blessed by a member of the clergy. If you think you're being followed, try taking shelter in a church. Neither Hellhounds nor demons can step foot on holy grounds.

"Why don't Hellhounds just go after regular human beings?" I asked. "They were once part-Reaper, so they'd have the same abilities. Wouldn't it be easier to just kill a human, bring them back to life, and then bite them?"

"Only Mages and pureblood Reapers were ever known to bring the dead back to life. It's not a talent Changelings and Hellhounds possess."

That foreign feeling stirred beneath my skin, pulling at my insides, as if it could sense what I was thinking.

The bird that hit the house.
The bird that had been dead.
The bird that I'd brought back to life.

How?

CHAPTER 10
Seven Nation Army

Adam offered to drop Reese back off at the mall once we were finished, promising to take me home afterward. I stole a look in the backseat, seeing Reese rubbing the back of his head tenderly. He obviously still hadn't fully healed yet. Just as he brought his hand back down, the streetlights overhead highlighted the sliver of skin exposed between his sleeve and fingerless glove. I froze.

Reese noticed where my eyes had settled, and he suddenly yanked the fabric of his shirt down.

We pulled into the parking lot a few minutes later. Reese didn't say another word, bolting from the Jeep.

"You're welcome," muttered Adam under his breath.

I opened my door as well.

"Kat?"

"I forgot, I need to pick up a delivery for my mom at the boutique," I said, gesturing to the building. "Carly and Daniel are here. I'll grab a ride with them."

"I can wait," assured Adam.

"No. I could use a little space, some time to process

everything. I'll be fine. Thank you." I hurried off to the front entrance, hearing Adam's Jeep drive off behind me. Confirming he was gone, I looked over my shoulder and bolted sideways through the parking lot. Finding my way back to the Cineplex, I spotted Reese hastily walking towards his truck parked in the far back of the lot.

"Hey!" I called out, running up to meet him.

He stiffened, but didn't turn.

"What is that?"

"What's what?" He tried to sound purely annoyed, but it was obvious he was flustered.

"Don't play dumb with me." I snatched his wrist, pulling up his sleeve. "What is this?"

Reese yanked his hand away, frantically shoving the material back down. His voice fell quiet as he nervously looked around the desolate parking lot. "Nothing. It's just a tattoo. Let it go."

He started making his way back to his rusty old truck, but I cut him off. "Bullshit. Those symbols," I said, pointing to his arm, "They mean something. What?"

Reese rolled his eyes and scoffed, as per usual. "Why do you care? Everything you need to know, your boyfriend already told you. I'm sure you'll find him to be far better company than me. Okay?"

Heat started to singe the inside of my left hand, and I could feel blood rushing to my ears as he plowed past me again. "What the hell is your problem?"

He stalled, but didn't turn around to face me.

"All I ever tried to do is be nice to you, and you treat me like shit! Why?"

"Get in the truck." The words were barely audible, and I wasn't sure if I heard him right. But he nodded over to the vehicle just the same, unlocking both the doors.

"No," I snapped. "Not till you tell me what's going on."

"I am. Get in the truck," Reese growled through clenched teeth. "Please."

I reluctantly rounded the old beater and climbed into the passenger seat, slamming the door a bit more forcefully than I had intended. Reese got behind the wheel, but didn't say anything.

"Well?"

"I can't risk being near you," he finally grounded out, his breathing ragged and sharp.

"...because?" I urged, seeing him fall silent once more. When he didn't answer, I kicked the passenger door open. "Unbelievable."

"I'm not trying to be an asshole," Reese muttered.

"And yet you've achieved it admirably," I quipped, climbing out.

"I'm not a Reaper. Or a Changeling."

I froze again, my foot failing to connect with the pavement.

"And I'm not a Hellhound," he quickly added, clearly spotting the evident look of fear in my eyes. There was something on Reese's own face I'd never seen before, except for the night at the gas station. He looked...scared.

My hand slid off the door handle, and I apprehensively settled back into the seat.

Reese already seemed to be regretting what little he had already said, but he nevertheless pulled up the sleeve to his tattooed arm. Just like me, his entire forearm was covered in patterned metallic ink. "They're runes. When a Mage comes of age, he or she receives their own distinct set. Each rune represents a unique ability. The more powerful the Mage, the more powerful their runes will be."

"Mage? I thought-"

"We were eradicated centuries ago? Not quite." He huffed. "What your good friends failed to tell you was that when those benevolent angels fell from Heaven to change them into Reapers, those same angels weren't allowed to go back to Heaven. Once you leave, you're earthbound. Their bodies became mortal, and they had to wait to die for their souls to return to Heaven.

"While they were here, they, too, bred with human women, but their offspring was virtuous. Just as there are good and bad people in the world, there are dark Mages and light Mages. While a dark Mage summons their powers through demonic energy, a light Mage draws their energy from the elements. We're not evil. Or vampiric.

"But that didn't stop Swieten in his holy quest; he and his men killed all Mages, including Light. They believed any Mage could use his or her powers for evil, so it became decree amongst Reapers to execute every last one. No one suspects them to still be around, and the last few of our kind wish to keep it that way," said Reese.

"So if Reynolds found out about you, you'd..."

"Be sent to a Texas cakewalk?" he finished. "Yeah. Dead as a doornail."

A new wave of nausea hit, and it wasn't from being hungry.

"I'd appreciate it if you didn't tell anyone about this. About me."

I nodded, but he glowered at me. "I promise. I won't say anything."

"Not even to Adam. I mean, you can't even mention the possibility of Mages, at all. If he so much as thinks about the chance that we still exist—"

"I said I promise."

"It's easier said than done." To say Reese was disquieted by the confession would be putting it mildly. He kept fidgeting about, and if he pulled any harder on his hair, I was pretty sure he'd end up with a bald spot.

"Yeah, well, I'm pretty sure it's in both our best interests that I keep my distance from Adam," I clarified.

"And why's that?" he grumbled, hardly convinced.

I pulled up the sleeve of my shirt, showing him my new, dazzling—and completely unwarranted—artwork that I'd been so diligently hiding.

His face went pale.

Not the reaction I was hoping for.

He grabbed my arm, turning it every which way to examine the markings. "When the hell did you get these?"

"About two and a half hours ago."

Reese's eyes practically bulged from his head. "All at once?"

"Yeah, and it hurt like a MoFo." I told him all about what happened on my way to Slippery Pete's, and the color never returned to his cheeks. Something was up. "What is it?"

"I've never seen these runes before." He continued to ogle at the markings with equal parts fear and fascination. "My father's journals cataloged every rune he himself collected and had ever come across, so I can double-check it, but none of them are ringing a bell."

"I thought your father was a Reaper..."

"I never said that." A mischievous grin pulled at his lips. "Part of the upside to dealing with people who think they know everything: they make assumptions. If Adam and his father want to believe that, I have no objections."

"Why didn't you want me to tell them what happened, with the Hellhound in the alley?"

His amusement vanished at the mention. "You heard what they said back there. As a Changeling, you're a liability to them, even more so now that you know the identities to half a dozen members of their charter. If they learn you've been directly targeted by Hellhounds, you're more than a liability. You've become a threat. And I can guarantee you, they're not the types of people that leave loose ends."

"You seriously think Adam or Mr. Reynolds would actually do something to me?"

"Them? No. But I wouldn't put it past one of Reynolds's cronies." He motioned to my arm. "And that only makes things more complicated. They'd kill a Mage, no questions asked. But a Mage that could potentially be bitten, who will use their magic for demonic warfare? You'd be dead before you hit the ground."

"Gee, thanks, Debby Downer. Any other words of encouragement you'd like to share?"

"Be on your guard. Considering your newly acquired runes, it's safe to say that whoever resurrected you is a Mage as well. We don't know who they are or what they want, so you're gonna have to be vigilant."

"Wow, you're officially a human depressant. You know that?"

"Hey." He returned my arm to my side. "We'll figure it out. Okay?"

"*We?*"

***

Yeah, the thought of counting on Reese for help sounded about as pleasant as a kick to the teeth. I *had* hoped that the idea would look better in the light of day, but oh boy, was I wrong. All I came to find was that I was truly out of options. Confiding in the only real father figure I've had in recent memory was off the table, and I was now officially afraid of Adam.

What I'd give to be invisible.

It seemed like everyone wanted to talk to me the moment I got to school the following morning. I'd literally flung myself into the janitor's closet to avoid running into Adam when I saw him coming down the hall. The weather even seemed to agree with my misery. Though it was well after sunrise, it barely looked like dawn had arrived. Low rumbles teased of impending storms in the distance, but none had reached town…yet. Relieved to get into class without any further incidents, I exhaustedly plopped down into my desk and put some music on to drown out the chaos. Between my racing thoughts and the fear of levitation-inducing nightmares, I secured yet another sleepless night under my belt.

A few minutes later, I could see Carly slide into the seat beside me out of my peripherals, but I kept my eyes focused on my textbook, listening to Jack White sing about the hounds of Hell.

Seriously?

Music was usually my favorite form of escapism. But the more I listened to my playlists, the more and more I noticed how biblically rife so many songs were. Everything somehow referenced demons, angels, devils, and Satan himself. I couldn't escape it.

"Hey." Carly outright pried the bud from my ear. "What happened to you last night?"

"What?"

"Daniel said you were at the mall. Why didn't you say hello? I really could have used your advice on this sweater I found."

"I'm sure it was cute," I mumbled, rubbing my eyes tiredly.

"Well, it better be. I'm wearing it," she jabbed.

I finally gave her a look-over, noting that she was in fact sporting a new cashmere cardigan. "Oh...yeah. Looks good."

"So?"

"What?"

"Daniel also mentioned that you were there to meet up with someone," she urged. "Care to elaborate?"

I slumped down into my seat, as if it would actually help me disappear. "Not really."

Car out-and-out whimpered. "You didn't seriously hook up with Adam, did you? God, I knew you'd cave! The way you were looking at him before gym...I should've just punched him in the face. Or the jewels. That would've been better."

A gentle warmth spread across my chest, and my eyes involuntarily shifted to the doorway.

No, no, no, no!

Six feet of Victorian allure sauntered in the doorway, leaving me both breathless and horrified. What was Reese doing here? He didn't share this class with us, and the only time he'd ever sought me out in school was when he was invisible. That pirated grin of his tipped up a notch as his eyes settled on mine. He wouldn't try to make me look crazy... Would he?

Just look busy.

Just look busy.

If I ignored him, he'd go away.

I grabbed my book bag off the floor and preoccupied myself with taking out notebooks I didn't need, opening them up and pretending to concentrate on the material.

My desk jostled slightly as Reese took a seat in front of me, resting his arms on the edge of my desk.

"Fancy running into you here."

My teeth ground, but I refused to pay him any mind.

"What? Not even a 'hello'?"

Carly cleared her throat. I stole a sideways glance, seeing her eyes wider than a king-sized bed. "Oh. My. God!" she mouthed.

Wait...

Reese made another remark, and when I didn't reply, Car gawked at me like she wanted to take a two-by-four to my head. She shifted her eyes back and forth between me and Reese, giving me confirmation that she could more than see him, too.

"It appears you misplaced this," said Reese, sliding something on top of the notebook laid in front of me.

I finally looked forward, seeing it was my cell.

"Understandable, amid all the to-do." He said the last word with particular emphasis, signifying an undertone that made Carly choke on her morning latte. I knew exactly where her mind had gone. Right in the freaking gutter. And it wasn't like I was in the position to clarify what he really meant. You know, rescuing me from an Underworld assassin and all... "Seemed like the gentlemanly thing to return it."

What game was he playing at? I just gawked at him confusedly, and of all things, he smiled back at me with a kindness I hadn't seen since we first met well over a year ago. Thankfully, there was a good five minutes left before class started, leaving most of the seats around us still unoccupied, but the conversation was not lost on Carly or Vanessa, who I now just realized was seated behind Car.

"Thank you," I said at last, taking the device off my

desk and putting it into my book bag. Where had he found it? I knew I lost it sometime last night, but it could've been anywhere.

"Oh, you might want this back as well." Reese lifted up something else in his hands I hadn't noticed. My jacket. He'd gone back to the alley and found them both…for me?

Okay, something was up. Either Reese was suffering from some kind of brain damage after last night, or Mr. Hyde had decided to let the dear doctor make a rare appearance today. Because this was beyond freaking me out.

Reese was actually being…nice. Shell-shocked, I opened my mouth to say something else, but there weren't any words.

"Try to stay out of trouble, Princess." And just like that, Reese swept out of the seat, giving me a wink Carly and V were sure to misinterpret, before heading out the door.

"Holy crap on a cracker!" blurted Vanessa. "Seems you *did* have a busy night."

CHAPTER 11
Angry Angel

For the first time ever, I couldn't be happier to get to English class. I planted myself into a seat in the far corner of the room, relieved that none of my friends shared the period with me.

The last I needed was more of Carly and V's interrogating. Why had I run out on Car? When did Reese and I get so chummy? And most importantly, how the hell did he end up with *my* clothes? They had a million questions, to which I had not one reasonable answer.

The fact that rumors were already beginning to spread didn't make things any easier. In no time at all, things had snowballed out of control. Even with only the handful of people who had overheard my conversation with Reese, the story mutated all too quickly into a beast of its own. What started simply as a recalling of me meeting up with Reese at the mall somehow turned into a raunchy tale on how Blackburn and I had apparently gotten down and dirty in a boutique dressing room. Yep, people officially sucked.

And of course, there were so-called "eye-witnesses." Always a friend of a friend of a friend. In consequence, I was doing my best to zone out as much as possible.

"Skank." The word emanated into every corner of the room, and I turned toward the commentator to see the Queen Bee herself, Ava Ashford, looking back at *me* from the opposite side of the classroom as she continued in her discussion with some other cheerleaders.

I settled back in my seat and focused my attention on the blackboard, trying to ignore the remark.

"You know she was sleeping with Blaine," Ava continued. "My aunt lives across the street from the Ryder's estate, and I saw Kat's car parked in his driveway from Friday night till Saturday morning the weekend before the accident. And you've seen the way she's like with Adam. No way are they still not hooking up. She was screwing them both. And you hear about her and Blackburn? Stacey overheard the two of them talking last hour about how they hooked up at the mall or something. Montgomery's burning through men faster than a kid playing with sparklers." Her voice was so loud that I swear the Biology department could hear her!

"Yeah, but she doesn't really seem like the type though," said Erica Shiffer, thankfully coming to my defense. "If she was hooking up with Blackburn, then why would she bother stringing Adam along?"

"'Cause the girl's obviously effed up," remarked Ava.

A tingling sensation rippled up my left arm. I refused to meet her gaze as I looked around the room, dumbfounded by the fact that no one else seemed to be paying attention to this blatant, loudmouthed discussion. Was everyone deaf, or were they just trying to pretend like they didn't hear any of it?

"Apparently, she's going anywhere she can for a good lay," Ava continued, "even if it is with trailer trash."

"Excuse me?" The words pierced through the air and they caught everyone's attention. It took me a second to even realize that they had come out of me!

Ava and her posse looked at me confusedly, as if I shouldn't have been privy to their brash discussion.

"What's your problem now?" Ava scoffed at me, like I had no right to address her.

"What did you just say?" My voice had become unusually harsh, to the point that it didn't even sound like me.

Ava glanced over at the other girls with a surprisingly puzzled expression. Everyone was looking at me like I had just Hulked out and smashed through the wall.

"She heard us?" whispered one of the girls to another.

"You've practically got microphones taped to your hands," I remarked, seeing all their faces with the exception of Ava's go pale. "Please, share that last thought again."

I rose from my seat and sauntered over to the front of the room towards her. The entire class had gone pin-drop quiet.

Ava still looked a bit caught off guard by my stance, but she straightened up and gave me her best toxic smile. "I said," she annunciated with venom practically oozing between her teeth, "that you're a total skank." She boldly cocked her head to the side, seeming to size me up. "You really are pathetic, aren't you?"

A handful of the students sneered and laughed under their breaths. Something under my skin crawled, and without permission from my brain, my body took over. I smiled back just as wickedly as I strolled right up to her. "Funny, I could swear your boyfriend said the same thing about you at Jake's last party, considering the fact that he had his tongue down the throat of that blonde from Jefferson High and not yours."

Ava's eyes practically bulged from her skull as the entire class gasped. I even got a chorus of "Oooohh"s.

"You bitc-"

"Sticks and stones, sweetheart. Don't throw what you can't take in return," I said. "And a piece of advice, verbal diarrhea isn't attractive on anyone." I closed the distance between us. "But I have a feeling that if we took a look into your own *little black book* that we'd discover that a lot worse things have been in your mouth other than your words."

Now, the whole room was filled with "Oooohh"s, before cutting abruptly short as footsteps trotted into the room behind me.

"Good morning, class," replied an unfamiliar, rather handsome man. By the restrained grin on his face, it was obvious that he had overheard my last statement. Ava cast me a lethal glare, and my insides churned. And just like that, my mind finally seized control over my body and a wave of nausea hit. *Did I honestly just say that to Ava?!*

The man walked over to Miss Garrison's desk and pointed to the blackboard behind him. "As you can read, my name is Mr. Salzmann, and I'll be your substitute for the day. So, take your seats, and knock it off with the death stares," he remarked. "You guys can all return to your '9-O-2-1-Oooohh no, she didn't' drama after class. Got it?" He laughed, and the warm chuckles from the other students helped ease the tension as I retreated to the other side of the classroom and took my seat again.

Mr. Salzmann started his lesson plan, but my attention span had already been spent. I could still see Ava out of my peripheral vision giving me the stink eye.

"Okay," announced Mr. Salzmann after his lecture, "I'd like to hear some of your thoughts on the subject. Anyone have an opinion they'd wish to share?"

Fellow classmates chimed in with their opinions, and our substitute turned to the blackboard to jot down some of the key points. Against my will, I turned to look at Ava as she motioned something out of the side of my vision. She returned my stare, poking her tongue into the side of her cheek and moving a closed fist in a horizontal motion. Seriously? Was she twelve? I rolled my eyes with a forced laugh like it didn't bother me, but I could feel a stirring in my gut boiling up into my chest. My grip tightened around my pen to the point that the plastic started to bend.

Just as Ava unscrewed the lid off the drink on her desk, I tossed my pen down on my desktop with a little more force than I intended. Suddenly, Ava's water bottle seemed to be ripped clean from her hands, splashing its contents all into her lap. She shrieked as she leapt up from her seat, and Salzmann handed her the lavatory pass so that she could go get cleaned up. The other students started to buzz about with whispered remarks and Salzmann had to usher everyone to quiet back down. I couldn't help but find some mild satisfaction that karma seemed to play in the matter, but something icky told me it was more than a lucky chance.

The class quickly regained order, and the newfound calm seemed to be too much for me, because I couldn't fend off the lethargy sliding its way into my fatigued limbs. I hadn't slept in days. Reveling in the darkness found behind my eyelids, I could hear the chatter around me fading into the background.

My body instinctively jerked, forcing me out of my approaching dream state. I couldn't sleep now. Not in the middle of class! God only knows what would happen. I couldn't risk levitating in front of everyone.

But relief was short-lived as my eyes shot back open. I wasn't in English. I wasn't sitting in my desk. I was suddenly standing upright…alone. Outside.

Don't panic.

Don't panic.

Dried leaves and broken twigs cracked beneath my feet as I staggered forward, greeted by nothing but a chorus of chirping insects and an eerie screeching I prayed was only an owl. Did owls come out during the day? With the storms coming into the area, the sky was dark enough that it looked like twilight. But where was I? How did I get here? There were trees as far as the eye could see in every direction. That wasn't saying much though, because visibility was pretty much nonexistent outside thirty feet with the thick embankment of fog rolling in.

I shrieked as a burning pain suddenly seared my left forearm. Yanking up my sleeve, I saw that same upside-down Y symbol inked into my skin glowing red again.

What did this thing mean?

The last time it had acted up was just before that Hellhound attacked. My blood ran cold in realization.

I was in danger.

Everything had gone quiet. Even the low chorus of chirping insects died down. I dug into my pockets for my phone, only to realize I'd left it in my book bag beside my desk. Laughter broke the silence, whirling me around. By the echoes ricocheting off the vast woodlands, it must have come from a distance. Another bout followed, this time a much higher pitch. Definitely a woman. Only, she wasn't laughing.

"Please!"

That invisible tether in me urged me forward.

"Please, stop!"

I was definitely going to regret this...

Keeping low amongst the thicket, I tiptoed towards the hysteria, still hearing healthy fits of laughter. And it was coming from multiple sources now.

"That's not how you say it, idiot," snorted a masculine voice.

"You think you're so smart? You try reading it then," gnashed a different voice. Another male.

The ground sloped up, and I peered over the top of the hill side, seeing a flat, open stretch of field. ~~Seven~~ eight people I counted in total, all men...with the exception of one. A blonde adorned in what looked like a white silk nightie. She wrestled against the guy holding her, his arm securing her around the neck. It was hard to tell from this distance, but they all appeared to be around my age, college students at the most. The blonde clawed her nails and beat her bound fists against the guy holding her, and he merely laughed, suddenly pinning a knife to the side of her face. She immediately stilled, silent tears still streaming down her face.

"Please, Will... You don't have to do this! Please, just let me go," whimpered the poor girl, looking to another member of the group.

The guy in question, Will, snickered and snatched a piece of yellow parchment from another one of his buddies. "Let's see... Ah... 'Purr san-gwin...nose offer...tye-bye et sacrifice-ee-umm'...ugh..."

"For God's sake, give me that." The guy holding the blonde lobbed her over to Will and took the paper from him. "Were you morons giving each other blowjobs when the Boss read this to you? It's 'Per sanguine nos offer tibi et sacrificium quod Magister.'"

They all began chanting the phrase, rather ineptly at first, but they eventually fell into sync with one another. The bits of debris littering the grass around them spontaneously burst into flames, ensnaring them in a ring of fire. The symbol on my arm singed my skin like a hot poker, and I couldn't bottle the pain. It wasn't more than a small squeal, but everyone's heads shot in my direction.

Shit.

Two of the men walked right through the growing flames, their pant legs catching fire. Neither so much as blinked before charging right towards me. It was too dark for them to have seen me, but if I took off running, they'd have no problem spotting me. So I hunkered down, ducking beneath the dead log beside me that was pinned against a standing tree. Every inch of me froze, trying to blend into the foliage as barreling footsteps stopped at the brink of the drop-off.

They couldn't see me…

They couldn't see me…

Leaves rained down all around me, sliding down the hillside as the guy trampled their way down. I didn't even dare taking a breath, feeling the log above me bowing as feet stood atop it.

"K-r-r-r-r-ick! K-r-r-r-r-ick!" Fluttering ignited overhead, and I strained to see the white and brown wings of a barn owl swooping toward a nearby tree.

The weight lifted off the log, and I could hear their footsteps trudging back up the hillside. "It's nothing," the voice directly above me called out.

I needed to do something, but what? It was seven against one. The symbol on my arm ignited again, forcing me to bury my cry into my balled up fist. I pinched my eyes shut, trying to hold back from all-out screaming.

"You guys done screwing around?" The voice was right in front of me.

I immediately flung my eyes open, only to find myself standing inside the blazing inferno, facing the backs of the men. I recoiled, but couldn't leave. The fire ensnaring us inside this circle came up past my waist.

"Just kill her already, and let's get this show on the road," huffed Will lazily, looking more annoyed than concerned at the blonde captured in his arms. The group began chanting again when the girl throttled her head back, hammering Will right in the nose. His grip loosened just enough for her to break free. She took off running, leaping right over the soaring blaze. The blonde yelped as her bare feet tickled the top of the flames, and she crashed into the grass on the other side of the clearing. But it didn't stop her. Hauling herself up with her bound hands, the blonde sprang up and continued running.

"HELP!"

Her tiny frame dropped out of sight as Will caught up to her, tackling her into the ground. The blonde rasped, trying to refill her lungs with air that refused to come. He'd clearly knocked the wind out of her. Will tossed her wilted body over his shoulder and hauled her back inside the circle. She convulsed, still struggling for air as she kicked and thrashed in his arms. I was right in his line of sight, but Will didn't pay any mind to me, dropping the girl on the ground before patting down the flames riding up his pant legs.

"Per sanguine nos offer tibi et sacrificium quod Magister. Per sanguine nos offer tibi et sacrificium quod Magister." Will plucked out a pocketknife, pressing the blade against the blonde's throat.

"Please...don't-"

The boy blinked, his eyes flashing gold. "Per sanguine nos offer tibi et sacrificium quod Magister."

One swift slash, and red filled my vision.

A hand gripped my shoulder and I flung upright, knocking my desk over in the process. Mr. Salzmann raised both his hands and stepped back, clearly startled.

What the hell was that?

"Are you okay?" asked the substitute. Every eye in the room was focused on me, making me all the more aware of my current state. My heart threatened to explode right inside my chest, a surge of adrenaline racked my body, making my entire frame quiver in its wake, and bile rose in my throat. I was going to be sick.

CHAPTER 12
Rolling in the Deep

I spent the whole next period in the nurse's office with a small flashlight burning purple spots into my eyes. Based on my physical symptoms, Nurse Delgado determined that I had experienced a panic attack. Obviously, I left out the part about the murder in the woods. As soon as the manic anxiety began subsiding, I was sent back to class. I needed to bide my time until I could talk to Reese. It wasn't like I could just saunter into the middle of his class and start an open discussion about demons and magic and homicide.

"You forgot *again*?" Carly laughed, hauling me toward my car the moment school let out.

"What're you talking about?"

"The country club. Your meeting with Mrs. Marin. It's in twenty five minutes." She opened the driver's door, gesturing me inside. "Your mom will kill you if you blow this off again."

Crap.

That was the last thing on my mind. I needed to get help. But after what Reese had said, I knew he was right. I couldn't go to Adam or Mr. Reynolds, and I certainly couldn't go to the cops. Mystic Harbor was surrounded by forestlands on all sides, save for the coast, and I hadn't the slightest idea where this had happened, or who was involved, or how I had gotten there.

"Hey, space cadet." Carly waved a hand in front of my face, snapping me once again out of my trance. "Woodstone, twenty-four minutes and counting. Get a move on."

I regrettably headed to the back and checked my trunk. Thank God. The dress Mom had picked out for me to wear was still wrapped in the garment bag. Seemed Reese would have to wait.

I pulled up in front of the Woodstone Country Club, and a valet greeted me as I stepped out of the Camry. He handed me a ticket and drove off into the parking lot, leaving only me and my nerves at the entrance. I immediately ducked into the bathroom to change, gaping at my reflection in horror. Donned in a pencil skirted, high-necked detailed black dress and matching ankle booted heels, I looked every bit of the sophisticated, Barbie-esque young lady that my mother always hoped I would be...except for the fact that the dress was sleeveless. When Mom had chosen it, I didn't give it a second thought. Now...I was in serious trouble. Metallic tattoos were sprawled all down my left forearm. In plain sight.

And the only thing I had to cover up the designs was the red leather racing jacket that Reese had returned to me, which was considered "street apparel" by country club decree. They'd force me to take it off the moment I went into the club's restaurant, and it would take too long to drive home to get something more suitable.

I was screwed.

My phone rang, and I tore it out of my purse. It was probably Carly. Maybe she was close. Maybe she had a jacket or a pullover I could borrow.

"Where's the fire?" It was...Reese.

"What?"

"You texted me '911'. What's up?"

Of course, now he got my message.

"A lot of things are 'up,'" I groaned, scouring the bathroom as if a miracle was somehow resting inside the nearby stall.

"Where are you?"

***

Reese had been just down the street, so it took him no time at all to pull into the parking lot of the country club. The pair of valets approached the old beater truck with a snicker, until it dawned on them that one of the two had to park it.

"Interesting style choice," Reese mused, looking me over as I met him at the curb. Like an idiot, I had my left arm wrapped up in the fabric of the shirt I had changed out of as if it were a cast.

"I have to be inside in five minutes, and my jacket violates the dress code. I can't go in there like this," I said, flashing him a glimpse of my runes.

He regarded me, not with mockery or amusement, but with empathy. "Here."

Reese drew back his shoulders, letting the rich damask fabric of his black blazer slide off his frame. I staggered back a step in bewilderment, but that didn't deter him as he wrapped the jacket around me.

"Will this do?"

Letting my bound shirt fall away, I put my arms through the sleeves and hugged the blazer around myself. Overall, it was obviously too long and a bit too wide, even considering Reese's slight build, but there was something charming about the look. A woman in a man's jacket always had a certain chivalrous appeal to it, like a snapshot out of an old movie when a gentleman realizes his date is cold.

Even better, the patterns of the jacket complimented the design of my dress. Sure, it wouldn't blend in with the convention of the club, but the blazer certainly didn't look like street clothes either.

"Thank you."

Reese reached into my/his jacket pocket and pulled out a chain. "Here." He placed it in my palm, and I fingered the pendant.

"A cross?"

"It's Celtic," he confirmed, reaching around me and clasping the chain around my neck. "But more importantly, it's silver. Always handy to have on your person. Only the purest of evil is affected by it. You touch a demon or Hellhound with that, and it'll burn 'em like a roman candle."

"Again, thank you."

"Was this the emergency?"

My teeth gritted as I tried to find the words that didn't make me sound crazy. "I saw someone get murdered when I was in English," I whispered.

"What?"

"I was sitting in my desk, and the next thing I knew, I was in the middle of the woods. There was a group of guys I'm pretty sure were Hellhounds, and they killed a girl."

"Did you recognize any of them?"

I shook my head. "The only name I caught was Will. And that hardly narrows it down. What happened to me? No one seemed to notice that I had vanished from class..."

"Did you fall asleep by any chance?" He didn't need me to confirm, seeing the answer on my face. "I think you may have had an out-of-body experience, like astral projection. It's a rare gift, even for a Mage. Could anyone see you when you were in the woods?"

"I...I don't know." I thought it had been my shriek that had caught their attention, but what if it had been the owl? And Will didn't seem to notice me either. "What do we do? Should I tell Adam—"

He immediately shook his head.

"But I have to do something, tell someone. What if we could bring her back?"

"You can't. To resurrect someone, you have to perform the enchantment on them immediately after they pass. And it's not like whoever killed her is going to be hanging around the murder site, so it wouldn't do us any good telling someone."

"Something else is wrong," I muttered.

"You're not gonna tell me you see dead people now, are you?" He smiled slyly.

"No, smartass." I gave him a light shove, and he laughed heartedly. Had I just been...playful? I shook the thought from my mind. "It's hard to explain, but...it's like I'm losing control of myself."

His left brow cocked up. "Come again?"

"One minute I'm perfectly fine and the next...I'm saying things I'd never say in a million years."

"This isn't about what happened with Ava, is it? 'Cause she got under your skin?"

"You heard about that?"

"I'm invisible. Not deaf."

"Okay, fine. Yes," I admitted. "But it's more than that. I'm worse than Ava. It's like I suddenly don't have a mental filter. Whatever comes in my head is coming out my mouth, and it's not pretty. Not to mention, there've been other incidents."

"Such as?"

"Things keep happening to people when I get pissed off at them. Like in English with Ava's water bottle. Then in AP French, her friend, Diana, was giving me a hard time as well. Just as I made a remark back to her, the mount pole from the overhead projector suddenly fell off and smacked her in the head! Madame Maillard had to send her to the nurse because it hit her that hard!"

"Karma?" Reese suggested lightly.

"Here's the kicker. Just as she got up from her seat, I again couldn't help myself and said, 'Don't let the door hit you in the ass on your way out.' And guess what happened?"

This seemed to earn his attention, because he snorted as he tried to bury his laughter. "Seriously? It actually *hit* her?"

"The door swung closed so hard, she almost face planted in the hallway!"

"Wow, you're the driving force behind a lot of mischief today, aren't you?" Reese chuckled.

"That's not all." I pulled up the sleeve of his jacket. "These tattoo things keep glowing. The skin starts tingling or it outright burns."

The amusement fell from his face.

Okay, not the reaction I was hoping for.

"What does that mean?"

He studied my arm for what felt like an eternity.

162

"That doesn't make sense…"

"What?"

"You're activating the runes."

"How?"

"Honestly, I have no idea."

***

In all of Reese's experience, a Mage shouldn't have been capable of igniting a rune without training, so he was clearly at a loss in regard to whatever was going on with me. The warm, enticing fragrance of cinnamon greeted me as I passed back through the lobby, along with an array of autumn decorations inside an elegant, lodge-themed interior. Following the signs that directed me down the left corridor, I came to the Harbor Bistro.

I was rather preoccupied with the thought of my runes that I barely paid mind to Mom's horrified gaze from across the table as I took my seat in the restaurant.

"Honey, surely you must be warm in that…thing," she prodded, her eyes widening even further. I guess she wasn't a fan of vintage outerwear.

The place was actually a little chilly, and I found myself snuggling into the lingering warmth left from Reese's body heat. "I'm good." I expected Mom to give me another ugly glare, but I hadn't anticipated the sharp jab to my shin. "Aaah!"

The woman just kicked me!

Mrs. Marin looked to me confusedly over the rim of her gigantic reading glasses. "Are you alright, dear?"

"Peachy," I winced, rubbing the tender spot of impact.

For the next hour, I laughed and smiled on cue. There

really wasn't any need for me to be here. I could have used a freaking cardboard cutout. I didn't speak once. I just nodded and complied with everything expected of me. Karma had apparently decided that I wasn't in enough pain, because it was like I was suddenly sucker punched in the gut.

Blaine's mother. The only time I'd seen her since the accident was at the funeral, and we hadn't spoken. I had hoped to keep it that way, but she was making a beeline right for our table. Everything from the salon styled shoulder length blonde bob and sleek onyx suit made her a figure to be both admired and feared. All the men in the room marveled over her, while the women, no matter their age, tried to avoid eye contact with her as if she was a grizzly bear on its hind legs, ready to strike down anyone who looked at her crossly.

"Charlotte," she announced, exchanging air kisses with Mrs. Marin. Her cool gaze drifted over to my mom. And then me. She gave a curt nod. "Ladies."

I attempted a polite smile, but couldn't bring myself to say anything. What words were there? 'Sorry for being partly responsible for your only son's death'? My nervous eyes traveled away, taking a sudden interest in the patterns woven into the carpet. She continued talking to Mrs. Marin, something about wanting to set up a new charity fundraiser in Blaine's honor.

"Oh, Sybil, that's a wonderful idea," Mrs. Marin concurred. "He would've loved that."

My nails bit into the palms of my hands so hard, I was surprised I hadn't drawn blood. I could picture his face. The contempt he and I both shared towards the snobbery our mothers masked as compassion.

He would have hated that.

I could see his face....

I could see his face....

I pinched my eyes shut, hoping to wash away the image. But all I could see was that night. That one faithful night that—unbeknownst to me—had put all of this into motion. Why did Adam have to leave me at that party? Why did he have to leave? If only he had stayed, none of this would have happened.

"I am sooo sorry," pleaded the server, scrambling to pick up the broken remains of the shattered flutes. A drunken Mr. Harding had practically tackled the poor girl as he ambled over toward his greatly peeved wife, knocking the server right off her feet. As a result, my legs and shoes were now soaked in Champaign. It really was par for the course. Adam abandoned me, again. Why? Why? Why? On top of that, Mom was treating me like a show horse out on display, and everyone was already drunk off their asses. And it was only seven o'clock.

"It's okay." I knelt down, helping the girl gather up the pieces of glass onto the serving tray. Plenty of feet passed by us, but no one else seemed inclined to lend a helping hand. Once we were certain we'd picked up every last fleck of glass, I followed the server into the kitchen and dumped the mess into the trash.

Masses of long curly locks fell into the girl's eyes as she rushed around the counters, continuously apologizing. "I hope I didn't ruin them," she whimpered, pointing at my shoes.

"That makes one of us," I laughed, taking the bundle of cloth napkins she handed me to clean myself off. "I'm pretty sure Satan invented these."

I achingly pried the towering stilettos off, wiping up the inside soles where some Champaign had gathered.

"Oh my God," gasped the server. I followed her gaze down, seeing the bloody insides of my feet. The heels had been torture,

and apparently more than I had imagined. Mom had just bought them for me, the insides an inflexible, hard plastic material that chafed the sides of my feet with every step. They'd been hurting, but I didn't think it was this bad.

"Let me go fetch you some Band-Aids."

"No, no. It's okay—"

"Really, I insist. It's the least I could do," said the server, darting for the hall.

More servers, both men and women, came and went from the kitchen. I limped over to the corner, trying best to get out of their way as they swapped empty trays for ones with freshly stocked appetizers and alcohol. Everyone else from the party was too busy socializing in the rest of the magnificent manor that I thankfully found myself alone.

"Where the hell have you been?" growled Mrs. Ryder. I startled at the sound of her voice, turning to see Sybil scowling at the base of the side staircase. Slow footsteps clomped down into the kitchen and a handsome black-haired boy emerged from the shadows. "The party started over forty minutes ago. Everyone's been asking about you."

The young man, who couldn't have been much older than me, stood lazily slouched in a dark blue suit as Sybil came up and started fussing over his tie.

"Remember to ask Sabrina how her trip was, and don't forget to talk to Lawrence Appleton, and—"

"I know, Mother," the young man huffed as Sybil tightened his tie in excess. "And I know how much you want me to look like a human Ken doll, but unlike him, I'm required to breathe." He yanked at the tightly bound tie like it was a noose, loosening it enough again so that it didn't appear to be choking him.

"Straighten up, and smile," she ordered through gritted teeth.

The raven-haired boy animatedly hopped to attention and

smiled as broad as he could, widening his eyes for additionally asinine effect. I had to clamp my hands to my mouth to suppress my laughter, relieved to see neither still seemed to notice I was there.

"Will you knock it off?" Sybil growled. "You look deranged."

"Then I should fit in just fine," he countered.

She merely cast him a tested look. The boy deflated, letting his features soften until they resembled something more natural.

"Better." Sybil ushered him out through the swinging kitchen door towards the ruckus of people.

I stood there still waiting for the server to return, catching glimpses of the handsome young man as servers continued in and out of the kitchen. His smile seemed sincere enough, so long as nobody really paid too close attention. It never faltered, remaining plastic and unwavering, a sign that it was well rehearsed. But the smile never quite reached his eyes. I knew that look all too well. I wore it to every party Mom dragged me to.

He continued surveying the room, appearing to map out the quickest way to get the hell out of there. The young man slinked back into the kitchen not a moment later, sighing exhaustedly as he yanked his tie clean off and relinquished a string of swear words.

"Rough night, I take it?"

He whirled on his heels, looking back at me like a deer caught in headlights. "Oh...shit."

I chuckled.

"Sorry," he murmured, ruffling a hand through his perfectly groomed hair enough that it left it properly tossled. "I'm just...uh...not feeling very well."

"Uh-huh." I still couldn't quite rid myself of my smile as the server returned with two large Band-Aids in hand. I thanked her, and she startled at the sight of the man. The server murmured *something incoherent before quickly grabbing a tray and fleeing.*

I turned my attention back to the black-haired boy who was now looking at me quizzically. He took notice to the blood on the insides of my feet and moved in closer. "God, what happened?"

"Seems like neither of us was built for high society," I chortled, holding up my heels to declare them the culprit.

"Seems so."

I padded away some of the blood trickling down my foot with the cloth napkin I still had in hand, limping toward the side hallway. "Would you happen to know where the closest bathroom is?"

"Here, let me help you with that."

I barely had time to straighten up when he effortlessly swept me up into his arms. A shrill shriek escaped me as he carried me across the kitchen, setting me down on an empty countertop. He laughed softly, angling me so that my legs dangled over the sides.

"You really don't have to do this," I said, watching him peruse the lower cabinets for rubbing alcohol and a few cotton swabs.

"Nonsense. As your host, it's my duty to see to my guests. Not to mention, it buys me some time from having to go back out there," he laughed, nodding to the swinging door. The boy smiled, and for the first time, the gesture reached his eyes. Soaking the cotton with some alcohol, he knelt down and lightly dabbed it on the blistered skin. I immediately flinched, and he laughingly caught a hold of my foot in case I kicked him.

"Sorry," I gasped, feeling blood rushing to my cheeks. It didn't help that my feet were extremely ticklish.

"Even if you hit me in the mouth, it'd still be less painful than the party."

"Blaine, don't think I didn't see you come in here," announced Sybil. Her curt tone was cut short as she took note of

him placing the bandages on my feet. "Oh…hi."

My cheeks reddened all the more as I slid off the countertop. "Hi, Mrs. Ryder."

"I see you two have met." Her smile couldn't get any broader.

"Not officially," said the young man, rising to his feet. He extended his hand to me, "I'm Bl—"

"This is my son, Blaine," declared Sybil, rushing to our sides.

"Blaine," he reiterated, trying to muzzle his laugh.

"And this is Katrina."

"Kat," I corrected.

"Gemma's daughter. The one I was telling you about," said Sybil.

Blaine's eyes widened. "Gemma? As in Gemma Montgomery?"

"Yeah, that's my mom."

"I would have introduced the two of you sooner, but Blaine spent the last year abroad before going to his summer internship in New York," added Sybil giddily. She entered into a small spiel before Vanessa's mother interrupted with some conspiratorial gossip she wished to share with her. "Oh, excuse me. You kids have fun now."

"What?" I finally asked after they left, seeing Blaine still gawking at me, awestruck.

He shook his head. "Nothing… It's just—you're not what I was expecting."

"What'd you mean?"

"I'm not really sure. I met your mother last summer before I went away, and she was…ah…"

"Toffee-nosed?" I suggested.

He sighed. "That's a nice way of putting it. Yes. And around these parts, the whole 'like mother, like daughter' saying

169

pretty much sums everyone up."

"Well, I'm sorry to discredit the proverb."

"I'm not."

Drunken mirth roared from the other side of the kitchen door, and we both shuddered.

"I'm pretty sure they could scare hyenas with that laughter," said Blaine, running another hand through his hair. "And I swear to God, if I have to listen to another one of Mrs. Patterson's sexcapades, I'm gonna impale myself with the ice sculpture out back."

"You have to admit, she's lived a very spry eighty-nine years," I chuckled.

"Has she run out of material yet?"

"Oh, no. And she gets more explicit with alcohol."

"If you're trying to convince me to go back out there, you're doing a terrible job."

"So it's safe to say you aren't happy to be back home?"

"It wasn't particularly promising, until about five minutes ago." He extended his arm out to me. "You wanna get out of here?"

"My mom would kill me if I left."

His brilliant smile never faltered. "That's not what I asked. What do you want?"

Blinking, I could only see vague shapes through the tears clouding my vision as I snapped out of the memory. Sybil was long gone, and Mrs. Marin and my mom were already deep in conversation. I didn't bother excusing myself, sliding out of my seat. Walking as fast as my heels would allow, I darted out of the restaurant, only to find Ava and her posse hanging out by the front entrance.

I couldn't leave without having to run into them, and

the bathroom was right there as well, so I couldn't hide out either. And considering that my face was covered in tears, I suspected there was more mascara bleeding beneath my eyes than actually on my lashes. I probably looked like a raccoon or a watered-down clown. I backtracked through the corridor, thankful to find that the balcony overlooking the golf course was empty. My trembling legs barely managed to carry me outside.

"What do you want?"

Gripping the wall, I sank to the floor, my back pressed against the closed door to grant me what little privacy I could have in a place like this. I curled into myself, burying my head into my hands, crying harder than I'd allowed myself since the funeral.

What did *I* want?

I wanted to live in the old cramped two-bedroom apartment I grew up in. I wanted my dad to lose his position at the firm. I wanted him to go back working a nine-to-five job, when he didn't have to write himself reminders to spend time with his family. I wanted to go back to a time before Mom confused having bragging rights over her friends for happiness. I wanted the Adam I used to know, the carefree boy who used to camp out with me in our tree fort all summer long. I wanted to go back to a time before death marred the sweetest kid I ever knew. I wanted to be ten years old again, when love didn't come with conditions. But more than anything, I wanted to go back to a time before I inadvertently killed the nicest guy I'd met in this godforsaken town. Everything I wanted was what I could never have.

A strong vibration suddenly rippled up my arm, and I opened my eyes to see bright blue lights pouring out of Reese's left sleeve. Another rune was glowing, this one a peculiar horn-shaped symbol.

"Ego sum hic ut accipere vos a haec miseriae."

I snapped up to my feet, furiously wiping the tears from my blurred vision. That voice. It was nothing more than a whisper, but I knew it. I recognized that low, silky quality.

The figure from my dream…

I looked around, but it was clear that no one was there. I ripped open the balcony door to only find that the hallway, too, was empty.

Perfect.

Just what I needed, to be hearing voices.

CHAPTER 13
America's Suitehearts

Reese shot me a text later in the evening, promising to contact me if he found anything in his father's journals that could identify any of my runes or explain what was happening to me. Sadly, my hopes had fallen by the time I woke up the next morning without another word from him.

A pop quiz in French turned out to be the one bright spot of my day so far, which wasn't saying much. The rumor mill was in full swing, and now I seriously wished I had Reese's ability to turn invisible.

"Stalker alert."

I jumped at the sound of Eric's voice, inattentively unaware he'd even been behind me.

"What?"

"9 o'clock." He nodded to our left where Reese was standing a good ten people ahead of us in the lunch line.

"He's not even looking over here," I pointed out, grabbing an empty tray.

Eric laughed, seemingly at my ignorance. "Blackburn's been stealing glances at you all day. If he had laser vision, he would've burned a hole through you the moment you stepped through the front door."

My heart did a traitorous summersault in my chest. Had he really been looking? Anytime I crossed paths with him today, his head was always down, either buried in a book or fiddling with his camera. Reese was wearing a black pinstriped blazer with large, intricately embroidered cross symbols on the sleeves that matched the color of the exposed red stitching on the lapels. He turned just the right way that I could read the front of his shirt. *"Normal People Scare Me."*

I did my best to bury my smile as I turned back to Eric. "He's not so bad."

Eric's eyebrows shot up so high, they disappeared beneath the shag of hair hanging over his forehead. "Please tell me you're joking. Because if not, I'm gonna have to suspect that either you've been replaced by an alien pod person, or you're just as crazy as Blackburn now."

"Thanks."

"And what's with this?" Eric grabbed my free hand, looking at the fingerless gloves in amusement. "You start taking fashion advice from him, too?"

"No, I'm just cold," I said, ripping my hand away. That was total bull.

Carly had already given me crap about my new accessories the moment she saw me in the parking lot this morning, since the only people who ever wore them around here apart from Reese were the handful of stoners who spent most of their days higher than kites. With my sparklingly new—and totally unwanted—sleeve of tattoos, I didn't have much say in the matter. Even though my long-sleeved shirt covered my arm, the cuffs still didn't come far enough down to hide the inky designs stamped on my hand. Having spent all day yesterday trying to hide my hand in my pocket wasn't what you'd call fun. So I stopped by Target on my way to school to pick up a cheap pair of knitted gloves, cutting off the tops of the fingers with the Swiss Army knife I had buried in my glove box.

To make matters worse, the faculty decided to crank the heat in the building, forcing me to either sweat bullets underneath all the fabric or risk exposing myself. Also, my gym locker was right in the middle of everyone else's. There was no way nobody wouldn't notice the tattoos if I got dressed in front of everyone, forcing me to change into my uniform from inside the bathroom stalls yet again. I needed to come up with a different plan. Maybe invest in some good theater-grade make-up.

"Why is Reese crazy?" I asked.

"Hello, gas station. Remember?"

Okay, Eric did have a point. I thought the same thing at the time. "But all you guys said the same things about him long before that. And don't tell me it's because he's a West Ender."

"No, I say that because Harry Houdini over there just weirds me out. Trust me, if you grew up having to go to school with him, you'd know what I mean."

I rolled my eyes.

This didn't do me any favors, because Eric's expression blanched. "Alright, I'm not one to buy into idle gossip here, but seriously." He leaned in, lowering his voice. "Is there something going on between you two?"

Great, someone else who'd jumped on the Kat's-a-skank bandwagon.

I just scoffed, snatching up some plastic utensils.

I still wanted to talk to Reese to ask if he found anything out about my runes, but I couldn't find an opening.

The only class we shared where we sat anywhere near one another was Physics, and we didn't have that until tomorrow. As for lunch, talking to him was apparently out of the question. Mystic Harbor's cafeteria had its own system, an intricate operation that mapped out its hierarchy. The most popular students, like Ava Ashford and Becky Sorensen, sat at the table nearest the long window overlooking the fountain in the courtyard below. The other jocks, cheerleaders, and socialites, which included my friends, were positioned at the tables beside them. The farther you were from the Queen Bees, the further your popularity status tanked.

With the torrential downpour, eating outside on the football field bleachers was out of the question, which explained why Reese resigned himself to actually staying in the cafeteria today. He planted himself down in the last lunch table on the far end of the room. The few mathletes who had been sitting there took one nervous glance at him and quietly slipped out of the bench to the next available table. There obviously wasn't enough room to accommodate them all comfortably, but that didn't stop the trio from squishing themselves in as if the table was the last available lifeboat on a sinking ship.

It had now become impossible to ignore Reese. Every time he was near, I'd feel that flushness creep across my chest before I even saw him in the hallways. And for the very first time, I actually noticed him. Not just him as a person, but the way everyone else reacted to him. Now knowing what he could do, I figured out pretty quickly that he mostly roamed the hallways—invisible, because Reese slipped through the crowds without so much as a blink of an eye from our fellow classmates. However, anytime he entered a classroom or the cafeteria, it was obvious that everybody could see him because they all shrank away from him like he was a highly infectious plague. The only people to ever address Reese were loudmouthed jocks who never missed out on an opportunity to harass him. He never did anything to provoke these attacks, yet name-calling and forceful shoves were plentiful. Hell, my own friends partook in it. Seeing it made me sick, but the fact that I'd been blind to it up until now made me sicker.

There was one unspoken—but highly regarded—rule in Mystic Harbor, and that was: never challenge the status quo. Mom lived by this tenet like it was her life source. Yet there I was, about to rock the boat so hard, it'd probably capsize. I handed my money to the lunch lady and started making my way around Ava's table, seeing Carly and Daniel move over to make room for me and my tray. But I kept walking.

"*Kat?*" Carly shouted after me. I didn't stop.

"This seat taken?"

Reese took a break from stabbing the slop of ground beef on his tray to look up at me, and immediately froze.

CHAPTER 14
The Devil Within

Reese's eyes widened, only to narrow a second later. He looked around me, and I didn't need to see for myself that others were staring. The natural ruckus of the room had suddenly fallen to a low chorus of whispers.

"What are you doing?" he asked, clearly suspicious.

"I'm joining you." I didn't wait for an invitation, putting my tray down on the opposite side of the bench from him. "Though I can't say I really have an appetite. I'm pretty sure this food was prepared as a pretext to a dare."

'Mystery Meat Monday' was the unofficially coined term for the funky, uneatable main course slapped onto our plates, a collection of all the leftovers from the previous week.

I took a better look at the thick chunks amid the pinkish slime. "Uh…when did we last have meatloaf?"

Reese grimaced, poking at the gunk on his own tray. "Too long to still be edible." Surrendering, he finally tossed the plastic spork aside and ate a slice of bread instead. "Why are you here?"

"Looked like you could use some company."

He continued to eye me with evident doubt, but didn't say anything.

"What are you reading?" I finally asked, trying to fill the awkward silence lingering in the air. Reese propped up the book he had laid out on the table just long enough to flash me the cover. Charles Bukowski's *You Get So Alone at Times That It Just Makes Sense.* "So…how's your Physics report coming along?"

"Fine."

I tried out a couple more questions, still only getting one word responses. "Don't talk my ear off, now," I muttered.

He didn't so much as lift his eyes as he flipped to the next page. "I'm just waiting for the other shoe to drop. Why are you talking to me—here? There are these things they invented called cell phones. You may have heard of them."

"Ha-ha."

"Not to mention, you already have my number. The whole reason I returned your phone to you when I did was to avoid this very situation."

Ouch. "You really hate me that much that you can't stomach sitting with me?"

"What?" He looked up, confused. "No, I meant this." His eyes shifted across the room. "I'm not particularly fond of being a spectacle, and I really think you underestimate the killing powers I possess when it comes to one's social status."

"I'll take my chances. Besides, if you were really concerned with not drawing attention, I'm pretty sure you wouldn't dress like that," I pointed out.

He relented, closing his book. "Let me ask you, what would your reaction be if you saw someone dressed like me, who spends their days performing random acts of illusions, suddenly vanish out of thin air in the middle of class?"

"I'd be taken aback, sure, but I'd find it pretty cool."

"And what would you do if you saw your everyday jock or cheerleader vanish into thin air right from their desk?"

"I'd...probably scream and run away," I admitted.

"Precisely. Around here, the weirder you appear to be, the less people pay attention when something unexplainable happens."

"Do you lose control of your abilities?" I whispered. "Is that gonna happen to me?"

"To one degree or another, yeah. It's kind of unavoidable. Light Mages evoke their magic through concentration. The harder you focus on something, the more power you expel. So by simply focusing on your studies, you may accidentally make all your reading materials levitate off your desk. It takes practice and discipline, but even I have a slipup every now and again."

"That's hardly comforting," I mumbled. "Did you have a chance to look through your dad's journals?"

"Came up empty." Reese finally sighed. "Look, I don't know if you're doing this to make a point to those self-righteous assholes you call friends, but you really don't need to commit social suicide to do so. I don't need your pity, Princess."

"Okay, why do you keep calling me that?"

"Princess?"

"Yeah, do you really think I'm that spoiled?"

"Not at all."

"Then what is it?"

A sly smile crept across his face. "You really don't know?"

Even though I didn't regret not eating more from the cafeteria, my stomach certainly did. I'd dumped my tray with most of the food still on it, forcing me to take refuge with the vending machine. Sure, the snacks were far better tasting, but it really didn't do much to crave my appetite. Reese seemed to be suffering from the same problem, because we both practically tackled the machine the moment lunch let out.

"Sugar works best to fend off the cravings," he whispered, grabbing a Mountain Dew and two packs of Skittles. "It still doesn't work as well as having a solid meal, but it'll hold you over."

"Is that what's wrong with me? Is my blood sugar crashing?"

"Sort of. Our bodies heal so quickly because our systems run faster, including how we process things. So we need to eat and drink more frequently. Think of it as having a metabolism on cocaine."

Lovely.

He tossed one of the packets of Skittles at me. "Any more questions, you know where to find me, Princess."

His boyish smile was undeniable. He really wasn't teasing me. The moniker was that of...approval. The skin atop of my left hand began to tingle as I grabbed a Dr. Pepper from the vending machine. By the time I got down the hall, the sensation dulled. Ducking into the bathroom, I took off the glove from my hand, seeing the ink glowing ever so slightly. It wasn't the same symbol that had been acting up yesterday, and nothing strange seemed to happen with this one, so I guessed that was at least worth something.

Things really weren't shaping up to get any easier though. The light dimmed down by the time I made it to my next class, but I had to wait until the very last second to slip into Calculus, as to avoid being barraged by God only knows who for my little lunchroom indiscretion.

"What the hell?" Vanessa mouthed as I took an available seat, purposely on the other side of the room from her and Eric.

I didn't answer, fixing my gaze on the blackboard. The moment class let out, I bolted. I couldn't seem to escape everyone, because Kelsey tentatively approached me a few minutes later, dialing in the combination to her locker a few feet from mine. "Hey."

"Hey."

Please, don't say it. Please just don't say it.

"Listen, about lunch..."

Crap.

Kelsey could be worse than Carly sometimes when it came to gossip and social status, so I imagined my fuse would blow after about ten seconds. "Let me guess, you think I should stay away from Reese, because I'm popular and he's apparently bat-shit crazy?"

"No."

I preemptively rolled my eyes before my brain managed to truly process the answer. "Wait... 'No'?"

She gave a small smile. "I think it was kind of cool, actually."

My jaw dropped so far, I could have kicked it with my shoe.

"Reese seems like a decent guy from what I've gathered. Sure, he's got a chip on his shoulder, but can you blame him? With all the elitist, holier-than-thou bullshit that goes on around here, Blackburn's treated like he's a Sith

Lord or something. Just because you're from the 'other' side of the tracks doesn't make it the 'wrong' side."

"Wow..." I tried to say something—anything else—but I couldn't find the words. It was honestly that shocking.

Kelsey gave a halfhearted laugh. "Yeah, I know. You're probably thinking you're hallucinating, hearing me say this, but you know how it is. If my mom caught word of it, she'd shipped me off to get my head examined."

"I hear ya'." Another warming sensation crept across my chest, and I looked down the hall just as Reese came around the corner. Dr. Fritz immediately flagged him down, handing something over to him in a small, brown paper bag.

"Those your meds?" barked out Trace Bolton, Mystic Harbor's epitome of the dumb-jock stereotype.

His buddies joined in on the running commentary, and my stomach roiled. Dr. Fritz shooed them away to no avail before she disappeared into the stairwell, leaving Reese once again at their mercy.

"So what are they, Buffalo Bill?" Bolton further taunted. "To quiet the little voices in your heads? To fend off delusions? You see little green men?"

The rest of his posse kept the remarks coming, and Reese just shook his head.

"Come on, Barnabas Collins," snickered Trace. He threw a beefy arm around Reese's shoulder, plucking at the collar of his rakish dress shirt. "Tell us, what's your deal, man?"

Reese immediately shrugged him off. "You know how they say, 'every village has its idiot'? Well, I was told the pills would help me see only one." His gaze drifted across the entire lot of them. "Appears they're not working, because I can't keep count of you guys."

A few bystanders laughed, until Trace shot them a

daring glare.

I shrunk back, leaning over to Kelsey. "Has it always been like this?"

"With Reese?" Kelsey winced as she stole a look behind us. "Yeah, but it's still not as bad as it used to be. When we were younger, Trace really gave it to him."

"Are you serious?" My stomach roiled at the thought. If the guy was even half the size he was now, I couldn't imagine...

She nodded. "Yeah, and trust me. That guy was never small."

I grimaced all the more.

"Along with the relentless name-calling, Trace and all his friends thought it would be funny to make Blackburn into their new dodge ball target. So during recess, they used to grab him and throw him up against the side of the building where the teachers couldn't see. They started pelting Reese with the equipment. It wasn't anything new. Trace did this to him all the time. But on one particular day, Bolton decided that dodge balls wouldn't cut it. His whole posse started nailing Reese with basketballs, and Trace even pitched a baseball at him. Cracked his ribcage."

"Oh my God."

"The rest of us were afraid that Trace would go off on us, so we stayed out of it. Out of nowhere, Bolton wound up on the ground. Nobody saw what happened exactly, but Trace ended up with a busted lip and a broken front tooth. He claims he tripped and fell. Rumors started, and certain bitches like Ava Ashford couldn't resist taking advantage of the incident. You know how everyone's all weird and superstitious when it comes to Reese?"

I nodded.

"Yeah, well, Ava told everybody that Reese used

'black magic' to attack him. After that, Blackburn was deemed the local leper. It's stupid, but considering his...*peculiarities*, the stigma stuck, even after all these years."

"Explains why he doesn't trust anyone around here," I mumbled. "Were any of the guys a part of Trace's group at the time?"

She outright cringed. "Daniel always felt bad about what happened, but Eric and Mark just shrug it off as juvenile stupidity."

Another piece of the puzzle had fallen into place. It made sense now why Reese had such a gripe with my friends. Why he did everything to avoid them. Why he judged me for hanging out with them.

The warning bell sounded off overhead, so Kelsey and I started making our way to History. Adam was leaning against the desk beside mine as we entered the room, and that weird force inside of me yanked backward, urging to run out the door. After the other night, I'd made it a point to avoid him, but it seemed he had other plans.

"We need to talk," he said lowly as I approached.

Had he somehow seen my runes? My stomach broke out into nauseating somersaults. "What about?"

"You know *who*. Privately."

"No. Just say what you want to say."

Adam stole an annoyed glance over at Kelsey, seeing her still standing at my side. "I just think you should keep your distance from Blackburn is all."

"Is that right?"

"I don't want to see you get hurt-"

I scoffed. "That's rich coming from you."

"What's that supposed to mean?"

"If you're really that concerned with who your ex is

spending time with, then maybe you should have worried about that before you pushed her away." It was a cheap shot, I'll admit it, but he had really hurt me. The fact that he suddenly took interest now just left me suspicious and all the more pissed off.

Adam's jaw grounded. "Despite what you might think, I really am looking out for your best interest."

"Is that why you didn't say anything to me about what happened after the accident?" He opened his mouth, but I pressed on. "You *knew*. You knew what was going on with me, and yet you said nothing. You *did* nothing."

He gave me a pleading look, so I finally relented, pulling him into the corner of the room.

"You saw what I was going through, with the cravings. You treated me like I was just being paranoid when I told you about the guy in the hallway. You knew I would be hunted," I growled.

"I didn't know for sure if you really had been changed—"

"Bullshit. You attacked Reese at the mall without any evidence. You called your dad for reinforcements. You *knew*." Tears threatened to spill over my lashes. "You were my best friend, and you abandoned me. I loved you, and you pushed me away. I trusted you, and you lied to me. I don't care about what you think of Blackburn. He's the only one here who's actually been honest with me."

"Kat..." He reached out to me, but I recoiled.

Kelsey seemed to recognize my discomfort, because she immediately darted to my side from across the room, hooking her arm around mine. "I think it's time for you to leave," she said to Adam. She then guided me away to the other side of the classroom when Adam made it clear he wasn't going to move.

"Thank you," I mouthed to her as we took our new seats.

It appeared I wasn't the only one changing around here. For as long as I knew her, Kelsey didn't put up a fight when it came to social construct. She did what was expected of her, and she always acted like a lady, even when you could see she loathed it. She never butted into other people's business. Yet, here she was, telling off our star boxer.

The theme from *Dracula* blared throughout the classroom, killing my moment of relief. I frantically dug into my purse, hoping to silence the phone before Mr. Hopkins came in and confiscated it.

"Wonder if Reynolds will still be your white knight when he discovers the truth."

It was another text, from an unknown number. And there was a video file attached.

"Stanley," begged Mrs. Corvets's voice off screen. "Stanley, get over here, and stop harassing the poor girl!"

The spaniel cowered down at my feet. I was dressed in a familiar black dress. Vanessa's. It was the one I borrowed for Blaine's funeral. The feed seemed to be coming from the bushes lining the side of the house. Just as before, the crumpled, feathery body in my hand contorted, setting its snapped bones back into place, springing to life.

"Kat? You okay?" asked Kelsey.

I immediately threw my phone back into my purse, seeing more students file into the room around our desks. "Yeah."

"What was that?"

Based on the angle I'd been holding up the phone, she couldn't have seen the video, so I shrugged as nonchalantly as I could. "Just some ass-hat trying to harass me."

Whoever this was was definitely an ass-hat, but that's

not what scared me. The fact that this person was apparently stalking me, filming me, taking pictures…I couldn't begin to fathom who would do something so sick. I needed answers.

Thankfully, my anxiety was tranquilized after class began. Half the students wound up fast asleep halfway through Mr. Hopkins's mind-numbing lecture about the Neolithic Revolution, and the rest of us barely managed to keep our eyes open, that is, until Chelsea Parker suddenly screamed.

"No more marshmallows!" grumbled Duncan Hall, dazedly waking up from his nap. A loose sheet of notebook paper still clung to the side of his face from where his head had been resting on his desk. The room filled with a chorus of chuckles.

"Ms. Parker," annunciated Mr. Hopkins, still shooting an irritated glare over at Duncan, "care to share something?"

Chelsea's friend, Molly, appeared just as ill, looking at her own phone. And just like that, every other cell in the room started lighting up…except mine. Despite Mr. Hopkins's obvious objection, even Kelsey caved into curiosity with everyone else and checked out the new notification flashing on her screen. Her free hand flew to her mouth, masking a gasp. Before I could ask, everyone's eyes slowly settled on me in horror.

Had my mystery stalker sent that video to everyone? What if this person had more damning evidence, like Reese killing that Hellhound? I contemplated bolting for the door, but instead grabbed Kelsey's phone right from her fingers.

"Kat, don't-"

It was another picture of me—from the accident. But unlike the previous photo I'd been sent, I wasn't laying on the pavement. Here, I was still strapped in the passenger seat of Blaine's Mustang, my lifeless, blood-spattered body slumped against the door. The room was so quiet, you could hear a pin drop. I numbly set the phone back down on Kelsey's desk, fearing my shaking legs would give out beneath me as I stood up. I could feel my own cell vibrate from inside my bag, but I couldn't bring myself to look at it. Before Mr. Hopkins could object, I grabbed my things and ran.

CHAPTER 15
Alive

Taking refuge in the bathroom, I tried collecting myself amid my phone blowing up with texts from everyone. I had apparently gone viral. Just as I was about to mass delete all the messages, a particular one caught my eye. Again, the sender was listed as *Unknown*.

The attached image was all too familiar. Blood, shattered glass, crushed interior. The car crash. Only this time, it wasn't a picture of me. It was Blaine. His limp frame sat slumped in the driver's seat, his blood spattered face resting against the deflated airbag of the steering wheel. *"The thief comes only to steal and kill and destroy."*

My blood ran cold, and another weird tingling feeling prickled at my arm. I hiked up my sleeve to see a tiny P-shaped symbol glowing. The sight of it only made my heart beat faster. What the hell were these things? What did they do? I pinched my eyes shut, slamming my foot against the stall door.

I only did it to blow off some steam, but it really only made things worse. The moment my heel connected with the door, it went flying. The door didn't just kick open. It flew clear off its hinges, collapsing onto the damp tiled floor in front of the sink.

Not only that, but the metal was dented in…from where my foot had hit it.

What was happening to me?

My heart rate kicked up to a tortuous thunder. My inner core now felt oddly cold. My palms were sweating. My chest was tightening. And my entire body was shaking. I couldn't breathe.

I needed to get out of here.

Throwing inhibition to the wind, I took off running. Classrooms whizzed by me in a blur as I made my way to the ground level. Rounding the end of the hall, it felt like hitting a brick wall as I ran smack dab into someone.

"Hello to you, too," sighed Reese, catching hold of me before I wound up on my ass from the impact. His grip on me tightened as he pulled me back upright, and I had to blink several times to rid the blurriness from my eyes.

My vision finally refocused, seeing Reese staring uneasily back at me. His thumb ran over my cheek, and that's when I realized it. I was crying.

"Hey…"

I tried pulling away from him, embarrassment scorching my cheeks. But he wouldn't let go.

"*Kat?*"

"I'm fine," I blurted, the words coming out with a strangled yelp.

"What happened?"

Hot tears continued pouring from my eyes, and I knew if I opened my mouth again, I'd begin full-on sobbing.

Reese's hands were suddenly cupping my face, forcing me to look at him. He brushed the mess of hair from my eyes. "You wanna get out of here?"

I barely managed a nod.

***

If someone told me last week that I'd be spending the afternoon with Reese, I would have found them the phone number to the local nuthouse. Yet, there we were, heading down Main Street in his rust bucket truck, on the way to his house no less. When I finally managed to collect myself, I showed him the pictures I received from the car accident and told him about the creep in the hoodie who just so happened to show up right after I got the first message. After throwing in the bit about the glowing red eyes, he didn't need more persuading to agree with me that this wasn't just a prank. Reese assured me he would do what he could to try and trace the sender's location. I still couldn't bring myself to tell him though about what happened in the bathroom.

Passing the harbor, we drove down to Mystic Harbor's boondocks where the magnificent coastal manors eventually devolved into kempt colonial subdivisions. I tried keeping my expression neutral, but my unease still didn't go unnoticed by Reese. He stole several glances over at me with a smirk. It was void of any real amusement, but a look more of discomfiture. Given the grandeur of my home, I could only assume the ramshackle state of his own had left him with reservations of taking me there. I imagined most of the houses in the West End probably looked like something the police would raid on an episode of *Cops*.

Century old elm trees loomed overhead, creating a leafy archway over the rural backstreets. The car took an unexpected turn onto a narrow gravel path, and we rode up to a quaint, two-story cottage resting at the end of the stretch. The lawn was immaculately groomed, encased around the thick collection of trees that bordered the property. There was even a small garden by the front porch filled with hydrangeas and some seasonal roses that accented the dormer windows and open veranda.

"Wait..." I outright looked around, confused.

"What?"

"This is your house?"

"Last time I checked," said Reese, now clearly uncomfortable. "What were you expecting?"

I tried not to laugh. "Honestly, I don't know. It's just...how everyone talks about the West End, I guess I pictured something out of *The Warriors*, you know? Some seedy underbelly where all the windows are barred and everything's covered in spray paint."

He snorted, trying to bury his amusement. "Seriously? The worst place in the area is down by the old factories. Sure, there are some unsavory folk around there, but they're not all meth heads and gangsters as you may have imagined."

The low hanging sun left limited light to showcase the property, but I could still see it well enough to know I'd been wrong.

I opened the door and stepped outside. Reese backtracked to the front porch and unlocked the door with an invitation for me to follow him. The smell of freshly baked cookies lingered in the downstairs, making the rustic décor feel all the more homey. Washed-out brown carpet and bucolic furniture covered the living areas while handcrafted wooden tables and chairs sat in the kitchen. Mounds of books lay spread across the coffee table, there were coats hung on the backs of multiple chairs, opened mail sat on the tops of the counters, and a large wool blanket was sitting in a balled up lump on the three-piece sofa sectional. Mom would never allow such details to go unchecked. The house was still tidy and clean in its own right, but it was clear that people obviously lived here.

This is what a home was supposed to look like. Unlike the $5,000 Italian silk upholstered sofa that Mom never even let me sit on, Reese's worn couches practically beckoned me to curl up and take a nap right then and there. Every inch of this place was cozy and welcoming.

Footsteps galloped down into the foyer, turning my attention back to the door.

"Peanut? Is that you?" A woman who looked to be in her late thirties came into the family room dressed in hospital scrubs. She stopped dead in her tracks, her hands tangled up in the mass of coffee-brown hair she was trying to wrap into a bun. "You're not my son."

Reese ducked back out of the kitchen, offering me one of the soda cans he had in hand. "No, she's not," he laughed. "Mom, this is Kat. Kat, this is my mom."

I politely extended my hand to her after she fixed her hair, only to squeal as she suddenly yanked me forward and ensnared me into a massive hug. I hadn't exactly been raised in an affectionate household, so random hugs clearly caught me off guard.

"It's a pleasure to meet you," I choked out, awkwardly patting my pinned-down arms against her sides.

She finally released her grip and gave me a proper onceover. "Well, now. Just look at you. Sweeter than a honey bun."

"Minus the toothache," I half laughed.

"Is this the girl you were telling me about?" Reese's mom asked, turning her attention back to her son.

Redness suddenly flooded Reese's cheeks. "Kat's my lab partner. We were just going to work on a project."

Based on the peculiar smile she was sporting, Mrs. Blackburn seemed to be in on some kind of inside joke. Considering all the things Reese had said to me over the past year, I could only imagine what he had told her about me. She checked the watch on her wrist, and her eyebrow ticked up. "A bit early for school to be out. Early dismissal?"

"...Sure."

"You've always been a terrible liar," she laughed, leaning in to kiss his cheek. "Dinner's in the oven. Instructions are on the counter. Don't ruin your appetite on sweets."

"Will do." Reese returned her kiss and walked her to the laundry room. She gave me a wave before heading out into what I realized was the garage. A moment later, the house rattled as metallic workings clanked and shuddered. Everything suddenly fell quiet as the garage door slammed back shut upon her departure.

"Peanut, aye?"

Reese gave me a warning glare, but a hint of a smile still tugged at his lips.

"Should I ask?"

"She's called me that since I was little. You know, like Reese's Peanut Butter Cups," he mumbled.

I laughed. I couldn't help it.

He gave me a light jab with his elbow. "Shut up."

"That's kind of adorable, actually. The only thing my mom calls me apart from my own name is 'smartass,' and I'd hardly consider it as a term of endearment." I looked out the front window, watching dust kick up into the breeze as Reese's mom drove down the gravel driveway. "So...she really doesn't have a problem with you ditching class...or leaving you here alone with a girl?"

"She trusts me," he simply shrugged, ushering me towards the basement stairs.

I eyed him, then the pitch-black oblivion at the bottom of the stairs, and then looked back to him again. "Ah...is this the part where you hack me up with an axe and shove my body into the crawlspace?"

"Don't be silly." He moved around me and headed down, casting me a teasing grin. "There's no room in there."

"That's reassuring." I reluctantly followed after him, seeing yet again another surprising motif.

Countless strings of golden Christmas lights were hooked all across the perimeter of the basement ceiling in wave patterns, illuminating the collage of punk rock band posters and logos consuming every inch of wall space. Speakers were positioned in the corner alongside an electric guitar, countless printouts lay stacked across a small computer desk, and there was a sketchpad sitting on top of the...bed?

"Do you live down here?" I asked uneasily.

"Most of the time, yeah. My mom used to do laundry down here," he said, pointing to a door on the opposite side of the room. "That is, until she wound up breaking her ankle when she fell down the steps. Since then, she kind of has a fear of coming down here, so she let me do with the space as I wished after I brought the washer and dryer upstairs for her."

"Is she a nurse?"

"Yeah, she's working the second shift at the hospital. Won't be home till at least eleven." Reese pulled out the small paper bag Dr. Fritz had given him earlier from inside his book bag, dumping the contents onto an old fold-out card table. Little black cylinders rolled out across the cracked leather surface. "Turn the computer on," he instructed before disappearing through the doorway he'd just pointed to.

I did as he asked, taking a seat in the chair parked at the desk.

"I still have a traditional bedroom upstairs, but since I put in the darkroom, I spend most of my time down here anyway. Hence the bed," his voice echoed out to me.

"Darkroom?"

He poked his head out, a rare, natural smile tugging at his lips. "Come in here."

Reese ducked back inside, so I got up, seeing the sprawled out cylinders close up. They were film canisters. It took a moment for my eyes to adjust to the dim red safelight of the darkroom, but once they did, I was met with an amazing series of photographs hanging up across the space.

"Dr. Fritz found this old '60s Pentacon for a steal, and I've been helping her develop the film," he clarified, closing the door behind us.

"They're gorgeous," I said, taking a particular liking to a photo of a motorcycle burnout. "Are these all hers?"

"No." His beaming smile became curiously coy. "These ones are mine, actually."

"Seriously?"

"Is it that surprising?"

I shook my head. It really wasn't. Any of the photos he contributed to the newspaper were far too artful for the likes of the *Mystic Harbor Tribune*, and it was evident anytime someone else took the pictures instead. More often than not, the images looked like they'd given the camera to a monkey in comparison.

Reese seemed so in his element in here. Whatever reason we had for initially coming down in the basement was lost on both of us as we got caught up in the entire experience. I asked a billion questions, which Reese was more than happy to answer, and he even taught me how to work the equipment so that I could develop the film myself.

By the time we left the darkroom, the natural light that had been coming through the few basement windows was gone. For that short while, we'd both seemed to have forgotten about everything else. As consequence, reality hit hard once we refocused our attention back to the matter at hand. I handed my phone over to Reese for him to upload the images I had been sent, and he lost me with all his techno-babble in under a minute.

Reese took the singular chair in front of the desk, leaving me with the choice of either sitting on the floor or his bed. I chose the latter, hoping he didn't notice the shade of crimson I was sure my cheeks had turned.

A half hour later, he got up from his chair. "Well, one thing I can tell you is that both images were taken from the same phone. Bad news, it's a burner. Untraceable," huffed Reese, planting himself down on the bed beside me.

"Perfect. Some stranger brought me back from the dead, seems hell bent on harassing me, and I haven't a clue why." I looked over at the monitor, shuddering at the image of me all mangled up on the pavement.

Reese bumped me with his elbow. "Hey, we'll figure this out. Okay?"

I nodded absentmindedly.

"What's up?"

My vision started to blur the longer I stared at the monitor. "Why wasn't I turned into a Hellhound? Why didn't the person who brought me back infect me? How did I even get *these*?" I dug my fingertips into my forearm, as if I could somehow wipe away the ink staining my skin.

My phone vibrated across the top of the desk. Reese reached up to hand it over to me, but froze at the sight of the screen.

"What?" I took the device from him, seeing a new text message. From: Unknown.

"For I know the plans I have for you."

CHAPTER 16
I Know You

The truck jostled as we drove over a set of railroad tracks, snapping me out of my trance. I had assumed Reese was taking me home, but none of the scenery now looked remotely familiar. "Where are we going?"

"To get something to eat."

I shook my head, rubbing the sleep from my eyes. "I should really—"

"Eat something?" he suggested. "It's nonnegotiable. Firstly, your stomach's growling like a ravenous dog. Secondly, I have the distinct feeling if I drop you off at home you're just going to spend the whole night obsessing over this. You need to unwind, for both our sakes." Reese gave me a cockeyed grin, turning the old beater onto a pothole riddled road. At last, an old neon sign flickered up ahead.

Rockabilly Bob's Bar & Grill.

I could hear Wynona Carr's "Please Mr. Jailer" playing the moment we reached the gravel parking lot. The outside of the joint looked like an old dive bar, but sleek 1950s décor greeted us once we stepped inside. Framed posters of rock 'n' roll musicians and classic hotrod cars lined the walls while vintage booths and barstools were mapped out across checkered vinyl floors. Even the waitresses were dressed in retro red striper uniforms.

Reese led me to the back of the restaurant where the lights were significantly dimmer. We rounded the bend, coming to the entrance of a gaming hall.

He tossed me a pool stick. "Pick a table." Reese vanished back into the diner area and returned a few minutes later with two milkshakes and a gigantic platter of nachos. "Best in the state."

He wasn't kidding. Between taking turns at the pool table, I still managed to devour half the plate and my entire shake in ten minutes. It was obvious Reese was trying to keep the conversation lighthearted, but it didn't do much to take my mind off the new dizzying array of questions.

"So what's the deal between you and Adam?" asked Reese, sinking another ball into a corner pocket. "If you don't mind my asking, that is."

The mention twisted my stomach, but not for the reason I had anticipated. I jabbed Reese with the end of my stick as I made my way around the table to set up my next shot. "It's complicated."

"Well, I don't fancy myself to be an idiot. I'm sure I can keep up just fine."

"If you must know, Adam and I had been best friends growing up. We were practically glued to the hip, until about five years ago."

"Come again?"

"We were both raised in a little town in upstate New York called Everett. Back in the good old days when my mom still clipped coupons and painted her own toe nails," I better clarified. Reese looked at me confusedly, and I laughed. "Despite what my folks might lead everyone to believe, my family didn't come from money. My mom was an ordinary housewife and my dad was on the bottom of the totem pole at work. The only reason they were even able to ship me off to boarding school was because I received an academic scholarship."

Now Reese laughed. "So you really aren't a princess then."

I shot him a look, but couldn't hide my smile.

"Is that when you and Adam fell outta touch? Because you were sent away to school?"

Any amusement I had vanished at the recollection. "Not exactly. Everything pretty much went to shit after Adam's mom was killed."

"Killed?"

"Fire," I explained. "The Reynolds's place was really old, and the electricity wasn't always reliable. The fire department suspected that the pilot light had gone out, and a spark in a nearby outlet ignited the explosion. The downstairs literally blew up. Mr. Reynolds was out with some buddies watching a game, and Adam and I were at my place. Adam's mom wasn't so lucky. She'd just returned home to make dinner. Nathan never forgave himself for not being there to save her.

"Not even two weeks after the funeral, he and Adam were gone. One of my dad's old friends had just started up his own company and offered Nathan a position with his security firm here in Maine, so the two packed up what little they had and left town. Pretty much overnight, I lost almost everyone I loved. Mr. and Mrs. Reynolds were like second parents to me, and Adam was my best friend. Then, to add insult to injury, my folks shipped me off to boarding school come the end of the month, where I went to live with perfect strangers nine months out of the year. And I never heard from Nathan or Adam after they moved, not until I came to live here in Mystic Harbor."

"Why did you guys...you know? It's obvious Adam still carries a torch for you, and he's been shooting me unrelenting death glares the past few days. He seems pretty protective."

"There's a reason why Carly nicknamed him 'Casper'. I finally decided to end things with Adam after he ditched me at a dinner party. We were there together for ten minutes before he pulled his whole Spider-Man disappearing act, and the guy never came back. He left without so much as an explanation, and no one heard from him all weekend. It wouldn't have been so bad...if this hadn't become something of habit. Adam flaked on me all the time. We'd be out having fun, and then he'd suddenly run off. Guess it makes sense now, considering everything. It's not like you can tell your girlfriend that you left her so you could go all *Buffy the Vampire Slayer* on creatures of the Underworld."

Reese didn't look particularly comfortable, and I couldn't blame him. But he was the one who asked. "So, now knowing what you know, you think you two will...?"

I shook my head. "Adam isn't the same. He'd always been funny and silly and teasing when we were younger. What happened with his mom though really hit him hard, and I can't imagine the lifestyle he leads now is particularly easy either. He has his moments where I get to see the old Adam, but they're far and few. Honestly, I think nostalgia is what kept us together. At least for me anyway." It was the most open answer I'd given about our breakup. "Honestly, I hated it when I first moved here, and Adam wound up being the one familiar thing amid all the nauseating dinner parties and political fundraisers. I wasn't used to this lifestyle. Home for me used to be a crammed two-bedroom apartment, and then it became the academy. Coming here honestly felt like stumbling into an alternate reality. It still does. Adam was the only normalcy I could cling to. But that particular night when he had ditched me for the hundredth time...I had had enough. And I hated him for it, for the rippling effect it caused."

"Why? What happened?"

"It was the night I met Blaine," I barely whispered, watching Reese's shoulders go taut. "If Adam had stayed with me at the party, Blaine would've just been another charming host. Someone I never would have given a second thought to. Someone I wouldn't have snuck off with."

That last remark sent a cocked brow at me.

I jabbed Reese with my cue again. "Not like that. As it turned out, he hated soirées as much as I did. The moment we found an opening, we escaped. Together. Wound up spending the night barefoot at the beach." The back of my eyes burned at the memory. He really had been a decent guy. "If Adam had stayed, I wouldn't have gotten to know Blaine. We wouldn't have started hanging out, and he wouldn't have ditched his friends that night to come to the bonfire...to see me."

I tried to keep the slight tremble in my hands at bay as I lined up my next shot.

"Here." Reese moved behind me, adjusting my stance in front of the table. His hands settled on my hips, and I could feel my skin tingle...only, it came from my arm.

I looked down at my left side, seeing the tattooed ink on top of my hand glowing even beneath the fabric of the fingerless gloves. He then wrapped his arms around me.

"You're losing control of the cue on your backswing. You need to slow down when drawing it to you." Reese demonstrated, repositioning my hands on the stick. "Now, follow all the way through."

I did as he instructed, watching the red ball labeled 'three' land effortlessly into the center pocket. "You were right."

"When am I not?" he teased lightly, his breath stirring my hair as he remained behind me.

"I meant about my friends." I turned to face him, and any amusement fell from his face. "You were right to say that they're assholes."

It clearly wasn't what he expected me to say, because his eyebrow shot up yet again.

"I've heard some things about you, things they've said and done."

His body stiffened.

"Is that why you didn't want to be around me anymore? Because of them?"

He shook his head. "It's more complicated than that."

I drew up my glove, flashing him the glowing blue rune. "When isn't it?"

Reese's fingers brushed over the illuminated skin. Could he feel the vibration? "You ignited it."

It almost sounded like a question as he looked the rest of me over. He, too, was clearly at a loss for what it meant, because nothing else was happening. As he had said, they were supposed to do *something*. Was I defective?

Of all things, he smiled.

"What?"

"It's nothing." He gave a casual shrug, but still didn't let go of my hand, his thumb still gently drawing small circles over the tingling patch of glowing skin. The distance between us was rapidly closing, and I wasn't sure if he was moving in or if it was me. Our faces were now flush to one another's that I could see every shade of brown and gold woven into his bottomless eyes. They really were beautiful.

"Come on, man!" A clatter of loud voices suddenly boomed from the next table over, startling us both. We turned just in time as a girl laughingly stumbled into us.

"Sorry," the leggy brunette cooed, patting me on the shoulder as she caught her footing. "My bad."

"It's fine." I gave a polite smile, and she winked in return, a roguish grin teasing her lips. She was in head-to-toe leather, her feline brown eyes accentuated all the more by winged eyeliner and black eye shadow.

"I think she likes you," whispered Reese, trying to hold back his amusement.

I still couldn't take my eyes off the brunette as she headed down to a group of people who had just walked in. Something about her was uncannily familiar. Where had I seen her before?

She looked back over her shoulder, that feline grin still in place as she returned my gaze. Her eyes shifted over to the entrance, and her stare went cold. I turned around, catching a glimpse of a tall dark figure. That strange sensation stirring under my skin tugged at me, urging me to the open doorway.

"What's wrong?"

I didn't have time to answer. Making my way through the gaming hall, I headed back into the dining area, still feeling that pull as I surveyed the patrons. A fresh wave of warmth spread across my chest the closer I got to the parking lot. I stepped outside, feeling the breath catch in my throat at the sight of the hooded figure leaning contentedly against Reese's truck. The lighting overhead only consisted of a singular bulb hanging above the front entrance, so the parking lot was shrouded in shadows. But his sleeves were pulled up to his elbows. That much I could see, because glowing blue runes emanated from his left forearm.

As if in response, my own tingled with a dull roar, like an engine revving in anticipation before you floored it.

Footsteps galloped up behind me just as a van drove past. "Everything okay?" Reese asked, coming to my side.

I blinked, gaping at his old beater truck across the way. The hooded stranger was gone, my runes dying down at the realization.

CHAPTER 17
Don't Kill the Magic

Reese hadn't seen the stranger, but unlike Officers Blake and Stevens, he took my word for it. I knew no one was home before we even pulled up into my driveway. Mom had the lights set up on a timer, and only those select few were turned on.

"You gonna be okay?"

"Yeah," my voice cracked. "I'm sure I'll be fine—in there." In the big, dark, empty house… "Would you mind horribly coming in with me?"

Reese gawped back at me like I'd just declared myself to be the Easter Bunny. "You serious?"

"I know you always go into school early to work on the newspaper, and I know Kelsey would also appreciate not having to come hunt me down for my article later in the day. So I just thought I could maybe give you my flash drive…"

He pulled in his lips, trying not to smile. Why did he always have to make me feel like I was always the butt of some private joke?

"What?"

"After everything that's happened tonight, *that's* what's on your mind?"

"I kind of have a hard time shutting my brain down," I admitted. "You don't have to stay. Just come in…"

"And make sure there's no boogeymen hiding under your bed?" he finished.

"You *are* well-equipped," I said, nodding down.

He looked shocked at first, but then tried his best not to laugh. "Ooookay."

Uh-oh…

"What? No! That's not what I meant!" I could feel my cheeks burning with mortification. "I was nodding down at your *jacket*, not…"

Oh. My. God. Kill me now! Where was a demon when you needed one?

"If you say so." He patted my arm with a snicker before climbing out.

I was probably redder now than Elmo.

Mortified, I skulked out of the car and into the house. Reese offered to take a walk through the ground floor to make sure the coast was clear as I raided the box of Devil's Food Donuts sitting on the counter. I was starving. He returned a few minutes later, looking even more uneasy.

"Did you find something?"

He shook his head as I cleared my throat with a healthy swig of Dr. Pepper.

"What's wrong?"

"Nothing. You have a very…*lovely* house," he replied stiffly.

At last, I laughed. "No one's holding a gun to your head, you know."

"It's just…are your folks, like, anal-retentive or something?"

"Why?"

"Because it's not exactly what you'd call welcoming," he admitted, looking around at the furniture as if it was toxic to the touch. "This place puts a model home to shame. Everything's so...perfect. Not to mention pricey. Forgive me, but I don't exactly feel at ease in a room where I'd have to sell a kidney in order to pay for a broken lamp."

He *did* have a point. If someone so much as put a drink on the coffee table without a coaster, they'd probably vanish under mysterious circumstances. Mom didn't even let Dad or me venture into the parlor room out of fear that our footprints would leave impressions in the new luxury carpets she had installed last month. But that was just the way things were. I'd become accustomed to it, so I guess I didn't think it odd anymore. At least, not until Reese stepped through the door.

"It's not much of a secret that my mom enjoys being one of the elite in town. Everything you see is a reflection on her, so she wants it to be perfect."

"Everything, including *you*?"

As hard as I tried to salvage some kind of comeback, my mind came up dry. Instead, I closed the box of donuts and headed to the other side of the kitchen. Sure, that's not where I found them, but I needed an excuse to not look at him. He knew the answer.

"Let me go grab my flash drive." I slinked out and headed up the back staircase to my room. When I returned to the kitchen, I found Reese leaning against the island with a picture in his hands. "Here."

He took the flash drive, tucking it into his jacket. "Where was this taken?"

I looked at the image. It was the photo I had been using as a bookmark in Arthur Miller's *The Crucible*, which

I'd left on the kitchen table this morning. "That was my dorm room back at Stewart's Landing."

His eyebrow ticked up.

"The boarding school I attended before I moved here," I clarified. "Mom and Dad thought it would be good for us to spend more family time together after my dad got his new job here, so they pulled me out in favor of Belleview High."

Reese looked just as confused as I'd been when they told me the same thing a year and a half ago. "And how's that working out for you guys?"

I motioned to the empty room. "What do you think? It's…everything I expected it to be."

"Minus the murderous henchman of the Underworld."

"Yeah, I hadn't quite anticipated that." I smiled at the memory of when the photograph had been taken.

"You miss it there?"

"I'd been going to Stewart's since I was twelve, so up and leaving all my friends wasn't easy," I admitted.

"I like your shirt," he laughed. "I like your whole room, actually."

I was wearing a *Goonies* tee, and you could see a fandom of vintage movie posters plastered all across the wall. My best friends Eve and Dawn joined me on my bed, all of us donning knee-high *Doctor Who* socks with a massive bowl of popcorn in each of our hands as we sat down to watch a movie marathon.

"You look happy."

"I was." I grabbed the paperback, sliding the photo between two random pages before returning the book to the counter.

When I turned back to face Reese, I didn't have a

chance to react. He was suddenly standing directly in front of me, a gentle hand cradling the nape of my neck. His head lowered, and I instinctively tilted my own.

What was I doing?

What was *he* doing?

My heart began to pound furiously against my chest, and I was sure he would have been able to see it…if not for the fact that his magnetic eyes were focused on my face. Of all things, the back of my hand started to tingle with a strange electrical current pulsating up into my fingers.

Reese wasn't going to kiss me. He didn't *like* me. He—

He kissed me.

His lips brushed my cheek at first, tentative, as if to give me time to pull away. If I wanted. But I didn't. I wanted to blame it on my body locking up, blame it on pure and utter shock freezing me into place, but that wasn't it. Because the moment he brought his mouth to mine, I welcomed it. My back arched upward, eliminating the minuscule space still situated between us. His other hand cradled the small of my back, pressing our bodies flush together. A low sound came from deep in his throat, kicking my heart rate into overdrive. My fingers were suddenly raking through the back of his hair, combing the feathery locks. The soft caress of his lips deepened, and I finally pulled away.

"I don't understand…"

He was still so close, enough that his nose continued to brush against mine. Reese smiled ever so slightly. "Just stop thinking so much."

His hand slid from my neck, only to brush back the loose strand of hair falling into my eyes. And just like that, he left. His footsteps trailed down the hall, but I couldn't see him. *Now* I couldn't move.

Reese just kissed me.

Reese Blackburn.

The guy who infuriated me like no one else ever could just kissed me, and I'd let him.

Just stop thinking so much.

That kiss proved any chance of that impossible, because there was no way I couldn't *not* think about what just happened. Amid all the craziness that had been dumped into my lap tonight, all my thoughts now were on the curious boy who—against all odds—had just made me melt in his arms.

CHAPTER 18
Teenagers

The mouthwatering aroma of popcorn wafted the air as I went up to the concessions for my second helping. Unlike the dazzling new theater at the mall, the Stargate Cineplex was fairly innate to the vintage movie-going experience. Instead of plush recliners, they still had those hard foldout seats in the theater. An old marquee sign lit up the front entrance, and best of all, there wasn't reserved seating. I loved the spontaneity of being able to go to the theater on a whim. First come, first serve. Not like everywhere else where you have to plan a week in advance so you can assure decent seats.

My first week in town hadn't been favorable. I'd spent most of my time being dragged to dinner parties and political fundraisers by my folks. Tonight was my first night of freedom, and after seeing the sign advertising a from-dusk-till-dawn screening of the entire **Star Wars** *franchise, I knew exactly where I'd take refuge. Apparently, the force wasn't particularly strong in Mystic Harbor, because I shared the entire theater with only one other person.*

I stretched lazily as I looked over the concessions menu, feeling pins and needles spreading up my legs.

A pleasant chuckle emitted from behind me. "Feet fall asleep?"

I looked over my shoulder, meeting a pair of friendly amber eyes. Well, he was definitely unexpected. I had been convinced that no male in town owned anything outside of Ralph Lauren or the Brooks Brothers' brand names. Yet, the stranger before me couldn't be pegged by any label. He looked like how I'd imagine Dorian Gray might dress if he had been a modern-day rock star.

"A bit," I admitted, flexing my aching toes.

The coffee-haired stranger dropped his gaze to my feet with a smile. "Nice kicks."

Sure enough, we were both wearing black Chuck Taylors. The difference between the pairs was that his was branded with the anarchy symbol on the sides and top.

"So what brings you to our quiet little hamlet?" he inquired, brushing a loose strand of hair from his eyes. "Vacationing?"

"What makes you think I don't live here?"

"Everyone knows everyone around here, whether you want to or not," he clarified. "And considering the Prada sporting divas of Maine's coast, you don't exactly blend in with the pack." Mom would've blown a gasket if she'd seen me leave the house looking as I did. Torn up jeans, Led Zeppelin t-shirt, and all. The mention would have been an insult coming from anyone else in town, but approval flickered in the stranger's eyes, signifying it was entirely a compliment.

"Thanks," I smiled.

He nodded as a smile of his own spread across his lips. Between the dimples that formed and the adorableness of the cleft in his chin, the simple action lit up his entire face. "You know, if you want to avoid your legs from cramping up, it helps to sit in the first row of the main section. You can rest your feet on the metal bar of the walkway divider. Makes for a decent footrest."

"Wish I could, but someone's already sitting there," I said, gesturing to the doorway of my screening room. "It's only me and someone else, but I don't want to be that person who infringes on other people's personal space, especially when I have the whole rest of the theater to choose from."

"I wouldn't mind." His smile grew all the more as momentary confusion reached my face.

I sighed in understanding. "You're the other person."

"Indeed I am."

"Sorry, I didn't recognize you. All I saw was the back of your head when I went into the theater."

"Still a better sight than most of The Phantom Menace."

At last, I laughed. "Good point. But then again, you did pay to see it, so..."

"I paid to see the original Star Wars trilogy. Having to endure the unfortunate prequels just comes with the territory," he chuckled.

"So you wouldn't mind some company for Attack of the Clones?"

"Not at all." He extended his fingerless-gloved hand to me. "Reese."

Walking back into the lobby, we both winced as the early morning sun reflected off the freshly polished granite floors. I thought for sure I would've fallen asleep at some point, but Reese and I both spent the last eleven hours eating our weight in concessions, laughing the entire time. As it turned out, I'd met someone who was an even bigger Star Wars fan than myself, if that were possible. Fueled by a caffeine high from all the soda I'd ingested, I wasn't the least bit tired. Still practically in tears, we continued laughing over the 'Han Shot First' debacle as Reese and I headed across the foyer.

He held the door open for me, flashing me the smallest glimpse of a tattoo wrapped around his wrist between his glove and shirt cuff. I thanked him and walked out. Goosebumps perforated the back of my neck as I noticed the lone passerby on the sidewalk not ten feet from us. Based on his clothes and ruffled state of his once-neatly groomed hair, it was clear the twenty-something guy had obviously had a long night on the town. He stopped dead in his tracks, a wicked grin spreading across his tight lips. I followed his line of vision to see him focusing on Reese's tattoo as well.

"Friend of yours?" I asked Reese in a low enough voice so that only he could hear.

Reese took one look at the guy and froze, any sense of amusement slipping from his face. "No."

The stranger's smirk tightened as he lingered on the sidewalk for an instant longer, eventually continuing on his way down into the alleyway between a couple storefronts that hadn't opened yet.

That was weird, I thought. But the unease subsided the moment the man disappeared from sight. "You want to go grab something to eat?" I sighed, trying to lighten the sudden heavy mood. "I don't know about you, but I could go for some French Toast to wash down all that candy and popcorn."

Reese's eyes were still fixed on the mouth of the alleyway.

"Hey, you okay?"

"What?" he mused distractedly, finally returning his attention back to me. "Oh... Yeah, I'm fine. I just...have something I need to do." He was already making his way down the sidewalk. "Rain check, on the breakfast?"

"Sure."

He turned back to give me one last parting smile, but there was an inexplicable somberness in his eyes. "It was really nice meeting you. Kat." The way Reese said my name, I couldn't help but sense that he really wanted to stay. Nevertheless, he walked away. Something about the man had rubbed us both the wrong way, yet Reese seemed to be heading after him as he too eventually dodged into the very same alley.

***

I stirred awake. I'd spent countless times reflecting over the first time we met, and I could never figure out what happened between us. Now, I saw with new eyes. Something *had* happened that morning. Something he could only now explain.

But how was I going to ask?

Reese was guarded, to say the least, and I doubted he'd tell me outright.

Grabbing the tops of the covers draped over my torso, I was about to pull them up further when the theme from *Dracula* suddenly blasted from the nightstand. Receiving texts had become a new fear of mine, but I breathed a sigh of relief to see Reese's name on the screen.

"Pick you up at 7."

I lifted my head, seeing the clock that read *6:45 a.m.* Crap, I forgot to set my alarm. It thankfully didn't take me more than a few minutes to get ready, since I didn't bother doing my hair and I could pull off not wearing any makeup.

The downstairs fell silent as I made my way into the kitchen.

Never a good sign.

Just as I feared, Mom was sitting perched at one of the high stools with a full cup of coffee in her hands. By six o'clock, she was always a woman on the go, and the fact that she was sitting still only meant one thing: I was in trouble.

"Morning," I said, cautiously coming into the kitchen.

She stared down at me pointedly over the brim of her

218

reading glasses. "Care to explain something?"

"I learned all about Nonlinear Fubini's Theoremin in Calculus last week, so if you're interested in expanding your knowledge..." My attempt at a smile faltered as she glared back at me.

"Reese Blackburn."

Oh, crap.

Had she seen him leave here last night?

Did she think we'd been doing...something?

"I ran into Mrs. Ashford while I was on my run this morning. Word is that you and Mr. Blackburn have gotten awfully chummy as of late. Is this true?"

"We're talking," I admitted.

The glasses came off, and I instinctively cowered back. "Have you been listening to anything I've said? I'm running for president of the Woodstone Regency Society, and now you decide to befriend the boy who's written how many *defaming* articles about all their children?" She slammed her coffee mug on the countertop so hard I was surprised it didn't shatter on impact.

Double crap.

It wasn't exactly a shocker that Reese hadn't made any friends in Mystic Harbor, and the school paper certainly didn't help. But he didn't mind either, as he was the only one who actually called out certain individuals for abusing certain privileges. Like how some teachers were fudging grades for certain athletes so they had the GPA to play. Or how students were buying the answers to last year's Biology final after a certain cheerleader 'stumbled upon' a loose copy. Of course, nothing ever seemed to happen to the offenders, but it was gratifying to at least see someone airing their dirty deeds. Despite how much I wanted to punch him before, I always admired how Reese refused to be a cog in the Mystic Harbor machine.

"In his defense, his articles really aren't defaming if they're true," I countered.

"Katrina-"

"What? The children of your beloved Woodstone Regency Society have done a whole hell of a lot worse than write a couple honest articles, and you've never objected to me hanging out with any of them. If anything, *they're* the bad seeds, and you've been practically throwing me at them since we moved here."

"That boy is trouble." Mom rubbed her eyebrows, trying to regain her composure. "Maybe your father's right."

"...About?"

"After everything that's happened here, perhaps it would be best if you returned to Stewart's Landing for the remainder of your senior year."

"Mom...no."

"It might do you some good, to be somewhere where people aren't talking." With every excuse she listed off, my stomach clenched tighter and tighter. This wasn't about me. Not for my wellbeing anyway. This was about putting a stop to the problems I'd inadvertently caused her.

No, no, no, no. I couldn't leave. Not now. I'd lost everything. My parents, Adam, Mr. Reynolds. They'd all abandoned me when I needed them the most, and just when I had found myself a new family at the academy, they robbed me of that as well. It wasn't that I'd hate returning to Stewart's Landing. I still had great friends who went there. It had become my home. What made me sick was the all too familiar pit in my stomach that forced me to acknowledge my greatest fear. Did my parents really not care? The first time they sent me away, it *had* been for my own good. The academy gave me opportunities my parents couldn't provide for me at the time. But that wasn't the problem anymore.

It didn't matter how hard I tried. It didn't matter that I left all my friends without objection. It didn't matter that I spent the last fifteen months bending over backwards to make everyone happy. It didn't matter that I studied more hours at night than I slept to ensure I'd get perfect grades. It didn't matter that I stomached this nauseating social scene without protest. One slipup, and I was as disposable to them as a used dishrag.

"We just need things to calm down around here. What I'm trying to do is for everyone's best interest," Mom kept assuring. "With people like the Marins as friends, your father and I will have the clout to get you into whatever college you want-"

"And at what price?" I finally snapped. "You treat people like Reese as if they're trash, but you've never bothered looking past your own snobbery. He's a good person. I'd rather be on the wrong side of the tracks than have to sell my dignity to the highest bidder." My stomach was growling something fierce, but I buried the hunger down as I slung my book bag over my shoulder and stormed out of the kitchen.

Mom's heels clacked right behind me as she continued in her rant, cutting in front of me before I made it to the foyer. "You are not to see him again."

As if on cue, the front doorbell rang. I stole a nervous glance at the clock. It was only five to seven. Reese wasn't seriously here...was he?

Mom cast me one last cautionary stare before answering. Long blonde hair and a breezy canary yellow dress lit up the porch, and Mom immediately straightened up.

"Hi, Mrs. Montgomery." Carly said it sweetly enough, but there was hesitation in her delivery. She'd clearly overheard the conversation.

I could have tackled the girl with a hug as I pushed past Mom. "I have to get to school. Try not to pack my bags while I'm gone."

My mother would never dare keep the fight going so long as company was around, and I happily took my exit, slamming the front door behind me.

"What's up?" I asked, making my getaway down the driveway.

She bit her lower lip, only on the right side. A telltale sign she was nervous. "I just wanted to say I was sorry."

"*Sorry?*" I knew I'd been a bit preoccupied as of late, but had I really not realized we'd been fighting?

"We were all talking last night about some things." She winced. "And then taking into account what happened with the photo yesterday, it kind of hit me how insensitive we've been. You went through a lot, and I know I've been critical of you, rather than supportive. I mean, it's your business what you choose to do, with Blackburn or otherwise."

"Ah...thanks." Like Kelsey, it was the last thing I expected to hear from her.

"It's just...you've also been acting really weird, too. You know you can talk to me, Kat. About anything."

"There's just a lot going on right now, stuff I can't explain."

Carly cocked a groomed eyebrow at me as we came to a stop at the curbside. Yeah, this girl wouldn't be taking no for an answer.

She knew how to keep her wits when she needed to, but believability right now wasn't my greatest ally. And the fact made my heart sink. Car was my best friend, for better or for worst. Not being able to tell her anything wasn't helping anyone. It just put more distance between us. I missed confiding in her.

"Whatever's going on, I might be able to help," she further insisted. "I'm a good listener."

"It's complicated," I muttered.

She folded her arms, leaning against the streetlight. "And I've got time."*For you.*

"I'm being stalked, for starters."

Her mouth dropped. "Excuse me?"

"I've been getting creepy text messages from an unknown number. Plus, some freak in a hoodie is following me around. I already tried talking to the cops, but they refuse to hear me out."

"*Excuse me?*" Car blurted again. "Your life has turned into an episode of *Criminal Minds*, and I'm only hearing about it now? What the frack, girl?"

"You can't say anything," I pleaded.

"Say anything? Why aren't we *doing* anything?"

"What do you mean?"

"This is epic! Like, primetime drama." A huge smile burst across her face. "We need to start sleuthing, researching, investigating!"

I laughed, more out of disbelief. "You're excited by stalkers, and *I'm* the one who's weird?"

"What can I say? Morbid curiosity. But anyway, get a move on," she beckoned, pulling me towards her car. "We can start plotting our investigation on the way to school."

"I...uh, already have a ride," I winced, hearing the low grumble of the old beater before the truck even came into sight.

Carly's eyes widened as Reese pulled up to the curb,

but she clamped her mouth shut and nodded. "Have room for one more?"

Reese gawked at Carly for a long moment like she was an alien life form. "Sorry?"

"Can. I. Join. You?" she pronounced, deliberately slow. If she had any reservations, she clearly wasn't showing it. In fact, there was a teasing quality in her voice.

Reese gave me a sideways glance and laughed under his breath. "Just when I thought things couldn't get scarier."

After the events of last night, from the hooded stalker in the parking lot to that kiss in the kitchen, I had actually been dreading the ride, knowing full well of the awkward silence that would ensue. And that's precisely why Carly wound up being a godsend for the second time this morning. So long as she was around, there was no such thing as quiet. Reese's truck only had one row of seats, but it was more of a cushioned bench, which allowed all three of us to sit up front. And it didn't go ignored by either Reese or me as our thighs brushed against one another's as I took my place in the middle. We both stiffened. Yeah, this was going to be awkward regardless.

By the time we made it to Main Street, Carly had already come up with our sleuthing team nickname, which apparently was "BLT," as in Bacon, Lettuce, and Tomato. I wasn't sure who was supposed to be who...or how the hell that had anything to do with sleuthing, but I was too afraid to ask.

"Oh, could you stop here?" asked Carly as we turned onto the side street leading to the school. "I know we're a team now, but a girl does have to save face. No offense, but the guys would never let me hear the end of it if I rolled up with you two stone-cold weirdos." She was still giddy as she hopped out of the cabin.

Reese just shook his head.

"She takes some getting used to," I chuckled.

"You might as well join her," he sighed, tossing on a black fedora.

"Reese-"

He shrugged. "What? I'm just afraid she might forget where she's going. Not sure if you noticed during our delightful drive just now, but she's kind of A.D.D. The girl might wind up at the mall if you leave her unattended."

"I can still hear you!" called out Car from the sidewalk.

"I intended you to," Reese shot back.

"On that note..." I climbed out and joined Carly as she waved a dismissive, perfectly polished hand at him.

"I swear if my phone rings again..." Carly growled, prying the device out of her purse. The damn thing had been vibrating nonstop as it sat between us during the entire car ride.

At the same time, I could feel mine go off. It appeared both of our phones had been guilty, because thirty new text messages had flooded into my cell over the past ten minutes. We didn't need to open them. The moment we rounded the bend to the front of the school, we had our answer. Spotlights, camera crews, reporters, police cars, and men in blue drenched the entire entrance. The chaos of everyone trying to talk above the commotion only made it harder to understand what anyone was saying.

"Déjà voodoo," muttered Car. She had told me all about the media hype surrounding the Hersey bus disappearance, and this looked like a snapshot right out of her retelling. Only worse.

CHAPTER 19
The Kill

Brutality.
Carnage.
Horror.

They were just the handful of words I managed to make out amongst the clamor. Carly's fingers interlocked with mine as her other hand clamped itself around my arm. Any amusement she had a moment ago was gone. We pushed our way through the throng of people, and we were forced to duck as one of those microphone boom poles whizzed past us from an eager film crew member.

I shuddered, seeing Channel 5's Rebecca Weathers standing in front of the steps leading into the building with a camera primed right on her. She'd done more than her fair share covering my accident, implying on more than one occasion that I was likely under the influence of an unspecified substance. Even now I wanted to punch in those fake porcelain teeth of hers.

"The body of seventeen-year-old Casey Ann Radley was discovered late last night by her neighbor in Griffin

Park. Authorities are baffled by the lack of motive, as we've just learned that the young woman slain last night was drained of blood and then dumped not a block from her house. This town is in shock and nobody can quite believe the grisly nature of this crime, although this is not the first time this small community has endured such heartbreak. Only weeks ago was another student, high school senior Blaine Ryder, killed in a devastating car accident just outside Prescott Hills." The reporter paused, motioning to the light pole beside her where numerous missing persons' flyers had been taped. "And as you can see, there remains this constant reminder of the tragic disappearance of 21 teenage county residents…"

Carly squeezed my arm tighter as I looked to see Brittany's weather-worn paper portrait clinging pitifully to the rounded metal. But her face wasn't the only one that caught my attention. My blood ran cold.

Despite the madness brewing outside, it still paled in comparison to the pandemonium ensuing in the hallways. Some girls were crying while others were gossiping about all the possible ways Casey could had been murdered.

"I bet it was that freak, Blackburn," snarled Ava Ashford. "He probably had to use her as a virgin sacrifice…since someone else we know clearly couldn't be it." She cast me a pointed glare.

"Like you're one to talk," growled Carly. "We all know you're a whore of more than attention."

Malice flashed in the cheerleader's eyes, but she merely smirked. "Says the girl who's been ridden more than a carnival pony."

Carly suddenly sprang forward, nearly tackling Ava before Daniel snatched her up by the waist and pulled her back.

"Whoa! Down, girl." He towed her to the other end of the hall, refusing to release her till she calmed down. "As much as we'd all love to see a catfight, this really isn't the place for it."

Carly finally ripped out of his hold, seeing several cops making their way towards us.

"Ms. Montgomery," greeted one of the men as they passed by.

"Officer Blake," I gritted through clenched teeth.

He smirked, following the others into the principal's office.

"You know him?" asked Daniel.

"We've met. And I can guarantee you, if his sleuthing skills are anything like what I've witnessed, they'll have about as much luck finding Casey's killer as they will Jimmy Hoffa."

I kept my eye out for Reese, but didn't cross paths with him as Car and I made our way to the art room. Mark was already there, lying across one of the back tables. His eyes remained shut as he air-drummed to what we realized was Drowning Pool's "Bodies" as we approached the tableside.

"Perhaps not the most appropriate song of choice, considering the circumstances," remarked Car, prying one of the buds from his ear. "You know, with the *murder*, and all."

Mark blindly fished inside his pocket for his phone, his smirk unrelenting as he switched songs and unplugged his headphones. Sure enough, My Chemical Romance's "Helena" filled the room.

Carly swatted him in the chest. "You're going to Hell."

"At least I've earned my stripes," he chuckled, his eyes still closed.

"Perhaps you'd like to earn some extra credit as well, Mr. McDowell," announced Mrs. Brightberry, slamming an armful of boxes down beside his head. "Heaven knows you could use it." By her pinched expression, she'd clearly overheard the exchange, still scowling at the music blaring throughout the class.

Mark finally opened his eyes as a wound up section of decorative string lights plopped down on his stomach. "It's a little early to deck out a Christmas tree, isn't it?"

"It's for Homecoming," corrected our art teacher. "And unless you wish to sit out Friday's big game, you'll take up my offer."

This earned Mark's attention, as he snapped upright like a vampire springing free from its coffin. "Come again?"

"You're very well aware of our policy regarding one's GPA, Mr. McDowell. Since you have more of an affinity for slacking off rather than actually putting in any effort, your grade in here reflects it." Mrs. Brightberry pointed to the small stack of boxes piled in the opposite corner. "All the supplies for the Homecoming dance are being stored in the old weightlifting room. If you want the necessary boost in your grade, you'll go up there and bring the remaining supplies back down here."

Mark rolled his eyes, but he didn't dare make any further fuss. He knew he'd be screwed if she pulled the offer off the table. "Fine."

Carly and I volunteered to help, knowing full well that Mark would lose all motivation if left alone. We quickly learned that Mrs. Brightberry made you work for every ounce of extra credit. The old weightlifting room was on the third story, whereas the art room was stationed on the far side of the first. By our eighth trip back upstairs, we were exhausted. Car and I plopped down on an old weightlifting bench as Mark tried to prove his testosterone level by doing chin-ups on one of the few pullup bars across the way. The room was long and thin, lined wholly with mirrors on one side of the wall. It probably would have smelled as foul as the current weightlifting room if not for the homemade lilac-scented candles Mrs. Brightberry had brought in to freshen up the place.

Even with my newly acquired strength, my arms still screamed with fatigue as I made my way down the hall following dismissal.

"You'd think being invisible would have its perks in high school, but you know what? It still sucks," remarked Reese, crashing his frame into the locker beside mine as I lifted up my exhausted arm to dial in my combo.

"Uh-oh, High School Hell got you down?" I whispered.

"You know, the word 'hell' is applied far too liberally these days, yet here it is quite appropriate."

"I hear ya'. But I imagine things can't be too hard for the likes of you. You know, considering that you apparently know *everything*," I jabbed.

"I only store things of relevance up here," he chuckled, tapping on the side of his head. "And I can guarantee you, eighty percent of what you learn from a school desk will never be applied to your life once you're out in the real world."

"So I take it you won't be lending me a hand with my Calculus homework then?"

"Sorry, tangent half-angle formulas don't come in handy when you're trying to restore the balance between good and evil. It rarely ever requires mathematical skills."

"What a jip," I chortled.

"Asshole!" exclaimed Camille Browning. The curly haired brunette stampeded over to Trace Bolton and hurled his letterman's jacket at him as he stood about ten lockers down from us talking with his friends.

"Cam?" He managed to collect the coat in his grasp before it hit the floor.

"Stay the hell away from me," she demanded, turning around and walking away.

"Hey!" He lobbed the jacket over to Nate and followed after her. "What is your problem?"

"You're an asshole; that's my problem," she clarified. "The fact that I was dating you up until twenty seconds ago used to be one as well, but, thankfully, it no longer is."

He just looked at her confusedly. "What are you talking about?"

"I'm dumping your ass, Trace," Camille said, almost proudly. "I don't date douche bags that cheat on me with my best friend!"

"Oh, so that's what everyone was talking about first hour," remarked Reese softly. "You know, apart from the murder and all."

"I didn't hear this one," I said.

"Apparently, she had thrown a party at her house this past weekend, and someone recorded a video of Bolton, I suspect, getting down with a cheerleader, who obviously wasn't her," said Reese, pointing to Camille.

"Babe, just calm down," said Trace, cutting in front of her.

"You slept with her!" Camille whirled back around and proceeded in the other direction.

"Yeesh..." Reese and I both winced.

"Look, we were both drunk, okay? It didn't mean

anything," defended Bolton, rather indifferently.

"It meant something to me!" She finally turned and confronted him, the two of them right in front of us. "You cheated on me. It's that simple."

He rolled his eyes.

"And look at you," she scoffed. "You don't even care!"

"Cam-"

"You are such an idiot!"

"You're really blowing this outta proportion."

"Oh yeah? Spell 'proportion,'" she challenged.

Bolton didn't respond.

"My point exactly." She stomped away, leaving the hallway behind her to buzz about in gossipy whispers. "Moron."

"She was a better lay than you anyway!" he shot back, almost with a laugh.

Camille simply raised her middle finger, not even turning back to give him the satisfaction. Carly made her way through the crowd toward me, still gawking with the rest of the spectators.

"What the hell is going on around here? It's like the freaking *Twilight Zone*," she whispered. "Those two have been practically joined at the hip since freshman year. There's gotta be something in the water, because everyone's been arguing. Even Kevin and Angela broke up."

"What are you lookin' at, chief?" Bolton suddenly throttled a scrawny freshman against the lockers as the poor kid tried to discreetly slink past Trace.

I slammed my locker shut and prepared to move in to intervene, seeing Bolton ready to strike again. Reese swooped in though, grabbing hold of Bolton's arm just as the jock started driving it toward the freshman. He redirected its target, sending Trace's fist right into the locker beside the kid's head. The freshman yelped at the near impact and took off down the hall like a rocket as Trace whirled around.

"You got a problem there, freak?" barked the jock, unfazed by the devastating blow as he yanked his knuckles out of the now-dented locker face.

"Holy crap," blurted Carly.

Trace took another swing, this time directed at Reese's face. It came as no surprise that the magician quickly deflected it, quickly grabbing hold of the extended arm. He forced it just enough in an unnatural angle that it threatened to break, but he thankfully didn't apply further pressure.

Reese focused his eyes on the jock as he stepped right in front of him, pushing him up against the dented locker. "How about you run off to the weightlifting room, work your hostility off on an actual punching bag, aye?"

Trace's face fell neutral, his frame slackening. "Whatever."

Reese released his hold, and Trace shoved past, purposely knocking shoulders with the magician to throw him off balance. Reese didn't budge.

"Damn, talk about a knight in shining armor," sighed Carly as Reese returned to my side. Was that…admiration I saw? "That kid's face would've been a crater if you hadn't stepped in."

"Someone was bound to intervene. I just got there first." He casually shrugged, pulling his hat off to run a hand through his hair. I'd come to learn that was his telltale sign. Anytime he was either anxious or lying, he instinctively had to touch his hair.

The moment the incident started, everyone, including Trace's own friends, backed off. There was no way anyone else was going to come to that kid's rescue, and he knew it. A new knot formed in my stomach as I parted ways with the pair. I made my way upstairs to head to my next class, only to find Adam already waiting there for me.

Before I even approached, he pushed off the lockers and nodded over to the adjacent hallway.

"I take it you heard the news," I muttered dryly, following after him.

"Yeah, and it gets worse," he said lowly, handing over his phone.

He wasn't kidding.

***

I found Reese sitting on top of a cafeteria table as I followed in the procession of students flocking towards the gym. Principal Harris had ordered a mandatory assembly, in which the Sheriff was set to speak. Considering word of mouth, I figured Blackburn was invisible to the rest of our classmates. Everyone walked right past him without a blink of an eye, all the while speculating further on Ava's earlier assessment. Yep, Reese was now Prime Suspect Number One in the court of public opinion.

"We've got another problem," I whispered, pulling him clean off the tabletop. "Another girl, asides from Casey, was killed last night. A jogger came across her earlier this morning. In the woods, drained of blood. And it gets worse."

"Of course it does," he groaned, ruffling a hand through his hair. "What now? Is a hundred foot marshmallow man attacking the city?"

"The girl was one of the cheerleaders that vanished from the Hersey bus. Felicia Coldwater. Whoever did this kept her for over two weeks before they decided to kill her."

"Hellhound?" he suggested. "Maybe another Reaper found her-"

I shook my head. "Her throat was slit, and there weren't any stab wounds to her heart. They already got the coroner's initial report. She wasn't branded."

"That doesn't make any sense. Your run-of-the-mill demon only goes after humans to possess them, and a Hellhound would have ripped her apart to make it look like an animal attack."

"The kicker: there were occult symbols found on site."

His eyes narrowed. "Where did you hear all this?"

"Adam." I handed over my phone, showing him an image from the crime scene. "That's the girl from my vision."

Reese's eyes widened all the more. "You sure?"

"Positive. And the time of death was yesterday evening, an entire day *after* I had the vision. That's not astral projection. That's…"

"A premonition."

"Adam's dad wasn't able to identify the symbols they found, but he thought maybe you could. Have you seen these before?"

Reese grimaced at the photo, and I didn't blame him. The poor girl was sprawled out on the mud, her once white nightgown caked in muck and filth and blood. Vacant eyes bore up at the sky, still widened in a primitive state of sheer and utter terror. He took a long drag, trying to focus his attention on the one particular symbol drawn up around her.

It appeared to have been constructed from a bunch of pale rocks and some loose tree branches, making up a weird twisted symbol inside a star-encrusted pentagram.

"It's a dark sigil of some sort. You can't really make

out the engravings," he said, zooming in the photo as far as he could. "Looks like a...diamond, maybe."

"There's something else." I took out the folded missing person's flyer from my pocket and handed it over. "He look familiar?"

"Travis Freeman?" he read.

"Another student from the Hersey bus disappearance."

Reese studied the picture for a long minute, only to shrug.

"Imagine him with blonde hair."

The paper fell from his limp fingers. "The Hellhound from the alley."

"There's still eighteen of those students missing, and seven more of them I recognized from my vision in the woods. If the rest have been turned..." I couldn't finish the thought.

More questions clawed at my insides, begging me to voice them. It felt like playing mental double-dutch. I kept waiting for the opportunity to jump in and ask, but I just couldn't find the right moment.

"What happened between you and the guy outside the theater?" I suddenly blurted.

Reese's left brow arched in its trademark fashion, as if a hook pulled it up whilst his other brow remained perfectly flat. "I'm sorry?"

"The night we met...or I guess the morning after," I clarified. "And don't play dumb. What was he?"

He ran a hand over his face before ruffling it through his hair. I'd clearly struck a chord. "Hellhound."

"Did you kill him?" I murmured, happy that no one else was in ear shot.

Reese nodded. "Right after I left you."

"What happened between...us?"

His back stiffened.

"It's not like I expected for you and me to become besties overnight, and I know you don't like my friends. But that shouldn't have stopped us from at least hanging out. I mean, you pulled a complete 180 on me. You went from being the nicest guy in town, only to turn into the Abominable Asshat. Why?"

He backed away until his back rested against the wall, his features hardening. "When I followed that thing into the alley, I learned a little too late that he wasn't alone. If there's one thing demons and Hellhounds alike enjoy more than anything, it's killing and torturing their prey. And doing so to someone like me is pretty much their equivalent to Christmas morning. It's not just about causing the victim physical pain. They want to make you suffer in every way imaginable. And the guy that saw us together outside the theater thought it would be particularly amusing if he went back and snatched you up. I won't go into further detail about what they all planned to do next."

The lump in my throat expanded to the size of a softball. "But you killed them..."

"I'm scrappier than I look." Reese tried to smile, but the effort never made it past his lips. "Despite my good fortune, that morning still served as a sour reminder. When you're like us, anyone you care about becomes a potential target. It doesn't matter if they're your friend or even just the sweet old lady next door. If you care about their wellbeing, they'll have a bull's-eye on their back.

"And you were the first person I'd met in a long time that was genuinely nice. Everyone else around here is either afraid of me or they just think I'm a freak. Talking to you was easy. And that's exactly why I knew I needed to keep my distance. We wouldn't have just been casual acquaintances. I wanted more than that. And it would've been really selfish of me. You didn't deserve to be hurt like that, so I did what I could to stay away."

"And the reason for being such an ass…?"

"When it was obvious I couldn't avoid you completely, I figured I needed a different game plan. You were still really nice, and I knew I'd end up in the same problem if I didn't do something to keep you at arm's length. It felt really shitty saying the things I said to you, but it had to be done." Reese slumped back, half laughing at himself. "But what the hell do I know? You were with Reynolds for how long, and nothing happened to you…at least not until after you broke up."

"Hey, get a move on, the both of you," ordered Mr. Abrams on arrival, shooing us out of the cafeteria and into the gym. The conversation had clearly caught Reese off guard if he'd unknowingly dropped the veil keeping him invisible.

Carly waved to us from one of the upper decks of the bleachers, signaling for us to join the group. Daniel seemed neutral to the idea, but once Vanessa and Eric noticed who I was with, their expressions turned sour. Car just shook her head, mouthing *"ignore them."*

"It's okay," I mouthed back, taking hold of Reese's hand. Now, Mark looked like he was about to have a stroke, with V and Eric not far behind. I pulled Blackburn back toward the cafeteria entrance where we took our seats in the second row of the stands.

There were a handful of officers already standing on the half-court line, waiting for everyone to settle down. Mrs. Harvey provided them a microphone, and the gym quieted the instant the Sheriff stepped forward. He didn't tell us anything we didn't already know, and he didn't seem too keen on answering any questions. Afterward, Dr. Fritz suggested we take the time to express any feelings or concerns we had, which opened the floodgates. Attention whores like Ava Ashford jumped at the opportunity to have center stage, as they all tried to do their best Sunday School impressions, leading us in a variety of prayers.

Reese just shook his head. "I swear. Any moment now, one of them is gonna burst into flames."

Casey's legitimate friends finally got their turns to speak, and it wasn't pretty.

Lucy Cartwright entered into a hyperventilated state, her words nearly indistinguishable as she started squeaking out high pitch cries. Just when it seemed like it couldn't get any more painful, Ava returned to center court.

"I really think it would be appropriate that we have a moment of silence in recognition for our dearly departed classmates," she declared, swiping the microphone away from the last speaker. Lucy and the others who had spoken looked just as appalled by the apathy, considering the nicest thing Ava ever said to Casey was probably along the lines of, "You're in my way, bee-otch."

"To Casey." Ava paused, looking right at me. Her lip twitched ever so slightly with wicked intent. "And to Blaine, who was taken from us—so needlessly."

Sure enough, surrounding eyes began burning a hole in the back of my head, igniting a pleasing smile Ava tried (and failed) to repress.

When I was changing into my gym clothes for P.E. yesterday, I'd overheard Ava Ashford's posse talking about me like I'd murdered Blaine right in front of everybody and laughed about it. You'd think nearly dying—or in my case, *actually* dying—would earn a girl a little compassion around here. Instead, I was being treated like I was Ted freaking Bundy.

Everybody finally lowered their heads as the gym fell silent.

A shrill screech echoed from the hallway right by us, and I pitched my hands over my ears at the awful noise. It sounded like nails on a chalkboard, only amplified. I looked at Reese to see his gaze focused on the open doorway. We both looked around, seeing not one other person paying any mind to the racket. And that meant one thing: trouble.

Reese rose to his feet, ready to climb down the bleachers when I grabbed his hand.

He looked down at me curiously. "What?" he mouthed.

I nodded to the other end of the gym.

The ends of a long, tattered cloak gathered at the ankles of the lanky figure looming in the other open doorway. A large hood drew over this person's head, but I knew it wasn't the creep who'd attacked me before...unless he'd ripped off all the skin from his hands and grown razor-sharp talons for fingernails all of the sudden. It was the only exposed body part I could see, and it was safe to say I held no curiosity in wanting to see more. With unnaturally elongated, twisted limbs, this individual took a step forward. They tilted their head back a fraction, taking in a sharp inhale that resulted in another piercing shriek. Enough light captured the figure's chin, revealing a skinless jaw line.

"Is it just me, or does the school mascot look a little different?" said Reese.

"A bit."

CHAPTER 20
Before I'm Dead

Trampling down the bleachers, I raced after Reese out of the gymnasium. "What is that thing?"

The magician pried out a massive filigree blade from inside his militia coat, admiring the steel as he made his way through the cafeteria toward the adjoining hallway where The Crypt Keeper's cousin had come from. "Haven't a clue."

I grabbed him, pulling him to a stop. *"You don't know?"*

"For once, no, I don't. Shocking, I know." He tipped the brim of his fedora, effortlessly rolling it off his head and placing it on mine with a grin. "Just hang back and let me take care of Tall, Dark, and Creepy. Okay?"

He took another step forward, but I yanked him to a halt again. "No! You're not facing that thing. Not when you don't even know what the hell it is! What happens if you go all *Gladiator* on its ass, only to find out that none of your blades work on it?"

"Haven't thought that far," he said, continuing on his way.

"Maybe you should, because you're gonna wind up looking like a victim from *Saw*," I sneered.

"Well, if your boyfriend wants to help out, then he's

more than welcome. But as far as I can see, Reynolds's conveniently absent at the moment," growled Reese, motioning down the abandoned hallway. "Hate to break it to you, but right now, I'm the only person here who can deal with this. Just stay here. If anything happens, you run. Understand?"

He didn't wait for my response.

The cheering that sounded from the gym grew louder, drowning out the sound of his footsteps as he disappeared down the hall. A tug in my chest stole the air right out of me. It was that inexplicable pull I'd felt when Brenda got hurt in P.E., and it urged me forward. Considering how things had ended the last time, I didn't hesitate. Just as he was about to turn down the adjacent hallway, black mist ignited all around his frame.

I bolted after him. "Reese, don't-"

A loud thud echoed from the end of the hall, and I caught sight of Reese's body slamming against a set of lockers as I came around the corner.

"Okay, definitely not my best plan," the magician huffed, staggering up to his feet.

Despite its warped stature, the creepy figure moved far more stealthily than I'd imagine. It sprang forward, gripping Reese by the throat and yanking him clear off his feet. Whirling around, it tossed him across the hallway right into the brick wall like he weighed nothing. Reese lurched toward where his sword lay nearby, but the creature swiped a taloned hand down at his arm, forcing him to recoil before it tore into his flesh.

The metallic nails slammed down on the linoleum floor, slicing four long lines into the tiles. Adrenaline overcame me as I raced towards the action. A sickening mixture of rotten eggs and burnt meat batted me in the face upon arrival, making me gag. The creature remained with its back turned toward me as it scuttled after Reese. I grabbed the silver-infused blade off the ground, prepared to swing it. Only, the sword was a whole lot heavier than I'd imagined, and my arms were still killing me from art class. I clumsily drove the weapon through dead air.

Nice.

The momentum spun me around in a full circle, and I nearly dropped the blade as I steadied myself. With every movement, a small cloud of ash billowed into the air off the monster's burnt robe. I leapt to the side, trying to stay in the creature's blind spot as it lurched about the hall in pursuit of the Magician. I lifted the blade again, positive of my stance, and swung all-out at the figure's back. The cloth tore open, and the creature snarled as it staggered forward. I looked at the end of the sword, expecting to see blood on the tip. Instead, gooey red gunk hugged the blade, forcing my eyes to the spot of impact. I shrieked, stumbling back a step to see a section of fleshless ribcage bones with exposed muscle clinging to the skeletal frame.

The creature hissed, stealing a look over its shoulder. I staggered back another step, seeing the full extent of its face. It looked human; only the skull was a great deal longer. Its jaw appeared to be dislocated, as it hung crooked with a gaping expression. Patches of skin still clung to its face, but it was thin and flaky, revealing dehydrated muscle underneath that looked like spoiled turkey jerky.

The creature roared, and the tendons in its cheeks visibly stretched. It sniffed through the decayed remains of its nostrils. Empty eye sockets bore down at me from its seven-and-a-half foot stature, making me recoil all the more. Bones creaked as it twisted around and faced me.

"Et alterum ad dominum," the creature hissed like a

snake. It even had a forked tongue.

I swung the blade defensively, hoping it would make the beast recoil. Instead, it lurched forward, forcing me to swing again. Lacking the momentum and obvious accuracy, the blade merely skimmed its arm.

"Hey!" Reese barked, regaining the creature's attention. He had a new sword in hand, poised in a battle-ready stance.

A jeering sound escaped the skeletal figure, and it slashed a hand at the significantly smaller blade. The steel sliced off in four separate sections, where each of its fingernails connected with the blade, leaving Reese with nothing but a stump.

The boy went pale. "That's not good." He suddenly whipped the nub at the creature's face, and of all things, the fiend wrinkled its nose in surprise. Reese slinked to the side just as the creature feverishly thrashed its hands out where he'd just been standing, repeatedly clawing into nothing but air. And that's when I realized…it was blind.

Reese, now pinned in the corner of the hall, remained still and hunkered down, having realized the same as me. The creature relied wholly on its other senses. So long as he didn't make a sound, it couldn't pinpoint him. I dug into my pocket and pulled out a pack of gum, hurling it at the lockers on the opposite side of the hallway from where Reese stood. The thud caused the creature to whirl around, and it slashed its deadly set of nails into the metal sheeted lockers. Taking advantage of my distraction, Reese sprang up and darted over to me, but the creature reacted instantly to the sound of his footsteps.

Freddy Kruger's cousin sliced a hand out once more, and I drove my own blade up for another attempt. The fingernails grazed Reese's right side, tearing through the fabric of his coat sleeve, but my swing actually managed to deflect the nails from connecting all the way. The blade wedged into the creature's arm, and I gave a solid heave to free it. Only, the thing wouldn't budge. The sword sat lodged in decrepit bone, and the handle ripped out of my grasp as the creature wildly hurled its injured arm about. I ducked, narrowly managing to not get a head full of hilt in the process as the butt of the blade swung back in my direction.

My shoulder was practically ripped from its socket as Reese grabbed my arm and yanked me away. We ran down the hall, but once we reached the end of the corridor, Reese stopped me from turning back toward the gymnasium.

"We can't put that thing towards other people," he panted. "Regular humans may not be able to see it, but they'll sure as hell feel it if that creature takes a swipe at them."

Bones rasped as the ghoul lurched towards us. With no other choice, we went down the converse hall. Though a lot of the students were at the rally, there were still plenty of others loitering the hallways and classrooms. We passed emergency exits, but leading that thing outside wasn't an option. Alarms were rigged to go off if someone opened any of the doors, which would cause a flood of students to pour out into the hallways and put them right in the path of that thing.

Racing through the maze of corridors, I did my best to get that thing to the other side of the school. There was some halted construction going on in the west wing. With no workers and classes in that section, it was the least populated part of the building and our safest bet. Despite our quickened pace, the creature remained no more than a hall's length behind us. We came to the dead end of the corridor to the art room. An exit rested on the other side, free of alarms. Our ticket out of here. In all my time going here, never had the door been locked. Today of all days... I twisted the knob to no avail.

The gruesome smell of rotten eggs only grew stronger the closer the creature came. Reese wrenched the knob as hard as he could, but the damned thing wouldn't give. We both hurled our bodies at the door in a last ditch effort. Still, nothing.

"Come on!" I race back down the hall, right toward the decaying monster.

"What the hell are you doing?" bellowed Reese, following on my foot heels.

I motioned to the small passageway up ahead, midway down the hall. By just a hair's breadth, we managed to turn into the dark, ten-foot long corridor before the creature met with us. Our momentum sent us crashing into the heavy steel door. We ignored the WARNING: AUTHORIZED PERSONNEL ONLY sign and pried the rusted entrance door open. We snaked inside and slammed the door shut, throwing the metal lever lock into place. The pungent odor of burning oil and mildew greeted us as we trampled down a barely visible flight of steps. Dim fluorescent lights did little to illuminate the vast cellar space. Water pumps and electrical generators eventually came into focus. We were in the boiler room.

I knew the school had one, but I honestly didn't ever know where it was. There were several maintenance rooms with the same signs around the building, so by logic, it could've been behind any one of those doors. Yet, here we were. Trapped in the basement with nothing but a couple of barred windows near the ceiling.

Reese used the flashlight on his phone to help him

investigate deeper into the room. "By law, there *should* be an emergency exit in here somewhere."

The building was fairly old, and I could see the bars guarding the windows had some rust on them. It was worth a shot. I leapt up, clinging onto them. The glass could be opened, I guessed for air circulation, but the bars were firmly welded in place. I relentlessly clutched my fingers around metal, wrenching my body down with as much force as I could muster. It wasn't any use.

"This might not be the best time to mention this, but what does it mean if you see a freakish cloud looming around someone?" I gritted, still yanking at the bars.

"It's a prophetic aura. Tells you that the person in question is either going to get hurt...or die. *Why?*"

"There's one around you right now," I admitted, finally dropping back to the floor.

"What color?"

"Black."

Reese reemerged from the shadows. "Come again?"

Even with the darkness resting behind him, I could still see the swirling black mist clinging around his form. I didn't need to be told what *that* meant.

Reese's cursing didn't inspire any confidence as he darted back into the darkness. His flashlight finally stopped moving, now transfixed on an unlit EXIT sign...behind an old, busted rooftop HVAC unit blocking the entranceway. I raced over and we both yanked and pulled and wrenched our weight into it. The damn thing didn't budge an inch.

The door at the top of the stairs continuously pounded, and shrill screeching followed. Seeing as how that thing tore through locker doors like they were made of paper, I doubted we would have more than thirty seconds before that ghoul clawed its way in here.

I needed to think. Fast.

An array of equipment lay before us, and I started hitting every button and pulling every lever available. Engines roared and gears clanked and sensor alarms started beeping.

"What are you doing?"

"That thing can't see," I said, now dumping disinfectant and floor cleaner across the open space of concrete. "So we confuse it. It can't kill us if it can't find us."

The whole room was now filled with a barrage of mechanical roars and the pungent odor of chemical.

"All it has to go on now is touch, so we hide. The moment it moves towards the back of the room, we make a run for it."

Sure enough, a loud rupture ignited from the top of the stairs. The metal lever once locking the door clanged down the steps, its handle shredded right off. The door burst open, and as if it was floating, the creature swept down the stairs in one fluent motion.

Reese pulled me back, and I ducked behind an empty hot water tank as he crouched in back of some kind of large chiller. The creature whirled around, rasping at the air. The ends of his tattered cloak sat inches from the pooling disinfectant as it suddenly stopped. The creature lowered itself, snuffling in the potent tang through whatever remained of its nose.

Scrunching its face in what looked like disgust, the monster recoiled, batting a talon-clawed hand through the air as if to fan away the smell. It straightened back upright and slowly moved about the floor, still consciously avoiding the spilled chemicals. Cocking its head from side to side, it seemed confused by the whaling machinery. Only, it didn't come deeper into the room.

Its sharp shoulders slackened. *"Sponsae of Sitri."*

I stole a look over at Reese who just shook his head in puzzlement. His eyes grew as they traveled down the length of me.

Sure enough, a blue light was illuminating from beneath the left sleeve of my sweatshirt. I rolled up the fabric to see one of the runes glowing brighter and brighter. It was circular with an ornate U shape holding up three iron crosses. I still didn't have a clue what any of them meant, but I had a feeling the towering creep in front of me did, because he was staring straight at me.

Panicking, I slithered out from behind the tank, moving further back into the room. A bat of noxious air hit me in the face not a second before the creature suddenly manifested right in front of me.

I clumsily stumbled back, falling into a machine. My palms pressed against the plate cover behind me, and I yelped as the hot metal scorched the skin. The creature cocked its head, raising its clawed hand out to me. It even turned its palm upright so that its clawed fingers angled away toward the floor. Was it…reaching out to me?

The creature suddenly lurched back, hissing as it batted its talon around. Something was clamped under its throat. The skeletal figure whirled around in a frenzy.

Reese.

He was clinging to the creature's back, gripping a lead pipe from both ends as he dug it against the monster's windpipe. The beast threw its weight back, hurtling both Reese and itself into the far brick wall. Reese gasped, clearly having the wind knocked out of him. The pipe fell away as his body sank to the floor. The creature turned to him, its claws primed and raised.

I raced for the stairs. "HEY!"

Before it even had a chance to look at me, I hurtled the broken lever at the foot of the landing square right into the back of its head. The creature hissed something under its breath, striking a hand against the wall right above Reese's head. Blackburn sank down lower until he was practically lying on the floor, still struggling to refill his lungs.

"You want to kill me?" I barked, wielding a long rod of rebar. "Then have at it!"

"Kat...go," Reese choked.

Like hell.

Bearing in mind of the stealth it possessed, I swung at the creature the instant it stepped forward. And just like that, its skeletal hands caught hold of the steel well before it even came close to landing a hit. I twisted the grooved rod and yanked it back, watching the abrasive metal tear apart the remaining skin on the creature's palm and fingers.

That same disgusting red gunk clung to the end of the rebar as I ripped the metal away. I tried to lift it up to take another swing, but the creature gripped it again. Only this time, steam was coming out from the hand wrapped around the steel. Instantly, I let go of the rebar. An all new level of fear hit me as I watched the steel melt away in thick globs like wax from a sickly candle.

If Mr. Abrams was right in his teachings last year, then it took about 2,500 degrees Fahrenheit to liquefy steel. And this creature was doing it with the mere touch of its hand.

Speaking of hands, the beast reached its free one out to me again. A bright light suddenly blasted from my left arm as a fresh wave of adrenaline overcame me. The skin burned, and I instinctively thrust my hand up.

My fingers burned as light suddenly erupted from my palm, hitting the creature right in the chest. The monstrous being shot across the room, but instead of hitting the wall beside Reese, it went right through it, evaporating into an inky mist. Burn marks powdered the wall, low embers still burning amid the charcoaled residue.

The instant I lowered my hand, the light vanished, the glow from the runes returning to their shiny metallic branding.

"Reese." I raced over to him, falling down onto my knees.

"I'm okay," he muttered hoarsely.

And he was right. That weird aura around him had vanished as well.

"What did you do?" Reese muttered, coughing out the words grievously.

"I thought maybe you'd know." I helped him back up to his feet, turning him around to face the wall.

"Holy shit," he blurted.

I extended my arm out, showing him the collection of runes. He immediately recognized the one in question...

Because the very same symbol was burned into the wall, on a much bigger scale.

It took up nearly the entire space from floor to ceiling and stretched at least ten feet wide. That circle with the three iron crosses.

CHAPTER 21
Make Me Wanna Die

All I wanted to do was go home and curl up in bed, but Carly had insisted that Reese and I meet up with her at the library after school let out. I just started to doze off when a heavy thud hit the table. My head shot up to see a big office file box set in front of me.

"Break out your magnifying glasses, Sherlock," declared my blonde bestie in pure giddiness, removing piles of manila folders from the container.

"Whatcha got there?" I asked, nervous.

"Well, I stopped by the office supply store during Study Hall and got myself a corkboard. And like any good sleuth, I started mapping out the details from each of the cases to see if I could find any connection between the victims." She lobbed over a stack of files to both Reese and me. "Guess what I found."

"That you have way too much time on your hands?" Reese guessed, fingering through the good hundred pages of work in front of him alone.

She rolled her eyes. "Hey, I'm not hearing you contributing anything here yet, Edward Scissorhands. So shut your pie hole." Car dug deeper into the box and unfolded a gigantic diagram full of labeled squares. "As it turns out, they were related. Distantly, but related nonetheless."

"Seriously?" Now Reese seemed impressed.

"Fourth cousins, once removed to be exact."

"So what's all this for?" I asked, leafing through the first few pages. "Car, what the hell is this?"

"You. Or more specifically you and your family."

"I can see that." There were pictures and news ads and….medical records? "Where did you even get all this stuff?"

"With 'too much time,'" she cracked, casting Reese a glare. "And a…confidential source."

"Carly."

"What?" She batted her eyes innocently.

"Honestly, I'm afraid to actually know," I amended with a yawn. "But besides that, what does any of that have to do with me?"

"Seriously? The last time a murder took place here, e-mail wasn't even invented yet."

If only she really knew…

Bodies seemed to be dropping faster than a drunken sorority girl in stilettos.

"Whoever is behind this seems to be sticking to a pretty strict M.O., so it's safe to assume that there's a connection linking you to Casey and Felicia."

"But Kat's not from around here," said Reese. "I highly doubt that missing link is blood related."

"Eliminate the impossible before considering the improbable," countered Car, taking her place at the table. She remained in high spirits…for the first two hours.

We all had our heads on the table, leafing through more and more pages with bleary eyes.

"Can we take a break?" Reese pleaded. "I'm starving."

"Just a little longer," said Car. "We're on the verge of a breakthrough. I can feel it."

"I can feel the bottomless pit in my stomach," he murmured, tossing another file aside. "Is your life even half as mind numbing as these articles are? Because if so, I'm recommending you for sainthood."

"Thanks," I chortled. It's not like I could blame him. He'd spent the last forty five minutes reading about every publicized fundraiser I'd been dragged to over the past year.

"Seriously, look at this. Auctions, pledges, raffles, charity balls, galas, holiday luncheons, formals, weekly parties..." He tossed the news clippings aside, rubbing his exhausted eyes. "Do you have a life outside school and the country club?"

"What do you think?" I scoffed, tossing another file at him.

He flipped it open and immediately banged his head on the tabletop. "There's *more*?"

"The week I stayed home after the accident was the first time since moving here I got to actually sleep in."

"Jesus."

"Sometimes privilege doesn't buy you freedom. It only puts more restrictions on what you're allowed to do with your life."

"Stay positive," ordered Carly, grabbing a fresh batch of folders. Her stomach grumbled, and she winced. "Although, you've got a point. I really could go for a quick bite. Kat, you have anything I can nibble on?"

"All I have is a box of Tic Tacs."

"I'll take it." She seized hold of my purse and rummaged through the mess, trying to unearth the source of the infamous rattling.

"You okay?" asked Reese.

I looked up to see Carly's eyes wide, her fingers wrapped around a white paper cuff. It was the patient ID band I'd received in the hospital after the accident. The cuff had been way too big for my wrist, so I'd just tossed it into my bag the moment they gave back my things upon release.

Carly whipped the band aside and it smacked Reese in the chest. He studied it, but still looked just as baffled as me. The girl was flinging folders left and right, cursing as she continued in her search. For what exactly, we had no idea.

"Yahtzee!" Peeling through the pages, her eyes finally settled on a document and her face immediately paled.

Reese looked over her shoulder. "You find something there, Sherlock?"

"Try a whole lot of somethings." She slid each of the papers over to Reese and me. They were my family's medical records. "Look at the blood types."

"What am I missing here?" My parents were both O-positive, as was I.

"Did you ever need another blood transfusion after you were little?"

"I wasn't aware I needed it the first time," I said, taking the next paper she handed to me. Apparently, I'd been born premature and in consequence had been anemic. This was all news to me. "I'm still not sure where you're going with this, Car."

"When you were in the E.R., the doctor ordered new blood work for you, probably to see if there were any drugs or alcohol in your system. Notice anything odd?"

Reese took another look at the wristband, and the same expression washed over his face as it had with Carly.

I leaned over, snatching it from his hands. "That... That can't be right."

Plain as day, the cuff read, *TYPE: B-negative.*
"They can't be my parents."

***

"Hey, you guys could be, like, the long lost heiresses to a billion dollar empire, and maybe evil corporate CEOs have sent out henchmen to hunt you all down to keep the money for themselves," declared Carly.

"Or," Reese interjected snippily, "maybe the hospital just made a clinical error."

I shook my head. The more I thought about it, the less likely it seemed. Sure, every kid at some point wonders if they're adopted, but there were more than a few oddities I couldn't overlook. My parents had made their fair share of remarks over the years that they would've thought I was adopted if they didn't know any better. While both my mom and dad's sides of the family had either brown or hazel green eyes, mine were just plain off-putting. My pediatrician called it "central heterochromia." It was a mutation that caused an iridescent ring of yellow to hug the pupils, while the rest of my eyes were bright blue. Not to mention, while my parents had blonde hair, neither of theirs was nearly as white as my own. In fact, both of theirs were on the darker end of the color spectrum. Even odder, both my folks suffered from an array of allergies. My mom couldn't even take Advil, as it would cause her to go into anaphylactic shock. Yet, I never had a reaction to anything in my entire life.

If I wasn't really their kid, I highly doubted they even knew. The Montgomerys were one of those so-called "dynasty" families that were weird about potential spouses tainting their bloodline. This was so strong in fact that my grandparents threatened to cut off my eldest uncle's inheritance if he went through with marrying a barmaid he met back in college. Needless to say, he's still miserably living in a lap of luxury as a terminal bachelor.

Had there been a mix up at the hospital? Had I really been switched at birth?

Was it even a mistake?

If I was somehow related to Casey and Felicia, someone knew about the swap. Why else had I been targeted? Why kill Blaine, only to bother bringing *me* back to life? Maybe I really was a Changeling, in more ways than one.

We remained silent for the rest of the drive after Reese dropped Carly back off at her house.

"You sure you don't want to do something? Help get your mind off things?" Reese finally asked, rolling up to the side street of my house.

I shook my head. "I'll be okay. My folks...or whoever they are...they're home tonight, and we don't really get to spend a lot of time together."

"If you change your mind—"

I reached over and kissed his cheek. "You'll be the first one I call."

Considering Mom's rant this morning, I figured it would be best to not get caught doing anything more, especially right outside the house, so I blushingly said goodbye and climbed out. I still would have loved to see the look on her face though if she had caught us.

Mom had made my dad and me promise that we'd always reserve Thursday nights for family. So long as Dad wasn't away on business, we'd adjust our schedules accordingly and actually take the time to sit down for dinner and eat—together. I was supposed to be home by seven, and it was already a quarter after.

I prepared myself for a tongue lashing as I walked in the front, only to be greeted by silence. My heart immediately sank. "Hello?"

No response, except for Mom's Persian cat lounging on the entryway table. She let out a low growl at me as I hung up my coat.

"Belles?" I brought my hand up to stroke her, seeing the fur on her arched back and tail puffing up. She hissed, swatting a tiny paw at me, and I took the hint. I called out for my folks again as I headed into the kitchen, receiving no answer.

Shocker.

Given that there wasn't a trace of anything in the fridge but restaurant doggy bags, it meant I'd have to fend for myself. Rummaging through the containers, I found nothing but some old Thai food. I couldn't remember the last time anyone here even ordered that, so I figured it'd be best to stay away from it.

"Who's in the mood for delivery?" I queried to the empty kitchen, plucking off the coupon I had pinned up on the fridge. "No objections? Perfect."

I ordered two extra-large cheese pizzas and headed up the stairs. The guy on the phone said I had forty-minutes till they dropped off the food, so I had time to take a shower beforehand. I kicked the door open to my bedroom, lobbing my jacket on the nightstand as I grabbed some fresh clothes from my closet. All the blood drained from my face as I looked up at the mirror beside my dresser.

"Look at what we have here," cooed the brunette standing in the corner. In one swift motion, she crossed the room and shut the door. "About time you showed up. I've been waiting forever."

I whirled around, almost winding up on my ass as I stumbled backwards over my book bag. It was the girl from Rockabilly Bob's.

"What a pretty little thing you are. The Master's going to be very pleased with this." She practically salivated as she eyed me up and down like I was a hot fudge sundae. Her eyes burned a smoldering gold as her smile grew.

Crap.

She was a Hellhound.

"Any chance you'll believe that this is just a case of mistaken identity?" I laughed feebly.

"Afraid not," she cooed, taking her time as she sauntered towards me. "Could've spotted you a mile away."

"And why's that?" My voice cracked over each word.

"You're marked."

"Come again?" I looked over my shoulder, seeing the two-story drop outside the window. The chance that Mom's rose bush garden below would cushion my fall seemed unlikely. In fact, it sounded awfully prickly. The girl guarded my path to the doorway, knowing full well I'd never manage to snake around her. And even at the off chance I managed, she'd probably wolf-out and rip me in half with her teeth.

"You're marked," she reiterated. "You belong to him now, and the Master has his plans." She snarled, snapping forward.

I screamed like a banshee as I leapt sideways, trying to make a run for the bathroom, and all she did was laugh before a grip tightened on the back of my collar. In one swift motion, I was sent hurtling backwards, smacking my head against the bed post as I lost my footing and hit the floor. She strolled over to me with a pip in her step, staring down at me in cruel amusement as if I were an ant burning under a magnifying glass.

My hand slipped under my bed skirt, and surprise flashed in the brunette's eyes as I drew out my baseball bat from beneath the mattress.

"Aww, little Kitty Kat wants to play?" she teased.

Her continual taunting only propelled me further to slice the bat into the girl. I sprang up from the hardwood and all-out hurtled the aluminum, landing it right in the middle of her arm as she used it to shield her face. The force knocked her off balance, but she just as easily recovered. The girl blew the hair out of her eyes as she shrugged off her leather jacket, and I couldn't help but gag at the sight of the unnatural bend in her forearm. I'd broken the bone in half, the splintered end pushing against the inside of her skin as it threatened to break out.

I half expected her to curse or scream or do...something, but she just stared down at it with indifference. Not a smidgen of pain. It dawned on me far too late about what Reese had said. She was a Hellhound; therefore she didn't feel. Not only would she heal faster, but whereas pain would hinder someone's mobility, she was like a freaking Terminator! Not until I managed to beat her body to a point where it couldn't move at all would she ever stop. How the hell was I going to do that? I took another swing at her, but it proved to be in vain. She absorbed the hit to her rib cage like my bat was made out of nothing more than foam.

"You through?" she huffed exasperatedly, gripping the sweet spot of the bat as I tried recovering from the futile swing. The brunette pried the aluminum from my hands and tossed it across the room.

The breath caught in my throat as I took notice to the beauty mark on her left cheek. I'd seen that before...

"Brittany."

Her brows furrowed in confusion.

"That's your name, isn't it?" I muttered. "Brittany Lynch. You were on the Hersey bus the night it vanished. W-what happened to you?"

"I found salvation," she growled. The gold in her eyes turned yellow as she bared her teeth, and her canines lengthened as they pushed out from her gum lines.

I'd seen that look only once before, from the attacker in the alleyway. And that was after he'd shifted back into his human form. I had a feeling given her current appearance that things were about to get more hairy...or more furry.

Just as she moved in closer, the chain dangling from my neck bit at my exposed skin with an icy prick.

Could it work?

I grabbed the pendant and yanked on it as hard as I could. Thankfully, the necklace broke off, but not without a grunt from my end. It always looked so easy and painless when someone did that on TV, but in actuality it really kind of hurt.

"Here, play with this." I flung the necklace at her, and she caught it as it smacked her in the chest.

"Seriously?" She laughed, palming the cross in her good hand without any problem.

Oh shit...

With nowhere else to go and nothing else I could do, I retracted back to the windowsill. Thorn bushes, here I come.

Suddenly, Brittany howled, dropping the pendant from her hand. Smoke rose from her palm, and she thrashed backward as the skin reddened. "Bitch!"

Genuinely crippled by the scorching pain, the brunette doubled over onto the hardwood, digging her nails around the damaged flesh. I took opportunity with the distraction and leapt across my mattress, making it to the door. Just as I reached for the doorknob, a sweltering pain of my own registered in my right leg.

I tried to stay on my feet, but the leg buckled under me against my will.

"As they say, if the heel doesn't hurt, it doesn't help," the brunette sneered.

I dreadfully looked down, seeing the spike of her stiletto jammed in the back of my calf. She staggered up to her feet, laughing as she watched me crawl across the floorboards towards the doorway. I reached for the knob, but a grip tightened on my ankle and I was sent skimming across the hardwood. My vocal chords rattled as I relinquished an ear aching scream, feeling Brittany's bare foot pushing the stiletto deeper into my calf. She let out a sadistic chuckle, yanking the device from my leg in one quick, agonizing pull.

Clutching onto a chunk of my hair, the girl pried me off the floor, throwing me up against the wall beside my nightstand.

"Maybe I should just bite you now and get it over with," she hummed, wrapping a strong hand around my throat.

I scratched and clawed at her, leaving everywhere from her hands to her face maimed with nail marks, but it didn't do any good. Her grip tightened, squeezing the furious pulse pumping in my neck as she lifted me off the ground. I fought to keep conscious, but my vision inevitably clouded over with a tunneling gray haze as my feet kept kicking at the empty air beneath me.

She leaned in closer, her jagged breathing batting me in the face as a low growl rumbled deep in her chest. She was going to bite me. I'd turn into a monster.

CHAPTER 22
Raise The Dead

My fingers grappled at the objects on my nightstand, but a crash followed, and I assumed the brunette had swiped the countertop clean. The little bit of hope I had left drained from me as I clawed uselessly at her. She wrenched me off the wall, only to hammer me against it again with a breathtaking blow. Brittany whispered something, but the comment was lost on me. All I could hear was the rattling of the frames overhead. The entire section above me was decked out with framed award plaques. Faith surged in me once more, and I prayed Mom hadn't cheaped out. She'd paid no expense with the rest of the room, so it only seemed logical that this would be no exception.

I reached up, tugging at the bottom of a random plaque until the hook holding it broke from the wall. The frame fell into my grasp, and I brandished it firmly. Brittany anticipated me hitting her with it, but she only laughed at the effort. As if a Presidential High Honors Award would really do any damage...

Instead of hurling it at her, I yanked it down to eyelevel and shoved the plaque into her face. The girl howled, and I could hear her flesh sear as I mashed the Tiffany's sterling silver frame against her cheek. She shrieked, immediately dropping me. Brittany screamed out every curse word in the book as her footsteps ambled mindlessly across the floor. The girl sounded like an injured bull in a china shop.

I choked on the abundance of oxygen that flooded my lungs, welcoming each burning breath as my vision slowly cleared. A thunderous ruckus erupted across the room, and I looked up confusedly. Brittany's body was in a hurled heap at the bottom of my now-broken bookcase. What the hell did she do? Charge into it? All my precious hard covers and paperbacks lay sprawled out across the floor with the exception of only the top shelf. I staggered up to my feet, whimpering at the sting raking up my leg from the heel wound. Holy crap on a cracker! No wonder the brunette had freaked out. There was a long, two-inch thick charcoaled burn running down the length of her face, seared even on her eye. Books fell away from on top of her as Brittany achingly tried pulling herself off the floor. She got up on shaking knees and staggered back, rattling the bookcase once more.

"You're dead," she snarled.

I might have paid more mind to her gigantic canines if not for the gruesome state of her face. Her damaged eye already had a clouded white film over the cornea, and beat red veins raked the remaining surface. As she sneered, the burnt flesh on her cheek stretched, causing it to tear.

"Kat?" The voice called out from downstairs, and I stiffened.

Mom.

Brittany's cruel smile widened. "Second servings, I see." She pulled herself out of the bookcase, and the effort rattled the top of the stand, toppling over a mammoth volume. Just as she moved forward, the book fell, smacking her right in the head. A dazed expression met her one working eye before she collapsed onto the hardwood floor.

"Kat?" Mom called out again, this time anxiously. Her footsteps trampled up the stairs, sending my thoughts into a frenzy.

I limped across the room as fast as I could, throwing the lock into place on my door. I knelt down beside Brittany, seeing her breathing, but still thankfully unconscious.

"Thank you, Jane Austen," I sighed, picking up the trusty all-in-one volume. Who'd have thunk it? A book could literally save a life.

"Kat, is everything okay?" My door rattled as Mom twisted the locked knob.

Crap, crap, triple crap.

"Ah, yeah, I'm fine," I called out, trying to calm my shaken nerves.

"What happened?"

"Hmmm?" I looked around at the mess, feeling a new surge of panic arise.

"What was all the noise?"

Shit!

"My, uh, bookcase...it fell," I replied clumsily.

"Oh my god-"

"Yeah, but I'm okay."

"Well, could you open the door?"

"It's a bit messy in here at the moment."

"Kat." Her tone made it clear this wasn't a request, solidifying it with a knock on the door.

"Just give me a sec." Sweeping the books out of the way, I bent down and grabbed hold of Brittany by her underarms. The hardwood flooring gave me little resistance as I dragged her body across the room, hiding her figure behind the other side of my bed. Blood from my leg spotted the floor as well, so I frantically snatched up some laundry from my hamper and tossed the random articles over the various stains. I hobbled back over to the door and pulled it open, forcing Mom's knuckles to bat the air as she prepared to bang on it.

"Heavens." Gawking at the mass of books still splayed across the floor, Mom tried heading inside, but I stepped in her way.

"I'll take care of this," I assured.

She looked down at me crossly as I blocked her second attempt to move around me.

"Don't-"

She further examined me, and I was grateful to be wearing black pants so that she couldn't see the blood running down my leg. That still didn't stop her from noticing the dab of sweat on my forehead or my flushed cheeks as I struggled to conceal my pain. "What has gotten into you?"

"Nothing. It's just...you're not wearing any shoes," I quickly countered, looking down at her feet. "There's glass all over the place. I don't want you to cut yourself."

Voices echoed from downstairs as she noted the several shattered candle jars on the floor.

"Did you invite people over?" I asked wearily.

The question seemed to catch her off guard. "Oh, yes. Sophia and Ashley joined me for yoga, and they stopped by for a drink. Is that a problem?"

"No, I just ordered a pizza, and I didn't want to interrupt," I assured. "Go back down to them. I've got this."

She hesitated, but Mom eventually agreed, leaving me. I closed the door and locked it once again, racing back over to check on Brittany. The girl was still unconscious, laying haphazardly on the small area rug surrounding the bed, so I grabbed my purse.

Yanking out my cell, I dialed his number. "We have a serious problem."

I could hear the engine of the old beater rumbling from down the block, and I waved my hands frantically at the sight of Reese cutting through the Mandrakis's backyard.

"Is it really that hard for you to stay out of trouble, or were you just inventing an excuse to see me again?" he mused with his cell to his ear.

"Ask that to the body lying on my floor," I said, wielding an iron poker. Just in case Brittany came to, I was prepared to put her to sleep again. It didn't matter if she couldn't feel; a proper concussion still knocked you out.

Reese arrived within five minutes of my call, leaving me just enough time to stack my books in the corner and sweep up the remaining debris. He made his way under my windowsill, looking up at me expectantly.

"What do we do?" I whispered. "Should we call Nathan?"

He shook his head. "There's really only one thing we can do." Reese opened his coat and pulled out a sizeable blade.

I immediately shook my head. "No, you can't kill her."

"You said she was a Hellhound, yes?"

"Yeah, but I thought maybe... I don't know. Maybe Mr. Reynolds can keep her prisoner or something, interrogate her..."

"She won't tell him anything-"

"She's only seventeen," I snapped. "She has a family!"

His brows pinched together. "How do you know?"

"She's one of the missing students from Hersey," I muttered, feeling tears prickle the corners of my eyes. I'd seen her mother on the news begging for answers, pleading for her daughter's safe return.

"I understand your hesitation, but you can't do anything to save her. She's lost." The sympathy in his eyes confirmed his words. "And you won't be doing her any favors by handing her over to Nathan. You saw what he and his men wanted to do to me when they thought I was one of her kind. Reapers want to see them suffer. He'll brutalize her in every manner possible, prolonging the pain for as long as it takes until her body gives out. Do you really want that for her?"

I looked beside me to the unconscious girl. "Throw me a blade."

"Come again?"

"It's the only way to kill her, right? Silver?"

"Apart from removing her head," Reese admitted. "Though I wouldn't suggest the latter. It's a bit messy, as you can imagine."

"Exactly. Throw a blade up to me."

"Yeah, there's a saying about running with scissors that comes to mind. I'm pretty sure the same applies to chucking deadly knives," he argued.

I stepped aside, hiding behind the wall. "Just do it."

A moment later a sliver of silver came hurtling through the window, hitting the corner of my bed. The blade ricocheted off the mattress and bounced back at me. I howled as I scrambled away, only to realize the dagger was still encased in its holster. I gripped the handle, prying it out of its sheath. I hovered over Brittany with the blade tip primed at her, seeing her chest rise and fall. Sure, the girl had stabbed and strangled me, and my calf still hurt like a Mofo. But I'd already started to heal.

"I can't." I fell back, snatching up my phone. "I can't do it, Reese. I can't pierce her in the heart... What if I just stab her in the arm or something? She's allergic to the steel. Wouldn't that be enough?"

He sighed. "No, that'll just hurt her, not to mention make her really, really angry."

How could I kill an innocent person, someone who didn't have any control over their actions? It wasn't her fault what she'd become, just as it wasn't mine.

I snapped out of my train of thought, looking out the window. "Reese?"

Where the hell did he go?

A soft tap registered at the door, and I jumped, dropping the blade in my hand.

"You gonna let me in?" the magician whispered.

Seriously? How did he get in here?

I unlocked the door and grabbed him by the lapels, pulling him inside. Knowing him, he probably waltzed into the house without bothering to go invisible, just to make things interesting.

"That her?" he queried, spotting Brittany as he rounded the bedside.

"No, that's my neighbor. We got into a fight about who the best boy band was, so I clobbered her." I gave him a light backhand to the chest. "What do you think?"

He knelt down, studying her face. "Talk about a cat fight. What happened?" I pointed at the silver frame, and a small smile formed on his lips. It immediately vanished though as his gaze traveled up to my leg. "You're bleeding."

Before I could protest, he swept me up and settled me down on top of the bed. His fingers slowly glided up my calf, hiking the pant leg.

"I'm fine," I assured. "It's already healing."

"Did she bite you?"

I shook my head.

"We don't have much time," he murmured.

"Have you done this before? I mean…kill someone who *isn't* attacking you?" I asked weakly, looking at the girl's unconscious frame.

Reese eased my pant leg back down and turned his attention to Brittany once more. "It's merciful in comparison to what end she'll face elsewhere."

I couldn't bring myself to look. I climbed off the bed, making my way over to the rubble still sitting at the foot of my bookcase. A thunderous crack erupted, and Reese's frame came hurtling beside me. He bit down on a howl, prying out a shard of broken frame glass from his abdomen. I spun around. Brittany's burnt face sneered up at us as she staggered to her feet.

"There'll be nothing *merciful* in what I'm about to do to you," she spat, flashing Reese a wicked set of bloodstained teeth. But that wasn't the only thing bleeding. Blood coursed down her hand from where another large shard of glass was pressed firmly in her palm, the barbed end primed at Blackburn. She sprang forward. As if stepping outside myself, instinct seized control over my mind. I dropped to the floor, plucking up the dagger I'd dropped not a moment before. The girl was mere inches from plunging the jagged glass into Reese's neck when she suddenly gasped, hobbling backward.

It took a moment for my mind to finally regain command over myself as my eyes traveled down. My fingers were still wrapped around the handle of the dagger, now plunged in the left side of the brunette's chest. Warm liquid pooled over my hand and I gasped, recoiling back until I hit the wall. I was covered in her...in her blood. Just as I'd witnessed in the alley with her male counterpart, Brittany's pained expression turned brittle, as did the rest of her until there was nothing left but a pile of ash splayed across the hardwood floor.

My hand instinctively shot to my mouth, but I shrieked, slamming it back down to my side before my bloodied digits could connect with my lips.

"Kat—" Reese's arms caught hold of me as my knees buckled under. "Kat, you're okay."

"I just..."

"I know." He settled me on the floor, brushing the mess of hair from my eyes. My whole body shook, and he sank down in front of me, purposely blocking my view of the poor girl's remains. "Hey." Reese angled my face up to his. "Thank you."

CHAPTER 23
By the Way

I couldn't bring myself to do it. After taking a shower, I came back out into my bedroom. Reese had cleaned up everything, but as I sat on my mattress, my stomach churned. How could I sleep not two feet from where I had just killed someone? Every inch of me was still stained by an invisible taint. It didn't matter how hard I scrubbed at my skin, how much I lathered, how much soap I used. Brittany's blood was still there. I couldn't see it, but I could feel it.

"We can go back to my place, if you want," suggested Reese. "The bed in the basement is all yours. My mom won't know."

I shook my head, hearing voices still echoing from downstairs. "Mine would, if you could even call her that."

Reese followed me down the hall to a distant guest bedroom. A lush sofa sat in the corner beside a lofty bureau as a massive king-sized bed took up the rest of the space. Neither of my parents ever came into these bedrooms, and they hadn't come in to wish me goodnight since I was five, so I didn't need to worry about either walking in on us or wondering why I wasn't in my room.

I had been dreading the moment when I'd be left alone, and Reese didn't need me to ask. He slid off his tailcoat and shoes before removing his vest as well. In nothing but a half-unbuttoned dress shirt and black jeans, he settled into the sofa, draping his jacket over himself as a makeshift blanket. My other concern rested with having another uninvited visitor, so I flipped the door lock into place before nestling into the fluffy comfort of Egyptian cotton sheets.

***

I shrieked as arms safely ensnared me around my waist, hoisting me up before the rogue waves splashed my feet. I'd been swimming at several local beaches all summer, but even by the ocean's standard, the water was shockingly cold. Blaine set me back down in the sand once the waves receded back into the ocean. The moon's distorted reflection rippled in the surf as it hung low in the sky. No one had ever mentioned Devil's Bay before, and I couldn't be happier that Blaine had taken me here.

I had never seen water like this. With each wave that piled on top of one another, the ocean glowed—literally glowed—a bright neon blue. Bioluminescence he had called it. The marine life apparently emitted this mystical luminosity through photophores as a reaction to the disturbance in the water.

"You like it?" Blaine asked.

I didn't need to answer. He could tell by the ridiculous smile on my face that I loved everything about it, soaking in every detail as if to stow them away in my mind for safe keeping. I still nodded. "How come no one else is out here? I mean, it's so beautiful. You'd think the entire beach would be filled with onlookers."

"Well, that's kind of the thing. We're really not supposed to be out here," he whispered mischievously. I shot him an uneasy look. "During the summer months, we tend to get a lot of folks,

homeless and tourists mostly, that like to sleep out on the beach. This stretch isn't particularly well lit, so police patrol the area at night to kick out trespassers."

"So we're breaking the law?" I couldn't stop smiling.

"Kind of fun, isn't it?"

"Kind of freeing." I came to a stop, looking out into the water again. My gaze dropped to the ridiculous heels in my hands. I suddenly hurled a shoe. It disappeared into the night, only showing itself again by way of a splash in the water with glimmering blue lights swirling beneath the surface.

Blaine laughed, watching me throw the remaining heel. "Dare I ask how much those cost?"

"Asides from my dignity?"

"It really is mind numbing, isn't it? The parties, the gossip, all the bullshit." He sighed, nodding down at his pristine suit as he brushed the rogue strands of black hair from his eyes. "But hey, at least we don't have to wait much longer till we can get out of here."

The waves splashing up onto the shore seemed to stretch out, as if begging to kiss my feet. I didn't move. "You never really escape it though, do you?" It wasn't a question. "Sure, you go off to college, but it's one of your parents' choosing. You take the classes they've already decided for you, you get the degree they want, and then you're groomed to take over the family business. What choices do we really have?"

Blaine's expression turned sorrowful. He knew this all too well. "True love should never come with conditions."

"That's what they make you believe."

"Perhaps, but as they say, 'Yesterday is history. Tomorrow is a mystery. Today is a gift.'" He extended his hand out to me. "'That's why it's called the present.'"

A new smile tugged at my lips. "Quoting Alice Morse Earle, are we?"

He winked. *"We may not be able to control our futures, but we can decide what we do in the here and now. Fuck the lot of them, even if only for tonight. Let's paint the town red."*

***

Glass blasted into my face, the final roar of the car engine exploding like a cannon as everything around me crumpled in on all sides. Blood. There was blood everywhere. I couldn't move. I couldn't breathe. Every effort to refill my lungs ended with nothing but a rasp. And the pain. Not one inch of me was spared from the devastation. It was as if the vehicle had been put through one of those car crushers from the junkyard—with me still inside.

A strangled gasp next to me fought off the darkness threatening to overwhelm my vision. I could barely manage to move my eyes in the direction. Blaine. Blood masked most of his face, but he was still alive. Barely. Just as his eyes fluttered shut, two bright flashes illuminated the inside of the pulverized cabin.

Something shattered on the other side of Blaine. I tried cocking my head, only I couldn't. More glass splayed out onto my lap. What was left of the driver's window had just been obliterated. Shadows lurked from outside, but I couldn't make them out. What I could though...

A gigantic blade gleamed in the limited moonlight.
"The thief comes only to steal and kill and destroy."

I shot up from the mattress, hands clasped around my throat as I awoke with a violent gasp. Reese startled awake at the sound, and he was at the bedside in an instant. My breathing was so fast and hard, I was practically choking on the air.

"Hey." Reese's voice was low and unnaturally gentle

as he brushed away the sweaty locks of hair plastered to my face. "It's okay. It's okay." Sitting beside me on the mattress, he wrapped his arms around me, continuing to hum the words until my breathing slowed and the threat of wrenching subsided.

"He was still alive," I rasped. "Blaine...someone did that to him *after* the accident."

"Did *what*?" Reese whispered.

"He was decapitated."

His breathing faltered. "Come again?"

"Blaine," I muttered. "I overheard at the funeral that his head got taken clean off...along with other things."

"Are you sure?"

"That's what Danielle told her friends, and her dad's a police sergeant. So if anybody would know-" I shook my head in disbelief. "Who would do that?"

"The question's not *who*, but rather *why*? Someone's clearly out to make an army of Hellhounds. Why kill a perfectly good specimen?"

Whether the room was actually cold or not, I wasn't entirely sure, but a chill had sunken deep into my bones. Laughter. It had been coming from outside the car. Whoever had butchered Blaine had been laughing.

***

I stirred, my eyes burning through the frightening images of my dream state. It took me another second to realize that I was alone. I'd woken up briefly an hour ago to find an arm draped over me, holding me close as I lay nestled on my side. It was the first time I'd seen Reese's hands without his gloves on. His fingers were long and slender and rather elegant, like that of a pianist.

I turned over, greeted by nothing now but a cold bed sheet. Soft taps clanked in the distance, which I figured was Mom probably fiddling with the coffeemaker from the kitchen. Grabbing the tops of the covers draped over my torso, I was about to pull them up further when the theme from *Dracula* suddenly blasted from the nightstand. Receiving texts now had become a new fear of mine, but I breathed a sigh of relief to see Reese's name on the screen.

"I'll be back to pick you up."

Remaking the bed wound up taking me longer than going through my morning routine. Mom was rather anal about the order in which her accent pillows had to be arranged for each bedroom, and for the life of me, I couldn't remember it. Feng Shui was the least of my problems, so I eventually forfeited and just tossed the pillows at random. I just finished slipping on my shoes when my phone rang.

"Hey, I'm out front," announced Reese on the other end of the call.

"Seriously? Now? It's not even six thirty."

Sure enough, the unmistakable throaty purr of the truck's engine resonated from the driveway.

My stomach dropped. "Wait, don't—"

Too late. He'd ended the call. I tried redialing, but he didn't answer.

Not good.

I grabbed my jacket and bolted out into the hallway when the doorbell rang. Just as I reached the top of the stairs, Mom's heels clacked across the foyer.

"I've got it," I called out. "It's for me."

My stomach lurched as I heard the front door open. I made it to the bottom of the landing just in time to see Mom's eyes bore down at Reese like she'd just found a flee-infested mutt on her front steps.

Her smile was devoid of any genuine pleasantry as she asked, "Can I help you?"

Reese flashed a smile of his own, a very warm, boyish grin. "Hi, I'm here to pick up Kat. You must be her mother." He extended his hand, awaiting a handshake he quickly realized wouldn't be returned. "I'm Reese. Reese Blackburn—"

"I know who you are," Mom said curtly. Her eyes gave him a second look-over, and any pretense of a smile vanished as they settled on his jacket. He was wearing the one I'd returned to him, the same one I had worn to the country club. "What business do you have with my daughter?"

"Reese is my new tutor," I cut in, stepping between the two. "And he was kind enough to give me a lift to school, so we can get in an early morning session before class starts."

Mom continued glaring at him. "I thought you said you were all caught up with your schoolwork. Anyways, why can't Vanessa tutor you? She's on the honors society."

"Well, I'm actually in the top five of our graduating class," Reese politely replied.

Even I couldn't help but look at him doubtfully.

"And there's a big exam coming up in Calculus that Kat could really use help on," he added.

That part was true, and I had even mentioned—or more moaned about it—the other morning over breakfast. At last, Mom relented and backed away from the door, allowing me to step past her.

"Don't forget we're hosting the social tonight for the Woodstone. Seven o'clock," she called out as I followed Reese down the driveway. I waved back to signal I understood before climbing into the passenger seat of the pickup as Reese settled behind the wheel.

"Top five in our class?" I laughed quietly.

"What's funny about that?"

I'd learned his tells pretty well by now, and Reese was showing none. Holy crap! He wasn't kidding. "But...how? You don't even go to half your classes!"

He gave a knowing smile. "The only one I don't go to is French, and that's because I'm exempted due to my commitments for the newspaper. I take all the necessary exams during either Lunch or Study Hall. I've got a ninety-eight percent."

"You're serious?"

Reese nodded.

"Well, well, well. You really are full of surprises."

He winked, flooring the truck out of the driveway. "Oh, you have no idea."

We drove down the end of the street, but Reese took an unexpected turn once we hit Main.

"Ah, hate to break it to you, Columbus, but you're going in the wrong direction," I said, pointing behind us. "The school's *that* way."

"Not the one I have in mind." Reese turned onto another road, and I realized where we were going. The highway.

"Care to fill me in?"

"Have you ever heard of Dr. Jonathan Madsen?"

I shook my head.

"He's a theology scholar who just so happens to be holding a lecture at Whitmore University."

"So...?"

"I've got a good feeling," he simply shrugged.

"A feeling?" I gawped. "You're gonna drive a two-hour roundtrip for a 'feeling'?"

"That..." He reached into the backseat and tossed me a paperback. "And this."

"*Decoding Demonology & Occultism,*" I read across the spine. I turned it over, and sure enough, it was written by the good ole doctor.

To our surprise, we managed to make the trip there in less than forty-five minutes. Creighton looked like many of the other New England campus towns I'd visited, filled with quaint village shops and grocery markets next to multileveled banks and hotels. Monuments of men dressed in colonial clothing rested on various street corners as several artillery cannons greeted us on the lawn of the local library. And I wasn't entirely sure which period they were supposedly a part of. Maine seemed to house memorials from many wars spanning over multiple centuries. Most of Mystic Harbor's monuments were in dedication to the Civil War, but other places also paid tribute to everything from the American Revolution, the French & Indian Wars, and even Aroostook.

We at last rolled up to a set of opened filigree gates with the word Cumberland inscribed into the rote iron workings. Taking the long, winding road north, the front of the magnificent building eventually came into view. The place looked more like a freaking castle than a college. Just like Belleview High, Whitmore was an old school, only much bigger. A stone façade and gigantic columns loomed overhead as we parked the car. Reese reached over me to open his glove box, fetching out what looked like an ankle brace of some sort.

"I want you to carry this," he confirmed, plucking out a dagger from inside his jacket.

"Seriously?" I wasn't the biggest fan of knives to begin with, and after what I'd done to Brittany, it was the last thing I wanted to ever have to use.

"It's better to have what you don't need." He slid the knife into what I now realized was a holster. Relenting, I rolled up the end of my pant leg, letting him strap it around my ankle before we headed into the building.

Inside past the massive oak main doors sat gleaming marble floors, a rich crimson area rug, and soaring ceilings fit for a Renaissance cathedral. A bulletin board hung nestled in the corner, and a map of the school was printed on the right side. I headed over to it, but just as I approached, a flash of imagery swept into my vision.

"What is it?" asked Reese.

"I'm not sure..." I turned around and froze at the advertisement board in front of me.

"Folklore & Anthropology Seminar, Speaker Dr. Jonathan Madsen," read big, bold letters.

For the first time in a long while, I actually felt like I was on the right track. We asked one of the students if they knew where Dr. Madsen was teaching, and he directed us to the east wing. Sculpted vaulted ceilings and warm wall sconces made up every hallway inside with carved stone and woodwork only emphasizing the school's regality. Finding the lecture hall in question, I slowly pulled open the back door upon hearing the commanding voice talking on the other side.

"The Book of Enoch referenced demons as the evil spirits of the Nephilim. These were the half-breed offspring of human women and the male angels that fell from Lucifer's rebellion. Christian theology suggests that demons are the spirits of evil angels. Others will say that they're malevolent specters that were once human. And some even suggest that demons were created by the hands of Satan himself."

Reese and I quietly crept into the back row of the stadium raised seats, taking focus to the man standing center at the pitched floor below by the projector. Dr. Madsen looked exactly like his photo on the placard with the exception that his hair was now a little longer, still neatly slicked back. He put up a number of slides on the overhead, asking the class if they could identify each of the depictions shown above. Students chimed in, listing off a number of demons from Caim, Balam, Paimon, Azazel, and so on. All of which I knew nothing about.

"Does anyone know what this represents?" Madsen asked next as he put up a drawing of a pentagram with a star and goat head placed in the middle. He had an accent I couldn't quite ascertain. Perhaps Dutch or Danish.

A girl raised her hand, and he called on her. "It's considered a diabolical symbol."

He nodded in agreement. "Yes, it is. Do you know why?"

"When inverted, the pentagram mocks the five holy wounds of Christ," she replied. "Same as an upside-down cross."

"Correct. But the inverted cross simply signifies one's denial of Christ. This pentagram has a particular function, one that's been used since the Middle Ages," said Dr. Madsen. "Does anyone know its purpose?"

Everybody quietly exchanged glances, but no one raised their hand.

"Nobody?"

I hesitantly lifted my hand.

"Yes, the girl in the back."

"Circle of Containment?" I suggested, seeing the

blatant similarities to the one I'd seen while Reese had been flipping through one of his dad's journals.

His eyebrows piqued. "No, but that's a very good guess. It's actually a Conjuration Sigil. There's a reason why knowing a demon's name is so important. Containment Sigils are used to permanently exorcise a demon from a person by calling out the spirit's true name. With a Conjuration Sigil, it has the opposite effect. When a conjuror draws this symbol and calls upon the demon by name, it summons that particular demon to that very spot, meaning you now have control over it."

Madsen flipped the lights back, making us all wince at the sudden brightness. "If you have any questions, feel free to ask. My door's always open."

Here was our chance.

"Excuse me, Doctor Madsen," I said, as sweetly as I could. It was important we didn't draw any extra attention. "Do you have a moment?"

He looked up from the materials he was gathering up and smiled back. "I think I could spare one. What's on your mind?"

I looked over at Reese, suddenly unsure as to how I should word this. "This might sound odd, but..."

"We were wondering if you could tell us what this might be," Reese stepped in, placing a sketch out on the desk.

My eyes shot back up at Reese. He mentioned how he liked to draw, but I had no idea he was that good. He'd rendered an exact illustration of the creature from the boiler room.

Madsen paused for a second before reaching out for

the drawing.

"It's for a graphic novel we're working on," added Reese as casually as he could. "We just want to be thorough, so I guess we were just curious if you'd ever come across anything in your research that might look like this."

The doctor studied the image. "You know, I just might have."

Reese and I both shared an excited glance, trying to repress from outwardly sighing.

"I'll have to take a look through my studies, of course. And I have another lecture starting shortly, but if you have time later..."

"Yeah, that'd be great."

Reese and I spent the next hour or so roaming campus before heading to the library as we were instructed. Whitmore's library proved to be just as magnificent as the rest of the school, if not more. Cathedral vaulted ceilings rested overhead, intricate stone and oak paneling filled the walls with detailed carvings of angels, numerous candelabra wall sconces lit the outside aisles of the bookshelves, and the floor was brightly polished marble.

A librarian directed us to a small oak furnished room at the back of the library behind a section of studying tables where Madsen was already waiting. We headed inside, and the doctor closed the door behind us.

He'd taken the chair beside the entrance, so Reese and I took our places on the other side of the research table. Madsen suddenly lobbed a coin at the both of us. We each caught them, seeing intricate patterns embossed on the surfaces.

"Well, you're not Hellhounds, so that's at least an

upside."

The coin. It was made of silver. "How did you-"

An unmistakable click registered in front of us, and we both paled as we raised our heads to the good ole doctor…and the barrel of the gun now aimed between us.

So much for a good 'feeling'.

CHAPTER 24
Fallen

Reese and I slowly drew up our hands.

"I wouldn't recommend doing that," my companion said. "Everyone saw us walk in here. The moment you shoot, they'll sound the alarm. They'll know it was you."

"That's where you're mistaken. They won't, because they won't hear any of it," remarked the doctor, nodding overhead. We angled our heads to see the gigantic face of a clock. The second hand moved, but no typical ticking was being produced.

"You put a ward over the room," Reese gritted.

"A what?" I murmured.

"Magic. It prevents anyone from eavesdropping so long as they're outside the projected range," he clarified. Like what Reese had used in our own school's library.

"Magic?" My eyes traveled to the doctor's left arm, and the man immediately withdrew it from the table surface. "You're a...a Mage."

"And this is loaded with bullets made from Angelorum steel," growled Madsen, repositioning the gun on me. "Doesn't matter what you are. I pull the trigger; you die."

"It seems we got off on the wrong foot here," I said

shakily. "All we wanted was a few answers."

He smirked, but there was no amusement behind his eyes. "This isn't my first rodeo, girl." The doctor cocked his head, looking to Reese. "Interesting accessory you're sporting there."

Reese looked down bemusedly at the vintage pocket watch hanging from his vest.

"I meant the inside." Madsen gestured to his jacket. "You should do a better job concealing your hardware if you really wish to play junior assassin."

I gave a sideways glance, and sure enough, I could see the outline of one of Reese's blades resting against his torso through the fabric.

Crap.

"Let me take a wild guess; your Regent sent you two to knock me off. Is that it?"

"Our...Regent?" I looked to Reese again for clarification.

"Sir, we're not Reapers. We don't have an affiliation." The doctor sneered, but Reese slowly raised his left hand higher until the fabric of his sleeve fell down his forearm, revealing the metallic ink.

"By the Angel..." The doctor heaved a relieved sigh. That is, until he turned his attention to me. "What about you?"

"Same," confirmed Reese.

"I'd show you, but I'm kind of afraid to move," I said weakly, still seeing the gun aimed at me.

Madsen finally had the decency to lower it, allowing us to drop our hands as well. Reese removed his jacket and rolled up his sleeve, showing the doctor his runes. Madsen returned the gesture, and I could make out several matching symbols on each of their arms. None of which I had.

"How did you find me?" asked Madsen.

"We weren't looking for you, per se. We just wanted to know if anybody could tell us what that thing is," said Reese, nodding to his sketch on top of the table.

"Why do you want to know?"

"Because it attacked us."

Any relief the doctor had vanished. "How did you fend it off?"

We shared another puzzled side-glance. "We don't really know what happened. It just kind of…vanished."

Madsen settled back in his seat, his skin going gray. "It's a spectral warrior called the Moraine, recognized as a chief assassin and henchman of the Underworld. The Moraine is known for maiming and paralyzing its victims before devouring their livers, and it can only be summoned or recalled by its master. The high prince of Hell, Sitri."

"A demon?"

"Dark Mage."

My blood ran cold. "And he's the only one who could get the Moraine to leave?"

Madsen nodded, but with hesitation. "Sitri, and whoever may bear his mark."

"His mark?"

"It's said to be something of tradition. The emblem is used to herald someone as his mate."

You're marked. That's what Brittany had said.

The hooded stranger in the parking lot.

He had runes. Runes that my own had responded to.

I could feel Reese's eyes burning a hole through my profile.

"Have you ever seen this before?" asked Reese, his voice crackling over the words. He handed over his phone with the image of the scorched symbol burned into the boiler room wall.

Madsen swallowed hard. "That's it. That's the mark." He dragged a hand over his face. "Has anything else happened? Anything out of the ordinary? Increased demonic activity? Any other spectral figures?"

My chest tightened the moment Reese opened his mouth. Would he tell him? Could we really trust Madsen?

"An entire bus of students disappeared a few weeks back. One of those students was killed a couple nights ago, and two more kids were turned into Hellhounds. We don't know what happened to the rest." Reese swiped to the other photo I'd forwarded from Adam. "And this was left at yet another murder."

"It's a sacrificial ceremony of some sort. A summoning like this would only be used to break one of Hell's seals. I can't make out the inscriptions though." Madsen's entire body shuddered at the mere image. "If Sitri's mark is topside, then it means he already is as well. Whatever his plan is, this is only the beginning. More creatures like the Moraine will come."

"What do you mean a 'seal'?" asked Reese.

"Unholy power resides in Hell. The only way to bring it here would be to break the spell binding it there. Every seal has a specific code that needs to be unlocked for it to work." Madsen studied the picture all the more. "Given the Moraine's unfortunate appearance, it's safe to say that Sitri performed that ceremony to bring that beast here."

"Who is he?" I finally managed to ask, feeling my insides constricting tighter and tighter. "Sitri, I mean."

The doctor began to speak, but abruptly stopped. A glimmer of understanding flickered in his eyes as he studied me. Studied the fear that even my strongest mask could not conceal. "May I see your arm?"

I didn't move. Couldn't move.

"Please." There was an inexplicable sense of earnestness in his gaze. He knew what it was like to be hunted. He knew what it was like to live in constant fear. He knew what I was. Madsen rounded the table, kneeling in front of me.

"Kat…" Reese's voice was barely audible.

Despite my apprehension, I gave Madsen my arm. His fingers caressed my wrist, steadying the slight tremble that rattled through the limb as he pushed up my sleeve with his other hand. His eyes became pensive as he rotated my arm, taking in every symbol.

His lips tightened, his face going taut at the sight. He wasn't afraid. He was…concerned. Concerned for me. For a stranger.

A single tear escaped down my cheek. "What are they?"

"They're Enochian runes."

Reese pinched his eyes shut.

"It's the language of the Fallen. Of the angels banished from paradise. I recognize several of their etchings. Like this one." His fingers traveled over the upside-down Y. "It's Naudiz."

I just looked at him blankly.

"The omen rune. It reacts to impending distress." Madsen finally held my gaze. "You weren't born a Mage, were you?"

I shook my head, feeling that foreign energy pulsating beneath my skin. Beneath his mark.

"Hey." Madsen gently tipped my chin up, as if reading the thought right inside my eyes. "You may have been marked by darkness, but you still have humanity in you. You haven't been claimed."

"*Claimed?*"

"Bitten," answered Reese. "You haven't been infected with the demonic virus."

"Exactly." Madsen tugged my sleeve back down. "Sitri may have imprinted on you, but he chose not to turn you. Not yet anyway. It may be a mercy, but it's a highly feeble one. The moment he finds it suitable, he'll come for you."

"Is there a way to stop him?"

"Apart from killing him, probably not. And that won't be easy, especially considering that no one knows what he even looks like. But he appears to be working on a schedule of some sort if he didn't wish to claim you when he had the chance. If you put a damper on his plans, it might buy you more time to find out who he is."

And kill him.

CHAPTER 25
Broken

I had underestimated how many journals Reese's father had kept. It was the freaking Encyclopædia Britannica of demonology and folklore. No wonder it took Reese so long trying to find anything. Unlike the Encyclopædia however, these journals didn't have any real organization to them. It was all very random. One page would talk about a particular demon; the next would be about how to exorcise a different one entirely. It seemed his father just documented everything as he went along, which didn't make research particularly easy. When we returned to Mystic Harbor, we spent the rest of the school day in his basement, flipping through the countless volumes to no avail. Not one mention of Sitri.

Great, some evil lord of the Underworld had deemed me as his hellish bride, and I hadn't the slightest clue who I was dealing with. The question kept gnawing at me, relentless in its pursuit to find an answer.

Why me?

Why did this demonic prince pick *me* of all people?

If he was looking for an evil, malicious bitch that thrived on unholy power, surely he would've targeted Ava Ashford. Instead, I was the lucky winner to be bound to a scaly red-skinned creature with horns. At least, that's what I was picturing.

And the journals were only reinforcing my fears. Every depiction of a demon in its natural form included dragon wings, a serpent tail, a goat's head, or worse.

I mentioned to Madsen of my recent discovery concerning my parentage, and he didn't seem particularly surprised given the circumstances. Blood Magic appeared to be the most powerful form of sorcery known to man, and specific individuals held more powerful blood based on their lineage. The chance I was linked to at least the girl killed in the summoning ceremony seemed highly likely. If her blood was significant enough to enact dark magic, then certainly a Mage with that same blood in their veins would prove to be most formidable. I'd been engineered into becoming the perfect weapon.

"Got him." Reese's voice startled me out of my stupor as he sat down beside me on his mattress.

I crooked a brow at him, seeing the title on the book page opened in his hands. "Bitru?"

He lobbed the journal at me. "Keep reading."

"Sitri, commonly referred to by rank as Bitru, is a Great Prince of Hell and the leader of sixty-six legions of demons. As a demigod of darkness and chaos, he uses trickery and deception to create pandemonium wherever he may go. Sitri is also blessed with the ability of foresight, making his wisdom the prime temptation to summon him. It is highly advised not to attempt conjuring this Prince however, given that his powers of persuasion are often used against those who summon him. His influence is nearly impossible to resist, thus turning anyone he captivates into his unwitting servant. He is the Crown Prince of Lust and is said to be dangerously charming and unnaturally handsome." My eyes continued scanning the page, feeling the knot in my stomach expand to the size of a baseball as I read a particular passage. "One of his many skills is illusion, in which he can disguise himself as anyone he chooses. Furthermore, he can take possession of any human vessel, but it can hold nothing more than a fraction of his potential. Only upon claiming his rightful mate can he take his true form, therefore unleashing his supreme power and wrath upon mankind…"

My hands fell limp in my lap, forcing Reese to take back the book before it slid from my grasp.

Well, this was just dandy. It wasn't like I was expecting Sitri to be the ruler of teddy bears, puppies, and rainbows, but really?

"Makes sense why the Moraine wanted me dead, and why Sitri didn't bother bringing back Blaine," said Reese. "There's no room for possible competition, seeing as how *you're* the key to breaking his final seal."

"I'm *what*?"

"When his so-called 'mate' is marked, she apparently has to go through something known as the Great Rite. It's a multilevel ritual of some kind that's used to unlock the seal trapping Sitri's power in Hell."

I fell back against the mattress, jamming a pillow over my face.

"I don't think asphyxiation is the answer," Reese chuckled.

The weight of the bed shifted, and I could feel the heat from his body running down my entire left side. I finally pulled the pillow away, turning over to see that Reese was indeed lying next to me. "What is the answer, then? We have no idea how to find Sitri. Even if we come across a black-eyed person, how can we tell if it's actually *him* and not just another run-of-the-mill demon? I doubt he's gonna be sauntering around with his runes on display."

"If Sitri is as strong as these texts suggest, he probably won't have black eyes anyway," Reese sighed inwardly, lobbing the journal to the side. "He'll be able to conceal his demonic nature, even from the likes of us." I moaned again, ready to slam his pillow back over my face when he caught hold of it and ripped it away. "We've got time to figure it out. The Great Rite can only be performed during a Sanguine lunar cycle.

"A what-what-what?"

"A Blood Moon," he clarified, "which isn't marked on any foreseeable calendar. We'll figure it out, okay?"

"*How?* If he's that powerful and clever, he could possess anyone! Hell, he could be you for all I know."

The widest smile broke out across Reese's face. "Is that what you think?"

"Well, you *have* been uncharacteristically pleasant to me lately," I jabbed, trying to snatch back his pillow. He extended his arm away teasingly, leaving it just out of my reach. "And how do I know that you're not using some unholy power to mask your *real* runes?"

"So you're accusing me of being the Crown Prince of Lust now?"

"Perhaps I am." I laughed at my attempt to wrestle his arm back towards me. It was no use. He didn't concede so much as an inch.

He continued staring at me with that fixated grin of his, chuckling at my pitiful effort. "Having some trouble?"

"Against your abnormal brute strength? Yeah." I sat up and reached over him, but his arms were so much longer than mine that I still didn't stand a chance of regaining the pillow from this position.

"As for the other things?" Reese further prodded.

"What other things?"

"Do you find me 'dangerously charming'?" he quoted.

"You can be, when you want."

"And 'unnaturally handsome'?"

"Perhaps," I laughed, my fingers grappling at a corner of the pillow as I lay over him.

Reese rolled over, taking me with him in the process. Tossing playful elbows, we tried wrestling the pillow from each other's grasp until our scuffling sent it toppling off the bedside. Reese's whole body went rigid, and I looked down to realize why. I was straddling him at the waist, our faces mere inches apart. "Is that right?" He'd suddenly gone breathy.

My long blonde tendrils cascaded around his face, and his tattooed hand reached up, sweeping away one side of the locks behind my neck. His fingers rested on my nape, the delicate caress urging me closer.

The theme from *Psycho* suddenly blared beside us on the bed, instinctively setting me upright. "Shit," I murmured.

"What is it?" Reese could see my phone lighting up, but clearly couldn't see who was calling. "Is it *Unknown*?"

"Worse," I confirmed. I didn't need to see the screen. I'd specifically set the individualized ringtone to that chilling theme, because it seemed the most appropriate as of late. "It's my mom."

"You tell her yet about your blood work?"

I shook my head.

I didn't have time to even answer before she sneered, *"Where the hell are you?"* on the other end.

"Out."

"Well, I need you to get back home! The social starts in an hour. Did you remember to pick up your dress?"

"My *what?*"

A professional string of expletives followed. "I ordered you a new dress from Collette's over two weeks ago just for the occasion. I left you how many reminders!"

I immediately groaned. "Is this really necessary? I mean, this is like the thousandth dress you've gotten me, and I've only ever worn them once. Besides, none of the girls are gonna be there. Kelsey and V are working tonight, and Carly's with the student council to set up for the Homecoming Dance tomorrow. It's not like anyone's gonna miss me if I'm not there."

"Carly's in an after-school activity?" whispered Reese, trying not to laugh as my mom continued ranting on the other end.

"Car already said she was gonna clock in an hour and then bail," I confirmed, holding my hand over the cell's speaker. "She's just using it as an excuse to get out of having to go tonight."

"Smart girl."

"I don't care what Carly's doing. Her mom's not running for Regency President! What you do is very much a reflection on *me*," she growled. "And don't even think of bringing that boy! You've done enough damage as it is."

Reese's amusement quickly turned into a scowl.

"Trust me, I won't," I countered, feeling him stiffen all the more. "I wouldn't subject anyone as decent as him to your special breed of torture."

A ghost of a smile returned. "Stay," he mouthed.

I wanted to say I was strong enough to stand my ground, but one mention of Stewart's Landing had me woefully waving my white flag. Though Reese had been kind enough to take me to Collette's before dropping me off at home, he still hadn't spoken a word since we left his place.

Sure enough, Mom was waiting at the front door, her arms crossed over her chest as the old beater truck rumbled into the driveway. I mumbled a quiet thanks to Reese and climbed out of the cabin. Mom had some choice words, but they fell on deaf ears as I shoved past her.

It took me a good ten minutes just fussing with the special coverage concealer I had picked up at the store to hide my runes. After that, I fixed up my hair, freshened my makeup, and slipped into the incredible champagne colored cocktail dress Mom had chosen. I hated it. She had apparently ordered it with boning built in, and the midsection was corseted with absolutely no give. I was pretty sure it was crushing my internal organs.

A knock registered at the door, and I groaned. "I'll be down in a sec!"

Another knock.

"For the love of God, *what*?" I practically pried the door off its hinges, only to be met with striking amber eyes. "*Reese*?" When he didn't make a move, I snatched him by the lapels and yanked him inside. "What are you doing? If my mom sees you—"

He just shrugged, shoving his hands into the pockets of his jacket. "I walked right past her. She didn't even blink."

"Congratulations," I groaned, disappearing into the closet. I sifted through the entire shoe collection, and still no luck. Where did I put those blasted heels?

I came back out into the room to scour the floor when my gaze traveled over to the bed. Reese was lying atop it, his upper half propped up by his elbows. The look would have been sexy...if not for the icy glare he returned as his eyes kept traveling over my body.

"What? You don't like it?" I motioned to the dress, expecting some kind of reaction. A smirk, an eye roll, something. But Reese's expression remained hardened. I attempted a feeble laugh, but the effort honestly hurt. Surely, this bodice was going to crack a rib cage. *"What?"*

"You look ridiculous," he scowled. "And in a great deal of pain."

"What's that old saying? 'If it doesn't hurt, it doesn't help.'" I sighed, still seeing no give in his temper. "It's really not that bad. I've honestly had to wear worse."

"Why?"

"Why what?"

"Why do you keep doing this to yourself?" His words bit like a rattle snake. I actually retreated back a step. "I understand that you don't want to disappoint your mother, but dressing up like some haughty debutante isn't going to win her affection."

It was as if he slapped me across the face. "You do what you have to for the people you love."

"And what has she done for you lately, besides threatening to ship you away?" Reese's gaze hardened all the more. "It's no wonder you haven't said anything about your blood work."

My breathing hitched, but I pushed past the growing lump in my throat. "She's one of the elite in this town. As she said, what I do is a reflection on her, and this means a lot to my mom."

"A party? That's worth bullying your own daughter over?"

"You don't get it," I finally snapped. "What else does my mom have? I haven't lived with her for most of my adolescent years, her husband spends more time away on business than he does at home, I'm going away to college next year, and she hasn't had a job in nearly twenty years. She's lonely. But I see the way her face lights up when people congratulate her on things like this. I don't want to take that away from her. It's the only time she's ever happy anymore."

He scoffed. "So bragging rights, then? It all makes sense now."

"What?"

"Everything. Like, for instance, why you don't have a bedroom," he clarified, noting my puzzled expression. "Sure, this is a room with a mattress and a closet and a door, but it's not a bedroom. A real teenager's bedroom has posters and movies and collages of your friends. The whole house looks like something right out of a luxury designer's catalog. It's fancy, but not the least bit inviting."

"That's not true."

"Really?" He motioned overhead. "What the hell is that?"

"A...light."

"It's a chandelier. And not an inexpensive one, I gather."

I could feel my cheeks blushing, but why? "Just because you have an apparent allergy to nice things doesn't make them cold. I happen to like my room."

"Tell me, what makes this different from the guest bedroom we stayed in last night?"

I opened my mouth, but I didn't have a rebuttal. Instead, I pushed past him and headed over to the dresser, rummaging through my jewelry box in search of the earrings Mom had told me to wear.

"What about the Wall of Achievement? Was that your

idea, too?" he further remarked, gesturing to the very wall next to me. The entire section of the room was decked out with all the framed award plaques alongside a lengthy shelve of every trophy and medal I'd ever won. "You know what I think?"

"If I say yes, will you go away?" I bit, turning to face him.

He slinked over, his shoulders drawn like a lion stalking his prey. I instinctively recoiled, my back hitting the frontend of the dresser. He stopped only once there was virtually no space even left between us.

"When was the last time someone asked you what *you* wanted?" His breath fell onto my lips as I angled my head upright to look at him, my eyes stealing a glance at his mouth.

"Why are you doing this?"

He braced his hands on either side of me, trapping me in as his fingers gripped the dresser top. Taking a small step back, he lowered his frame and leaned in, meeting me eye to eye. "Doing what?"

I wanted to kick myself again for marveling at his mouth. The admiration didn't go unnoticed either, because heat flashed in his eyes.

"Let go." He said the words almost breathlessly as he drew closer, leaving nothing but a fraction of an inch between us.

"Kat!" called out my mom's voice from downstairs. "Get a move on. The Andersons just pulled up front!"

Reese shut his eyes, his grip contracting around me. I whispered a pardon to him, but he only growled. "Don't."

"Reese, I have to go."

His features hardened as he finally looked at me. "You don't *have* to do anything."

"Please move."

Reese's arm disappointingly fell back to his sides as he straightened. "Why do you keep letting yourself be used like a puppet?"

"Excuse me?"

"You do everything everybody tells you to do, because you're so afraid to disappoint someone. What do you want?"

A clamp tightened around my chest. Blaine had asked me the same thing. Had inspired me to break free from all the polite, societal bullshit. Its answer had been the very thing that convinced me to go to the bonfire instead of Mom's last fundraiser. And that stupid decision had cost him his life.

Feeling red hot tears burning the back of my eyes, I plowed past Reese, grabbing a random pair of heels off the floor. "I don't have time for this."

"Yes, because you can't flaunt a trophy around unless it's perfectly polished," he growled.

"What is your problem?"

"This isn't you."

"How would you know? You don't know me!" I sneered.

"Perhaps you're right." His voice was low and riddled with ire. I could hear my pulse pounding again in my ears. "Perhaps I misunderstood the girl I met that night at the theater, because I never believed her to be some Barbie doll with a spine of a collapsible folding chair."

Any apprehension I had drained from me immediately. The inside of my arm radiated with such intensity that the makeup couldn't conceal the burning blue light. I dropped the heels in my hand. The air resounded with the deafening wallop as my hand smacked Reese across the face. The slap jolted his head to the side. I waited for him to react, seeing his cheek already reddening from the impact. But he didn't say anything.

Chocolate-hued strands hanged in his eyes, casting shadows across his features as he slowly turned to face me. Anger surged through me again as Reese wordlessly moved in closer. I retracted, trying to keep some distance between us, but my back hit the wall. I slammed my hands against his chest to push him back. He didn't budge.

His breathing remained steadied, but it grew heavier, stirring the ends of my hair. He was too close.

My hand grew readily hotter, and without a second thought, I took another swing at him. It stopped a mere inch from connecting with his face. He'd caught hold of my wrist. I brought up my other hand, but he claimed that one too. I writhed under him, forcing Reese to pin both of my hands against the wall. The space between us was nothing more than a slither that disappeared against our ragged breaths as our chests heaved. I nearly screamed at the dress's boning piercing into my sides.

Reese kept scanning my face, seeming to calculate my next move. Waiting for me to kick or thrash or yell. But I didn't move. His eyes lost their edge, replaced by an unnerving softness. Without warning, I stood on my tiptoes and pressed my lips to his.

His mouth immediately molded to mine. This wasn't a chaste, innocent kiss. Not like how our first one had started out. Each of our lips was demanding and fierce, and neither of us was pulling away. Reese's grip around my wrists slowly eased, sliding up to my hands to interlock our fingers. It wasn't enough.

I ripped my hands free from his, only to find my fingernails digging into the taut muscles between his shoulder blades. His left hand settled on the small of my back, pressing me completely against him as his other hand cupped the side of my face. We were wholly flush, his touch scorching every inch of me.

My mother's shrill demand rattled me free from my ecstatic delirium as she barked my name so loudly, it even startled Reese. His fingers caressed the curve of my cheek, brushing away a stray strand of hair that toppled into my face.

One last kiss, and he finally pulled away. I opened my mouth to protest, but he was already opening the door. "Let me know if you ever change your mind."

Left in the desolation of my bedroom, I looked to the heels resting on the floor. Time to face the music...

CHAPTER 26
Love is Blindness

"Kat, there you are." Mom sighed, but the breath faltered upon her doing a double take. The color drained from her face as she weaved her way through the small crowd at the foot of the stairs.

The other ladies followed her line of vision, and Mrs. Hoffmann coughed as I suspected she choked on some gourmet cracker spread. Yep, nailed the outfit. I'd splurged at a vintage clothing store in New York during our last family trip, and the lonely articles had been sitting in the back of my closet collecting dust for the past eight months with nowhere appropriate to take them out.

Leather leggings, spiked stilettos, a studded leather jacket, fingerless riding gloves, an onslaught of eyeliner, and an off the shoulder Sex Pistols graphic t-shirt. Sure enough, Mom looked like she was about to have a heart attack.

"Honey," she gritted through a forced smile. "What on earth are you wearing?"

I batted my eyelashes innocently. "What? You don't like it?"

"I hardly find it appropriate for the party." Her eyes

flared, and on any other day in my life, the look would have petrified me to my very core.

"That's alright," I retorted. "I'm not staying."

Mom grabbed me, her talon-like false nails digging into my leather clad arm as she tried dragging me away. I didn't move. "If you honestly think after a stunt like this that you're not going back to Stewart's Landing, you've got another thing coming," she growled under her breath. "One word to your father—"

"'True love should never come with conditions.' But since you've made your position so clear, I'll make mine. Two words to Dad, and I'll be the least of your problems." Her face scrunched in confusion as I leaned in, lowering my voice. "David Monaghan."

Her grip immediately fell away.

"Perhaps I'll spare a few more words for better clarity, like 'Room 731 at the Biltmore, Monday's at one.'" A familiar tingling warmth curled around my left arm as I watched the blood drain completely from her face until she was paler than egg shells. I plucked up a chocolate covered strawberry from a nearby serving dish. "Don't wait up for me."

And just like that, I strolled right past her and through the gawping crowds of stunned onlookers.

"Have a good one, ladies," I cheerily called out, sauntering to the door.

***

The familiar trek through the West End took me to the front entrance of a quaint cottage where a rusty old beater truck sat parked in the driveway. Galloping up to the porch, I rang the doorbell, startled at the chime. Beethoven's fifth symphony echoed from inside. Not ten seconds later did a shadow pass the entryway's draped window. The door eased open.

Reese's gaze immediately dropped, scoping every inch of me. "Wow."

My blood red lips stretched, and he shook his head.

"I mean, hi." He laughed, but it was breathy.

"May I come in?"

He leaned a forearm against the doorframe, as if to bar me passage, but his impish grin was all fox. "What if I say no?"

There wasn't a moment of hesitation. My fingers gripped the lapels of his jacket, pulling him down to me. Before any sense of rationality had a chance to catch up with my body, I crushed my mouth against his.

For the longest moment of my life, he didn't react. I finally pulled away to see him looking back at me in complete astonishment. And timidity finally crashed into me.

What was I doing?

My face heated with embarrassment as I turned to head down the front porch when his hand grabbed my wrist. In an instant, I was spun back around, finding Reese right in front of me. He drew me in through the doorway until our bodies were flush against each other as his lips captured mine.

A thrilling wave of electricity swept through all my extremities, inciting the shiver that had me gasping. His kiss deepened, and every inch of me went flush as his hands trailed up my sides. My own hands pulled at his jacket, forcing it off his shoulders. He haphazardly tossed both our jackets at the coat rack in the corner, immediately taking control of my waist. I fiddled with the front of his crimson brocade vest, undoing each notch blindly as his mouth softly grazed over my lips.

With one swift motion, Reese kicked the front door closed, pinning my body against it. The cool October air penetrating the steel surface only reminded me of just how much every cell of me was on fire. I needed him. I wanted him. I wanted every inch of him on me.

As if reading my mind, he picked me up so effortlessly, it was as if I weighed nothing more than a feather. Reese pushed off the wall, and my legs wrapped around his waist as he carried me through the foyer into the family room, setting me down on the empty couch.

Soft leather greeted my back, and I gasped as he laid his body over mine. "Wait…"

He finally pulled away, his vibrant eyes wide with apprehension. "What's wrong?"

I actually cringed for not having thought of it before. "Your mom isn't home, is she?"

He smiled beamingly down at me. "You really think I'd be doing this if she was?"

A shudder rippled through him as my fingers grazed the hard contours of his stomach. The deep, desperate moan resonating from the back of his throat only incited my hands to further explore his body. He pulled himself up enough to remove his vest, unbuttoning his dress shirt as well.

Reese's peculiar choice in fashion had definitely accentuated the slightness of his frame more than I would have guessed. Quite deceptively so, because underneath the layers of clothing was a slender, yet handsomely well-toned abdomen.

"You know, I think my mom was right," I whispered, trying to bite back my smile. "You really are trouble."

"Is that right?"

"Yeah, but my favorite kind."

Reese chuckled, laying back over me as I slid the shirt off his shoulders.

We both laughed, and my smile didn't cease as his fingers slid under the hem of my shirt. Arching my back, he eased the fabric up and slid the shirt out over my head. His lips caressed my neck, and he took his time as they descended to my collarbone. His hand gripped my thigh, and my fingers teased through his hair. Reese eagerly retraced his path, meeting my lips once again. His kiss deepened, and I had to fight off the impulse to moan as the skin on top of my hand tingled.

Just as my nails began to dig into his upper back, a series of blasts erupted from all around us, and the entire room was swallowed up by darkness. Asides from parting our lips, Reese and I remained stock-still in place, wholly clueless as to what just happened.

Reese sighed, fingering the glowing blue rune on top of my hand, the only source of light now. "Did you just...?"

I opened my mouth, but I wasn't sure what to say. Had I really taken out the electricity?

I followed his gaze to the stand beside the sofa, seeing flecks of shattered glass strewn all across the tabletop. The light bulb set within the lamp had burst. Reese retracted off me and we both surveyed the room in the limited light. Every last bulb had literally exploded.

But it wasn't just the room. Even the street light at the end of the driveway was out. Reese headed out to the front porch for a better view down the stretch. "The whole block is pitch-black."

Looking out into the black oblivion of the property sent chills raking up my spine. The feeling only worsened when Reese tried to call the electric company. Neither of our phones had service. Reese was more curious than concerned, insisting we take a trip to see how far this electrical disruption had hit. The entire West End was down. Not one house or store had service. It wasn't until we drove to the mall that we saw any signs of electricity.

Though the parking lot was completely shrouded in darkness, we could see lights on inside through the windowed entranceway. It wasn't until we headed in that we realized it was just the emergency reserve lights that were working. Despite the venture being a bust, Reese and I couldn't help but find amusement in our surroundings. We outright laughed at the hysteria breaking out across the storefronts. It seemed that some of the cash registers weren't backed up to an emergency power source, and irate customers like Mrs. Madison couldn't grasp the logic as to why their credit cards wouldn't work at the check-out counter.

Reese slinked up behind me and ensnared me into a hug, kissing my neck as we headed across the upper deck overlooking the plaza. A few familiar faces from school did a double take at us, and one girl even pointed.

"I told you," sneered her friend. "They were probably going at it again in the dressing room."

Reese buried another laugh into my shoulder, silently confirming my suspicions that he, too, had heard the rumors circulating about us.

"Oh, you have no idea," I purred, running my hand through his hair. I even threw a wink at the girls, leaving their jaws agape in disbelief.

We managed to keep our composure long enough to round the corner, only to burst out laughing once the coast was clear.

"You see their faces?"

Reese drew me in, burying my laugh with a teasing kiss. "You're a very bad girl, you know that?"

"No, I'm just happy to not give a damn," I corrected, sighing as I felt my cell vibrating for the billionth time. Curiosity finally got the better of me, because I pried it out of my purse.

"Your mom?" Reese safely guessed.

Only...it wasn't. "No, it's my dad."

Never a good sign. Mom must have started a five-alarm fire to actually incite Dad's concern.

I tried muzzling the annoyance in my voice to a minimal as I answered with a curt, "Hello?"

I was met with a string of expletives on the other end. Not a promising start to a conversation.

"Is she there?" I could hear Mom howl in the background.

"What's up, guys?" I replied in an absurdly sugary tone that only made Reese snort back a laugh.

"The police are here. That's *what's up*!" Dad barked.

"Come again?"

"They're here to see *you*," he snapped.

"What for?"

"They're looking for Riley—"

"Reese," Mom corrected angrily. "His name's *Reese*. They're looking for Reese."

"Again, *why*?"

"From what we can tell, they're looking to arrest him for Casey Radley's murder," Mom sneered, obviously having taken the phone away from Dad. "Please tell me you're not with him."

I hung up.

"Kat?"

I staggered back a step, out of Reese's hold.

"Hey, what's wrong?"

"We have to go," I muttered.

"Why? What happened?"

"You're being framed for murder."

CHAPTER 27
Whispering

"You don't seriously expect me to turn myself in?" Reese protested.

"I know you didn't do it," I clarified, trying to pull him towards the frozen escalator.

"Yeah, but they sure as hell don't," he growled, planting his feet firmly in place. It didn't matter how hard I yanked on his arm. He didn't budge. "Wait...how do *you* know?"

"Well, I'm really not in the habit of making out with suspected serial killers for starters. Secondly, I saw the police report that Carly's contact sent her. Casey was killed somewhere between eight and nine that night. The same night you took me to that restaurant. You didn't drop me off until a quarter to ten. I'm your alibi."

Knowing how the cops operated in this town, even I had to admit I wasn't overly comfortable with the situation. But what else were we going to do? If Reese ran, it would only make him look guiltier. He finally relented, following behind me.

All it took was one face though to wipe away any

other thought. I slammed to a halt, causing Reese to crash into my back.

"*Kat?*" Reese called out to me as I turned around and pushed my way back through the crowds, but I didn't stop.

I finally reached the passerby in question, grabbing his arm and spinning him back around.

"Can I help you?" asked the man, taken aback and rather perturbed.

I looked into his eyes, feeling the cold dread of sheer and utter panic wash over me. "S-sorry," I muttered. "I thought you were someone else."

He politely smiled. "Oh."

I kept staring at his eyes, and it made him laugh nervously.

"You okay?"

"You don't wear contact lenses by any chance, do you?"

"No. Why?"

I whirled back around, crashing immediately back into Reese.

"Kat, what are you doing?" he whispered, looking over my shoulder at the black and blue haired Goth.

"We really have to go. Now!"

***

"Goddamn it, answer!" I cursed, trying to redial as I leapt down the escalator stairs.

I hit the landing and took off like a rocket, hearing Reese in hot pursuit. We battled our way through the crowds until we finally reached the parking lot.

"Mind filling me in?" he called out as I practically crashed against the side of his truck, still too preoccupied with my phone.

"His eyes are blue," I panted.

"Come again?"

"The guy in there. The one who was possessed, his eyes are blue."

"So? Demons don't usually stay in one person for any long length of time. It's moved on to possessing someone else. That's hardly news."

"Daniel said they were brown!"

Reese's face paled. "What are you talking about?"

"When I first ran into that guy, Daniel was with me. I couldn't see his eye color, because it just looked black. Daniel told me they were brown! Why else would he say that—"

"Unless he couldn't see the color either..." Reese slammed the keys into the ignition, and we floored it out of the lot.

"Hey, you've reached Carly. Leave your name and number. If I like you enough, I'll get back to you," the teasing voicemail laughed into my ear.

Whatever sparked the power outage must have tampered with cell service as well, because it took a good five minutes for any of my texts to even read, *"Sent."* And I found even worse luck when I tried calling Adam, receiving another failure message that said, "We're sorry, the number you are trying to reached is currently not in service."

"Goddamn it!" I punched my fist into the passenger door, and Reese outright jumped in his seat, seeing the knuckle-sized dent I left in the metal.

"Just take it easy there, Hulk," Reese urged. "You said it yourself. Carly was thinking about heading home early.

She could be in the shower for all we know."

"She's not."

"How'd you know?"

"I just do." That weird stirring under my skin was coiling itself around every muscle, propelling me forward. The closer we got to the school, the stronger it grew. "Do you really think Daniel could be Sitri?"

Reese gripped the steering wheel tighter. "Possibly. Only upper level demons can cloak their nature from us. With how much time you've spent around him, you would've seen past it at some point if he was anything less. Or he could be a Hellhound…"

"Yeah, but we would've noticed that. I mean, you saw what the other Hellhounds were like. Daniel's been acting normal—"

"So long as they aren't triggered by anything to make them angry, Hellhounds can still act like themselves, at least on the surface. Hell, there are some Hellhounds born with the condition, and they manage to live amongst society without detection. It's not wholly impossible for Daniel to hide it." He hesitated. "What if Carly was already turned? If Daniel really is one, he's been that way for how long now—"

I actually laughed. "We're talking about the girl who cries every time she watches an animal rescue relief commercial. Hell, she got choked up yesterday over a YouTube video. Carly's the poster girl of emotional."

"Point taken," he sighed, finding what little relief he could in the matter.

My gaze fixed outside the passenger window.

"We don't even know if Daniel's planning on doing anything, to her or anyone else. I mean, he's had more than ample opportunity to attack."

My eyes remained glued to the sky. I'd seen a few

harvest moons in my life, and they'd all been a washed out red. This one was bleeding an unnerving, effervescent scarlet. "You see anything in the forecast for a Blood Moon?"

Reese leaned over, seeing the circular sphere hanging overhead. "Shit."

Muffled music reverberated through the metal door as we approached the gym entrance. Reese eased the door open just far enough for the two of us to slip through. BASTILLE's "Requiem for Blue Jeans" played overhead on the loudspeaker, but no other sounds filled the gymnasium. No clamor, no voices, not even a footstep. It was impossible to close the door quietly, so I gently wedged the wooden triangle by our feet behind the frame to leave it open just a crack.

Leafless plastic trees adorned with pale decorative bulbs were aligned down the endlines of the basketball court, and the only real source of light came from the music-synced LED spot lighting solutions system mounted in the center of the gym. The lights eased between blue and red as the song's ominous drums echoed across the space. Two sets of fog machines continued pumping out masses of thick gray clouds that now engulfed the entire floor up to the middle of my calves as Reese and I stepped out into the gym. At first glance, everything looked normal, until you took inventory of the decorations. Only a handful of balloons had been filled, and dozens of wound up string lights were still stacked on the lone bottom bleacher that was pushed out. Then there was the large banner clinging to the wall, tacked up on only one end, as the stepladder beneath it sat toppled over on the ground.

Where was everyone? I recognized at least ten of the cars in the parking lot including Carly's.

Reese turned to say something to me when he suddenly seemed to stumble over his own feet, disappearing into the layer of fog hovering above the floor. I ran to help him, only to be met with the same fate. My feet blindly collided with something solid, and I face planted onto the hardwood. The force stirred the fog just enough to clear out the immediate space. I gasped, scuttling across the floor until I crashed into Reese. He seemed to realize the same thing I had, because he pried me up and we both stumbled back toward the bleachers.

"Tiffany..."

Reese nodded. "Eric, too."

"No." Without thinking, I snatched up the clipboard behind us and raced over to where Reese had fallen, fiercely fanning the fog until it cleared. My hand shot to my mouth, forcing my palm to eat up the scream I couldn't repress. Reese was right. Long shaggy locks were tangled across Eric's face, his eyes fixed in an empty stare. His body lay contorted, his neck snapped in the most unnatural angle. Just like Tiffany's.

I started frantically batting the air, trying to clear away the rest of the floor. Reese joined me as more and more classmates appeared beneath the fog, all their necks snapped. But no sign of Carly.

"She's not here," said Reese, watching me pull out my cell. "We need to go."

Justin Timberlake's "Sexyback" sounded off behind us, and a heavy metallic *clack!* followed as we both whirled around towards the side exit.

"Oh, what's the rush?" mused Daniel, gleefully twirling the ends of a chain in his hands.

Reese and I immediately bolted to the other end of the gym, shoving our weight into the push bars of each dual door leading to the hallway. Neither opened. The chain rattled behind us, but it wasn't coming any closer. Something thudded, and we both turned around to see Daniel had used the chain to fasten the side exit shut with a large padlock snapped in place.

Every expletive exploded in my mind as Reese and I continued throwing ourselves into the doors.

"Come on, Kat. Won't you stay? Our boss will be with us shortly, and he's just dying to see you," Daniel laughed, pulling out a bedazzled pink rectangle from his pocket. Carly's cell. "We really appreciate the heads up, too. Saved us from having to come and hunt you down ourselves."

My stomach dropped.

I told Carly in my texts to her that we were coming here.

I'd given them everything they needed.

CHAPTER 28
Tonight

"Where is she?" I demanded.

Daniel knew what I meant. "Somewhere around here, along with that idiot, McDowell. They got lost in the commotion, but we'll find 'em soon enough. There's really nowhere else to run. Every exit's blocked, locked, or bolted shut."

Carly and Mark had both gotten away, at least for the time being.

"Why kill everyone else?"

"Couldn't really help it." Daniel shrugged. "If anything, it's your fault."

"*Mine?*"

"Well, you are the one who broke Hell's seal after all. Triggered the Blood Moon into effect." He took a long drag of air and sighed. "And how wondrous it was. All that energy surging through your veins, just begging for release. It sent us all into a frenzy, and well..." Daniel casually gestured to the floor. "You see what happened."

"Who's *we?*"

"Trace, myself, and some other folks you may have

seen around town," he chuckled, pointing to the missing person's flyers still plastered across the activities board beside the door.

The rest of the Hersey basketball and cheerleading teams.

"But enough about us," insisted Daniel, motioning to me. "You've been very, very naughty lately, haven't you, Kat?" It really wasn't a question. He beamed from ear to ear, the smile jarringly happy.

"What do you mean *she* broke the seal?" asked Reese, stepping in front of me as to shield my body from Daniel. "Kat didn't do anything."

Daniel threw his head back and laughed. "Oh, how naïve you really are. Even with all your resources, you still haven't got a clue."

Reese stole a look over his shoulder, seeing me as equally confused.

"She's been slowly breaking it since the night she was resurrected," Daniel purred. "Kat first had to prove that she was worthy of her hellish groom-to-be. And what better way than to have her commit the unforgiveable? Gluttony, sloth, wrath, envy, pride, greed and —"

"Lust," I muttered. "The seven deadly sins."

"Right you are. And you definitely tried our patience, I'll give you that," sighed Daniel. "Committing the first was always going to be the easiest. The transition into a Changeling made it impossible for you to resist the urge to eat so much. But for a girl always on the go, we knew the second would be the biggest challenge. So how could we stop you in your tracks?"

A thousand pound weight slammed into my chest. I couldn't breathe. No, no, no, no.

"That's right, pretty girl," Daniel crooned. "Just as I

predicted, you moped about in your misery and guilt over Blaine's...untimely demise."

"*You*," I spat. "You killed him just for that?"

"We don't do anything without reason." Daniel paused, surveying the floor with a snicker. "Well, most of the time, anyway."

My eyes pinched shut, forcing repressed tears to run down my cheeks. I was going to be sick. Blaine had been alive, and they killed him—not because he was a threat—but just because they wanted to make me *despondent*. All my mind's eye kept conjuring up was Blaine. I could see him now. The dimples that formed when he genuinely laughed. Those perfect, bright white teeth. Those crystallized blue eyes that were nearly translucent. And now...

Now, Blaine was six feet under. Because of *him*.

I made no effort to hide my anger, my horror, and it only made Daniel smile wider. "Awww, you really cared about him, didn't you? That's so sweet."

"I didn't break the seal!" I sneered.

"Oh, but you did. Granted, it took you longer than most. Dark Mages channel their power through their emotions, so this should've been a cakewalk. Nowadays, people seem to break commandments like they're speed limits. We anticipated you completing your Great Rite at least a week ago. But it's here nevertheless." He playfully kicked a stray balloon, letting it drift off into the accumulating fog. "You can deny it all you want, but you know it's true. The little lightshow on your arm there should have been the indicator."

My runes. The pieces slowly started to slide together.

My ravenous appetite.

The week I spent wallowing in bed.

The text message that taunted me over Blaine's death

and the anger that had me kicking the bathroom stall door clear off its hinges.

My longing for my old life.

Me slapping Reese in my bedroom, when I let my *pride* get the better of me...

My desire to stay here that I'd resort to blackmailing my mother just to ensure I wouldn't be sent away.

And then Reese and me on his couch.

"I did it," I muttered, almost inaudibly. I really did do it.

"Gotta say though, the boss isn't too happy about the final one. He really had hoped that you'd check that one off the list with his help, not with...whatever the hell you'd call *that*," said Daniel, cocking his head as he examined Reese. "I mean, really? Blackburn? No offense, but just look at the guy."

"Wow," Reese muttered. "And to think, you're considered the nice one of the bunch."

The inside of my arm vibrated, and I immediately recognized the sensation. Wrath.

Daniel cocked his head, noting the vibrant light illuminating out of the sleeves of my leather jacket. A smile crept onto my face, and his amusement vanished as I whirled around, kicking the dual doors. Just as before, my foot slammed into the steel and they burst open. I grabbed Reese and we bolted into the hallway.

"No, no, no!" The rune immediately started dissipating, and by the time I reached the chained emergency exit, the light was gone.

"Can you reactivate it?" bellowed Reese, seeing me hike up my sleeve.

"I don't know how!"

He slammed his body into the door to no avail. We

didn't have the luxury of waiting any longer because Daniel was charging right for us. Reese yanked me down the connecting corridor, taking every turn and bend through the series of hallways in the hopes to lose him. Daniel's footsteps weren't more than twenty feet behind us.

We rounded the next corner, and Reese suddenly threw me sideways. I yelped, only to find his hand pressed against my mouth as darkness swallowed us up. A thin slit of light peeked out from the bottom slat in the door, and I quickly realized where we were. The janitor's closet.

Footsteps trampled towards us, and a shadow zipped past the doorframe as they continued down the hallway. Reese dropped his hand, but pulled me closer. "We need to get to the main offices," he whispered.

"Why?"

"Because they have landlines in there. We can try calling for Reynolds again. Right now, we need a cavalry, and we need it fast."

He slowly eased the door open and poked his head out. Only the reserved lights were on in the entire school, so it made it harder to see amongst the shadows in the hallways. And it was hard to keep an ear out, because we could still hear the music from the gym. Adam Lambert's "If I Had You" echoed down the hall, and the clapping rhythm sounded like reverberating footsteps, only spiking my anxiety further.

Reese eventually seemed satisfied, because he waved for me to follow as he stepped out into the hallway. We backtracked down a few halls and took a shortcut through the pool. I hit Reese's arm, still afraid to say anything. He turned to me and I pointed up to the observer's platform. He nodded.

Tiptoeing across the border of the lanes, we headed

up the bleachers to the upper deck. The lights were off in the overhead office, but the reflective glimmer from the pool still highlighted the objects on Coach's desk. A landline phone. Reese twisted the doorknob. It was locked. Before I could curse, Reese held up his finger, handing his blade over to me before digging into his back pocket for his wallet. He plucked out a gift card and slid it into the crease of the door, pushing the plastic down on the latch. It clicked. Reese shot me a small smile, turning the knob.

Okay, even now I was impressed.

We headed in, and I closed the door behind us as he rounded the desk to the phone.

"Holy shit!" He suddenly ducked as a metallic pole came hurtling at his head. The beam smacked into the filing cabinet behind him, and he swiftly grabbed it, wrenching it forward. A mass of blonde hair flung out from the shadows, stumbling right into him.

Reese clumsily caught hold of the person, only to be immediately shoved back. "Carly?"

Another stealthy figure emerged, and the business end of a baseball bat caught the light.

"Watch out!" I bellowed.

Reese promptly stepped sideways, rushing the attacker. His hands blocked the attempted swing just before he hooked his arms around the assailant, driving them both into the far wall. They disappeared into the shadows, and I blindly felt around for the light switch. The overhead lights crackled on, causing everyone to wince.

Reese finally looked up at his attacker who was still pinned in his hold against the wall. "*McDowell?*"

"Get off me, you freak," Mark sneered, shoving Blackburn away.

Carly's face lit up at the sight of me, but Mark quickly

yanked her back.

"Don't," he warned, snatching up his fallen bat. "They're probably like Danny."

"What happened?" I demanded, looking to Carly.

Her chin trembled and her entire frame was shaking. "Daniel… He…he killed Eric…and Rob, and Jennifer, and Tiffany…" She could barely talk. "His eyes…"

Reese headed back to the entrance, taking back his blade from me. Carly shrieked, and Mark quickly raised his bat in response.

Reese didn't pay any mind. "Show us your necks."

"*What?*"

"Unless you want this buried in your chests, show us the back of your necks," Reese ordered, priming the blade in his hand.

Carly hesitantly swept her tangled mess of hair to the side, pulling it away from her neck. She turned around, revealing untarnished, milky white skin.

"You, too," said Reese.

"Why?" Mark growled.

"It's the only way to know for sure that you're not one of them."

"*How?*"

"That weird tattoo," muttered Carly. "Daniel's had it for weeks…"

"Show us *your* necks then," countered Mark, motioning to Reese and me. We both took turns showing them, and Mark finally relented. We were all clean.

Reese lowered his blade, heading back to the desk.

"It's no use," said Mark, grabbing the cord to the phone. It had been cut. "We had the same idea. We tried the other offices too, but it's the same thing."

"What happened to Daniel?" Carly uttered, shakily

bringing her hand to her mouth. "When he started attacking everybody, we tried stopping him, but nothing worked."

Reese and I both shared uneasy glances.

"What?" Mark charged over to us, blocking our way to the door. "I just witnessed my best friend on a murder rampage, sporting fangs and glowing yellow eyes. Okay? We're past the point of the whole 'you wouldn't believe me if I told you' bullshit."

"Look at what we have here."

We all stiffened.

"An appetizer, my main course, a little dessert, and the girl of the hour." Trace sauntered his way around the pool, heading towards the bleachers with an axe brandished in hand.

Mark slammed the door shut. "Help me move the desk."

"We can't barricade ourselves in here," said Reese.

"Why?"

"You don't want to be in a confined space with him. Trust me."

Carly grabbed her metal pole again, which I now realized was a cleaning rod for the pool, and we all hurried out the door.

Reese ordered for us to aim for Trace's head as we reached the bottom of the bleachers.

"So, which of the three little piggies am I to eat first?" Trace beamed, twirling the axe about gleefully. It seemed someone had already tried attacking him because his sleeve was torn and blood dripped down his arm. As expected, he didn't feel a thing.

I stepped forward.

"Kat," Reese snapped.

"He just said it himself; he can't kill me," I said,

raising Reese's sword. "Isn't that right?"

Trace smirked. "Kill? No. Maim? Well, let's just see how things go. Shall we?"

"Screw this." Mark suddenly flew past me, ready to nail Trace with his bat. His friend laughed, effortlessly ducking. McDowell flew past him, clumsily trying to regain his footing.

"Nice try." Trace brought up his axe, all set to drop it right into Mark's shoulder blades. The hatchet swung back around however just as Reese's dagger came hurtling at him. The bit clipped with the blade, and the momentum sent the dagger flying up into the bleachers. Reese charged him. Trace parried the strike, the top of the axe connecting with Reese's sword. Spinning the axe over his head, he hammered it down at Blackburn, and the profound force sent Reese's fighting arm to the floor. Trace made a line drive at him, and Reese somersaulted sideways, sprawling out on the tiles.

"Just like old times," Bolton snickered. "Only this time, I'm the one who'll be knocking your teeth out. Right after I rip out your spine."

Mark took another swing, but Trace leveled his axe right at the sweet spot of the baseball bat. The wood cracked in half, leaving Mark with not much more than a nub. Reese sprang up from the ground, throwing another dagger at him. It lacked any real accuracy, but that wasn't the point. It took Trace's attention away from Mark, who was now defenseless. Blackburn wasted no time reengaging Bolton, and Trace's blasé manner only made the magician imprudent in his strikes. He needed to pace himself. Despite his bulky build, Bolton glissaded in every step with perfect form. Meanwhile, Reese was rushing, meeting too many close calls.

Trace hurled the axe down again, primed at Reese's head. Mark threw the remainder of his bat at Bolton's face, giving Reese just that split second he needed to sidestep the strike. The axe barreled down into the floor, crushing right through the tiles. Reese swung at him, but Trace deflected, hauling up the axe once again. Blackburn barely managed to raise the sword in time, catching the top of the axe right on the end of the blade. Bolton pressed down further, and it proved to be too much. Reese couldn't hold the weight. The axe dug right into his left shoulder.

Any rationality I had was gone as I ran right for him.

"No!" Reese begged me. "Go!"

Trace nailed the heel of his foot right into Reese's chest. The force set the steel tearing out of his flesh, and the air was knocked out of his lungs before Reese had the chance to scream.

"What's the matter, Houdini? You should be used to getting your ass kicked by now," Bolton laughed, grabbing Reese off the floor by the front of his jacket. He threw the magician like he was nothing more than a sack of flour.

Reese's thin frame crashed into the bleachers, and his body fell limp.

I charged at Trace, viciously swinging at him as hard and as fast as I could. Bolton only continued to laugh, somehow managing to grip the hilt of the sword. When it was made clear I wouldn't let it go, Trace shoved me back. The colossal force sent me hurtling across the slick tile, and I only stopped upon slamming into the far wall. I tried catching my breath so I could stand, but I just croaked on a strangled gasp.

"Who's next?" Bolton looked to Mark, seeing him still without a weapon. He snickered, actually tossing aside his axe. "Come on, McDowell. Let's see what you've got."

The linebacker rushed at Trace, preparing to tackle him with an annihilating blow that left even the best players on the football field buried in the ground. He extended his hands and drove them upward across Trace's chest, ready to demolish him with maximum leverage. Instead, it was like he hit a brick wall. The moment Mark collided with Trace, neither moved. Mark's feet scraped against the ground, trying to gain an inkling of momentum, but Trace still didn't budge.

Bolton raised his arms above Mark's hold, driving his elbows down onto his friend's upper back. The impact sent Mark crumpling into the ground with a wheeze. Trace booted him over with a snicker, effortlessly snatching a hold of the metal pole that came hurtling right at the back of his head. He turned around, twisting the pole right out of Carly's grasp.

He howled with laughter. "Really? That's the best you've got?" Trace grabbed the bar with both hands and snapped it over his knee like it was made of straw. "'If she only had a brain,'" he singsonged.

"Speak for yourself," I sneered, finally staggering back up to my feet. I swung the blade at him. The weight of the steel made me undoubtedly clumsy, but I kept slicing it through the air every time Trace teased us with a step closer.

He pounced forward and I swung Reese's blade as hard as I could, hearing him howl. Trace staggered back, pressing his fingers tightly into his palm. Blood seeped out. It may have only been a scratch, but hell, it was better than nothing.

Trace's eyes flashed an all too familiar yellow, and a low, guttural growl rose from the back of his throat as his canine teeth lengthened. He lunged at me.

Not good.

I frantically flung the sword up at him, and it cut into his arm, but he didn't stop. Trace's hands were suddenly clasped around my throat as he slammed my body against the wall. Tiles broke all around me, and my vision blackened from the devastating impact to my head. I tried keeping hold of Reese's blade, but the impact rattled me hard enough that it fell from my fingers. Metal clamored behind us, and glass shattered somewhere else, but I couldn't make anything out.

A sickly squishing sound suddenly filled the quieted space, and Trace immediately dropped me. My vision recovered just as he turned around. Reese's dagger. It was buried in the left side of his back.

"*You*," he sneered. Bolton knelt down, revealing the culprit. Mark was crumpled on his knees, still struggling to regain his own breath. Trace grabbed him in one fell swoop by the neck, prying him right off the floor. McDowell was sent catapulting across the room, his body airborne before he plummeted into the water.

"How'd you like me now?" gritted Carly. Trace barely managed to turn as a heavy metallic wallop reverberated across the space. His features fell in confusion, traveling down to the blonde's hands. She brought up the fire extinguisher again, nailing him square in the face. The hit literally spun him around, and he toppled over right into the pool. "Bastard."

Mark broke the surface of the water, still on the other end of the lanes. "What the hell happened?" he gasped, seeing blood fanning out across the water where Trace's motionless body bobbed.

I left Carly to explain as I hurried over to the bleachers, shaking Reese's frame. He groaned as he came to, his hand immediately pinning to his shoulder. Trace wasn't the only one bleeding. Reese's shoulder was drenched, and I could see the mutilated flesh peeking out between the slashed fabric of his jacket.

"I'm okay," he assured, woozily climbing up to his feet.

"Don't scare me like that," I sighed, planting a kiss to his cheek. We ambled down from the bleachers, but we both froze.

"Get out of the water," Reese muttered.

Carly and Mark turned to us, and now I was screaming.

"Get out of the water!"

Trace's tanned body was lost beneath a growing black mass of fur developing under the water. He was shifting!

CHAPTER 29
Mama

I grabbed Carly's hand, forcing her to follow us as we all bolted to the other side of the pool. "Mark, get out!"

A snarling muzzle roared as it breached the surface of the water, and all the blood drained from Mark's face. He immediately plunged under, sculling beneath the lane dividers. His head reemerged not two feet from us, and we all reached for him. The black mass of fur shot through the water and charged the surface like a great white. The hound's teeth were as equally ferocious, each canine at least three inches long. Everyone grabbed hold of Mark's arms, hauling him up. We all fell back on the sidelines, losing our footing as the hound's muzzle sprang up onto the tile.

"Holy shit!" Mark thrashed the heel of his foot, clocking the impending beast right in the snout. He scuttled back just far enough to evade the snapping jaws as they repeatedly clamped together, the curved canines begging to tear through flesh down to the very bone. The hound's slick paws slipped on the tiling, unable to haul its body up onto the poolside. It continued snapping up at us, only to slip back under the water.

I grabbed Mark's arm. "Come on!"

We climbed back to our feet, hearing tiles shatter behind us as we bolted for the nearest door. Trace had found his way out of the water. Reese yanked the heavy metal door open, and the four of us piled into the locker room. The hound struck the closing door in full force, inadvertently slamming it shut in the process. Razor sharp claws tore into the barrier, unable to pry it back open. Howling and thrashing resonated from the other side of the door, and we all bolted through the aisles of lockers to the side exit. Mark ransacked the shower rack, snatching up a handful of bath towels on our way out. His waterlogged sneakers squished and squeaked with every step, forcing him to abandon them not ten feet into the hall.

Footsteps galloped from an adjoining passage. We pressed our backs to the wall, trying best to melt into the darkness as we slid over to the stairwell. Mark cursed under his breath, seeing the blatant trail of water he was leaving behind. A guy called out down the corridor, and we all froze. Laughter immediately followed.

"What the hell happened to you?"

"Piss off," barked Trace. A fresh set of squishing footsteps pounded down the hall right for us.

We bolted up the stairs, checking each of the classroom doors along the way as we darted through the main hallway on the second floor. Everything was locked.

Bolton's voice boomed from the lower level. "Check all the exits!"

"We already did," replied his companion.

"Do it again!"

Carly motioned to us, pulling one of the dual doors open.

The library.

All the lights were off, so we only had the small flashlights from our phones to help illuminate the vast space.

"Waterproof, my ass." Mark hit every button on his cell to no avail. It was clearly dead. "Well, there's four-hundred bucks down the toilet."

Silence greeted us as we headed through the computer lab department. Mark motioned to a nearby cubicle, but Reese shook his head. "EMP knocked out the internet too."

Taking refuge in the librarian's station, we locked ourselves inside Mrs. Hastings's office. Between the hysteria and wasted energy, we either collapsed into empty chairs or right onto the carpet.

Mark ambled over to the wall, sliding down to the floor. Reese and I came to his side, immediately seeing the blood coursing down the nape of his neck from his hair.

"I'm fine," McDowell grumbled, cringing as he dabbed the beaten spot on the back of his head. "Some of us are worse off." He nodded to Reese, noting his gashed shoulder.

"Thanks," Blackburn muttered, "for everything back there."

"Don't mention it."

Reese nodded.

"Seriously, don't mention it. I can't have people thinking Bolton bested me. I have a reputation to uphold." The two chuckled as Reese took a seat beside him.

Catching my breath, I snatched up the landline receiver sitting on Mrs. Hastings's desktop, dialing in the phone number for Mr. Reynolds's bar. It was the only other landline I knew that could be reached.

"….Hello?" A thick wave of static overwhelmed the

voice on the other end.

"*Adam?*" I tried speaking as loud as I could without shouting. "Adam? Can you hear me?"

"K...Kat? Is that...?"

"Adam, we need help. It's Daniel. He's a Hellhound. We're trapped in the school-"

"Hello? Hel..."

The static roared, drowning out Adam's voice entirely. "Can you hear me? Hello!" I bellowed. "Hello?" The call cut out. It took everything I had to not slam the receiver down.

"What the hell's going on?" asked Mark. "What happened to Bolton in the pool?"

"He's a Hellhound," muttered Reese, applying pressure to his injured shoulder. "He and Daniel were infected with a demonic virus. It's kind of a long story, but the cheat sheet version is that they're raving, shape-shifting lunatics now controlled by an even worse raving lunatic who wants to kidnap Kat." He handed Mark his only other longer blade and instructed on what to do with it before giving Carly a small dagger.

Silent tears trailed down her cheeks. "What'd we do now?"

"We go to the north wing," muttered Mark, using the other towels in his hands to mop up his dripping frame as best he could. "If we can find a way inside one of the classrooms with a window, the bushes lining the building just might help break our fall."

My throat double-clutched. "You want us to *jump*?"

"You have a better idea?"

We all startled, instinctively ducking down as the main doors to the library slammed open with an ear-splitting bang. Everyone buried their phones into the carpet and shut off the lights. Windows lined the whole front of the office, so Reese was able to steal a quick look between the slatted blinds at the bottom of the sill.

He held up two fingers, signifying how many people he had seen. "We have to move," he mouthed.

Things crashed and slammed and banged and boomed in the front departments of the library as whoever ransacked the place. By the sounds of it, they were toppling over bookshelves.

"The Boss is gonna flip shit if we don't find her before he gets here," one of the intruders barked.

A female sighed. "It wasn't our job to babysit her. Daniel's the one who let her get away. But regardless, he already called in the rest of the troops for support. The whole gang should be here in ten minutes tops. We'll find her."

"*Gang?*" Mark mouthed. We all shuddered. It was hard enough fending off Bolton, let alone an entire mob.

Reese waved at us, slowly easing the office door open as the voices trailed off into what sounded like the computer lab. We each slinked out, keeping ourselves low to the ground. Stalking over to the closest aisle, we froze. The talking had abruptly stopped. The four of us practically army crawled into the History section, ducking behind the towering shelves. We strained to hear anything, but the entire place was silent with the exception of our panicked breathing. Carly even pinned a hand to her mouth to try and suppress the sound.

The main door was wide open. If we made a break for it now...

I didn't have time to finish the thought. A wisp of shadow zipped past the shelves, and Mark was suddenly airborne. His body crashed right on top of the checkout counter.

"Come on!" He groaningly rolled off the tabletop, collapsing onto the carpet. "Why am *I* always the one being treated like a human keg-toss?"

"Well, well, well. Look who we have here," purred the female, standing over us. We scrambled to our feet, and the strange woman immediately bellowed. She staggered back, gripping her stomach. Reese sliced his blade at her again, and she recoiled with a hiss.

Carly and I blindly stumbled backward, only to hit a solid wall of flesh. We whirled around. The shadows made it impossible to see anything distinctive about the towering man, but his glowing yellow eyes were unmistakable. Beefy mitts ensnared both our throats.

"Which one is she?" the man barked, exchanging glances between Carly and me.

Things clanged and crashed behind us. Clearly Reese was keeping his partner busy. Sadly, the two of us couldn't say we were putting up much of a fight. We kicked and thrashed and clawed at the brute, only to be thrown against the bookshelves beside each of us.

Reese screamed, and I could see him out of the corner of my eye. The woman had him pinned against the wall, digging her clamped fingers into his wounded shoulder. Vibrations rippled up my arm, and I suddenly threw my fists forward. They connected with the man's chest, and he rocketed backward, hitting the adjacent bookshelf so hard that it toppled over, causing a domino effect across the entire library. I was instantly at the woman's back, pinning my hand against her throat. In one swift movement, I sent her skidding backward across the carpet.

"Damn, Montgomery," Mark choked, staggering up to his feet. "Remind me to never piss you off." Snarling immediately erupted from behind him. We didn't need to be told twice. Our new acquaintances were shifting. The four of us bolted out the door so fast that we all nearly lost our footing from sheer momentum.

Twenty feet down the corridor, and everything ruptured behind us. I stole a look over my shoulder, seeing the splintered fragments of the library door explode across the hallway as two massive hounds burst out of the entryway. Within seconds, they were right on our heels. Reese whirled around, throwing one of his silver stars. The metal buried right into the animal's snout. It immediately came to a halt, thrashing its paws up at its face in an attempt to rip it out.

Blackburn tried to throw another one, but the remaining creature bounded right at us. Mark shoved Carly and me aside and swung at the hound, forcing the animal's face away. It still threw its weight into McDowell, knocking him to the ground. The beast sprang on top of him, baring its hideous canines.

"Run!" he ordered.

Like hell.

Brandishing Reese's pocketknife, I leapt at the two of them, ready to drive the blade into the hound when it inexplicably whimpered. The blackened fur vanished in an instant. Nothing but the hound's human form hovered above Mark, and then that petered out too. The petrified young man just lay there, still holding the angelic steel in his hand. He'd stabbed the beast in the heart.

Realization must have finally settled in, because McDowell sprang up from the floor. He violently shook himself out, trying to free the mound of ash that now covered his entire body. The effort did very little, as the filth clung determinedly to his dampened clothes. He abandoned the effort however once he looked down the hall. A similar pile of ash fell to the ground just ahead of Reese. The light caught his blade, revealing an equally bloody foible.

Blackburn nodded to us, but froze in his tracks. "Where's Carly?"

Mark and I turned on our heels, so certain that we'd find her standing there.

But there was no one.

We all took off down the hallway to the connecting corridor. Our heads twisted from side to side, looking down every direction. She was still nowhere in sight.

"*Carly?*" I called out as softly as I could. Three hallways later, and I was shaking, my head drowning in all the horrors it could conjure up.

Where was she?

"Testing, testing," crooned Daniel's voice over the P.A. system in a sickeningly sweet tone. "Attention, all Mystic Harbor students. Will Katrina Montgomery please report to the gymnasium immediately? Your friend is waiting for you."

My blood ran cold.

"Say hello to our audience, would you?" he mocked.

"Kat, don't!" Carly bellowed hysterically from the background.

"How's about a little swap meet?" Daniel further insisted. "Kitty Kat for Car-Car."

Reese snatched my arm the instant I stepped forward, dragging me back to his side. "This is exactly what he's counting on, for you to be impulsive—"

"*I'm not leaving her.*"

"You heard what Daniel said earlier. Sitri's on his way. You'll be walking right into his trap," Reese growled. "That's why *I'm* going. You and Mark find a way out of here."

Before I could object, the P.A. system pitched back on. "Just to make things a bit more expedient, I'm gonna set the buzzer for two minutes. If *Kat* isn't here," Daniel emphasized my name, "you're gonna need to bury Barbie here in a closed casket. Or better yet, perhaps I might sic her on you after I take a bite out of her neck."

All our grips loosened around the blades in our hands. Seeing what Daniel had become was hard enough; I couldn't begin to imagine how painful it must have been for Mark to watch his best friend turn into a monster. Every muscle in my body knotted at the thought of having to witness Carly go through the same thing. This was *my* fault. I was the one they were after. And I wasn't about to let my best friend die…or worse. Not for me.

CHAPTER 30
This Means War

Slow clapping resounded across the gym as Mark, Reese, and I all walked in through the double doors. Fog still engulfed the floor, stirring with every step we took. Daniel wasn't anywhere in sight.

"Yoo-hoo." A sharp whistle echoed overhead, and our heads shot up to the overlook. Daniel continued clapping, even with his arms wrapped around Carly's trembling frame. Those blazing yellow eyes glowed in the limited light, sending a chill up my spine as he leaned down toward Car's neck. "Just in time," he laughed, the game buzzer counting down the last ten seconds.

It didn't escape any of our attentions that the hallways were conveniently Hellhound-free on our trek back here.

"Don't be shy, Kat." Daniel beckoned me up to the weightlifting overlook. "Come, join us."

I didn't so much as look to the side stairwell as I remained glued in place.

Daniel sighed. "And to think we had a deal." He kicked a section of the wire mesh railing, and the metal blasted right out of place. We leapt back as the section crashed down on the hardwood floor not five feet ahead of us. Daniel threw Carly forward, whirling her back around to grip her by the throat. He extended his arm, and she was forced off the exposed ledge.

"Don't!" I begged, watching Carly choke on a gasp as he held her out by nothing but the throat. Her acrylic nails dug into Daniel's arms well after drawing blood, but he only laughed. She kicked at the empty air beneath her feet, desperately trying to regain her ground.

"Make up your mind, Kat," hummed Daniel. "Agree to my terms, or Barbie takes your place."

"Which is it?" I growled. "You gonna bite her, or kill her?"

"Kill her," he clarified. "Then I'm gonna wait for your betrothed to get here, in which he'll bring her back. And then I'm gonna bite her."

Carly's hands started slipping from Daniel's arms. She was losing consciousness. He tightened his grip, and her thrashing legs fell limp. Any sense of self-preservation vanished as I bolted across the room to the staircase.

Daniel clicked his tongue, waving his finger at me in disapproval. "Not so fast there, sweetheart. Leave your weapons down there, along with your entourage."

I looked over my shoulder, seeing McDowell and Blackburn still standing right behind me.

Reese shook his head, the rest of the blood in his face draining as his eyes bore into mine. "Kat..."

I handed Reese's sword back to him, holding up my empty palms. Daniel nodded, motioning to the stairs. I remembered what Reese had once said. Hellhounds had spectacular hearing, so I didn't risk saying anything to him as I walked into the doorway. Once I was amerced deep enough in the stairwell that Daniel could no longer see me, I mouthed to Reese and Mark, praying they understood before making my way up the cement steps.

"There she is!" Daniel announced as I stepped out into the workout center with my hands raised over my head.

He pulled Carly back over to the platform, but kept a fist still clamped around her throat. She barely managed to drag in a decent breath as her feet planted on the ground, and the lack of oxygen had tinged her face with a sickly mix of purple and blue. Cold metal snaked down my sleeve as I lowered my hands.

"Let her go."

"You sure about that?" Daniel thrust his arm out again, forcing Carly right on the brink of the ledge. Her toes curled, barely managing to cling to the lip of the brink.

"You know what I mean."

He grinned. "Come closer, and we'll negotiate."

"Kat, don't," Carly choked out.

I forced a small smile. "It's gonna be okay."

Daniel's grin grew to an outright smirk as I walked over to them both. I came within arm's reach, and sure enough, he flung Carly backward, her tiny blonde frame dropping out of sight. I lunged to the railing still in place, leaning over to see Carly splayed on the ground...with Reese and Mark sprawled out beneath her. Groans erupted from below, and Daniel sneered in disappointment as the guys pulled Carly up to her feet.

"*Catch her*," I'd mouthed. And they had understood.

Car yelped as she put pressure on her right foot, and Reese quickly caught hold of her before she tumbled back to the floor. Daniel snatched a hold of my jacket, prying me over to him as he let out an ear-aching whistle. There was no doubt that he'd just called for reinforcements.

I let the cool chain stuffed in my sleeve slide out into my palm as I bellowed, "Go!" I jammed the cross necklace into Daniel's face, and he howled as the silver seared his cheek. Breaking free from his grip, I bolted to the door, practically falling down the stairs to the gym. The double doors burst open, and figures piled into the entryway. Countless yellow eyes gleamed even through the swelling fog that now billowed up overhead from the sudden rush of air. Reese shoved Mark and Carly back toward the side exit. Mark raced over to the door, driving Reese's spare sword down on the padlock.

Carly shrieked as Trace emerged and charged at her. Reese hurled his last dagger, catching him right in the chest. Bolton staggered back, his fists clamping around the steel in confusion. Just like the others, his body disintegrated into a pile of ash. Reese barked at her to run, and Carly clumsily hobbled towards the exit just as the padlock brokenly clanged to the floor. Mark yanked the chains out of the door, flinging it open. He swept Car up into his arms, and the two disappeared outside.

Knowing where my fallen classmates rested, I managed to gain an edge over my attackers as I darted across the gymnasium. Everyone else stumbled or outright fell over the bodies amid the blinding haze. I followed Reese's instruction, ducking as he swung his blade through the air. And I didn't dare steal a glance behind me, hearing what I knew now to be flesh slicing open. A hand brushed my back, and I jumped, only to find Reese at my side a second later. The chilling October air took my breath away as we raced out the side exit. Not three steps later did Reese suddenly vanish from my peripheral vision. I whirled around, seeing a hulking young man throttle Reese against the side of the building.

Blackburn brought up his blade, but he wasn't fast enough. The stranger grabbed Reese's wrist, twisting it until it snapped at the most unnatural angle. Before I could reach him, arms ensnared me from behind. I thrashed and kicked and flailed, only to feel a sharp single stab to the side of my collar.

"If only you played nice," Daniel laughed wickedly with a sneer.

My vision clouded over, giving me just enough time to see the stem to an empty syringe being ripped out of my neck.

"Sweet dreams."

The muscles in my arms screamed as I came to, finding myself suspended up by the wrists. My feet dragged on the floor, and I found I could stand upright to take the weight off my aching arms. I couldn't see anything, assuming amid my disorientation that I was in a dark room. But as I shifted, I could feel the fabric. There was a sack draped over my head. Like I was a hostage. A prisoner.

And that's precisely what I was. Shackled and hooded and left alone in the deafening silence.

The restraints clamored as I yanked at them. Metal on metal. Was I wearing...handcuffs? My fingers traced over the material and up to whatever I was fastened to. A cold metal rod, about three feet long. Even with the hood over my head, I could still smell something, ever so faint.

Lilac.

I knew exactly where I was.

The old workout room. I was handcuffed to one of the pull-up bars.

Shit.

Mark had still used it when he came in here fooling around, and the damn thing never budged. Given that he weighed nearly twice as much as me, I seriously doubted I'd be able to pull it out from the wall.

Which was probably why my captor found it fitting to chain me up here. Plus, I was on the top floor of a presumably empty building where nobody would hear me screaming for help.

Perfect.

Goosebumps raked my exposed arms, and the thought only sickened me all the more. Someone had removed my jacket. What else had they done? I continued fussing about, only stopping once I heard the door squeak open.

"Aww, look who's awake," laughed the familiar voice. Daniel.

I still couldn't see anything with this stupid sack over my head, but the light pouring in from the hallway illuminated two silhouettes as they walked into the activities room.

A long, noisy exhale. Someone didn't sound too pleased.

"Oh, lighten up. Where else was I gonna put her?" sighed Daniel, presumably talking to the other individual. "Besides, she's perfectly fine. Arent'cha, Kat Nip?"

He brushed a finger under my chin, and I blindly thrashed my legs up to where it sounded like he was standing. I only kicked at the air, making Daniel laugh all the more.

"Screw you," I gritted.

He clicked his tongue. "Such poor manners, especially when I come bearing a gift for you."

"Unless it's a gun for me to shoot you in the face with, I'm not interested," I snarled.

"Oh, I beg to differ."

The ends of the sack tugged around my neck, and I instinctively jerked, half expecting to be strangled. Instead, the bag lifted from my head. Only one section of the lights was turned on in the room, but I still winced at the sudden brightness that flooded my vision.

I'd been right. A brief glance around the room, and I could see the stacks and the wall of mirrors, not to mention my reflection across the way. Sure enough, I was handcuffed to the pull-up bar. Bastard.

But that's not what I was looking at.

Gaping at the sight, my mind fought to find answers. But I couldn't even form a single question. This wasn't real. This *couldn't* be real.

I had to keep blinking, waiting for the phantom to erase from my vision.

It wasn't leaving.

I wasn't…breathing.

I couldn't quite digest the unnatural blonde hair, but I knew those cheekbones. I knew those crystal blue eyes. I knew *him*.

"…Blaine."

CHAPTER 31
Sucker For Pain

Everything about him was *off*. The hair, the clothes, the way he carried himself. The Blaine I knew always looked perfectly polished. Prim, proper, always a gentleman. Hell, that's why his nickname had been 'Gatsby.' This person, this imitation, was *not* him. He laxly leaned against the doorway, hands in pocket. Where perfectly groomed black hair used to be now rested bed-head, bleached-blonde locks. His head-to-toe Armani attire had been replaced by faded black jeans, beaten up riding boots, a black leather jacket, and an untucked, half-unbuttoned dress shirt. I just continued to gawk stupidly at him, my brain unable to process what stood in front of me.

His lips tipped up into a pirated grin. "Hey, Kit Kat."

I finally managed to tear my eyes from him long enough to look at Daniel, seeing the side of his face still marred by the silver I'd burned him with. "What the hell is this?"

Daniel motioned to Blaine with an exaggerated Vanna

White gesture. "Your present, of course. Don't you like it?"

Blaine just looked at me, expectantly. He sighed at last when it was clear I wasn't going to answer. "You seem surprised, and reasonably so, but I thought for sure you'd be happy to see me again."

"How is this possible? You... I mean, the police reports... You were decapitated."

He and Daniel shared a knowing, Cheshire grin.

"We have what you'd call, 'friends in *low* places,'" said Daniel.

"Not to mention a few members of the police force in our pockets to fudge some facts," added his cohort. "With the way death is treated around here, it's best to convince everyone that you *won't* be coming back, especially with the likes of Reynolds snooping around. And nothing sounds more absolute than beheading."

"Where's Reese?" I growled. "What did you do to him?"

Blaine cast me a mocking smile. "We took care of him."

Daniel outright laughed, seeing the blatant horror in my eyes. "Relax, Kitty Kat. Not like that. The Boss thought it would be in poor taste to start your new union together by offing your previous beau. Even if it is Blackburn." He cocked his head in amusement. "You really do have lousy taste in men, don't you?"

Blaine clicked his tongue. "Now, now. No reason to be mean. I'm on that list too, remember."

"I, for one, have to admit. I'm quite impressed with you," said Daniel, crooking a finger at me. "I mean, I always knew you had tenacity, but *this*?" He eyed me up and down, shivering his shoulders theatrically.

He brought his hand up again to my chin, and I

instantly snapped at it with my teeth. Daniel startled back with a laugh. "That's the spirit. I'll admit, I wasn't sure what the Boss saw in you at first, but I stand corrected. Quite the little fighter you are. You just might make a fine, ferocious princess after all."

My body quivered at the very thought. Of what their 'boss' had planned for me.

I couldn't give them the satisfaction of seeing me scared. I looked back to Blaine, trying to bury the sheer terror beneath all the anger. "Who did this to you?"

"Did *what*?"

"Dyed your hair," I countered with equal moxie. "What'd you think? Who turned you?"

Blaine smiled guiltily. "I have what you might call a…preexisting condition."

"Meaning what?"

That smile quickly turned feline. "You're a smart girl, Kat. Figure it out."

My heart sank in my chest. "No."

He whimpered mockingly. "Afraid so."

"But you can't be. I know your parents. Our moms play tennis together for crying out loud!"

"Being a 'mom' doesn't necessarily make a woman a mother, if you catch my drift."

"Adopted?"

"As I suspect you're already familiar with. And to think, my folks were so happy at first, having an adorable bundle of joy that never cried. It wasn't until a bit later that they realized the wiring upstairs just wasn't quite right," he remarked, tapping the side of his head.

"But…how? You guys aren't exactly what you'd call upstanding citizens. You're more like gremlins on crack."

"Years of practice on my part. Clinically, I'm what

you'd call a sociopath. See, demonic entities such as myself still feel emotion. Our range just isn't very expansive. And the pesky ones we can just turn off."

And to think I cried over this man. This whole time, he'd been one of them. A Hellhound, by birth. I could see it on his face. Cold, callous, apathetic.

He strode closer, and I shrank back against the wall.

"Awww, what's the matter, pumpkin?" he pouted, brushing his fingers down my jaw line.

I writhed away, shuddering at the contact.

"Don't be like that. I don't bite." A fiendish grin crept across his face. "Well, not hard anyway. Not when I mean to play nice."

My eyes shifted back over to Daniel, seeing his cell pressed against his ear.

His malicious grin stretched from ear to ear. "Slippery little thing she is. Thanks man."

"Dare I ask?" Blaine crooned.

"Hate to walk out on this precious little reunion, but the boys think they spotted my girl," confirmed Daniel, sliding his cell back into his pocket. "And I'm positively dying to sink my teeth into her."

"Your girlfriend, or more presumably your ex, is hardly the priority here."

"Why? Are you kids in need of a chaperone?" he laughed to his friend.

"I can manage just fine," confirmed Blaine.

"Well, then it's settled. That is, unless you prefer me to stay and watch."

The pounding in my chest only worsened. I wasn't sure what was more horrible: being trapped in a room with two of Hell's minions, or being left alone with just *one*.

Blaine cut his partner a sharp glare as he shrugged off

his jacket, and Daniel threw his hands up in mock surrender. He waltzed out the door, a cheerful whistle echoing down the hall as his footsteps faded into the distance.

My eyes remained pinned to where I'd last seen Daniel, unable to bring myself to behold Blaine again, feeling his own gaze fixed on me.

"You really are a sight for sore eyes." His hands cupped my face, forcing me to finally look at him.

I didn't lash out this time. There was no one here to rein him in. All it took was one wrong move, and Blaine could snap at any moment. I was now solely at his mercy.

"And I really am sorry about the restraints," he huffed, looking up at the cuffs holding me captive. "We just couldn't risk having you run off again. You understand."

"What do all of you want with me?" I gritted, trying to fend off the tears burning behind my eyes.

"Right now?" His hands ran through my hair, gently brushing the loose strands from my face. "Right now, I want you."

My heart, my head, my chest; everything contracted, suffocating me slowly as Blaine rested his forehead against mine. His obnoxiously long, thick lashes fanned the tops of his cheekbones as his eyes fell closed. He really was beautiful. And that very thought churned my stomach. They said that Satan disguised himself as an angel of light, so it only seemed fair that menace would appear in the guise of temptation.

"Don't be afraid," he whispered. His voice. He always managed to sound so calm. Even now it still held that soft timbre, making each word more persuasive than the last.

He opened his eyes again, searching mine for...I wasn't sure. Acceptance? Surrender?

Unable to move, my knees gave in as he bore down

on me, delving his mouth into the side of my neck. A scream strangled in my throat, leaving me with nothing more than a gasp. The sound only encouraged him.

I froze, awaiting the painful prick of canines to puncture into my neck. Instead, his lips molded to my bare skin, suckling on the exposed flesh. He left a trail of kisses from the top of my shoulder till he reached my earlobe, nibbling on the bottom with his teeth.

"Just give in." He was nearly breathless.

"Why? So I can become a monster, like you?" I finally jeered. It was all I could do, save for screaming.

Blaine looked genuinely disappointed. "Either way, you're going to become one of us. The only question here is if you're willing to embrace it?"

"I'd rather you kill me."

Blaine sighed, and it sounded like he was trying to bury a chuckle. He continued teasing with the skin along my neck, inhaling my scent. "Don't say that. Besides, you didn't seem to enjoy it too much the last time. I've never seen someone fight so hard to stay alive. And then you were so defiant against me. Almost wasn't able to bring you back."

I froze. "What did you say?"

The revelation constricted every ounce of me, and Blaine felt it. He brushed his nose along my jaw, kissing my chin. "Which part?"

"You... *You're* my Maker?"

He smiled. "Well, of course. Who did you think it was?"

I'd been so focused on trying *not* to look at him that I had missed what was right in front of me. His left hand.

Blaine's eyes followed to where I was gaping, and his smile grew all the more as he hiked up his sleeve.

Black metallic ink painted his entire arm. And the

runes. They were an *exact* match for my own, down to the tether wrapped around his ring finger.

"Sitri."

Wicked delight blazed in his eyes. "Someone's been doing their homework."

I shook my head. "No."

"*No* what?"

"You can't be him. You're from *here*."

"No, I was *raised* here. My parentage on the other hand," he sighed. "Well, let's just say it's unconventional."

"That was you, stalking me?"

"I had to keep an eye out on my girl." He was practically beaming, continuing to plant small kisses on my neck.

"You tried attacking me with a tire iron!"

"I was trying to keep you safe," he corrected between kisses. "Between Blackburn and Reynolds snooping around, I didn't have much of a choice. I was forbidden from revealing myself to you until the last stage of your Rite, so it was the only way I could make contact. I *had* hoped your suspicions would've convinced you to stay clear of them both."

My head was swimming, unable to process it all. "How did you even know I'd be there on the road, or at the school, or in the restaurant?"

"Tu es meus verum coniunx."

"*What?*"

"I'll always know." Blaine met my eyes again. "So long as you're near, I'll always be able to sense you."

"Why *me*?"

"Why not?" His fingers teased with the hem of my shirt, his knuckles brushing the skin of my navel. "You said it yourself, how much you despise this place, this way of life.

The parties, the exhibition, the pretension. No more. We can start over."

Where?

In Hell? With an eternally damned soul?

"If it really was you who brought me back to life, then why didn't you change me right there?" I demanded. "Why wait till now?"

"You saw what happened to the others. Making both transitions at the same time isn't too kind on the mind. Sure, it still brings about loyal followers, but as you said, they can be a bit too rambunctious for their own good. It's best to take things a little more slowly. Like us."

His hands gripped my waist, pulling me closer. Too close. Petrified and in a whole new league of disbelief, I remained frozen. What was happening? This couldn't be happening.

Any moment I would wake up from this nightmare. I'd wake up in a cold sweat, feverish from how real it felt. Because this *couldn't* be happening.

I tried to shrink back, but he wouldn't allow it. His hands seized my waist, pulling me back to face him. My feet knocked against his, and I nearly gasped. Had he felt it? Nothing in his eyes indicated he did. A thrill of hope exploded inside my chest at the feeling of my ankle...and the holster strapped around it. Reese's knife. There was a very good chance that Daniel had found and confiscated the blade after he tied me up, but...what if by some miracle, he hadn't?

Anything else wouldn't do any real damage to Blaine, and it certainly wouldn't slow him down. If I stood any chance getting out of here, I needed to make my move. Only, I couldn't reach for it. Not with my hands still cuffed to the bar.

And that glimmer of hope immediately drowned beneath the suffocating upsurge of horror that flooded every inch of me as I realized what I had to do.

One deep inhale, and I let all the tension drain from my limbs as I leaned into him.

His breath suddenly caught, clearly taken aback. Blaine continued working his hands along my waist, and I knew he was testing me, testing to see if I really was game. Fending off every instinct to writhe away, I ground my hips against his. He had to know. Surely, he must have known I didn't want this...

I couldn't do it.

If anything, I was going to vomit. Just as I started to turn away, Blaine's fingers dug into my hips, and he drew me back against him. His lips suddenly claimed mine, and a fire set ablaze in my mind. Startled and horrified, the scream nestled in my lungs threatened to burst right out of my chest, forcing my mouth open. But just as my lips separated, he dove in further, deepening the kiss. Blaine's hands followed down the form of my figure, admiring every dip and curve until he gripped the back of my thighs. As if I weighed nothing, he picked me up, having my legs straddle him on each side.

"You're so beautiful," he breathed. Blaine pressed my back against the wall, and every inch of us became flush. I could feel his heart hammering in his chest. For a guy supposedly incapable of emotions, he surely seemed to be feeling...an awful lot. His kisses became more and more hungry, sending an electric charge between us I hadn't expected.

My legs tightened around his hips, pressing him even closer. This earned him a surprised moan, and my teeth bit down on his bottom lip just enough to break the skin. The pain didn't leave him unaffected.

No.

It incited the mania all the more. His lips feverishly kissed down my neck, nuzzling back into my nape as his opposing hand cupped my face. My eyes caught sight of the mirror across the way, and I could see the sheath exposed beneath my hiked pant leg, the blade still peeking out of the top. I was in the perfect position. All I needed was—

An unmistakable metallic grind ignited above me as my wrists were set free.

I gasped, instinctively wrapping my arms around Blaine's neck as my weight suddenly dropped. He fastened his hold around me, cupping my backside to assure I wouldn't fall an inch. I could feel the hum of a rune vibrating against my thigh. He had set me free. A bright, playful smile immediately lit up his face. A genuine, affectionate smile I had once grown accustomed to. A smile that *shouldn't* have been possible. Not from a heartless, demonic overlord.

No.

I crushed my mouth against his. It was the only thing I could do to rid myself of the sight, feeling the fury of contradicting emotions suddenly pulling at me from every direction. He was a monster. A monster who had *killed* me. Any doubt I had was obliterated. I had a job to do, and I was going to do it. I was so close.

But he was attuned to every inch of me. Everywhere I touched. It wasn't just about getting to the knife. I needed enough time and the element of surprise to successfully stab him. If his reflexes were even half as good as Reese's, he'd be able to stop me well before the blade came anywhere near his skin. And I only had one chance. The moment I struck, the ruse would all be over. No chance of regaining his trust and getting the hell out of Dodge. One shot.

My fingers ran through his hair, surprised by how soft it was. Given the harsh dye he must have used to bleach it, I figured it would have felt like straw. Instead, my hands combed through it without objection, each strand as silky as a raven's feather. I slowly eased my free hand down his neck, careful not to move too quickly. He still shuddered, his breathing quick and anxious, as my fingers grazed his shoulder.

I gasped at the vibration that simultaneously incited between his left hand and my own. A blue light ignited on the top of my hand, the same rune that had ignited when Reese and I were on the couch. Lust.

Given my unknowing run-in with Blaine outside Rockabilly Bob's, I already knew that my runes reacted to his, and he had just triggered mine by way of his own. Overwrought heat spread through every inch of me, and the very thought sent an equally chilling shiver down my spine. He clearly misconstrued the tremble that raked my body, because Blaine's hold on me tightened, drawing me closer. My nails clawed into the taut muscles encasing his shoulder blades, only encouraging him more. His mouth quickly reclaimed my own.

My hand was far enough down Blaine's back. All I had to do was bring my foot up, and I could grab the knife.

But could I do it? Could I bring myself to stab him?

He deserved it, more than anyone.

But I remembered the feeling of having to plunge that very same blade into Brittany. The look of unbridled horror on her face. Having to watch the life leave her eyes. Knowing I was responsible.

The air left my lungs as I drew up my ankle.

Blaine's whole body suddenly went rigid, his lips pulling away from mine.

Shit. Shit. Shit. Shit. Shit. Shit.

CHAPTER 32
Going To Hell

A low, guttural sneer emanated from the back of his throat. "You never fail to disappoint." The primal frenzy brewing behind Blaine's eyes vanished in a blink, replaced by a cold, calculating mask, wicked smile and all.

The shadow lingering in the doorway shifted, and every inch of me went as stiff as Blaine as I peered over his shoulder.

Adam.

Gun readied and aimed, he faltered back a step at the sight of me. At the sight of me with my legs wrapped around Blaine's body. My hand tangled in his hair. At the heavy, panting breaths exchanged between us.

"Reynolds, how lovely of you to join us," jeered Blaine, not even bothering to look over at him. He had known Adam was there the moment he entered the room. "Sorry, love, but the fun's over."

His hands fell away as I disentangled myself from him.

Adam's face was paralyzed in a hundred different degrees of confusion. "Kat...?"

The sound of my name on his tongue seemed to make Blaine visibly ill, because his breathing hitched as he finally took his eyes off me and looked over his shoulder.

Adam clearly didn't realize it had been Blaine, because recognition hit him like a bucket of ice water being dumped over his head. His grip tightened as he snapped the barrel of his gun back at eye level.

But Blaine was faster. One moment I was pressed against the wall, the next I was pried forward, only to be thrown back against the taut muscles of Blaine's chest and torso. He was using my body as a shield between him and Adam. "Easy there, Wyatt Earp. Wouldn't want something to happen to this little vixen now, would we?" He only had one arm wrapped around me, but it was enough to pin my hands down to my sides. Blaine teased the skin on my neck with the very tips of his fingers, and goosebumps perforated down my entire nape as I wrestled against him. He was too strong.

And Adam's eyes missed nothing. Blaine's sleeve was still rolled up to his elbow, displaying every last rune. He looked back to me, and his aim shifted...right to the center of my chest. "How do I know you haven't already?"

He thought I'd been turned. And as horrified as I was, I still couldn't blame him. Not after what he just saw.

"Adam, please," I barely muttered, breathless as tears poured from my eyes.

"Come on, Reynolds. Can't you see you're scaring her?" Blaine mocked, burying a laugh into my ear.

His head perched right over my shoulder, and I shivered at the contact, the intimacy he possessed as he trailed soft kisses up the side of my neck.

Adam must have seen the unreserved panic in my eyes, because his aim fixed back to Blaine's head as I pleaded for him to shoot.

Blaine merely clicked his tongue. "Awww, that's not very nice."

"Let her go," ordered Adam. "Let her go, and I'll let you walk away."

"Oh, okay." Blaine started to loosen his grip on me, and I prepared to bolt, only to have his arm tighten around me again. He laughed. "Is that the same promise your old man made poor little Casey? That he'd let her 'walk away'?"

Adam's stance suddenly faltered, and his name was all I could manage to utter, seeing his jaw tighten. *What was he talking about?*

"Yeah, Reynolds, why don't you educate dear Kat here on the finer points of how your beloved pack takes care of business?" A low growl emitted from Blaine's throat as his mouth found its way back to my neck. "Tell her all about how your father's cronies staged Casey's death so that she looked like she'd been attacked by the same person who killed that Felicia girl."

"He's lying," Adam finally snarled.

"Am I?" Blaine laughed, but it didn't have a hint of amusement. "'Cause I seem to remember things differently—"

"Don't listen to him."

"But it's such a good story," Blaine further prodded. "See, poor Casey had an asthma attack a few days before her untimely demise. Unfortunately, paramedics didn't make it to her in time, but thankfully a dear friend of mine did, after the fact."

"Don't—"

"But," Blaine annunciated, "he didn't turn her. Not

yet. Sadly, word somehow got back to Reynolds's buddies that she *may* have been a possible Changeling. And I have a pretty good feeling you know how the rest of this goes." He could feel the tension leaving me as I fell limp in place. His arm coddled me closer. "That's right. Daddy Dearest just couldn't stand the risk of having another Hellhound walking around that he'd rather order her death sentence than bother trying to keep her safe."

"That's not true," I muttered. *It couldn't be.*

"And what's to stop one of your thugs from killing Kat?" he directed back to Adam. "Your men know she's a target now. Whether I turn her or not, she's still a liability. A threat just waiting to happen. If I let her go now, Kat's as good as dead."

I could see the anguish in Adam's eyes, but I *knew* him. He would never hurt me, and he'd never let anyone either. It was why he wouldn't risk taking a shot at Blaine so long as I stood between them. But Blaine...his repositioned hold around me had freed my arm just enough.

I slowly drew my foot up, almost imperceptibly, my fingers grazing the tip of the blade strapped to my ankle.

Blaine suddenly seized my hand. "Now, now. No need for bloodshed, love. Save that for later."

Fury riddled every last nerve in me as I thrashed, kicked, and flailed to no avail. Why couldn't I ignite any of my runes?

"Because I don't want you to hurt yourself," Blaine whispered, steadying me in his hold.

Did he just...?

I couldn't even process the thought when a deafening blast tore through the air, scaring me stiff.

"Enough!" bellowed Adam.

Blaine only seemed more amused, admiring the bullet

hole now lodged in the wall beside us. "I'm gonna take a wild guess and say that those aren't made of Angelorum steel?"

"Silver. And they'll do the job just fine if I plant one between your eyes."

"Indeed," he mused. "Only, we both know you're not going to try. Not while I've got your little sweetie here."

Adam repositioned his aim, for my shoulder. If Adam fired, the bullet would go through me and into Blaine. And the silver would put him down, even if only long enough for me to break free from him.

"Do it," I whispered.

"He won't. He's too much of a coward."

My eyes suddenly darted to the door. "Adam..."

His reaction time was flawless. Not a split second after Daniel sprang in through the doorway did Adam unload a slug right into his shoulder. Daniel staggered back, but only laughed. It took him a few seconds to register the severity of the gunshot, because he suddenly collapsed to his knees. The bullet must have gotten lodged in him, because I could see smoke emitting from his back as he hunched over, hollering in agony.

A barrage of footsteps echoed down the hall, forcing Adam's attention back to the doorway. Blaine hauled me sideways to the backdoor entrance, only to let go of me. I stood still for a second, confused. He suddenly shot his hands up and closed his fists. Sparks rained down as every light bulb in the room and hallway exploded, letting darkness swallow up every corner of the open space. My hands blindly reached for the doorknob, wrenching it every which way until it finally gave in. I stumbled inside the dank, musty stairwell, only to find that it too was pitch-black. I slammed the door shut behind me, trying to feel my way down. The cement stairs were awkward. Too high and yet not long enough. I didn't have big feet by any means, but my toes still hung off the ends of each step, causing my stomach to lurch with every rung.

I only made it halfway between floors when the door slammed open from above. I could hear hands grip each of the banisters, and in one fell swoop, feet planted themselves right beside me on the platform. Holding my breath, I recoiled into the corner. The pair of feet pivoted toward the next set of stairs, and just as quickly hit the next landing. Hinges creaked as someone pulled the second floor door open, their footsteps vanishing in the distance. I finally let out a shaky breath, feeling my way down to the level.

"Kat?" someone hollered from the other side of the door. The voice was muffled, but...it sounded like Adam. He'd been the one in the stairwell.

I yanked the door open, peering into the hallway. It seemed Blaine had wrecked the emergency lights as well, because only the eerie glimmer from the streetlights outside illuminated the corridor through the windows.

"Ad—"

I barely had time to register the silent sweep of wind that rushed at me from the darkness. A hand clasped around my mouth as a familiar hold grabbed me from behind. I tried screaming anyway, but Adam's voice was too far away to hear my stifled shrieks. Blaine pulled me up off the ground, hauling me back inside the stairwell. Blue lights shone in my eyes, but they weren't from *my* runes. The tilted Z symbol on Blaine's arm glowed, illuminating the closed corridor. I managed to pivot my right foot on the wall in front of us and used it to push myself backward, driving all my weight into Blaine. He tried steadying us, but the force was too much. His back slammed into the opposing wall, knocking the wind right out of him.

Without my feet beneath me, I dropped to the ground, smacking my ass on the concrete floor as he let go of me. I shot up and bolted back out the door. "ADAM!"

My legs were moving so fast, I thought I might lose control of them. I charged through the corridor, leaping down and jumping up the split level stairs of the second story. Just as I called out for Adam again, his frame rounded the corner at the end of the hall. Relief drained from me as the dual doors dividing the corridor between us suddenly bolted shut.

"Kat!" Adam met me in seconds, throwing his weight into the barrier from the other side.

I desperately yanked at the handles, already knowing it was no use. The unseen force rippled all around me, fastening the doors in place. I couldn't control my hysteria as hot tears streamed down my face, my palms slamming against the unforgiving steel.

"Run." Adam was barely audible. All color had drained from his face, his eyes fixed over my shoulder through the small laminated window built into the door. "Kat, get out of here!"

"That's good advice," drawled the voice behind me.

Not bothering to turn around, I bolted to the classroom door closest to me.

Locked.

I darted across the hall to the opposing one. Same thing.

No...no...no.

I couldn't breathe. My lungs were heaving so fast, but my sobs kept robbing me of air. Adam's agonizing screams only further unraveled me as he desperately kicked, slammed, hurtled every ounce of himself into the steel to no avail.

I slammed my fist into the door one last time, praying something would finally give. Nothing.

"Kat..." Blaine's soft voice made my knees buckle, and I cried. I screamed until there wasn't any air left in me. I cried even after my voice gave out. I crumpled to the floor, dignity be damned.

There was nowhere left for me to go.

The faintest heat began spreading up my arm. I opened my fist, finding a small humming light sitting in my palm. It crackled, glinting blue, red, gold, and shades I wasn't even sure had names. I rose back to my feet, turning to face Blaine.

He took one look at the light in my hand and froze. "Kat, don't—"

The promise of hope flickered in my chest. If he really had marked me as his mate, then I shared his abilities. I *could* take him on.

The halls filled with another scream. My own. My entire arm suddenly felt as if someone had dipped it into boiling water. White light flashed in my vision, and arms caught me before I blindly collapsed on the floor. The instant Blaine's hands touched me, the pain stopped.

Everything stopped.

"Kat? Kat!"

I gasped, and my vision finally cleared. Wild, icy blue eyes loomed over me, wide in what looked like...worry. The air had cleared. Not just the energy that I had produced, but his as well. I blinked a few times, and Blaine's features softened, reinstating that lopsided grin.

"Don't scare me like that."

The doors slammed behind me, and I whirled around, seeing the material bow. Without Blaine's magic reinforcing the door, it was finally giving way. Only a few more hits and it would buckle in.

Gun shots erupted from below us, echoing across the lower halls. Swarms of footsteps immediately followed.

"We have to go." Blaine grabbed hold of my arm, pulling me backward.

I tried regaining my bearings, but the floor was suddenly off kilter. It slanted in all the wrong ways, making me stumble over my own feet. With every step, the ground seemed to tilt in another direction. "What did you do to me?" I rasped, still struggling against Blaine's grip.

"I saved you from blowing up the entire city block," he huffed, dragging me to the stairwell.

Broken bits of the lock exploded across the floor as the dual doors burst open. Blaine cursed under his breath, resuming his stance where I was—yet again—his human shield. And I could see why. Adam barreled down the hallway, his gun firmly in hand.

Any hesitation he had before was gone, replaced by an unnerving resolve. "Let her go now, or I'll shoot her." He wasn't kidding. Adam really was willing to put a bullet into me if it meant taking Blaine down. If it meant stopping him from damning me.

Blaine's breathing was suddenly uneven, worsened all the more as Mr. Reynolds's voice called out from the other end of the building.

"They're surrounding the place. You leave now, you just might stand a chance of making it out of here alive. Alone," declared Adam, taking aim to the right side of my chest.

"And what about her?" growled Blaine, pulling me

closer. "The only reason your men haven't killed Kat was because she served a purpose. They needed her to flush out their target. They know now who's pulling the strings here. Your father has no use for Kat. He'll kill her."

"If she leaves with you, she'll be as good as dead." Adam cocked the revolver. "Last chance."

Blaine didn't move.

And neither did I.

I didn't even have time to gasp as an unmistakable, earsplitting blast detonated in front of me. Blaine's hold on me tightened, whirling me around in one fluid motion. He rasped, his body shuddering as he stumbled forward. Blaine caught himself on the wall beside us, inadvertently pivoting us back around so that we faced Adam again. A low hiss seeped from Blaine's shoulder, intensifying to a sickening sizzle. The bullet hadn't passed through the front of his shoulder. I saw what exposure to silver did to Brittany's skin for merely touching it. I nearly wrenched at the thought of what it must have been doing to Blaine's insides.

Adam prepared to take aim again as Blaine's breath warmed my ear.

"This is going to hurt," he whispered.

"NO!"

He was holding me too tightly. I couldn't move.

Two slender spears simultaneously sliced into the side of my neck. I choked on the strangled scream lodged in my chest, deliriously yanking up my hand to hit Blaine, to push him away, to get his own hands off whatever he had just stabbed me with. Every muscle in me fell slackened, my fingers only getting so far as to brush the side of his cheek. His cheek.

My hand limply slipped down to my side. I couldn't move. I *really* couldn't move. My muscles weren't even tensing, struggling against his hold. I was paralyzed in place, my body only held up by the grace of Blaine's arm snaked around me.

His mouth was on my neck. His...his...his fangs. He'd bitten me.

CHAPTER 33
Animal I Have Become

Blaine was still biting me.

The next gunshot barely registered over the blood pounding inside my ears. Blaine's weight staggered and we both fell back. Adam kept yelling something, but I couldn't hear him. I couldn't hear him over my own screams. Every nerve ending fired as the acidic poison propelled its way down my neck, down deeper, down lower. I was burning from the inside out. My veins pumped molten gold. My lungs breathed fire. My skin was melting off. Every muscle contracted so tightly around my bones, I could swear my entire body was about to shatter from within.

And it only worsened. Another wave of unspeakable pain ripped through me. The raw agony tearing through me, and I couldn't even verbalize my anguish. I convulsed, gasping on silent screams. Screams that had no home outside of my chest.

"Accept it," Blaine coughed from behind me. He wasn't dead. "The harder you fight it, the more it'll hurt."

"SHUT UP!" Adam's frantic eyes scanned over my body as he pulled me up into his arms. "I can fix this...I can fix—"

A raw laugh. "You can't stop it."

"SHUT UP!"

Footsteps echoed from the adjoining corridor. Adam quickly set me back down, yanking off his bloodied flannel shirt. He jammed the crumpled fabric into my neck and over my shoulder.

Russell suddenly appeared behind Adam. He took one look at me and his fingers instinctively clenched around the sword in his hands. "What the hell happened?"

"That piece of shit over there tried using Kat to escape, so I shot her," Adam panted, still unable to look at Blaine. "The bullet passed through her and hit him, but I planted in another for good measure."

Russell nodded, his lips tipping up in satisfaction as he slammed a hand onto Adam's shoulder. "Well done."

Mr. Reynolds came into view next. He bent down to get a better look at Blaine, his brows knitting in confusion. "Where have I seen him before?"

"You stopped by his funeral service," sneered Adam. "His name's Blaine Ryder. He's a Mage."

Russell brushed past us with a scoff. It took not five whole seconds before he leapt back into view. "Holy shit. He's not kiddin', boss."

Boss.

The title reverberated in my head, making my veins burn more avidly. Was that what Blaine was going to be to me now? My boss?

Yes, because you're one of them now.

I gasped, pinching my eyes shut. I couldn't mask the pain rippling through me, and Adam knew it. He immediately swept me up, my legs dangling over his left arm as he secured my upper half in his right.

"Where do you think you're going with her?" barked Russell. "The wound will heal on its own. We need to ask her more questions."

Adam only stopped to look at his father. "It'll take hours for the wound to fully heal. I'm not gonna let her suffer like this. She needs something for the pain."

Mr. Reynolds nodded. "Take her to the compound."

"Sir—"

"Take her to the compound," he reiterated, shooting a warning look at Russell. "The rest of us will meet you there shortly. We have some questions for our new friend here."

Blaine choked out a laugh. "As much as I'd thoroughly enjoy that, you won't get anything useful out of me."

"Oh, I beg to differ," said Mr. Reynolds, eerily calm. "And even if that is the case, we'll certainly take pleasure in having you as our guest."

Adam turned our backs to them as I could hear what I knew now to be flesh frying. Blaine gnashed out a grievous, bitten down scream.

No, no, no, no.

Kill him. Kill him now.

My nerves were so sensitive that the bitter October air hit me like a thousand pins prickling all over my body as Adam carried me outside. He pulled me closer to his chest as a violent shudder ran through me. People raced past us to head inside, but I couldn't make out anyone's face. I could barely move.

Where was Reese? Had Blaine been lying about

sparing him? What about Carly? Did Daniel catch up with her?

I must have said something out loud, because Adam whispered softly, "They're okay."

Adjusting my weight in his arms, he unlocked the back door to his Jeep Wrangler and set me inside. I lay across the seats, still convulsing from the pain and the cold. Adam draped his jacket over me before climbing up front. All I could see were streetlights and the tops of trees whiz by as we drove to God only knows where. I'd been clinging to the hope that Adam would give me whatever painkillers he claimed to have, but he finally admitted he couldn't give them to me. He didn't want to risk having the drugs calm me enough that I'd involuntarily let the virus take hold.

It felt like an eternity had passed by the time the car finally came to a stop. We were in a parking garage. Adam gently eased me from the backseat, taking me inside whatever building the structure was attached to. Cold fluorescent lights loomed overhead, and all I could see were cement walls and ceilings. Where were we? A military compound?

Adam took us upstairs to a small room and laid me down on an old mattress. There weren't any windows, and the light was from a desk lamp. "You'll be safe here. The building's been fortified to protect from attack, so none of Blaine's guys will get in."

I didn't have the strength to ask more as I desperately bundled up in the worn comforter. Adam went to the armoire in the corner and pulled out a couple more blankets to cover over me. The pounding in my head grew worse. Even with my eyes closed, the room kept spinning. Adam's voice eventually trailed off as I couldn't fend off the exhaustion anymore.

***

My insides danced in a flurry of nerves, but there wasn't a trace of the fever. I stood facing a wood paneled wall, flinching at the familiar hands brushing my skin. I turned just enough to glance behind me at the black tousled locks and gleaming pale blue eyes in the candlelight. The desolate room chilled my bare legs, but Blaine's touch scorched my skin. What was he doing here? Why was his hair back to its natural color? And it was so much longer, the ends nearly brushing his shoulders. His fingers combed through my own hair, sweeping it away from the right side of my neck. Where he had bitten me. Why wasn't I running? Why wasn't I screaming? My body refused to listen to me, acting on its own accord.

He pulled down the collar of my linen gown past my shoulders, exposing my entire neckline. When had I changed clothes? Blaine's lips pressed to the back of my shoulder blade, slowly moving their way up my neck as his hands caressed my waist. He whispered something warmly in my ear, but the words were lost on me. What was this? How did he get to me? Why wasn't I afraid?

His breath cascaded down my jaw, and a traitorous impulse took hold of me. I angled my head and raked my hand through his tangled mane as our mouths met. His fervor had taken control, because his kiss deepened as he turned me around to stand square with him. Tearing off his shirt, he drove me back against the wooden wall and I moaned from the ecstasy his mere taste gave me as his hands dropped down to my thighs.

"STOP!" I finally reclaimed my voice, only to bellow out into the cool compound room.

"Kat? Kat!" Hands gripped my shoulders, and I shot up from the mattress, furiously batting at them. "Kat, it's me!"

Finally regaining my senses, I looked up, seeing Adam standing over me. I collapsed back into the bed, feeling everything from the sheets to my clothes completely soaked through. I was wearing my outfit from earlier, my Sex Pistols tee clinging to my sweaty frame. Every bone in my body shook and quivered. Fire still ran through my veins, but my outer core was frozen. The only thing that felt warm was the mass of tears now rolling down the sides of my face, absorbing into the already damp pillow. The sight proved to be enough of an assurance for Adam, because he sat down beside me, the old bed groaning under his weight.

He rested the back of his hand against my forehead, his jaw setting even tighter. "You're burning up."

My words came out uneven through chattering teeth as I asked, "Where is he?"

"Reese is at the hospital with Mark and Carly. They're all okay," Adam assured.

It should have given me some sense of relief to hear that, but I just shook my head.

He understood. "You don't need to worry. He's down in the cellar, shackled in silver—"

"I need to see him."

Fear struck those deep blue eyes as they widened, and he involuntarily jerked back as if I might...as if I might bite him.

"He's the only one who really knows what's happening to me. You have to take me to him. I need to know the truth. I need to know..." *if Adam should just kill me now.* It might be more merciful.

"I can't do that—"

"Then I'll go on my own." I flung the blanket off, immediately regretting it. The cold air sliced into me, making me shake even harder. I tried climbing off the mattress, only to have my legs give out on me. Adam was quick to react, catching me before I toppled into the nightstand.

"You look like shit," he murmured.

"Thanks."

His eyes were still sharp, but he let out a steadier breath. "You'll be lucky to get down the hall before passing out. The moment anyone sees you, they'll know something's up."

"Then help me."

Adam bit out another curse as he wrapped his jacket around me. The warm leather fabric swaddled me tightly enough that it actually managed to repress my trembling body from full-on convulsing. His sturdy grip secured me under my arm as he hauled me out of the corridors. Most of the time, my feet didn't even touch the ground. He only set me down when we crossed an occasional passerby. Adam always nodded, and I made sure to keep my head down. I swiped away the beads of sweat dampening my forehead for the billionth time as he carried me down to the basement level.

We rounded the bend, and a brawny man, around thirty, immediately pinned a hand to Adam's chest. "You can't be down here."

"I'm on orders from my father. Leave," he ordered. "Now."

The man hesitated, giving me a wary onceover, but left the way we came and headed upstairs.

The air was thick and damp, reeking of mold and mildew. Adam guided me past several empty stalls equipped to look like old prison cells. Instead of a door blocking off each small space, thick metal bars rested between us and the inside of the enclosures. The cells were stripped of everything except for steel brackets mounted into the walls.

We approached the fifth compartment, and I had to stifle the urge to vomit. A part of me thought it would make me feel better to see Blaine like this. But staring at him, staring at the blistering red burns that charred his exposed chest... I staggered back.

"I was wondering when you'd pay me a visit." Blaine's eyes weren't even open. He sat on the floor, his back resting against the far wall. Chains sat around him, the ends hooked into the thick brackets I now realized were for securing his shackles. They rattled as he moved his hands ever so slightly across the damp cement floor. His wrists... The skin was literally charcoaled black where his wrists were bound, steam simmering off the silver manacles.

Bile rose in my throat as I finally lifted my gaze to his face, only to find him already staring back.

His nostrils flared as he surveyed me. "Well, you look rather worse for wear. I take it you haven't given into your baser instincts yet?"

"How long do I have?" I gnashed, trying to mask my pain with the bitterness that already coated my lips.

"*How long?*" he repeated drolly.

"How long does this last for? When will I...?"

"If you resign yourself to it, it'll be over in a matter of seconds."

"And if I keep fighting it?"

"Then I'd seriously begin doubting your competence." He rolled his eyes as I grimaced. "Hate to break it to you, love, but you've looked better. And no,"

Blaine said, cutting Adam off the moment he opened his mouth. "There isn't a cure. Her body will eventually concede, willing or not. She's got twelve hours, a day at the most."

"What is she going to become?" gritted Adam.

"She's an extension of me now. She'll become faster, stronger, more agile." A seared hand flicked to my concealed arm. "She'll finally be able to put that beautiful artwork to real use."

"Not a Hellhound?" The words were like poison on my tongue.

"Those insufferable things? God no. They're far too aggressive for my palate," Blaine jeered. His amused grin cast into a vulpine smile as his eyes danced over my body. "I appreciate passion of a different variety. One you're very familiar with."

I glowered at him, shifting away from the bars.

"Don't be coy now." He teased at the chains binding him, even as they seared deeper into his wrists. "I was quite impressed by what you could do without the use of your hands. And I'm particularly aroused at the prospect of seeing the fullest extent of what you could do *with* them.

"I'd sooner choke to death on my own vomit."

"No need to pretend, Kitten. You know you enjoyed it." His smile only grew bigger, especially as he turned his attention to Adam. "Hell, Reynolds saw it for himself. Did she really look that disgusted?"

I looked over at Adam, and sure enough, he was scowling. *Did he honestly think I enjoyed that?*

"I'll take his silence as an endorsement."

All he wanted was to get a rise out of Adam, and he was doing just that. My tolerance was nonexistent as I finally barked, "Why me? Why do any of this?"

"Awww, where would the fun be in telling you that?" Blaine crooned. "Besides, a boy's allowed to have some secrets, isn't he?"

"Yeah, well, those secrets are gonna be following you right into the grave, because that's where you'll be by sunrise," gnashed Adam.

"Oh, I wouldn't be so sure of that." He haughtily rested his burning wrists on his propped up knees. "Not if you wish to spare Kat from sharing in that same fate."

"What is that supposed to mean?"

"She's my mate now. Our lives are one and the same. Linked for eternity. If you kill me, she'll die too."

I wasn't breathing, and by the silence beside me, I wasn't sure if Adam was either.

That was why he had bitten me. Blaine could have tried making a run for it at the school when Mr. Reynolds had the place surrounded, but he could just as easily been caught—and shot dead on sight. Now, this way, he had a guaranteed ticket to freedom. Adam would have to let him go, and furthermore, do everything he could to make sure his father wouldn't find Blaine after he did.

"Bullshit," Adam spat.

"Perhaps," Blaine cooed. "But then again, there's only one way to find out. Are you *really* willing to risk it?"

A heavy iron gate clanked from the other end of the hall, and we all startled. Russell's voice boomed across the cellar, urging Adam to throw his fresh overshirt at me. He patted the fabric across my face, wiping up the chilled sweat dampening my forehead. I tried steadying myself as best I could as the footsteps came closer. Russell rounded the bend of the corridor, and he stopped short when seeing us.

"*Why is she here?*" His eyes shot over to me before settling on Adam. Adam opened his mouth, but Russell didn't wait for his response. "You know better. We can't risk her getting too close to that vermin."

"I highly doubt he's strong enough to snatch her through the bars," said Adam. "He'd be lucky if he could stand."

Russell merely scoffed. "Best be on your way. Your father wants to speak with you in his office."

Adam stole a look at me out of the corner of his eye before nodding. "Sure, just let me take her back to my room first-"

"That won't be necessary," interrupted Russell. "We're heading out to the safe house. Transport just arrived."

Before I knew it, Russell's beefy hand seized me around the arm.

"Don't-" Blaine sprang forward, the silver chain wrenching him back to the floor.

Startled by the outburst, Russell yanked me away from the cell, hurling my body into the cement wall on the other side of the hall. "'Lucky' my ass. Go get Jenkins back down here to pay this scum another visit, this time with the full workup." He kicked a heavy boot at the bars. "Let's see how he fairs with colloidal silver injections."

"You can't let them take her," Blaine seethed, his indignant eyes fixed on Adam as Russell pried me away. "Don't let him take her!"

"*Now*," ordered Russell. Adam paused for a brief moment, as if he might challenge the command. My heart sank though as he mournfully headed in the other direction. I wasn't sure if it was the darkness taking root in my gut or just good old intuition, but nothing about this felt right.

Blaine's deafening screams rang in my ear as Russell dragged me back down the way he'd come. I struggled under the brute's hold, feeling his firm grip tightening all the more the moment I tried pulling away from him. He shot me a dark look.

"You don't have to treat me like a disobedient dog. I can walk myself," I said, trying to mask my dread as mere annoyance.

"It's for your own safety," he assured, dragging me out through the iron gates. We headed up the steep cement steps, coming to the entrance where four white cargo vans sat parked out front. Russell directed me to the third one, opening up the back door. "The drive shouldn't take more than twenty minutes. Just stay put, and we'll be on our way in a few."

"What are all these for?" I asked, pointing to the rest of the vehicles.

"It's just a precaution. The rest of the crew will be hiding in the backs of the other vans, locked and loaded. So if Hellhounds try to ambush us on the road, they won't know where you are. And we'll take them down before they even get close to you."

Unless I wanted my shoulder ripped from its socket, I had no choice but to climb up into the empty van as Russell yanked up my arm to hoist me inside. There was a small foldout seat in the back corner, and I strapped myself in. He shut the doors behind me, locking them from the outside.

This was so not good.

There weren't any windows in the cargo bed, sending me into complete darkness. Indistinct voices clamored outside, and not a minute later did the engine roar to life.

What was I going to do? Adam had abandoned me. Did he have another plan devised? With all the guys coming on this trip to the safe house, it meant that the compound was now lax on security. Was that what he anticipated, setting Blaine free at the opportune time? Every last ounce of hope I had clung to that possibility. If not, Blaine would surely be dead long before I had a prayer of getting back here.

The cabin jolted as we accelerated, and a strange numbness swept over me.

CHAPTER 34
Until the End

The darkness dissolved as metal bars formed in front of my face. I was suddenly standing, now looking out into the basement hallway. Chains softly clattered behind me, and I spun around to see none other than Blaine still sitting on the floor. I was in his cell! On the wrong side of the bars!

I expected him to look up at me with that cocky grin, an innuendo already laced in his words, but he didn't budge. Didn't bother to pay any mind to me. I staggered back, expecting to crash into the caged bars. Only, I didn't stop. I had to catch myself as I fell out into the free side of the hallway. The bars were still intact, but I'd just floated right through them as if they were made of air.

I hesitantly reached out to touch the bars. My fingers passed clear through them. I waved my hand from side to side, watching my entire arm go through the railing. Was I...a ghost? Had I died in the car ride?

"Blaine?"

He didn't respond.

I slowly eased myself back into the cell, slipping right through the barrier. I waved my hand in front of his face, calling out his name again. His head lifted, and I stumbled back. Had he heard me? He let out a jagged breath, letting his head fall back against the cement wall. Tremors continually ran through his body, and his eyes pinched shut as he tried adjusting his scorched wrists in the manacles. I couldn't believe I even considered it, but I knelt down beside him and rested my hand on his shoulder. He had to feel me, right?

Yet again, my hand fell right through him.

Footsteps reverberated from the main stairwell, startling me back upright. Blaine sighed, almost laughing, but it was raw.

"Come to kill me yourself?" He glared up between matted blonde locks of hair at the visitor in question and scoffed. "I thought you only sent out your lapdogs to do your dirty work."

Mr. Reynolds grabbed the iron folding chair resting against the far wall and dragged it over in front of the cell, taking a seat. His unflinching gaze homed on the young man. "No, I've come to look evil in the face."

"Well, that's ironic."

"You nearly killed three of my men just bringing you here."

A fiendish grin painted Blaine's mouth as he chuckled. His body had gone taut, suppressing any signs of the agony he clearly exhibited not a minute ago. "Well, you have me dead to rights there."

Reynolds's features hardened as his teeth ground. "He should have killed you when he had the chance."

"Your son?"

"Your father."

Blaine's mock amusement washed from his face, replaced by incredulity.

"He deserved the death he got," Nathan spat, "bringing a monster into this world."

"Takes one to know one."

"I'm not the monster here."

Blaine's jaw wrenched as resentment heated his eyes. "You honestly believe that, don't you? After everything you've done...and your conscience is still clear."

"What exactly are you accusing me of?"

"Kat told me all about you, about how you were like the father she never had. She doesn't realize how truly fortunate she really is." The ire behind his eyes was unmistakable as his brow ticked up, reading Reynolds's expression. The air grievously heaved from his lungs. "Tell me, will you be the one to kill her, or are you as spineless as I think you are?"

Mr. Reynolds didn't say anything, his face now unreadable.

"Your lackey, then?"

"Why are you after Kat?"

Blaine's knuckles turned white as he balled his hands into fists. "Why are you?"

"I'm not."

"I saw you at the hospital," Blaine growled.

Nathan stiffened.

"You injected something into her I.V. before I so rudely walked in on you. What was it?"

My stomach turned, and I had to brace a hand against my chest. What was he talking about? The memories snapped back into place. When I first woke up in the hospital, I had heard two distinct male voices. One telling the other that I wasn't allowed to have visitors. Cinnamon and cigars. Mr. Reynolds had been in my room. But the other... the male nurse in the medical mask and scrub cap. Black hair; he had black hair. And he refused to look at me. *"Shhh, you're okay now,"* he had assured.

Mr. Reynolds seemed to put the pieces together as well. "...You."

"She's a lot stronger than she looks, isn't she?" A feline smile. "So what was it? Potassium chloride? I can only assume, given her heart slowed, along with her breathing. And she wasn't exactly light on her feet when she woke up later."

Potassium chloride? I'd learned about that in freshman science. It was what they used to kill people through lethal injection!

"And you still believe *I'm* the monster." Blaine glowered.

"We do what's necessary."

In one swift blur, Blaine lunged at the bars, the silver chains stretched as far as they could go. The shackles weren't long enough for Blaine to make a snatch at him, but the outburst sent Nathan reeling back nevertheless. "She hadn't been turned, and you fucking knew it!"

"She was already dead," Mr. Reynolds finally snapped. "Thanks to you. It's unnatural, what she became. *You're* the one who took her life away."

"I brought her back!"

"Out of selfish need, no doubt. What I did, what needs to be done...that takes sacrifice."

"Sacrifice?" Blaine seethed. "You're a fucking coward! You're not doing any of this for the greater good. It's out of fear." His pale eyes glinted, seeming to soak up all the light in the room. And his jaw. It trembled ever so slightly. "You said it yourself, she's like a daughter to you."

"I killed my own wife!"

Blaine stilled.

"Adam's mother was a Changeling, and just like Kat, she'd been targeted by Hellhounds." The only time I'd ever seen Mr. Reynolds outright cry was at her funeral, but even now, the very mention of her still brought tears to his eyes as he stared at the wall. "I came home one night to find half a dozen of our friends splayed in the kitchen, their throats torn clear out of their necks. And there was Madeline, sitting at the table, covered in blood, picking bone and flesh from her nails. Whistling. She'd been bitten. And as consequence, she killed all the other members of our pack, just because—as she put it—she 'got bored.' The only reason she didn't kill Adam was because he'd snuck off to see Kat before his mom came home." His gaze hardened as he looked back at Blaine. "I do what I have to."

My body lurched as a high-pitched squeak struck the air. Darkness engulfed me once more, and it took me a moment to remember where I was. What had that been? Astral projection? Even wrapped up in the warmth of Adam's jacket, my whole body shivered from the unbearable coolness in my core. I slumped against the side of the van, pinching my eyes shut. It didn't matter what I did; the world kept spinning around me as if I was trapped in a tilt awhirl.

Maybe Blaine was right. If I surrendered to the pain, maybe it would hurt less. But I refused to allow it. The darkness coursing its way through me could very well consume my body, turning me into something even more horrific than a Hellhound. I couldn't let it take hold of me.

The van shifted as I heard the front door open and

close. A moment later, Russell unlocked the cabin doors, gesturing me out. It wasn't much brighter outside. Low rumbles of thunder resounded overhead, and the bleak landscape illuminated for a split second as lightning tore the sky open. Trees sat in the distance, nothing but a lush green field stretching out around us.

"Where are we?" I muttered, trying best to collect myself as I unbuckled my seatbelt.

Russell didn't answer.

I staggered toward the backend, clearly seeing now that none of the other vans were there. Amid the burning in my veins, I couldn't mistake the hot release of a rune igniting on my arm. I was in trouble. Russell wrapped his beefy mitts around my wrist, yanking me down to the ground. The only reason I didn't eat a mouthful of grass blades was because he kept my arm suspended up, once again threatening to tear my shoulder out of its socket.

I'd barely managed to regain my footing when he started dragging me around the van. The vehicle was still turned on, its headlights cascading across the desolate field. Up ahead, I noticed the ground gave way. It was a hole.

I slammed my feet into the uneven soil, but it didn't slow us down. It only made Russell pull harder. "What are we doing out here?"

"Cleaning up the mess your boyfriend made." He gave me one last commanding yank, throwing me out in front of him. I caught my balance not more than a foot from the gaping hole in the ground. Again, Blaine was right. Mr. Reynolds had issued my death warrant, and Russell was about to make good on it.

I turned around, the headlights blaring into my eyes. The outline of his shadowed figure was unmistakable, particularly the long blade wielded in his hands. "Why didn't you just kill me in the van?" I surprised myself saying that, but it wasn't worth keeping up pretenses anymore. We both knew the score.

"Why bother having to tow your body when I can just make you walk here?" he retorted so matter-of-factly, nodding to the hole. "Plus, it saves on clean up. Blood would be hard to wash out of the van. And it seems wrong to stain the grass."

Well, that was a lovely sentiment.

Thunder shook the earth beneath our feet just before a bolt of lightning struck a nearby tree. We both jumped as the sky suddenly exploded with a flash as if a miniature bomb had gone off. The electrical bolt raged for just a second, somehow reflecting bright blue, hot pink, and fiery red all in one short swoop. The tree split in two, the unstructured half crashing to the ground as flames still tickled the charred lumber.

Unsure if I had really been responsible for it, I still used the distraction to my advantage. Lurching sideways, I dashed around the hole, away from the light.

A peculiar feeling suddenly washed over me. I couldn't explain it. It was as if I'd been here before, as if I knew what I needed to do. I took a step back and dropped out of sight, right into the cavern.

My stomach, as well as everything else, lurched as adrenalin kicked in from the freefall. The drop was a good fifteen, maybe twenty, feet down. Once again I crashed onto the soot-covered floor. Lightning struck again, highlighting the damp room. All the skeletons, all the remains. Hellhounds turned to ash when they were killed, meaning only one thing. These were Changelings, people who posed a threat to the order. This was where the innocent really went when they "disappeared."

Russell's head peeked out from atop of the hole, and I all-out screamed, scrambling out of sight as the trigger pulled. The singular sound of a gun blast exploded across the hollow space, leaving a high-pitched ringing in my ears. I could hear Russell curse as I faced the shadows of the three passageways. A swallowing draft kicked up the ash around me from the center opening, just as it did in the vision. This time though, I didn't hear footsteps.

Instinct told me to leap away, but that meant placing me back into the line of fire from up above. There wasn't a chance in hell I was going down *that* passage. Instead, I darted into the corridor to my left. I made it a whole ten feet in before the stench burned my nose, practically knocking me backward. I didn't need to see it for myself to know what putrefaction lay ahead in the dead, stagnant air. Something, or more like someone, was decomposing. I ran back out to try the last passage when I noticed the same foul odor right at the mouth of the opening. I had no choice. If I stayed, I was dead.

Up top, it had gone quiet. The bodies down here had been moved, which meant there was a way to get out. And a way for Russell to get in. If I had any chance of beating him to wherever this came out, I had to move. Fast.

Feeling my way through the center passage, I could smell the fresh fragrance of evergreens coming from up ahead, but blindly stumbling over the rough terrain didn't exactly help me on time efficiency. The path seemed never-ending, and I still couldn't hear anything above the low roar of thunder.

The slightest hint of light poked out at last around the dank bend. The moon still shone through the stormy sky, helping illuminate the landscape. An overgrowth of moss and fern clung to everything nearby, from the rocks to the tree lines. The mouth of the cave sat on an incline, the ground sloping dangerously down to a small pond.

I couldn't see any clear path that Russell might come from, but the surrounding landscape appeared empty. Climbing down, my vision swayed as I got snagged on a rogue tree branch. Wrenching myself free, I lost my footing and wound up tumbling to the bottom of the hillside. Plummeting right into a buttonbush, I woozily peered around.

Still, no one was in sight.

Pulling myself up, I made it over to the pond when my entire body locked up. I willed myself to move, but the fever in me hissed with fury, as if sensing my resistance. The harder I tried to move, the fiercer the fever sent that wave of fire to burn through my veins. I choked out a silent cry, collapsing into the ground. Red flooded my vision as my body seized up again.

Move.

Move.

Move.

I had to move.

My airways even felt like they were being singed. I couldn't move. I couldn't breathe. I couldn't...I couldn't die. Not like this. Not alone in the woods.

"Well, well, well. Look at what we have here."

I began to cry for a whole other reason. It was Russell. I was turned the other way, but I could hear his boots crack over all the loose foliage. Not more than ten feet away.

Move.
Move.
Move.
...Attack.

A wallop blasted behind me, and all I could do was flinch, expecting a bullet to tear through my body. Instead, a large mass hurtled past me, crashing somewhere in the overgrowth ahead. I could feel the magnetism, the energy coursing through the air. Magic. But...had I done that somehow?

Heat spread across my chest. Not the fever. That familiar, comforting warmth.

Reese.

Russell's frame staggered upright, and I could see the gleam of his sword in hand. He brushed himself off and reeled toward me, his face contorted with confusion. His eyes traveled behind me, and he froze.

"Miss me?"

No.

It wasn't Reese. That voice...it was Blaine.

CHAPTER 35
Own Little World

No further words were exchanged. The two rushed at one another, steel clashing as they met each other's proposals. With the flash of lightning overhead, I could make them out amongst the shadows. Blaine didn't have a sword. Just two daggers primed in hand. Still, by a hair's breadth, he continued to avoid each of Russell's pummeling strikes, time and time again.

With the next attempt, Blaine narrowly escaped the sweeping blade by dropping to the ground. The brute swung his blade and prepared for the final blow, but Blaine chopped his legs around Russell's and rolled over. The force knocked Russell to the ground as well. Both of them tried to grab a hold of their mislaid weapons, and I could see one of Blaine's daggers a few feet from me. I tried to speak, but nothing more than a grievous groan escaped. Russell scoured the foreground, still not seeing where his sword had fallen. He suddenly sprang forward and tackled Blaine, drilling him into the ground with an annihilating impact.

They escaped my line of vision, and all I could hear

was a rasp of air as Russell climbed back to his feet. He staggered toward a clearing, returning with his sword in hand. Blaine was still on the ground, struggling for breath.

Come on. Use your runes.

Blast this son of a bitch into oblivion.

In my current state, I was lucky to lift a finger. But Blaine could do it. He just had.

Just do it again.

Lightning flashed, and I finally got a good look at Blaine. The guy was as pale as sheetrock, his own blood staining every inch of clothing. Whatever Mr. Reynolds had done to him with that silver, it had drained him.

Russell strolled back to us, sword raised like a guillotine ready to deliver Blaine's execution. The moment the Reaper reached his feet, the boy suddenly kicked his legs up towards his head, jack-knifing back upright in front of Russell's face. Slamming an elbow into Russell's nose, Blaine brought the man to his knees with a crushing blow to the left kneecap that made a sickening pop upon impact. The guy still rallied the strength to bring up his sword, forcing Blaine to cower back before it could slice into him.

Using every ounce of energy I could muster, I kicked the nearby dagger, and it skittered across the pebbled ground towards Blaine's feet. A whisper of a smile danced across his lips as he knelt to snatch it up. And just in time.

Russell came barreling at him, driving his sword through the air with devastating momentum. Blaine sidestepped by a hair's breadth, seeing sparks erupt from the blade as it slashed against the rock face behind him. That wasn't a normal sword. I could feel its power pulsating from the hilt.

Blaine ducked the next sling of the blade and pushed right up to Russell, barely managing to drive his dagger into the Reaper's side before the sword hurtled at him again. He tore the knife free from the brute's flesh, trying to use it in an attempt to deflect the attack. It only managed to slow its impact. The blade came right at him. Blaine threw his arm up to avert the full brunt of the blow to his chest, and the steel sliced him down the entire length of his forearm. A sickening hiss seared the skin as the flesh was carved open.

Blaine collapsed, a guttural scream ripping through his lungs as smoke actually billowed out from the wound.

That wasn't just silver in the blade. Something unnatural stirred inside it, absorbing the blood staining its blade until the sword spotlessly gleamed in the pale moon light.

Russell swiftly brought his blade up again, and I suddenly cried, "Stop!"

The Reaper cocked his head over his shoulder and smirked. "You want to go first? Fine by me," he sneered, snickering at the beaten boy writhing on the ground at his feet.

"No!" Blaine gritted through clenched teeth, watching Russell turn to me. He tried to get his knees under himself to stand, but he slumped back down, his whole body shuddering from sheer agony.

The faintest glow ignited from under my sleeve. Anger.

Focus.

I pinched my eyes shut, trying to picture what I needed to do. An invisible force slammed down on me as I managed to wave my hand. Whatever enchanted that sword didn't want me controlling it. It yanked itself in the other direction, ripping free from Russell's grip. The blade flung aside, disappearing into a collection of overgrowth.

Russell turned back to Blaine, clearly believing him to

be the culprit. "Stay put, you little shit. I'd hate for you to miss this." He snatched a handful of my hair and yanked me upright to my knees. I choked on a stifled breath as cold metal seized my throat. I gasped, but it served no good. Metal rattled as the grip tightened. It was a chain. Blaine's guttural screams bellowed across the valley.

Russell jeered, prying me up. My knees were now suspended off the ground, but I didn't have enough space to gain my footing. He continued to squeeze. Tighter and tighter. Gray began invading my vision as I reached up, clawing at his hands, his wrists. Anything to find relief.

But something else was wrong. It felt and sounded like a clothing iron was being dragged across my neck. It burned like hellfire! My fingers grappled at the chain, only to meet the same scalding.

"*What the hell?*" Russell sneered.

Even through my blurred vision, I could see it. Smoke. It was rising up from my neck.

"I fucking knew it. You blood whore!"

My body began convulsing. It was shutting down.

Save that for later. Blaine's words slammed into the forefront of my mind. *Save* that *for later.*

I drew my leg up and pried out Reese's knife. Before Russell could even figure out what I held, I reached behind me and plunged the blade into his thigh. I could feel muscles and tendons ripping apart under the drag of the dagger as I yanked it down.

Sweet relief finally flooded my lungs the moment I pulled the blade free from his flesh. The chain clattered to the ground, but a heavy boot hammered into my back as Russell called me every rotten name in the book. The impact knocked the wind right out of me again, and I face planted into the grass, gasping for air.

The world fell silent, except for a lone gurgle, as something warm splashed my back and hands. Still croaking, I rolled to my side, only to have Russell fall down beside me. His hands clasped desperately at his throat. The sickening wheeze that rasped from his severed windpipe sent blood spraying everywhere.

One look at my own hands, and I shot up from the ground, still unable to drag in a breath. I collapsed backward, furiously rubbing my hands against the grass and the fabric of my pants. His blood was all over me.

What had I done?

What had I done?

What had I done?

I killed him. I killed him. How did I kill him? Had a rune ignited?

"Hey."

I gasped, seeing crystallized blue eyes suddenly looming over me. Blaine. The hilt to Russell's creepy filigree sword dangled in his limp fingers. Just as before, the blood evaporated from the blade. He let it fall.

"You…"

His arms suddenly cradled beneath my back and the bends of my knees. He was trying to lift me off the ground.

"No," was all I could manage. I batted my hands and threw my elbows at him until he finally let me go.

"Kat—"

"Get away from me," I rasped, mindlessly crawling across the grass.

"Kat, stop."

The chain. It was lying in the dirt beside Russell's body. I immediately snatched it up, ready to hurl it at Blaine.

He groaned. "Kat—"

The instant my fingers wrapped around the fetter, I

cried. My skin sizzled, and smoke rose from the area of contact even after I dropped the manacle. *"What...?"*

Blaine's hands cradled my own. "It's silver."

No, no, no, no, no!

I must have said it out loud, because he pulled me to his chest, pleading with me to calm down. Hot tears burned my cheeks as I beat his torso, trying to wrestle out of his hold.

Only the purest of evil is affected by silver.

Only the purest of evil.

I wasn't evil! I didn't want this! I never asked for any of this!

"Make it stop!" I wept, bundling my fists into the fabric of Blaine's shirt. I was the one now pulling at him, burying my face into his chest.

He knew what I meant, and he only held me closer. "It'll get better—"

"You did this to me! You made me into a monster!" My balled up fists slammed against him, but he wouldn't budge.

"You need to calm down," he murmured. "You'll only make it worse—"

"Why?!"

And that was it. The fever roared harder than ever. Blaine's voice fell distant over my unbearable cries. I couldn't control myself anymore. Every inch of me ripped apart as my vision went black.

CHAPTER 36
Bring Me To Life

I didn't know how I got inside the SUV. I didn't know where we were driving to. I didn't even know how long I had passed out for. One thing I did know: Blaine was driving without any keys in the ignition. The very thought sent a strange wave of crackling electricity into my fingertips. Could we manipulate electronics too? My mind jumped back to the stranger landing on the hood of my car. He—Blaine—had shut down the entire dashboard by merely laying a hand on the vehicle.

The burns from my neck and hands had died down to a small ache, but the rest of me... I couldn't put it into words. Between the unspeakable pains tearing through me and the fever that was at its very height, it took everything inside of me to stay conscious. Blaine's hand cupped the bottom of my face, urging my bobbing head back upright.

"Hey, stay with me. You're gonna be okay. Just hold on a little longer." His voice was so assuring that it made me laugh. It came out as nothing more than a grievous sigh. Talk about déjà vu. For the second time, Blaine was driving me 'somewhere safe' as I sat in the passenger seat feeling like I was about to die.

His arm was bandaged in makeshift bindings that looked like a ripped up t-shirt. Blood soaked it all the way through, leaving tiny droplets to paint the center counsel. I whipped my face away from him, letting my entire body slump against the door. Everything blew past the window in a blur of black and blue hues. The moonlight caught the very tops of the towering oak trees, but darkness consumed everything below.

A single pale light flashed by in an instant, and I blinked to make sure I'd even seen it. Sure enough, another light flew past us as well. There was something on the other side of those trees. My vision dazedly swung to the front window just in time to see an advertisement sign that read, "Slippery Pete's: Best Bourbon in New England - 0.5 Miles."

We were down near the pier, right by the shopping district. I knew from the extensive bus ride I'd taken last week that the road up ahead would soon curve around a bend to the coastline where only recluse houses built into the hillsides occupied the area. As soon as we'd pass the docks, we'd be leaving civilization behind for miles.

Whatever Blaine had prepared for me wasn't going to be pretty. He was going to use me as some mindless weapon in his perverted plan for power, and I refused to just sit back and play victim. I'd been manipulative and toyed with long enough. I wasn't going to be anyone's captive. Not anymore. If I was looking for an out, this would be the best I'd get.

My fingers slowly pressed into the seatbelt release button. As soon as I felt the clip free, I leaned back toward Blaine, suddenly throttling my elbow up. His reflexes were better than I had anticipated, because he managed to turn his head away just enough that it didn't hit him in the nose.

My blow did, however, connect with his cheekbone. Before he even had the chance to react, I tore off the seatbelt and threw the passenger door open.

"Kat!" He reached for the back of my jacket, but I was gone.

My survival instincts turned out to be better than my calculations, because I completely missed the patch of overgrowth I'd been aiming for. Tucking and rolling, my world spun as I collided into the ground with an excruciating hit. My body skimmed across the roadside in a whirl, kicking up debris and gravel along the way. I expected the grass up ahead to cushion my blow, but I slammed to a halt the moment I reached the meadow, feeling my ribs break on impact. Every curse word spilled from my lips as I cried out, only making the pain worse as my lungs expanded. Peeling myself off the sizable rock hidden beneath the lush grass, I could feel the dampness pooling underneath my shirt. But I didn't have time to bleed.

The Cadillac's tires screeched as Blaine's voice called out from down the road. The vehicle suddenly came hurtling back toward me in reverse, urging me to take off into the thicket. Blindly stumbling over broken tree branches and taking low hanging twigs to the face, I ran as fast as my legs and lungs would allow through the shadowed forest.

Footsteps pounded into the earth behind me. Blaine was out of the car, and now in hot pursuit. The closer he got, the harder I pushed myself. I wasn't even breathing. It was the only way to minimize the crippling pain from my ribs. Every time I was forced to take an inhale out of necessity, I nearly fell to the ground in blinding agony. The mouth to an alleyway came into sight, and I didn't need to tell people to move out of the way. As soon as my bloodied and beaten frame came rocketing out into the shopping district, every last person shrieked and fell back from me.

It wasn't until I was around the masses of people that it hit me. Being in a crowd didn't barter me protection. Unlike ordinary people, Blaine wouldn't care if others saw him. He could attack me and drag me away without batting an eyelash, because his powers of illusion could make any human see what he wanted them to. A ninja, Santa Claus, Voldemort.

It didn't matter. The only thing that did was getting away, getting far enough away that whatever bond we shared lessened until he couldn't sense me anymore. I needed to lose myself in the crowd first, which didn't seem too hard. The district was made up of several streets, all looping about in a massive square, with a courtyard venue sitting in the middle.

I pushed my way into a vintage candy shop, going to the back where there was an additional entrance that connected with the next boulevard. Masses of people meandered about in the middle of the cobblestone street, only separating to let an occasional car pass through. The nightlife was in full swing, with everyone buzzing about the shops or heading towards the numerous pubs and sports bars down the stretch. Struggling to stay upright, I headed to the south end. The trolley system was at the front gates, and it was always packed, which seemed like my safest bet. Standing up on my tiptoes, I could barely see the wrought iron décor that marked the courtyard.

Crap. I was on the whole other end of the district. Trying to regain my pace, I forced myself between all the couples hogging up the street. A girl in a plunging white halter shrieked and even batted her dangerously long fingernails at me like I was infested with flees as I cut between her and her date. If I looked even half as grimy as I felt, the reaction was entirely warranted.

"*Don't.*"

I whirled around, nearly stumbling over my own two feet. The voice. It had come from inside my head, but it belonged to Blaine.

"*Don't run. You'll only make things worse.*"

Taking in a much needed breath, I buckled over, trying to relieve the pressure pushing against my ribs. I straightened, just in time to see bleach blonde hair peaking over the tops of the crowd. Shit. I spun back around, only to hear everyone behind me gasp. I looked over my shoulder, watching as everyone was suddenly swept off their feet and tossed in every different direction away from the middle of the street. With the sea of people now parted, Blaine stared back at me, in full view.

A guitar hummed in the distance, a blues melody that surely came from a street performer. They were guaranteed to draw in a sizeable curbside audience. It had to be coming from the courtyard. Further screams ensued as I battled my way through the masses of people, but I didn't dare look behind me.

Zigzagging between people, I was losing ground on him, and fast. My runes were blazing from beneath Adam's jacket, but I couldn't tell which ones I was even engaging. If Blaine wanted to play dirty, I wouldn't go down without at least taking a swing of my own. Zooming past Blacksmith's, a Wild West throwback bar, I tunneled my focus on one of the old-fashioned rocking chair sitting out front. Channeling the invisible force inside me, I yanked my hand back, watching the giant wooden prop fly from the sidewalk. It hurtled behind me, and I could hear the wood splinter on contact as it hammered into something...or someone. Sure enough, Blaine was laying on the cobblestone street, clearly in a daze from the impact. He barely managed to stagger back up to his feet by the time I disappeared into the madness of the courtyard.

The more people that screamed and shrieked at the sight of me, the easier it would be for Blaine to track me. Hunching down, I slowly weaseled through the huddled masses, keeping out of sight. Instead of moving against the crowd, I fell into the flow of it. The less of a disturbance I made, the harder I'd be to spot. I slinked over into a corner café, sliding into an available seat at an occupied table. The two women who had already been sitting there froze with their cappuccinos hovering just below their lips.

"Can we help you?" one of them managed to utter.

I curled over in the chair, relieved to finally catch my breath. A sharp snap shifted in my rib cage, forcing my hand to the beaten spot. I could only hope that it was the sound of my bones being put back into place. The pain dissipated enough that I removed my hand, and my bloodied digits didn't go unnoticed by my two new friends.

"Please don't," I panted, slapping one of the women's cell phones away as she prepared to dial. I lay my face down on the cool, steel tabletop. "I...need...to hide."

"From what? A doctor?" the other woman yelped, trying a little too late to lower her voice.

"An...ex." I guess it was sort of true. I managed to look up, watching nameless bystanders walk in and out of frame from the café's window. No sign of him.

I stifled a sudden cry as the base of my ring finger scalded with a fiery rage. Sure enough, cheekbones sharp enough to split a hair came into view from the other side of the windowpane. I muttered a curse as I turned away, trying to lift my head up off the table as discretely as I could. My nails dug into my hand, clenching around the skin that I

406

could see lighting up even under the guise of my glove. It was the weird entwined rune wrapped around my ring finger. Had I activated it, or had *he*?

Letting my hair fall into my face to obscure my features, I snuck a look around a mass of matted locks to see Blaine still standing there, his eyes scoping out the crowds.

"Damn it," I growled.

The two women followed my line of vision, and their faces contorted in disbelief. I could only imagine what they were seeing. Another twenty seconds or so passed, and he eventually walked out of view towards the north end. I slumped back in my seat, taking the last decent breath I could afford. After a solid minute passed, it seemed safe to say the coast was clear. Muddled messes of music overwhelmed my senses as the blues guitars from the street mixed with the hip-hop and dance songs pouring out of the bars and nightclubs. I couldn't even tell if the pounding in my chest came from my heart or the ear-aching thumping of three different bass numbers clashing into one another.

Slithering my way between people, I kept my head down, finally making some headway back towards the front gate. The courtyard was much more crowded than the streets, and I appreciated the additional coverage. Just keep moving, and stay down. Just keep moving, and stay down. The south end exit from the courtyard was in sight. Thirty more yards, and I was home free. A hollering pack of frat guys came barreling down on me, forcing me against the wall in front of some Creamery that offered Chicago-styled hot dogs. Squeezing by, I passed the narrow alleyway between the buildings, and I knew before I even felt the yank on my arm that it was a mistake.

"Well, look who wandered in. About time." Blaine tossed some kind of food wrapper into the dumpsters behind us as he pinned me against the brick siding.

Seriously? I was trying to stay conscious long enough to get away, and here this asshole was, idly eating a hot dog, just waiting for me to show up. He was right. I was out of my league. He didn't have to bother holding me with both hands. I started sliding down the wall, feeling my shaking legs caving out from under me.

Of all things, he propped me back upright. "My, my. You are tenacious, aren't you? Stupid, but tenacious nevertheless. I'll give you that much."

"How's your face?" I scoffed, barely mustering the breath to get the words out.

He smirked, thumbing his bruised cheekbone as he surveyed me over. "Better than the rest of you, I'd reckon."

I writhed about in his hold, but we both knew the effort was futile.

"Can we just skip pretenses here, or do you really want to keep this going? 'Cause either way, this all ends the same." Blaine's fingers gently brushed the matted hair out of my face.

I returned the favor by slapping him in his, but he caught my hand before it could connect with his good cheek.

"I'll take that as your answer, then." He sighed, almost mournfully, keeping my hand in his hold beside his face. "There's nothing here for you anymore. You do understand that, don't you?"

"Just because Adam let you go, it doesn't mean he won't come after you, not if you take me," I growled.

His features hardened. "Who said Reynolds let me out?" He could see my eyes widen, and his hold on me lessened ever so slightly. "He made up his mind, and I'm sorry to say it, but you didn't make the cut."

"You're lying!"

"He left you, just as everybody else has...or will. That's a fact."

"Reese won't," I growled, trying to suppress the tears burning the back of my eyes.

"Much good he'll do, considering he's hauled up in a jail cell right now." He moved in closer. "It's about time you accepted your new reality here. After the transformation's complete, this isn't going to be something you can hide. So long as you fight your nature, it's going to backfire on you, and it will expose you. You really think Mommy and Daddy dearest are going to be accepting of you? They'd jettison you from all decent society if you so much as got a B on your report card. What do you think they're going to do with a freak in the family?"

My legs started to shake even worse, and it wasn't from exhaustion. I wanted to tell him that wasn't true. But what if it was?

"I can help you." More than anything, it was the earnestness in his voice that startled me the most. "You don't have to be afraid, ashamed of what you are. You won't have to hide. I can teach you how to harness your gifts."

"You're psychotic," I barely managed to mutter. "I hate you."

"All in good time..." The slightest hint of a smile teased at his lips as he started to lower my hand, and the pleasure, the sick amusement he seemed to find in what he'd done to me, burned a whole new kind of ferocity inside me.

Every cell in my body raged with an electrical charge unlike anything I'd ever mustered before. The bright blue light manifested so quickly in my hand that Blaine barely had time to notice it. In one instant, he had me pinned against the brick siding of the alley. The next, he was gone. The discharge from my hand emitted a thunderous boom roaring through the air as it hammered into the side of his head, and the blast left Blaine airborne. His body rocketed clear out of the alleyway, hurtling right into the courtyard.

My heart suddenly clenched up, feeling as if someone reached right into my chest and squeezed the muscle until it almost burst in their hand. I gasped, crumpling to the ground. Was I going into cardiac arrest?

I looked over at Blaine, seeing his unconscious frame shudder for a split second. And just like that, the feeling lifted. He hadn't been lying about our connection. I'd felt it right then and there. Whatever I just did had stopped his heart, and in return, it stopped mine. Now knowing that our lives were tethered together, his survival meant just as much as my own. At least I could find relief, though miniscule, in the fact that he really was as strong as I suspected. He'd healed quickly enough to recover from that part of the blast, but he still remained unconscious on the ground.

Everyone nearby began circling around his body, but no one dared to touch him. They were all exchanging looks back and forward between me and him. Clearly, nobody could quite wrap their head around what they'd seen. A solid, 170-pound guy had been sent flying through the air by...me? Even if by some freak chance I happened to be a kung fu master, that didn't make sense...unless I was armed with a catapult, which I wasn't.

People began looking up at the rooftops, now murmuring about how he maybe jumped from one of the buildings. Apparently, no one had actually seen what had happened. I staggered back up to my feet, hugging Adam's jacket around me to avoid anyone seeing the blood pooling all over my shirt. The smell of mint soap clung to the lining, now making me sick. I ambled out of the alley with my head hung low, eying Blaine as I inched along the wall away from the spectacle.

"Hey, you! In the black jacket!" a guy called out behind me, but I didn't turn. "Hey! Someone, stop her!"

The mob moved in every different direction as people pushed their way through the masses of huddled bodies, and I eventually got lost amid all the hoopla as several bystanders called 9-1-1. More clicking and snapping resonated from inside my rib cage, allowing me my first decent breath. I pushed my way through the crowds until I found myself at the front entrance. I'd made it.

***

Sirens whaled from the parking lot, which I'd mistaken for an ambulance. It wasn't until I was standing at the gate that I realized it was a squad car. I didn't need to pull up my sleeve to recognize the familiar burn of one particular rune. A threat drew near.

Blaine said he had members of the police force in his pocket, and I wasn't going to stick around to see if these particular ones were. The trolley system would take at least forty minutes to get close to my home. I couldn't wait that long. Blaine could already be awake for all I knew. He, along with Mr. Reynolds, knew I'd give myself up rather than put my parents in harm's way. It was open season now, and they were prime hunting targets.

Then another curious thought ate away at me. How come this rune didn't activate when Blaine was around? It hadn't gone off even before he bit me. Surely he was a threat, more than anyone. Call me crazy, but damning your soul for all eternity certainly seemed like a hostile act. Yet, I hadn't received any forewarning.

It wasn't something I was particularly proud of, but

even I had to admit there were perks to having demonic energy. I slinked over to a parked Beamer and placed my hand on the driver's door. The lock popped up without resistance, same as the engine that roared to life as I climbed into the car. Add grand theft auto to my list of offenses. The moment I exited the parking lot, I floored it.

The twenty-minute drive to my house took an enraged nine. I pulled the Beamer up alongside the curb, using my sleeves to wipe off anywhere I'd touch just in case they'd dust the car for fingerprints later. I had enough enemies as it was; I didn't need the Fuzz coming down on me as well.

I rang the doorbell, and in an instant, it swung open.

"Oh my god, Kat!" squealed Mom, yanking me inside as she ensnared me in a hug. "Where on earth did you go? What were you thinking?" More questions ensued, but she didn't give me time to answer any. "We were scared to death!"

"I'm okay," I assured, managing to weasel out of her hold. "But we need to leave."

"What?" She got a better look at me, taking in the muck and grime and God only knows what else. "Kat, what the hell happened to you?"

"I'll explain later," I said, grabbing her and pulling her toward the stairs, "but you and Dad need to grab whatever you can. We need to leave. Right now."

Dad came out from the kitchen with a bottle of beer in his hands and immediately sighed at the sight of me. "Jesus, Kat, you're okay."

"Yeah, well, I won't be. And neither will you two if we don't leave!" I bellowed again, finally letting Adam's jacket fall open.

Mom yelped and fell back against the wall as Dad

sprang forward, both seeing the bottom half of my white Sex Pistols tee now soaked red.

"Did that Blackburn kid do this to you?" Dad started grabbing at every part of me, examining every inch for injury. He didn't find anything.

That bottomless pit feeling wouldn't leave my stomach. Adam didn't help Blaine escape. Deep down, I knew it. He was willing to take the chance that I'd die. I wanted nothing more at that moment than to rip his jacket off my body.

"Please," I whimpered, tears shedding down my dirt-ridden cheek. "We have to leave."

The front door pounded, rattling the Halloween wreathe hanging on the back.

"Don't," I whispered, prying both my parents away from the foyer.

Neither had the chance to challenge me when a familiar voice called out from the other side. "Mr. and Mrs. Montgomery? It's Officers Blake and Stevens. We need to talk with you."

My father pushed past me and hurried to answer the door.

"Dad, no-"

It was too late. He flung the door open, and they immediately stepped inside as I pulled Adam's jacket closed again.

"We have news concerning Mr. Blackburn, but we still haven't heard word about your daughter yet," said Blake. Both he and his partner froze, taking in the sight of me. "But it seems you already figured out the latter..."

I stepped forward. "What about Reese?"

"There was an incident at the school. Mr. Blackburn was admitted into the hospital for examination," confirmed

Stevens.

Mom heaved an exhausted, grateful sigh. "So he's in custody-"

"Not exactly," winced Blake. "He disappeared from his room."

"How the hell could you have let this happen?" roared my father.

"The room was guarded by two of our men. We honestly don't know what happened..."

I did everything to repress a smile. Reese had gotten away. He was okay. Free.

"In light of the situation, and the fact that your daughter's apparently returned home, we think it would be best to finish this discussion at the police station," said Stevens.

"Why? Are you charging her with something?" Mom shrieked, pointing to me. "She doesn't know anything."

He held up his hand. "Calm down. We're not implicating your daughter in any of this. But from what we can gather, she's better acquainted with him than anyone else in town. Kat might be able to point us in the right direction."

"Would you mind horribly coming with us? It shouldn't take too long," added his partner.

"Of course." Mom didn't wait for my reply, grabbing her jacket slung over the coat rack. Dad was only a step behind her.

Crap.

We didn't have the time for this. Despite probably sounding like an escaped mental patient, I had to tell them the truth in the car, before we got to the station. If there was still a miniscule chance I'd be able to convince them to leave town, I had to take it.

"Just let me change first," I finally mumbled. The officers remained in the foyer, talking with my parents. I hurried upstairs and yanked off Adam's jacket, throwing it to the floor. I couldn't even stand the thought of it being on my body. I quickly changed my shirt, catching a glimpse of myself in the mirror. I looked like Death eating a cracker. My face was as white as a sheet. Even my lips were drained of color.

One thing I couldn't ignore: the rune on my arm had never faded. Perhaps my manic anxiety was messing with the reading, but that aching suspicion that something was wrong wouldn't leave. A low hum buzzed over the air, and I spun around, seeing the front of Adam's jacket vibrating on the floor. I reached inside the exterior pockets to find nothing, but as the buzzing continued, I realized there was a secret compartment built inside. It was...Adam's cell. The screen was cracked, but I could still read the number dancing across it.

"Hello?"

A brief pause. *"Kat? Is that you?"*

"Reese?" I lowered my voice, shutting the bedroom door as quietly as I could. "Are you okay? Where are you?"

"I'm fine. I was released from custody," he sighed. *"I've been trying to call you forever, but you weren't answering. I saw Adam carrying you out of the school, so I thought I'd try my luck and see if I could get through to him instead. What happened to you? I overheard a couple of Reynolds's guys mention something about Blaine. Is he really still alive?"*

"What?" The phone nearly slipped through my fingers.

"Blaine," he annunciated. *"Was he really the one who attacked you?"*

I felt dizzy for a whole new reason. "Did you just say

you were released from custody?"

"*Yeeeeah,*" Reese laughed awkwardly, clearly baffled. "*The police questioned me when I was forced to go to the E.R. My wrist hadn't quite healed yet by the time they ran an x-ray, so I'm stuck having to wear this stupid cast for show. But anyway, I told the officers of my whereabouts and they found the surveillance footage of me and you at the restaurant during the time of Casey's murder. That's hardly the highlight of this conversation, Kat.*"

I bolted out the door, practically falling down the stairs to the foyer. Everyone looked up at me as I stopped short of the landing.

"Oh my God!" my mom gasped, her attention centered on my left arm. I looked down, realizing all too late that my fever must have sweated off the makeup I had covering up my runes. They were on full display.

But that was the least of my problems.

"*Kat?*" shouted Reese on the other end of the phone. "*You still there?*"

The room had fallen pin-drop quiet that not a word went unheard by anyone. A leering smile pulled at Officer Blake's mouth as I focused my vision on him.

"Shit." The word came out breathless, seeing his eyes flash black.

CHAPTER 37
Made Of Stone

Stevens rolled his own eyes at his partner and sighed. "Seriously? You couldn't even keep the veil up till we got her in the squad car?"

Both my folks looked at me, their faces paralyzed in confusion and an unrealized fear.

"What are you waiting for? Go get her," huffed Stevens, shoving Blake forward.

"With pleasure." He charged through the foyer, and I spun on my heels, unable to gain enough momentum to outrun him. Halfway up the stairs, he grabbed hold of my ankle, sending me face first into the carpeted steps.

Dad barked something, but the room fell silent once more at the unmistakable click of a gun being cocked. "Best stay where we all are," said Stevens, his friend yanking me down the flight.

"Reese!" I screamed, the phone sliding from my hand as I tried grappling at the railings.

Before I could get a steady grip, Blake flung me upright and grabbed me by the waist to haul me the rest of

417

the way down. I kicked and pushed, managing to jab my elbow into his windpipe. He croaked, trying to drag in a breath that wouldn't come. In an instant of blind panic, he suddenly flung me backward. My body plummeted down the stairs, my hands frantically flailing to grab onto something. No such luck. My ribs took a whole new beating, this time from my back as I crashed onto the hardwood floor of the landing. With the wind knocked clean out of me, both Blake and I were now gasping to catch our breaths.

"Well, if this isn't embarrassing..." Officer Stevens shook his head, half frustrated-half amused. Sure enough, he had his service pistol aimed at my parents, their trembling hands raised over their heads. "Come on, man. What does she weigh? A buck-ten at most? Just grab her, and go."

Blake dazedly made his way down the stairs, trying to inhale through his nose. His breathing rattled with a strangled cough. Despite the spasm in my diaphragm still robbing me of air, I staggered back up to my feet, clutching the entranceway table for support. I grabbed the Italian lead crystal vase off the countertop and chucked it at him. A rune on my arm ignited just before the vase left my hands, and I watched as it rocketed with unnatural momentum from my fingers. It flew right at Blake's head, the glass shattering into oblivion upon impact. He fell like a sack of potatoes, his unconscious frame tumbling down the last few steps before crashing onto the landing.

Stevens just rolled his eyes, repositioning his aim at me. I instinctively threw up my hand, and even with a good ten feet between us, the pistol flew out of his grip as if I'd snatched it away from right out in front of him. I swept my hand backward, expecting to catch it. Apparently, my skills needed a little more work, because the gun launched back at me with the velocity of a professional baseball pitch.

I ducked, hearing something smash behind me. With my luck, it was probably Mom's fine china. If I wasn't on the verge of being kidnapped by minions of the underworld, the thought of Mom's wrath coming down on me would have made me wished I was.

"Kat?" my dad muttered.

I didn't have time to look at him. Stevens focused his gaze on me, balling his hands into tight fists. He narrowed his eyes more and more until the entire house shook, rattling the frames right off the walls. I waited for something else to happen, but he finally dropped his hands in disappointment.

"Should've figured you'd be immune to a penance stare." His fiendish grin returned, looking over at my parents. "Guess you two will have to do."

"Don't even think about it," I growled.

"Well, it's a bit late for that." Stevens laughed, and my mom suddenly collapsed to the floor, writhing in pain. She cried out, clutching her head. Dad fell next her, trying to help in some way, but he wound up grabbing the sides of his own head the moment he looked back up at the officer.

The familiar blue light that I'd manifested in the alleyway sparked to life in my left hand. I raised my palm. With the slightest flex of my fingers, the familiar blast erupted, throwing Stevens across the room right into the fireplace. Mom and Dad dazedly looked up at me from the floor, their mouths agape with disbelief.

Peeling himself out from under the rubble of soot and broken mantle knickknacks, Stevens snickered despite his nose now being bent in the most unnatural, twisted angle. "Come on now. You can do better than that."

He sauntered back over, and I aimed my hand at him again, only to find it no longer glowing. I shook my entire arm out, as if it would somehow help recharge it. Still, nothing. The officer grabbed one of Dad's empty beer bottles, smashing the body of it against the top of the coffee table.

He fiddled the remains of the beer bottle neck between his fingers. "Let's show them what you can really do."

I was ready to lunge at any second, expecting him to make a move toward my parents. Instead, the officer turned the bottle over, dragging the jagged pieces of glass across his palm. Thin red slits appeared, quickly blossoming into bloody lines that coursed down the length of his hand and wrist. A part of me wanted to laugh. If his plan was to mutilate himself, I sure as hell wasn't about to stop him.

"Qui ostendunt tenebrarum," Stevens hissed, his eyes glazing over into their true inky black form. He came into the foyer, extending his bleeding hand out to me.

The pungent metallic odor hit me hard. The moment I inhaled the scent, stabbing pangs throbbed in the roof of my mouth. Gasping, I collapsed to the floor, feeling my gums tear open as I at last caved into the pain with a strangled cry.

"That's more like it," the officer cooed, yanking my head upright.

Mom took one look at me and screamed, scuttling across the hardwood until her back smacked against the wall.

I couldn't make sense of what was happening. I sprang up from the floor and tackled Stevens, pinning his body against the sill dividing the family room from the foyer. Without a guiding thought, my mouth immediately took aim to the side of his neck. I could hear his pulse pounding beneath his skin, and a ravenous hunger begged me to sink my teeth into it.

My whole body stiffened at the realization. I throttled

myself away. They weren't teeth. My mouth was still ajar. I couldn't close it. I staggered over to the mirror hanging in the entryway that now dangled for dear life by only one of its hooks.

"Beautiful, isn't it?" Stevens laughed. "Don't you think so, Mom?"

I clamped my hands over my mouth, unable to bear the sight. It still couldn't conceal my eyes. My glowing red eyes. Blaine's eyes. Finally letting my hands fall away, I gawked back at myself, at the inch-long pointed canines protruding from my upper jaw.

"What did you do to her?" my mother cried.

"Oh, don't look at me. This one comes courtesy of my boss," the demon chortled. "Her master."

My entire forearm set ablaze at the words, nearly every rune igniting in response. The demonic energy coiled itself around the flurry of emotions stirring inside me. Rage, despair, horror. I couldn't have controlled it if I'd wanted to, but that didn't matter in that moment. I wanted to unleash its wrath.

An eerie calm washed over me, my eyes fading back to their natural blue, my fangs retracting back to their normal length. Turning on my heels, I opened my hand. The demon didn't move a muscle, yet his body shot forward, his neck coming right into my grasp.

He snickered. "Time to feed?"

"No. It's time for you to say your goodbyes."

He strangled on a cackle as my grip tightened. Placing my other palm on his forehead, the pattern on top of my arm lit up. The demon was no longer laughing. Black smoke began pouring out of his eyes as ear aching screams filled every corner of the house. In a rush of heat, it stopped, and I let Stevens' body collapsed to the floor. The smoke lingered in the air, slowly settling around my feet. My hands fell to my sides, and the mist dissipated, as if seeping into the cracks of the floorboards. He was gone.

CHAPTER 38
The Blower's Daughter

Apparently, Mystic Harbor's train station wasn't what you'd call a hotbed of activity at eleven o'clock at night, because the only people to keep me company in the entire terminal were a couple guys from the cleaning crew and Sheila, the barista at the dank little coffee shop inside. Nothing better than the smell of ammonia and dirty mop water to go with some burnt coffee.

Footsteps echoed across the cracked tiled floors, and my body stiffened, feeling the warm flush creep across my chest. A moment later, the individual rounded the corner into the so-called café sporting an unmistakable Victorian militia coat. I hesitated, unsure whether to get up or not. Reese hadn't said much after I told him about what Blaine had done. Was he afraid of me now, too?

If he was, I didn't want to make this any harder on him. So I stayed seated, wiping the constant stream of tears from my cheeks.

He gave me a small, close-mouthed smile as he reached my lonely table. "Hey, Princess."

I tried to return the greeting, but the words got caught in my throat. Reese bent down, pressing his lips to my forehead. His face slowly lowered further until our features were aligned. Our noses brushed one another, but I pulled back as he tilted his head.

"Don't," I pleaded.

"*Don't* what?" Even now, his voice had that teasing tenor to it. Only, I didn't laugh.

"I don't want to hurt you," I whispered.

He knelt down, brushing the mess of hair from my eyes. "Then don't." His fingers trailed down one of my strands and froze upon settling on the side of my neck. He could feel it. The puncture marks.

"*I* wouldn't, not on purpose," I murmured. "But after the transformation is complete, I don't know what I'll be capable of, or whether I'll be able to control it. I could end up like Brittany."

"You won't."

"You don't know that."

"I know *you*," he affirmed, his eyes fixed on mine. "And there's nothing that says the demonic virus will have the same affect on you. Hellhounds are bred for the sole purpose of being ruthless and submissive-"

"But I've been sired to...*him*." I couldn't say his name. It felt like trying to swallow battery acid. "If the bond is anything like being sired into a Hellhound, he could make me do anything. Hurt someone...kill them. Kill you."

"You don't have to go through with this," he said, looking around at the pathetic station café. "You can stay with me."

I shook my head. "He knows about you. Your house is the first place he'll look. He's probably there as we speak. And as soon as Nathan realizes Russell's dead, he'll come after me as well. Right now it's best if you don't know anything. I can't risk you getting involved any more than you already have. Everyone knows now that...Blaine...is behind all this. A lone-wolf Reaper will be the least of their concerns."

Whether he wanted to admit it or not, he knew I was right. He couldn't very well leave town. It would only raise suspicion.

At last, Reese nodded pitifully, continuing to look around the empty space. "Where are your parents?"

"Right now they think it's best to just get out of town, so they concocted a story about having to visit a sick relative. They booked a hotel room in Portland for the night, hence the train ride. But Dad claims there's some last minute 'business matters' he needs to tend to before he can leave, so he's planning on meeting me in the morning. And Mom didn't feel comfortable leaving him alone in town, you know, as opposed to leaving your only daughter who's being hunted by *everybody* alone in a crusty train station." I rolled my eyes, but it didn't stop a fresh batch of tears from pouring off my lashes. "Blaine was right, about everything. He said Adam would turn his back on me, that I wouldn't be able to conceal my abilities... And my parents... They're terrified of me, just like he said they would be."

Reese cupped his hands around my face, cleaning away my tears with his thumbs. "First off, I could've told you that about Reynolds. Hell, I said it myself. He's a dick."

I laughed despite myself.

"And you'll learn how to control your abilities on your own. You've proven yourself to be more than resourceful. And despite what you see, your folks still love you. They're in shock right now. Just give them a little time, and they'll come around." I nodded, but he kept a hold of my cheeks. "Hey, I mean it. In spite of everything, they're still meeting up with you."

I looked over at the clock and regrettably stood up. "I don't think they really have another choice. It's not like they'd risk sticking around here while demons are attacking. The last thing Mom wants is for one of the ladies from the Woodstone Regency Society to see her daughter becoming a vampiric bride from Hell."

"I know it's probably not worth much, but you'll always have me," said Reese, lightly nudging me with his elbow as we started making our way toward the train platforms. "If you need anything...or even just want to talk, you give me a call."

"I will."

Reese turned me so that I faced him, and I didn't have time to react. He kissed me. Not like how he had earlier. And not like Blaine. It was soft, gentle, tender. Sweeter than anything I knew I deserved. "Let me come with you," he murmured.

"Reese-"

"Even just for a week." I started shaking my head, but he wouldn't have it. "After the massacre at the school, it'll be closed tomorrow. The cops already have the entire block roped off. And after the weekend, my mom can cover for me for a few days. The police would be stupid to question my absence, considering Carly and Mark vouched for me. I'm apparently the new resident hero, having saved my fellow classmates from Daniel's murder rampage."

"You guys didn't say anything to the police about me, did you? They don't know I was there when—"

"Relax, Princess. You're in the clear."

"Thank you." Curiosity got the best of me, even now. I had to ask. "Why do you call me that, really?"

Reese grinned. "Because you may or may not remind me of a certain snarky, kickass Alderaanian with a feisty temper."

I laughed. Actually laughed. "Princess Leia?"

He nodded.

I gave him a playful shove. "You're such a dork."

"Says the girl who knew what an Alderaanian was." He pulled me in, and this time I didn't object, reveling in the steadfast heat from his body. Reese felt the shiver run through me, only urging him to hold me closer.

The loudspeaker clicked on with a monotone voice announcing, "The next train at Platform 2 is the 11:14 service to Portland Transportation Center..."

"That's me." I lamentably peeled myself free from his embrace. "Listen, Reese, I don't know where my folks are planning on taking me after this, so...."

Reese understood what I meant. He dug into his coat pocket, fetching out a freshly printed ticket. "Good thing I'm coming along then."

"What?" I snatched the paper from him in disbelief. Sure enough, it was for the very same train. "But how...?"

"There were only two choices left on the board for tonight, and Wells seemed like an unlikely bet."

"Reese, I can't let you do this. Between Mr. Reynolds and Blaine...and God only knows who else—"

He merely shrugged. "I'll take my chances."

"Yeah, but we're gonna be on the road. You don't have any clothes, or even a toothbrush—"

"Good thing I also packed a bag."

My smile threatened to tear my face in half, and I didn't care. "You're kidding?"

"Just gotta get it out of my truck." He planted a kiss on my cheek before jogging off, giving me a parting wink for good measure.

Only the low rumble of machinery filled the silence until my stomach let out a monstrous growl. I hadn't eaten anything since lunch with exception to the single strawberry from Mom's party. My nerves were still wound so tightly though that I hadn't the time to acknowledge my hunger. Several vending machines rested in the far corner by an old payphone, so I fished into my pocket and retrieved a couple singles. Ice pricked up my spine though as a sharp metallic chime echoed across the vast open space.

The payphone.

Without so much as a thought, my hand reached for the receiver. It wasn't until my fingers were curled around it that I regained control of my own actions. *What was I doing?* That invisible tug deep inside my gut wrenched me forward, begging, pleading for me to take the receiver off the cradle hook. I tried pulling my hand away, but the sensation only worsened. I didn't have a choice. Every last cell in my body clawed against my skin until I finally surrendered. I pressed the phone against my ear, but couldn't bring myself to speak.

"Hey, lovely."

My grip tightened on the device, threatening to snap it between my fingers. Panic arrested every instinct within me as I spun in every direction.

His breathing was unmistakably labored as he rasped, *"You can relax. I'm not there."*

That much I did know. I couldn't sense him, but that didn't mean someone else hadn't been sent in his stead.

"Sorry for not being there to see you off, but I'm a bit under the weather." Blaine tried to laugh. Instead, a ragged cough greeted me from the other end.

For the most part, the entire platform was visible.

Nobody else was there. But even if I managed to get on the train without a problem, who's to say there wouldn't be a band of thugs waiting to snatch me up at the next stop?

"You won't be followed. I can promise you that much."

My whole spine stiffened. Could he really read my thoughts? How else had he known where I'd be?

"But you can't run forever." Any attempt to sound lighthearted was gone. *"The time will come when we'll need to consummate our bond. And I will come to collect you."*

Without having to look, I knew I'd ignited at least three runes, because light was exploding from my sleeve and my whole arm vibrated from the surge of restrained power. I wanted him here. I wanted him standing in front of me so I could bury my fist into his skull. I wanted to rip his heart clean from his chest. I wanted to kill him.

Warmth spread over me, and I furiously whipped around. The fear uncoiled at the sight of razor-cut brown hair appearing over the top of the payphone dock. It was Reese, jogging towards the platform with a large duffle bag slung over his shoulder as gears shrieked from down the tracks. The train was pulling into the station.

"I know you hate me," Blaine murmured. *"But you will change your mind, someday."*

"That's not today," was all I said, placing the phone back on the hook.

EPILOGUE

The onslaught of rain made it virtually impossible for Maddox to see anything as the wipers zipped across the windshield. Showers hadn't been shown on the forecast, but this sudden downpour came as no surprise. Something was wrong. Very wrong. And the weather always had a strange way of reflecting it. The tires kicked up rock fragments as he swung his Escalade into the gravel parking lot. Cutting the engine, he hiked up the neckline of his frock coat and raced out into the storm up to the front entrance of the establishment.

"Basin Street Blues" played in the distance as the smell of beer battered onion rings and char-broiled burgers greeted him upon entering. The 1920's throwback speakeasy held some fond memories that very few nowadays remembered. Unfortunately, the bar had recently taken up new ownership, making the clientele almost entirely of the demonic variety. The young man didn't mind his fellow workmates, but he still preferred to never mix business with pleasure.

"Welcome to Nucky's," began the hostess before

surrendering her gaze to the man hustling down the main hall towards her. "Oh, it's *you*." She scoffed, setting down the menus she had preemptively grabbed.

The young man brushed his sopping ashy locks from his eyes and shook out the rainwater clinging to his leather coat, making a deliberate mess on the floor. He hated having to deal with succubi like Eva. They were always holier-than-thou, like they were Satan's gift to the world.

"I need to see him," the young man shouted over the music and loud clamor of the club.

"I'm sorry, but he's in the middle of a game right now," she replied with fake pleasantness, casting him a nauseating smile. "He's not to be disturbed."

"Trust me, he'll want to hear what I have to say," the man remarked impatiently.

"Well, why don't you go join the rest of the mutts over there, and I'll let you know when your number comes up." She cocked her head over towards the bar where he immediately recognized at least a handful of his colleagues who were clearly already waiting to have an audience with the boss.

"Sorry, sweetheart, but I haven't got time for this." He plowed past her and pushed his way through the mass of people occupying the dance floor.

"Maddox!" The hostess squealed, racing clumsily after him in her towering heels. "You can't go back there!"

"Read 'em and weep, gents," declared the Englishman, laying down a straight flush onto the table of the private gaming room. Everyone moaned, tossing their cards back into the pile. The wood paneled space was engulfed in a calm haze of smoke as all the men took long drags on their cigars and cigarettes. As the entryway door yanked open though, the smoke swirled restlessly above the gaming table as the young man crashed to a halt upon arrival. His throat bobbed at the sight of his boss positioned at the other side of the room. Everyone fell quiet as they observed the lad.

"Sir, I am so, so sorry," Eva panted as she practically collapsed into the room. "I told him he had to wait—"

"Don't worry yourself, darling. It's plenty all right," replied the Englishman, taking a drag from the cigarette in his hand. His nostrils flared as he blew out the smoke from his nose, making his already intimidating expression look all the more dragon-like. "What can I help you with, Maddox? It's a bit early for your shift to be over, isn't it?"

"I'm still on the clock, sir," the young man replied sheepishly.

"Might I ask what the issue is then? Blaine requires an extra pair of eyes on him right now, and you're not doing anybody any good standing here," remarked the Englishman.

"That's the thing." The boy choked on the words. "There's been an...incident."

The Englishman practically growled as he tapped his cigarette against the lip of the ashtray in front of him, flicking off the accumulated ash. "Of course there was."

"Hey, Mad," said a scruffy ruffian in a black and white racing jacket coming into the doorway from the club.

"Val," the blonde boy addressed politely.

"Boss, that brunette at the bar was just asking about you," laughed Val with roguish delight, smoothing out his pompadour-styled hair before knocking back a shot on the table. "And she has a twin sister."

The Englishman buried his hands into his face

exhaustedly.

"Okay, what'd I miss? You guys look like you were all just splashed with holy water."

"Where's Blaine now?" snarled the Englishman.

Val groaned at the name-drop. "What the devil has he done now?"

"He's back at the manor," replied Maddox.

"Is that so?" The Englishman's left eyebrow cocked up as he glanced at his watch. "Did he change the girl?"

Maddox nodded.

"So the two are at the estate then?" His boss grinned. "Calling it a night for a private shag doesn't exactly sound too concerning. Sounds like our boy's doing his job."

"And taking pleasure in doing so," chuckled Val.

"It's not like that," corrected Maddox. "Blaine was attacked tonight."

The subtle chorus of laughs that had circulated amongst the room suddenly hushed.

"Attacked how?" asked Val.

Maddox pulled up an image on his phone and handed it to his colleague. "He was barely conscious when we dragged him into the manor. He'd been cut pretty bad."

"Holy shit," mumbled the ruffian, cringing at the grisly snapshot of Blaine's sliced arm. "He's fine now, right?"

Maddox shook his head. "The injury's at least an hour old, and it hasn't healed. At all."

"How bad is it?" asked one of the other men at the table as Val gave the phone over to the Englishman.

"The entire length of his forearm was knifed open with an Angelorum blade," said Val laboriously.

Everyone gasped, and Eva fell back against the wall.

"He's as good as dead," murmured one man. "No one

could survive the Angelorum's hellfire, not with a wound as extensive as that."

"We have another problem," said Maddox. "The girl is gone."

"*What?*"

"She wasn't with Blaine at the manor. And the guy passed out five feet into the doorway, so we couldn't ask him where she was. When he finally came to, he said he let her go."

"Whatever for?" growled his boss.

"They were ambushed by a pack of Reapers. At least twenty in their ranks. Given Ryder's current state of health, he knew he wouldn't be able to defend her if they tracked him down."

"But he knows where she is?" urged Val. Maddox didn't answer. He didn't need to. "Goddamn it."

"There's something else."

The entire room shared in a collective moan.

"The girl was with someone else when everything went down, and by the looks of it, they were a thing." Maddox retrieved his phone and pulled up another image, handing it to the Englishman.

Raelynd took it, his eyes widening in an instant. "You just couldn't stay away, could you?" he murmured to the image.

"What is it?" Val walked over and stole a glance at the photograph, snatching it from his hands the moment his eyes settled on the picture. "That's not who I think it is?"

Raelynd emitted a low laugh as he settled back in his chair, running a hand across his left eyebrow. "Well, well, well. What an interesting development indeed."

"What could possibly be funny about this?" Val begged, slamming the phone down onto the tabletop. "I told you! I told you right from the start; we should have taken Gabriel out when we had him. Now look at this! How did we not know about *him*?"

Raelynd's smile still did not fade. "I knew, very well."

"Are you serious?"

"Do I honestly strike you as the type to overlook such a detail?" the Englishman mused. "I did underestimate Gabriel though. Never thought he'd go to these measures. Seems we're gonna be in for quite the contest."

His contentment only boiled Val's blood all the more. "What contest? The game's over, and it never even began! Blaine failed us, and his allegiance is undoubtedly in question. Even if your man survives the Angelorum's injury, he's a liability!"

"Oh, my poor comrade. You cannot see the forest through the trees," addressed his boss grinningly. "Mr. Ryder doesn't need to be on our side for him to perform his services."

"What aren't you telling us?" queried Val, seeing a sly glimmer ablaze in the Englishman's eyes.

"Let's just say that his loyalty is not nearly as important as his lips are. As for the other matter," Raelynd cooed, pointing at the brown-haired boy in the photograph, "Gabriel's gonna learn his lesson the hard way. He's chosen to interfere. It's open season now, and casualties are guaranteed."

"You really think we'll be able to pull this off in overtime?"

"My dear Valor," purred Raelynd as black inked over the entirety of his gray eyes, "the game has only just begun."

ABOUT THE AUTHOR

Victoria Evers is a debut paranormal fiction writer who feels really awkward referring to herself in the third person.... When she's not vacationing in Narnia, you'll probably find her reading, watching horror movies, spending time with her AMAZING family, or daydreaming about the newest story in her head.

You can also find her at: https://twitter.com/victoria_evers

Made in the USA
Coppell, TX
23 January 2020

14920957R00246